THE DEAD OF JUNE

By

G. H. Ellis

ISBN: 1-4107-5375-1 (e-book)
ISBN: 1-4107-5374-3 (Paperback)

This book is printed on acid free paper.

1stBooks - rev. 06/06/03

ACKNOWLEDEMENTS

I wish to thank all my friends, who have sustained me with encouragement, and who never have suggested that I spend more time at work. Special thanks are given to Harriet, Scott, Pat, Alice, Andy, and Paul for reading and commenting on previous drafts. Most of all, I am grateful to Jan, my wife, for her ruthless editing, without which, the book would be unreadable.

JUNE 1, FRIDAY, The Breakfast Club

Life is an engine with a giant flywheel. As the flywheel gains momentum, the stronger it drags us along. For Maddy, the ambivalent decision to attend medical school was followed by the equally ambivalent decision to specialize in pathology. Today the turning wheel was taking her to the morgue at County Charity Hospital.

A familiar clawing and meowing originated outside the bathroom door. Maddy enjoyed the steamy air of the room after her hot shower with the closed bathroom door. This offended Tasmin, an auburn tabby who insisted on full run of the apartment.

She misinterpreted the impertinent cat's activities and put out a fresh bowl of food. Tasmin snubbed the offering by jumping into the kitchen windowsill and taking up a meditation.

Maddy confidently walked out of her apartment dressed in a bright red and blue blouse with matching navy skirt. The red geraniums and blue clematis blooming along the front steps echoed her color scheme in the sunlight. A squirrel hopped onto the sidewalk three feet ahead of her, raised its head, looked Maddy in the eyes, and then dashed off over the hood of Maddy's car, slipping slightly as its foot dislodged a parking ticket under the windshield wiper.

Sensations of nature vanished. "Goddamn it," she heard herself utter reflexively as she walked around to a side view of the front bumper. Indeed twenty-two inches of Honda Civic bumper and grill were ahead of the yellow curb paint.

She thought it ironic, the numerous awful jobs in the world. "This ticket-writing vampire stalks the night making lives miserable. I cut up dead people for a living. I doubt chopping up colon cancers and placentas is any more pleasing to the average person. Do people immediately cringe at the thought of me, as I do the parking-ticket cop?"

**

Maddy was in her last month of her third year. In one year the flywheel would change her direction. After residency she must either specialize via fellowship training or take on a permanent hospital position. Maddy had six months to work the next plan. Secretly she hoped to find forensics to be a calling, a vocation with meaning for remainder of her adult life. For now her focus was toward the next ninety days of forensic training. She stuffed the ticket into her purse and drove away.

The parking garage gate refused to allow entrance. After several seconds of musing about the personality of mechanical gates, Maddy realized her VISA card would never open the parking gate. She shook and probed her purse for the parking card, then shook and looked some more. Panning for gold had a higher probability for success than readily finding something in her purse. She promised herself to organize it.

Two city blocks of continuous parking lot stood between the large white marble University Hospital and an ancient yellow sandstone building from the turn of the century, County Charity Hospital. The white marble walls and tall pillars in front warranted the nickname, The White Castle, a derisive comparison with a commercial hamburger. Inside were the nobility of haughty professors, deans, and crème de le crème of technicians.

Despite Maddy's advanced standing, twelfth month of her third residency year, her only previous rotation at Charity had been a two-month hematology rotation. All her previous training had taken place among the medical royalty at University.

The serfdom of County Charity Hospital stood in stark contrast. City soot discolored the yellow sandstone to gray near the roofline, and black at the base. "Welcome to County Charity," a blackened and insincere placard hung over the entrance. The surrounding concrete sidewalks were cracked and littered with the accoutrements of the welfare class: gum wrappers, straws, small paper napkins, and smoking detritus. Burger King cups provided color to the monotonous arbor vitae landscaping.

Patients smoked in wheel chairs parked on black grassless patches of ground alongside the main entrance. The friends and family of the patients appeared more in need of the nasal oxygen than the wheel chair riders did. Likely their seats would be switched next week, Maddy thought. She pitied them. Not because they were poor, nor for their ignorance, but because the welfare class had nothing to fill their days. At least Maddy had a job, medical journals to read, and places to visit. She didn't love pathology, but she did like it more than any other job she could envision.

Maddy made her way into the basement, the natural morgue placement by any respectable hospital architect. "Position the morgue closest to the back door and dumpsters, and away from any patient contact," Maddy imagined the directive in an architectural textbook. She followed the signs to the County Coroner, Division of Medical Examiners.

At the entrance to the morgue was a waist high sign with black felt background and white plastic stick-on letters. Maddy recognized the type of sign often seen in a funeral home, the ones with arrows pointing to a room showing the body belonging to the family of the late Mr. Payingstiff. The sign at the morgue entrance was meant to be startling and for the amusement of the morgue staff.

"Welcome to County Morgue. Aids, Hepatitis, Tuberculosis, and other unknown hazardous pathogens abound. Be forewarned and enjoy your visit." Maddy chuckled at the thinly veiled black humor, undoubtedly the response to the demands of a risk management lawyer.

The orange steel door was heavy and dirty. Her gentle push failed to open it; a solid shoulder block succeeded. She stumbled into the morgue not knowing what type of human remains might lie in her path.

She had done nearly one hundred autopsies in her three years. Corpses no longer were macabre. After thirty or so post mortems bodies loose their creepiness and become fascinating surprise packages like wrapped Christmas presents begging to be opened. Maddy knew that thrill of sliding a scalpel through the belly and being the first to glimpse the abdominal landscape.

However, the ambiance of the County chamber was a new experience. It squeezed and knotted her stomach.

She was immediately relieved to see three empty shining steel autopsy tables and no bodies or body bags. The room was cold in contrast to the hot June morning. It would be ninety degrees outside by mid-afternoon, but the morgue room would not exceed sixty-six degrees.

Instantly she encountered a thin black man in lavender pedal pusher pants and coordinated purple and white

4

flowered shirt and neckerchief. He had earrings in abundance and a hint of clear lipstick. Dandy did not give full credit to the effort of his finery.

"Well good morning, little angel of pulchritude. Ain't you a humdinger, red, white and blue like old glory. Come on now, we got to get you into some scrubs and cover you up before Poindexter gets a look at them hooters. He'll be trying to string you up on his flagpole."

"Excuse me, I'm doctor...," she began.

"Gray. Dr. Gray. I know who you are. We got pictures of the residents. But if that's your regular look, you have a definite defect in photogenic representation, mmm hmm hmmph," he said without pausing, while pointing to the bulletin board where a picture hung of the current crop of sixteen residents from University hospital.

"Who's Poindexter?" Maddy sliced into his non-stop monologue.

"Poindexter is Barbie's nightmare prom date. Don't tell me you never played with dolls?"

"I know who *that* Poindexter is."

"Percival Mordecai, M.D., forensic fellow, our brand of the same. He ain't worth being anxious to meet. Now come on, Precious, we got a lot of work for you today. You got a crispy crème and a glazed. Poindexter's on tap for the Bismarck and the donut hole. Doctor God's gonna staff and sign out the pop tarts."

"What?" Maddy shook her head. The door quietly opened with the entrance of a six-foot man with dark hair. His athletic build was slightly tarnished by a bulging waist and graying temples betraying an age in the mid-fifties. He had piercing blue eyes and sharp handsome facial features.

"What did he just say to me?" she asked in her softest tone of voice. She imagined herself as Alice talking to the Mad Hatter, wondering if the attendant was from the crazy ward or the Twilight Zone. She gritted her teeth to prevent a daydreaming lapse.

"Don't mind Slurp. He and Richard are the most competent dieners in the state. They're your best friends for the next three months. Slurp's got a nickname and slang for everything. He calls our forensic operation, "The Breakfast Club." We have two staff pathologists, Dr. Green and myself. I'm Graham O'Dell. Dr. Mordecai is our fellow. Each morning Dr. Green or myself comes in, assesses the workload, and makes the assignments. Usually the resident gets the first and third cases with one of the staff, unless they are complicated homicides. The fellow does the second and fourth bodies. The second staff is responsible for the fifth and sixth cases," calmly explained Dr. O'Dell.

"And you better pray we don't ever get a day with more than six pastries, cause I turn into one ugly Twinkie," warned Slurp, with a downward flap of his wrist.

"Pastries?" inquired Maddy.

"Slurp's breakfast club. Today's menu starts off with one crispy crème. That would be a crispy critter, a.k.a. burn victim, from a house fire. Let's get that one out of the way because of the smell. The glazed donut is a pedestrian motor vehicle accident. The police blotter has it spun as two dueling drunks, one with a car and one walking. Car won as usual." As Dr. O'Dell explained the breakfast club jargon, Maddy stared at his shoulders.

"Bismarck? Let me guess, a Nazi war criminal?" Maddy offered to join the levity.

"Close. Actually it's like a submarine, a sunken ship, a drowning victim," smiled Slurp.

"Donut hole would be a gunshot wound?" Maddy continued.

"Isn't she cute? Dr. God, we gonna have so much fun with this one. Look at her, all dressed up like the American flag. Oh! United we stand." He hugged her.

"Slurp, calm down! Get Dr. Gray her locker and some scrubs," Graham said, followed by, "Now!" That syllable that sent Slurp bounding towards the door.

"Does he always talk so fast?" asked Maddy genuinely.

"I got a chemical imbalance," Slurp explained, popping his head back into the room.

"I'll say. Too much amphetamine in the morning. He's about right by noon, but worthless after four," continued Graham. His affectionate tone conveyed comment without condescension.

**

Slurp took Maddy into the women's locker room where two obese young housekeepers sat smoking cigarettes. One was dressed in scrubs, the other wore only a bra and panties. Neither reacted as Slurp walked through the women's dressing area.

He opened an empty locker and handed Maddy a key. "The hospital is non-smoking, but the alarms don't seem to work in this end of the building. Tops are on the bottom shelf, and pants are on the top. The resident locker has a clear plastic apron. You got to clean it yourself, Precious, 'cause housekeeping don't do windows," chuckled Slurp at his joke. The housekeepers rolled their eyes and blew smoke toward Slurp. He returned a kiss and a wink.

When Maddy returned to the morgue the scene had changed from inert stainless steel to the working frenzy of an ant colony. Like drones harvesting a pile of food, the green scrub-suited workers pulled bloody pieces of tissue at each station and moved between tables and scales.

Slurp was at the near table measuring something that resembled the center attraction of a pig roast. The middle table was bodiless, serving as a workstation for cameras and photographic lights. The far table held an obviously bloated corpse of green gray skin. The chest and abdomen were already incised and organs were flowing out one handful at a time.

The hands belonged to Richard, head diener. He was nearly fifty with gray hair and black beardless face. He had shining white teeth without tobacco or coffee stains. He talked softly and every word was important.

At the other side of the table containing the drowning victim stood a tall and gangly man. He could have been a young boy with nearly beardless chin, thin lips, and fine light brown hair. The early balding of the temples gave clue to an age closer to thirty-five than the face of a late teen. He held a magnifying lens over the neck of the corpse. Maddy envisioned that the lens filtered a nerd beacon and Percival Mordecai was its lighthouse. Percival paused, craned his neck unnecessarily, and stared at Maddy focusing too long on her chest. She knew it would be difficult not to call him Poindexter. His mouth gaped as if about to speak. Mechanically his craned neck returned to the study of the corpse. He did not speak.

Immediately, Slurp handed Maddy a series of x-ray films and began incising the corpse. It was about half human size with drawn up arms and legs. Hands were cocked fists. The surface ranged from charcoal black embers to dry green gray lizard skin. It smelled of the fire sale from Ayres department store when Maddy was fifteen.

"See this?" Slurp pointed to a hole in the abdomen with protruding loops of intestine. "Left lung, 450 grams," grunted the second assistant as one pound of pink and black sponge hit the cutting board in front of Maddy. "Right, 420," followed six seconds later. Slurp flung one lung into the water basin at the end of the table. "Floats."

"Stop!" came a commanding voice from the refrigerator wall that housed two rows of six body drawers. The voice was Dr. O'Dell who was viewing an open drawer with the exposed body of an elderly man of white hair and skin. He walked calmly over to Maddy. Slurp and Richard became still.

"Maddy, you are in charge here. Slow them down to your pace. First read the police report." Graham was also dressed in green scrubs, but as the day's staff, he wore no gloves or mask. He picked up the lined form from the desk next to the autopsy table. "Sixty-nine year old woman who lived alone was found dead in a house fire. She is a known smoker. What next?"

Maddy responded, "Manner of death, murder versus accident?"

"Or other. We x-ray to look for bullets, trauma, knifepoints, whatever. Next we look for external signs of trauma, then go inside. See anything?"

Slurp jumped in, "Got a hole in the belly with chitlins bubbling up like Mammy's pork ring pie."

Dr. O'Dell looked at Maddy who raised her gloved hands palm-side-up to shoulder height, signaling her uncertainty. "The arms are fractured," she pointed to the upper body x-rays.

Graham took the pictures and carefully explained how the fire caused drying and typical circumferential fractures. The contracted torso and pugilist posture were the result of tightened muscles and tendons. The abdominal slit was along the muscle fibers. The uninjured protruding gut ruled out a stab wound.

"He's saying her last cigarette went in the bed instead of the ashtray. OK, we got a lot to do today. Case closed; let's move on. The officer for the glazed donut is coming at eleven and I expect my boys to get their break beforehand," Slurp said.

Graham gestured, "It's all yours," then hesitated as he looked over the heart and lung on the cutting board. "Maddy, what do you make of the heart?"

As Graham asked his question he gently touched her shoulder and turned her toward the specimen. Maddy instantly lost focus to his hand touch. Navigating the next three months with her obvious attraction to Graham would either be pleasure or hell.

She cut through the aorta and pulmonary arteries to lift the heart out of the chest. It was covered with coagulated blood. She turned it over. Flicking off a blood clot revealed a jagged gray and yellow hole. For the first time that day she was comfortably confident and in familiar territory. She weighed the organ, cut through its four chambers, and isolated the coronary arteries. She held open an artery cross section for Graham's inspection.

"She perforated the posterior wall. I'd guess the thrombus in the right main and the wall infarct are about two or three days old," Maddy beamed.

"You ruled out homicide. Is this a natural or accidental death? Your name will be on the death certificate," Graham led her.

"Myocardial infarct, natural?" Maddy sensed this was an educational setup demanding humility.

"Does everyone die from a heart attack? It appears she still burnt herself up smoking," Graham continued, "Let's look at her trachea. Slurp, what's her carbon monoxide?"

"Sixteen percent. Mild soot in the trachea." The diener responded as he opened the lung tubes. Slurp pushed the bronchi too close to Maddy's face and she recoiled backward into Graham's catch, an unexpected pleasure.

"Well Maddy? It's your case. You are the county official, you've got to make the call." prodded Graham.

"Dead is dead. Does it matter that much?"

"Perhaps she had a double indemnity clause for accidental death. That would make a big difference to the family and the insurance company."

"Do you want me to flounder with this, or are you going to help me?"

Graham smiled. "This is a good first case. The police, attorneys and assorted bureaucrats want it clean and simple. Clean and simple rarely, if ever exists. I'd have the police question family and neighbors about any chest pain in the last few days to help with the timing of the infarct. But the low carbon monoxide level is not generally lethal, and the amount of soot in her lungs minimal. It shortened her life after her heart wall blew out, but not much. The blood around the heart, the tamponade, kills nearly everyone who perforates their heart at home."

"Say what? Gunshots we get a lot, but what's that tampon business?" said Slurp.

"Tamp-on-odd. If a heart attack kills a large part of the heart muscle, it can blow out like the sidewall of a tire. The heart is in a tight sack, the pericardium. So when blood is pumped into the sack it literally chokes the heart," said Maddy.

"Ergo," prompted Dr. O'Dell.

"Natural, acute myocardial infarct, mechanism of death: free wall perforation with cardiac tamponade."

"Good work."

Maddy did not feel that she had done anything, but appreciated Dr. O'Dell's confidence and grooming. He had led her to the words she would use to sign the death certificate. She felt her professional status heighten.

Slurp and another assistant returned to the corpse and removed the remaining organs, weighing each quickly and placing them on the cutting tray. They waited patiently as she sliced each organ. She fought nausea as each piece of tissue reeked with the choking smell of badly burnt barbecue pork drippings and ashes from the bottom of a grill.

Slurp quietly offered pity and encouragement, "You can go as fast as you like with normal organs. If there's something there, I know you'll see it."

"Thanks, Slurp." Maddy felt embarrassed to approach the next question. "Is that a nickname? I mean I want to call you whatever you prefer," she said.

"If you had a name like Eldred, you'd take any other name. And trust me, you do not want to know the origins of Slurp. Oh, my lordy, here comes Josef 'Stalin' Maconi."

A thirty-year-old policeman entered the morgue carrying a manila folder. He was stocky, average looking, not homely. His jaw was thick and his reddish-brown hair had a slight curl. A toothpick wiggled with movement of his lips.

"What the fuck is that?" was directed toward Dr. Mordecai.

He was finishing up the drowning victim. The doctor repeated his mechanical neck rotation. His eyes moved up and down over the policeman's uniform. Percival, despite his creepiness, was admirable in his ability to observe. He pointed out a yellow stain on the officer's sleeve and handed him a wet paper towel.

"I believe this to be an uncomplicated drowning. Uncomplicated except to the fisherman," Percival displayed his twisted humor. Maddy detected a sense of disappointment in the word uncomplicated. "Do you eat hotdogs for breakfast, Officer Maconi?" asked Percival. His eyes systematically scrutinized the officer's stained sleeve.

"I got to eat something before I come down here otherwise I'd get sick to my stomach. The low life scum in this place are disgusting. Oh, no offense, not all you *GUYS*, a term I use lightly," he said with a wincing sneer directed towards Slurp. "Hey, who's doing the old man run down by the drunk bitch we got locked up? She ought to be good for three to five for manslaughter."

Joseph Maconi wiped at the mustard stain with the paper towel. He spit on the stain, wiped it again, then licked it.

Dr. O'Dell had been watching and listening to this interchange from the doorway. "Dr. Gray will be conducting the post-mortem shortly after she's had a chance to finish the dictation on this case. Our dieners should be ready in about twenty minutes.

"Twenty-five," said Slurp.

"I'll have the body placed on cart two. Meanwhile you can collect fingerprints and take additional photographs if you like." Dr. O'Dell stared softly but powerfully at Maconi. Like two street dogs the power contest continued for several seconds until Maconi turned away.

"I'll be back," he said as he walked out the door.

Maddy took the police report of the accident with her to the dictation desk. She quickly completed the report and signed the death certificate. Proximate cause of death was listed as acute myocardial infarct with ruptured left ventricle. She listed manner of death as natural. The final line included the contribution and complication of peri-mortem accidental fire. She felt a professional glow of competence and service.

**

The accident victim was a sixty-four year old man. He lived alone in a downtown flophouse. The accident occurred on the access ramp to the interstate, a 40 mile-per-hour caution zone. Details of the scene were lacking except for the body, which was found adjacent the guardrail.

The driver was reported to have a blood alcohol concentration just at the limit of .08 percent. She was a fifty-two year divorced woman who worked as a secretary for a temporary service. She admitted to several drinks at a downtown bar with friends prior to the accident. The investigating officer noted she lacked signs of inebriation.

When Maddy rejoined the morgue team, Officer Maconi was flipping through the accident scene photographs. Slurp had sketched the pattern of injuries and immediately showed his work to Maddy.

"Here's the score for crumpledstiltskin: fracture of the left femur, left humerus, most of the ribs, and left skull. Pattern abrasion of the left thigh. There is a two-inch area of lacerated scalp across the left parietal-occipital area. The remaining abrasions look like road contact with imbedded asphalt and stone particles."

Slurp looked for a response. After a nod from Maddy, he stabbed a scalpel into the left shoulder and with one broad stroke had opened the skin from chest to pelvic bone.

In previous rotations Maddy performed hospital autopsies in a slow and methodical manner. The County Morgue attendants worked rapidly to finish as quickly as possible. They reminded her of a grade school field trip thirty miles to Columbus to visit a cattle slaughterhouse. Richard and Slurp cut and dissected humans at a butcher's pace of trimming out rib roasts. Quick completion meant they were free to leave for the day. Maddy fantasized headhunters visiting meatpacking plants for diener recruits. Perhaps they left fliers on windshields in the packing plant parking lot.

Time and energy were spent only on important details. For an accident victim, the important details were the patterns of injury and the impact evidence. Richard, the second attendant who was never formally introduced, was busy weighing and charting the organs and stacking them onto the cutting table for Dr. Gray. Maddy introduced herself to Richard at the conclusion of the first case. He had seemed uneasy as if some unwritten protocol of caste had been violated.

"You ready to staff, Doctor Maddy? I'll go get Dr. God," Slurp asked, as a professional courtesy that Maddy knew could not be refused. The use of her first name gave her a sense of being accepted by Slurp and Richard. Sometimes informality by a hospital employee was disrespectful or contemptuous. It felt welcome in the morgue at County Hospital.

"This is a slam-fucking-dunk manslaughter homicide and I don't want any death certificate with accident on it. That bitch is going from lockup to pen. So don't fuck this up, you hear!" ordered the fidgeting Officer Maconi.

Maddy wasn't sure what annoyed her the most: his coarse language, his general rudeness, or his threatening demeanor. No, the most irksome aspect of officer Maconi was his vendetta against the woman driver. Why the anger? Why was he so bent on jailing her?

Maconi had no idea he compulsively acted out unconscious rage under the guise of justice. An average student and poor athlete, he knew nothing of prestige. Even without the father who slapped him for talking too loudly or changing the channel on the television; even without the neighborhood boys who had slugged him for fun; even without the older brothers who teased him with practical jokes, he would have been no different. Joe Maconi was a predator, born with the sole purpose of hunting others.

Slurp returned with Dr. O'Dell. Richard placed the slices into a plastic garbage bag and returned the tissues of the bag to the belly cavity of the corpse. Richard sewed up the torso with baseball-style stitches using coarse multi-fiber string. The resulting package of broken limbs and thick seams of coarse twine now resembled a bean bag chair.

Graham examined the injury patterns of the left thigh and scalp, then asked her, "What do you think?"

Maddy responded in cautious obedience. "Well, the fractured hip is probably from contact with the bumper. There is a waffle like pattern at waist level, which is something on the car, maybe, the grille. I don't know about the scalp lesions."

"Good work. You've got an eye for these things. When new residents come through, it seems about half get it quickly; the others slow to never."

Maddy enjoyed the praise from Dr. O'Dell. She was not sure yet if "good work" was a token pet phrase or a sincere evaluation.

"What's the issue in this case?" he said.

Maddy froze. What issue? After allowing Maddy a few seconds of educational discomfort, and realizing no answer was forthcoming, Graham answered his own question.

"The police seem to think this is a homicide. By statute this is true if a driver, beyond the legal alcohol limit of point zero eight, drives recklessly. But there's a world of difference to the driver whether she's convicted of reckless homicide or D.U.I."

"Jesusfuckingchrist just sign the certificate. Let the legal authorities handle the fucking details," chimed a now familiar voice from the local P.D.

"Richard, any toxicology on the deceased?" queried the chief pathologist.

"Yes sir. Alcohol content .24. No drugs of abuse on qualitative screen."

"Well, Dr. Gray and Officer Maconi, it's time for a road trip. Slurp, after you change clothes, bring those Polaroids of the body and the camera. Meet me in the parking lot in twelve minutes. Officer Maconi, would you escort us to the accident scene and then to the parking pound?"

"Fuck me," sighed the investigating officer.

Percival Mordecai elected to accompany the field trip much to the chagrin of the diener team. Delaying the last case meant a late afternoon at best and a seven P.M. closing was highly likely. Richard volunteered to stay overtime for Mordecai's gunshot victim.

**

The team of four from the examiner's office followed the squad car of Joseph Maconi. His Italian ancestors had more letters in their last name, but Joseph didn't know about them, nor did he care. He considered ancestors along with guilt and remorse irrelevant items of history.

His nickname since childhood was the same obvious trite pasta noodle as his older two brothers. The brothers took over the family business of produce distribution. He was glad to get away from the family. He liked guns; and cops got paid to carry them.

Maconi enjoyed the perquisites of driving a squad car through the city streets. He led the morgue team barely stopping at traffic signals and using his flashing lights to pass slow traffic. Dr. O'Dell was experienced at following Maconi's display of road power. His sporty BMW-3 was up to the task of riding the wake of the squad car. The pair attracted disdain from the dutifully stopped commuters. Maddy was terrified; Slurp was bored; and Percival seemed lost in a lascivious contemplation of Maddy's amply stuffed blouse.

The site of the accident was an on-ramp with barely enough shoulder room to park a car. Maconi stopped the squad well away from the guardrail, obstructing the entire ramp lane and unnecessarily delaying traffic. Maddy heard Slurp murmur the word, "asshole."

Graham walked one hundred yards up the ramp, turned about and walked two hundred yards down ramp. He knelt down on the center of the lane and motioned Maddy to take notice. He instructed Slurp to take pictures of fresh skid marks. He inspected the rail all the way back to the car. He measured the top panel of the guardrail with a pocket spring rule and jotted down notes.

"We're done here," he said.

Maconi commented, "I told you there weren't nothing here to see."

"Let's go to the car pound," Graham said.

"Fuck!" said the policeman.

Five minutes later the two cars and entourage assembled in a crushed limestone parking lot. The boundaries were fenced with chain link sixteen feet high. A row of circular razor wire capped the fence top. At twenty foot intervals were notices of police property with warnings against trespassing.

The rusting seven-year-old Ford Taurus was parked innocuously alone in the front row. The white paint had numerous dents and scratches. Newly marred paint was evident along the mid-hood. Blood stained the bumper. Dr. O'Dell immediately inspected the trim section above the passenger side of the windshield. He pointed to Maddy and Slurp to take heed and pictures.

He asked Slurp, "Where's the hip shot?"

Graham pointed to a chevron on the Ford logo in the center of the grille and held the hip photo alongside. Maddy could see the tip of the chevron imprinted on the thigh obscured but not obliterated by blood, dirt, and torn tissues.

"What do you think?" Graham directed his question to Maddy.

She realized she was learning quickly, but unaware of the exact contents of the lessons. The first day on the forensic service had jolted her into a new dimension of pathology. Hospital pathology had straightforward questions with difficult answers. Was it malignant? How advanced was the lesion? What was the indicated treatment for size and stage of the tumor? She had learned in less than six hours that forensics was the reverse, the importance and difficulty was crafting the right questions, the simple answers would follow.

"He was struck in the center of the grill. The bumper broke bones on his side and the grille imprinted on his hip area. The scalp and head injuries, which killed him, occurred when he bounced up and hit the windshield strip." Maddy was beaming at having put together the injury pattern.

"But where was he standing or walking?" grilled Graham. "Where are the skid marks? How much room is on the side of the road?"

Percival broke his silence as Slurp packed his camera and photographs. "From the length of the skid marks, I'd estimate she was traveling at the limit of forty miles-per-hour, a speed recommended by the orange sign, but not required as would a white one. She stopped right after impact. The skid marks are in the center of the lane. The old man was in the middle of the ramp and there isn't room for her car on the shoulder. He was crossing and hard to see in dark clothes, that is why he was struck at the side. After hitting the center of the bumper, his head clipped the windshield trim before he rolled off the side of the hood to the guardrail. He walked into her, she didn't do anything wrong."

"Jesusfuckingchrist, she was point 0-point-eight. She deserves to go to jail. This is still a homicide, right, honey?" Maconi pointed his finger at Maddy. Before she could answer, Graham had his hand pushing Maddy's shoulder into his BMW. She again felt an instant inner excitement from his touch. Maconi's lips opened to reveal gritted teeth as the car pulled away. Percival took careful note, as he did of everything.

The BMW returned to the hospital at 3:30 pm. The trip from the car impoundment was a silent ten minutes. Everyone was exhausted and lost in thought. The entire road trip had lasted ninety minutes, but for Maddy had been a travel through the looking glass which seemed like weeks. If every day would be this stress-filled, she'd never make it.

Graham parked the car and handed Slurp a twenty-dollar bill, speaking after Percival was out of earshot. "Take Maddy out for a drink. Nobody should have a first day like this and no lunch. Sorry I can't join you. Good work, Maddy."

Two blocks away Maconi stopped behind a double-parked car with blinking emergency flashers. The driver had obviously entered the store for a brief errand. He booted a back wheel and called for an immediate police tow.

**

Maddy called Mina en route to the Internal Medicine Room and invited her to join them. A few beers with Slurp alone might draw strange looks. Another friend along would qualify as a girls' night out.

Mina was Maddy's closest friend. Chatty and frilly girls had always bored them both. Although no tomboy growing up, she mostly had played with boys. Maddy's brother was her best friend as a child. Maddy was a loner child interested in books, not dolls. It also explained why Mina could hold her interest.

Mina had been the football playing, BB-gun shooting girl of her Terre Haute neighborhood. She was the third child with two brothers. Puberty changed the games she played with boys, but not her preference for their company.

The two met during their second year of medical school while waiting in the dean's office for schedule changes. Living at opposite ends of the city, each wished to switch a surgery rotation with a shorter commute. Because the surgeons began rounds at five a.m., this was a common medical student request. Maddy confessed knowing she would never be a surgeon. Mina said she hated blood since her first period. They laughed, then agreed to a joint swap, which the dean accepted. As their paths continued to cross in the hospital hallways, a strong bond grew slowly.

**

The Internal Medicine Room was one mile from campus, nestled among decrepit row houses of the inner city neighborhood. The concrete floor encouraged and attracted peanut shells. A few stethoscopes and surgical masks hung over the bar in a minimalist attempt to decorate the low-lit dive. Between four and seven p.m. however, it was a lounge stop for many of the brightest minds in the Midwest. At other hours, it stood nearly empty and indistinguishable from any of a hundred similar inner-city taverns.

Mina was first to arrive. She killed a few minutes in the ladies room before ordering a pitcher of light beer and four glasses. She wasn't sure how many people would be with Maddy.

"God, does that look good," groaned Maddy as she hugged Mina. "Mina, this is Slurp, the greatest diener in the state. Slurp, Mina is my best friend from medical school. She's a dermatology resident."

"I'm your only friend. Hi, Slurp."

"Careful or I'll tell him what you're really like, slut."

"Bitch," retorted Mina who turned and smiled to Slurp.

"Whoa, you charm school dropouts. I love you both."

By the second pitcher of beer the day's events had been thoroughly retold. Mina's story de jour involved chasing and murdering over thirty pubic lice throughout the day following the opening visit of a particularly squalid young female patient. Her "rash" was merely the responsive excoriations to the arthropod trespassers, the density of which was sufficient to incite a mass migration that infested the examining room.

Maddy turned to Slurp, "Is that Maconi cop always that vengeful?" Slurp was silent, so she asked again.

"Give me a minute, I slow down this time of day." He took a deep breath before continuing, "There are different kinds of cops. Some don't do nothing. Some try to give you a break, and then there's Maconi. I see quite a few what I call mean cops. All they see is a world filled with criminals and killers and drug dealers. Don't matter to the Maconi's of the world if a few innocent people go to jail. The more you pack away the less you have to deal with later, they figure. To them, nobody's completely innocent. Just ain't been caught yet. If you hang out with losers, you're a loser in their eyes."

"Is Maconi the worst of the lot?" said Maddy.

"Maconi's had that chip on his shoulder as long as I can remember. All the way back to the Michael Johnson case. He wants action. Put them in jail or shoot them. He's got some stalking addiction or something."

Mina perked up. "That's where I've heard that name before, Maconi, and the Michael Johnson boy. I remember Maconi, because it's an unusual name. He was one of the cops investigated for the gunshot death of a sixteen-year-old boy in a squad car."

"Don't ever say nothing around Maconi. He thinks the investigators made his life miserable. He got put on the desk doing investigations for five years. He hates doing report follow-ups. Just recently he got permission to do beat work again. He's trying to get a regular squad. Right now he only gets out if they need some overtime," explained Slurp in a quiet voice.

"The Johnson boy was in the police car handcuffed, but somehow managed to get the officer's gun and commit suicide. That's the official police story that didn't flush in the black community. They went nuts with riots and police brutality marches. That was our first year of medical school. Don't you remember?" Mina said to Maddy.

This interrupted Maddy's concentration and vision of the woman driver ducking as the homeless wino caromed off the bumper onto the windshield.

"I was too busy studying neuro-anatomy. But it does kind of ring a bell. I remember hurrying late to a spinal cord exam and having trouble crossing a protest march in front of the university union."

"After all the shouting was over, the case against the police was dismissed despite the fact that no one could explain how a handcuffed kid could shoot himself. Maconi and his partner got the five year slap on the wrist," Mina added.

"And don't say nothing around Dr. God either. They about hung him. He said he couldn't rule it wasn't a suicide and stuck by his decision of manner unknown. I know he felt bad about it. The press about got him lynched by the NAACP." Slurp continued, "I always figured Dr. God just stayed out of it to help his buddy, Withers."

"Who's Withers?" Maddy and Mina chimed in unison.

"He was Maconi's patrol partner in the squad car when Johnson died. In my community, the brothers, not the boys, said it was murder then and it is murder still. Withers is still around. Comes in the morgue every now and then. Usually on the really big cases like when we get a Random Ranger serial killer case. He and Dr. God are funny. Sometimes you'd swear they was good buds, but other days they hiss and snarl like cat and dog. Any beer left in there for old Slurpy?"

"I'm glad you're a good beer slurper. I don't have to entertain other origins for that nickname," teased Maddy, as all three laughed loudly, uninhibited from the libations.

"Who's Dr. God?" said Mina.

"Dr. Graham O'Dell, chief examiner." Maddy then turned to Slurp, "Why do you call him God? He seems normal to me. I mean he's smart and competent, but isn't God a little much?"

"Smart and competent? Is he single? When do I get to meet this guy?" Mina immediately picked up on Maddy's enthusiasm.

"Ladies, control yourselves. Mina, I'm sorry, but Maddy found him first. I am a person, as I am sure you can see, who can tell when a man is looked at in that way. And Miss Maddy here, has been looking at Dr. God, with more focal power than a radio-telescope," said Slurp.

"Ho, ho, ho, and I don't mean the Santa Claus ho either," Mina flamed Slurp's roasting fire.

"Subject is changed!" Maddy tried to downplay and deny her instant attraction to Graham. "Mina, are you going to the P.A.P. Fest tomorrow? You said you'd go."

"I want to hear more about this God creature from the morgue."

"The subject is the P.A.P. Fest tomorrow."

"Excuse me, but I am grossed out. You mean to tell me you are taking your friend to get a Pap test? Paleeze, ladies, we are grown up adults. We can handle these simple inconveniences of modernity discretely by ourselves. Ladies of good company do not share certain private events. You didn't even go to charm school, did you?" Slurp shook his head.

They laughed, then Maddy explained they were not discussing a gynecological exam. "P, A, P Fest with an F is an acronym for Pathology Annual Picnic Festival. Get it? P.A.P. Fest is our annual departmental picnic. Haven't you ever gone?"

"The White Castle doesn't invite the Charity Morgue basement rats. Doctors God and Green get faculty invites. G.O.D. by the way, are initials of Graham, O, Dell. Plus it seems to fit, seeing he calls all the shots in the department," Slurp answered.

"So Slurp, how will I recognize this hot Dr. God tomorrow?" teased Mina.

"Dr. God is not as trim as Moi, but a young looking fifty-five. Not my type, but I can see some hot in there. Never met his wife. I don't think she's ever been to the hospital. Rumor is they are separated. That's a strawberry that could be ripe for picking." Slurp pinched Maddy's shoulder.

"Will you two quit?" blushed Maddy. She swatted Slurp's hand.

"Slurp, I'll let you in on a secret about Maddy. She likes the older ones."

"And Mina here doesn't have a type. She's always in heat!" Maddy stuck out her tongue.

"Gray-head chaser!" Mina returned the banter, as Maddy swatted at her with her purse.

"Ladies, the bar is closed. Mainly because Dr. God's twenty is wearing thin and you two are in serious need of crowd control. Now get along, and Mina, don't let those bedbugs bite."

Slurp was on a roll and knew the event sponsored by Dr. O'Dell was a success. Nothing relaxed new residents more than a night out with Slurp. Even the homophobic male residents usually responded with a newfound camaraderie that would make the next three months easier for everyone. "Now is I officially invited to this picnic tomorrow or is I not?"

27

"Absolutely," they laughed out together.

"See you tomorrow at eight." Slurp was still working.

"Saturday?" groaned Maddy.

"Sorry, but Friday night is date night for the grim reaper." Slurp got up and left the twenty. As Maddy stood up, Mina caught her arm.

"I heard Professor Comstock is retiring. He'll be there tomorrow. I thought you should know."

Maddy was taken back, "Retiring?"

"That's the grapevine. Can you handle seeing him?" Mina touched her arm again. Now it was cold.

**

Maddy's unconscious autopilot drove the car home. She was lost in thoughts of Professor Bruce Comstock. Her second year of residency had been a whirlwind of passion and intrigue. Comstock was professor of clinical chemistry at University. He was a marathon runner of sleek build with brown grayless hair and bright green eyes that mesmerized Maddy. His current research was attempting to determine the affects of blood constituent proteins on blood wall surfaces, particularly the heart and kidneys. Maddy's first rotation in clinical pathology was chemistry, a special world of serum proteins, enzymes, cholesterol, and aisles of expensive analyzers.

Comstock gave Maddy a tour the first day of the month. He innocently touched her shoulder while explaining the throughput for the gas chromatography mass spectrophotometry unit used in drug analysis. Maddy remembered the tingling excitement from his touch. She heard his gentle voice, a quiet reservoir of knowledge that inspired the department. The memory was scarily similar to the presence of Dr. O'Dell. She took a personal oath not to repeat the hassles of an affair with a faculty member.

"P, H, D? What's that mean? Pretty handsome dude?" She recalled flirting with him in his office. Compulsively without control, she asked Comstock for an idea for her residency research project. She wanted to be close to him.

On Friday of the second week, she repeated the pretty handsome dude line with door closed and blinds drawn. Minutes later clothes of different sizes, gender, and colors were mixed and strewn on the office floor. In her mind, Maddy re-experienced her pleasure position on top of Comstock holding the arm of his leather chair for balance.

Comstock's wife was a borderline psychotic with histrionic features, according to the university's brightest psychotherapists. Maddy had no idea what that meant. She, like ninety percent of her class, had ignored psychiatry in medical school. In practice it meant threats of harm by Mrs. Comstock to herself and to Maddy.

The most damaging threats were organizational, not physical. She confronted James Sweetbread M.D., president of the University Hospital physician's organization. Mrs. Comstock demanded he intervene to stop the affair and suspend Dr. Gray, lest Mrs. Comstock campaign for Sweetbread's dismissal as an immoral brothel keeper.

Sweetbread's position was a complex hybrid of politics. Technically, the Board of Trustees appointed him, but they were puppets, rubber-stamping the back room orders from the state politicos who funded University Hospital. Sweetbread's boat tolerated no waves from outside its wake.

Maddy and Bruce complied with the order. She was to have no contact with him. The order called for zero tolerance or they both would be expelled from the university staff.

Her only regret was never having told him, "I love you." She wasn't sure she had loved him or anyone ever, but it was a present she had wanted to give him. Comstock had told Maddy she was irresistible because she looked at him with desire, a look he never received from his wife. He had blamed their affair and predicament on himself.

At age forty-nine, he was too young for retirement. Did he still think of her? Did she miss him? She missed his gentleness, his goodness, and the sex had been great, also.

She had a lifelong passion for older men. At age fourteen she was smitten with a crush on her English teacher. Compulsively she brought him written questions putting papers in front of him while she leaned over his shoulder and gently massaged her newly discovered breasts on his upper back. The pleasure was not entirely all hers. It ended when she got close enough to his face and Maddy kissed him before he could withdraw. The English teacher moved Maddy to the back row of the class and prohibited her from coming in alone. The guilt and fear persisted. He quit teaching the end of that year.

She dated occasionally in high school and college, but had more enthusiasm for volunteering to help out male faculty, pre-requisitely twenty years her senior. Bruce Comstock was her second crush consummate.

The first occurred her senior year in college. She was serving a term as treasurer of the science division scholarship fund and spent a good deal of time in the comptroller's office. The lanky forty-four year old accountant and Maddy devised a special and personal way of dealing with "interest and deposits."

**

A police siren jolted Maddy into the present. She was one block from her apartment when blinding flashing lights exploded from her mirror. She glanced at the speedometer. She couldn't have been speeding. A moment later she was handing her license and insurance card to a startlingly familiar face, Officer Joseph Maconi.

"You have to come to a complete stop in this state. You rolled through the stop sign at Thirteenth Street, doctor. Don't you ever look in the mirror? I've had my lights on for three blocks."

"I don't even know what you're talking about. I was busy thinking, about work. I am sorry. Can we let this go? It's been a long day for both of us," she pleaded.

"I think a ticket will help you reconsider that death certificate you fucked-up today. I had to release the drunk driver bitch because of you. This ticket could be dropped as easily as a slight change on that death certificate. Have a nice day." Maconi walked away. Maddy angrily leaned out the window.

"This is extortion."

Maconi turned around and put a toothpick into his mouth, "This is how the real world works. Backs get scratched or stabbed."

**

JUNE 2, SATURDAY, The P.A.P. Fest

The June morning was bright and windless. Saturday traffic was light. Maddy reached the parking lot in less than ten minutes. Maddy thought how delightful the weather was for the picnic. As she approached the front entrance of Charity, she noticed the absence of the smokers and wheel chairs and wondered if the welfare class took off on Saturday. She imagined the aimless daily street wanderings of the jobless who gave themselves permission to stay home and sleep in on the weekend. Maddy grunted a curse as she missed her turn into the parking lot.

Maddy anticipated a light morning in the morgue. She had followed Slurp's advice to preview "The Breakfast Club" specials by tuning to WXCR, a local radio news station, en-route to the hospital. Any deaths from homicide, fires, accidents, or police action would require autopsy. The lead news item was a bloodless bank robbery that raised her hopes of reaching the picnic early.

The morgue was spotless stainless steel, which shined with the pride of Richard and Slurp's end of the day buffing. Twenty-four hours had eliminated the charred soot and smell of the fire victim, the musty odor of the drowned, and the dried blood from Dr. Mordecai's gunshot homicide. Like the night elves in the fairy tales, an unseen band of morgue attendants scrubbed clean the tables and floors after the pathologists retreated to their offices. Maddy made a mental note to thank them and praise their work.

Slurp was a fashion chameleon. The earrings were gone. Yesterday's lavender pedal pushers were replaced with red khaki slacks and black golf shirt complete with Nike swooshes. "Let me guess, Tiger Woods day in the morgue?" Maddy winked approval.

"P.A.P. Fest. No sense terrorizing the parents. Children got enough on their hands without having to deal with hysterical parents worried some faggot's going to touch their babies. Feel privileged. Today is one of the rare sightings of the Eldred."

Despite the well-lighted room Slurp's pupils were large and dark. Maddy had thought Graham was joking about the amphetamine, but Slurp had hit the starting line in full stride. "Now come along, Precious, Dr. Green will be in soon. We got six pop-tarts and one old man we might be able to get out of doing if we can A, S, C, V, D him past Dr. Green. Dr. God wouldn't give him a second look, but Green's as straight as a stick from Robin Hood's quiver."

"Stop it!" Maddy heard someone's order using her voice. It startled her that she had been so loud, but she was proud of her assertiveness.

She had an instant flashback of Dr. O'Dell touching her shoulder and advising, "You are in charge." Maddy composed herself.

"Slurp, one thing at a time. Pop-tart?"

"Those the ones we pull out of the drawer, toast the outside with our eyes, and they're done. Get it?" Slurp's eyebrows raised.

"Not exactly. How many bodies are there?" Maddy's mouth remained open to encourage Slurp to continue.

"Seven. Welcome to Saturday brunch."

"We have seven autopsies this morning?" Maddy's inflection squeaked on the seven. Her hope of making the picnic early was fading.

"Okay, Precious. I can see we are going to have to start with death-metic 101. Attention class." Slurp tapped his pen on the morgue cooler. "We got nine hundred thousand people in this city. At least one percent die per year. That's roughly ten thousand assorted pastries, of which two thirds die in hospitals, nursing home, or under a doctor's care. The police and coroner get the local doctor to sign the death certificate and thank glory we never see them. You following?" Slurp's bulging eyes threatened death if she said no.

"Not everybody gets autopsied in other words."

"Hallelujah! Keep that neuron in play." Slurp kicked back into high gear. "We got to do all the homicides. That's about a hundred and fifty. Two hundred when unemployment is high. Then all the insurance cases like car drivers, accidents, and drownings, another six to eight hundred. Now we get thirty-five hundred refrigerated admits each year, but I only got two staff pathologists, one fellow, and a resident. You're OK, but some ain't worth a squirrel's dick. We got four dieners, which on any given day is likely to be three due to personal life complications. And they'll quit if I try to squeeze in more than four cases a day."

"Slurp, take some air! I understand. Four autopsies times three hundred working days is roughly twelve hundred post-mortems maximum. You get out of doing two thousands, the pop-tarts."

"Breakfast is served," smiled Slurp as Maddy nodded in self-congratulation that she had maintained pace with her manic assistant.

Slurp pulled open the drawer and pointed to a bypass scar down the man's chest. ASCVD he wrote on the paper and pushed it toward Maddy. Her raised eyes prompted Slurp, "Athero-Sclerotic Cardio-Vascular Disease. Bypass scar, lives alone, died at home. They couldn't get a hold of the family doc." He tapped Maddy's elbow and she signed.

"I don't know this for sure."

"Precious, nobody knows nothing for sure. He's old; he's dead; and he's got a bad heart, which is certified by that scar. Are you are going to sign this line or are we going to have an issue?" Slurp demanded with his gun-barrel pupils blasted open with methamphetamine. Maddy signed the death certificate and Slurp snatched it out of her hands.

The next drawer held an obese woman with gray skin and bright red cheeks and lips. Slurp rolled the body onto its side to disclose no trauma, while he announced a lab report of carbon monoxide of 67 percent. There was a suicide note left and she had been under psychiatric care for seven years. This was her first success after three tries. No one, most importantly the coroner, disputed the suicide. Maddy signed the death certificate: *Manner: suicide, Cause of Death: carbon monoxide poisoning.*

Two nearly identical stories of uncontrolled hypertension were certified as hypertensive cardio-vascular disease by history. The bodies looked normal. The fifth death certificate listed epilepsy as cause of death. The forty-six-year-old man had stopped taking carbazepam a week earlier. He had no money for a refill. Maddy reflected how a few dollars a month and this person would still be alive. Then she wondered if he had overdosed.

"How do we know anything about how these people died. Can we get a carbazepam level to document he was off the drug: to make me feel better?" Maddy asked in frustration.

"O.K., Precious. We want everyone to feel good, now don't we?" Slurp rolled his eyes while performing a poke-the-syringe pantomime to another diener sitting on the center autopsy table. He respected her conscientiousness.

"I'm serious. How can I certify death on a normal looking body? They could have been poisoned, or had a stroke, or maybe they've got an undiagnosed cancer. I am not going to be part of this charade." Maddy felt slightly embarrassed but mostly righteous in her ranting.

"We are trained and hired by the citizenry to do the best we can. We investigate them all to some extent, which usually means a few questions and a quick look-see. We can't post them all, and I'm sure few minor murders slip through," said Slurp.

A voice spoke from behind Slurp and Maddy, "Good morning."

"Dr. Green. We were wanting your opinion exactly how to word the sign-out...," Slurp switched to his most obsequious deference to the charge staff. Dr. Green cut him off.

"Slurp, drawer six, we've got to do him. He's a diabetic on an investigational insulin pump. It's political from the drug company. Let's get crackin', it's picnic day."

"You and Doctor God going?" Slurped encouraged the banter as he pulled the body tray out and motioned to Richard to load the gurney.

"I wouldn't miss it for the world. My two-year-old loves to work the crowds. Dr. O'Dell has some golf outing with the big cheeses, Dr. Sweetbread and Congressman Burr. I'm taking Percival. He seemed terrified, but I explained a little socializing was part of the training experience, mandatory in his case," continued Green.

Maddy speculated that Dr. Green was the prototype of normal if such a person existed. He spoke with a happy and pleasant disposition without a hint of Pollyannish sappiness. He delighted in his son. He was nice looking and Maddy imagined many women might find him desirable, although she felt no physical attraction. He had his job and the world in perspective. He would try his best without anguishing over each detail. Would she ever have a career with purpose, which she loved?

Dr. Green was indeed vanilla Hoosier: a Protestant, Purdue graduate, church deacon, no speeding tickets, married with son, and Pacer basketball season ticker holder. His parents were strict but kind, and had provided him clothes and basketballs without complaint. Green saw homicide victims as rare tragedies in an otherwise wonderful world.

"Dr. Green, did you always want to do this, forensics?"

"Not at all. When I was a resident on rotation like you. I found it interesting. One of my earliest cases was a fourteen-year-old newspaper boy who was shot and killed during a robbery for two dollars. I felt like I needed to do what I could for him and his family. I just stayed on after residency. I can't say it was a calling. It was more like helping an old lady across the street."

The diener crew flew through the autopsy. Body diagrams were completed with notations of scars, tattoos, and arthritic deformities. The torso was incised. The four working hands of Slurp and Richard removed and weighed the major organs in less than fifteen minutes. Maddy personally removed the insulin pump and placed it into a plastic bag at the suggestion of Dr. Green, who correctly predicted a call from the manufacturer requesting its return.

No specific pathologic lesions sufficient for death were discovered. After the previous day's controversies and unexpected findings, the current case seemed boringly mundane. There were only mild atherosclerotic lesions of the coronary vessels, but Dr. Green convinced Maddy that the cause of death was diabetes complicated by ASCVD. Whether by seizure, undiagnosed heart attack, brain stroke, or arrhythmia he said diabetes was the likely underlying initiator. It warranted certification.

The phantasm of the dead man's life took her. She imagined the man smiling enthusiastically as the research doctor tried to explain how the insulin pump worked. The doctor would gloss over the unknown aspects of research and the possible dangers.

If the pump failed to deliver insulin the man would slowly develop hyperglycemic crisis as his blood glucose rose over several days. In contrast, if the pump overdosed the insulin, it was possible to die within hours for lack of sugar to sustain the brain. Insulin degrades quickly and dying cells immediately after death eat up glucose. No usual blood testing can confirm or refute a hypothesis of hyperinsulinism. The acceptance of the device was simply another complication of this man's diabetes, according to Dr. Green.

Maddy labeled this reasoning science fiction. Later she would accept the practical necessity of such speculation as a social duty of her profession. For the moment she was flooded with the realization that death investigation ranged from the intense F.B.I. technological crime war with dozens of forensic specialists to the pop-tart sign out at County

Charity morgue. Two thirds of deaths never even pass through the morgue drawer, then only a few are actually autopsied.

Maddy realized that a body's journey from death to cremation could conceal anything. The public trusted the police, the pathologists, the doctors, and the coroners. How easy it would be for any of these officials to disguise a murder. She was ready for a personal rescue from her Walter Mitty land. A shower and a picnic would suffice nicely.

**

Graham pulled his BMW into the bag drop circle at Whispering Pines Country Club, stopped the engine, popped the trunk latch, and stepped out to tip the bag boy. A blonde whiskerless college boy with short hair and a broad grin greeted the doctor. "Perfect day for golf. Who are you playing with, sir?"

"I'm with the University Hospital foursome. James Sweetbread is *with whom* I will be playing."

"You must be Doctor O'Dell," said the boy oblivious to Graham's lesson in the objective case, as he checked off Graham's name on a pairings sheet.

Graham pitied the young man who had to memorize the names of guests for no purpose other than sustaining the grandiose self-importance of a half-dozen overfed board members of The Pines. The boy returned the pairings sheet to his back pocket and answered with practiced deference, "You're starting on hole one with Mr. Sweetbread, Mr. Burr, and Mr. Corless. You will be riding with

Congressman Burr. I can take you to the range after you park your car."

Graham handed away two dollars with the same compassion for poverty that he felt when paying off-key street musicians for unrecognizable solos.

Mr. Corless was the self-enamored chief executive officer of EnvironTech, the state's second largest corporation. EnvironTech was a spin-doctored name for a toxic waste treatment conglomerate. Corless's company imported railcar loads of chemical, nuclear, and industrial waste from other states. It treated the chemicals and either diluted or buried the run-off in local farmland. Compared to other states, Indiana laws on toxic waste importing and disposal were almost non-existent. EnvironTech profits were derived in large part from this political competitive advantage.

His name appeared regularly in the newspaper, usually to point out his state-leading annual C.E.O. compensation of over $12 million. Equally often he was the newsworthy target of green protests. Graham had met him at a zoo fundraiser to which William Corless was the top contributor. Charitable contributions were his noblesse oblige, inconsequential sums to clean up a toxic image. Corless's greatest personal struggle was restraining his monologue of self-importance, his power mongering as a congressional puppeteer, and his art collection.

Sweetbread's position was owed directly to Corless, the C.E.O. who flexed his political muscle in the state legislature. Sweetbread loved controlling people. Six thousand employees including two Nobel laureates directly depended upon him for salary and advancement.

Power is food for creatures like Sweetbread and Corless. They not only love its taste; they hoard it in their pantries. Money is useful primarily because it can control people, large numbers of people. Control is the fuel of their souls. Corless purchased a Monet, not for love of water lilies, but for its power to turn heads. Charity events in black tie were the arenas to face off with fellow players in the game of power.

David Burr in subtle distinction was a power user. Like a gambling addiction, he thrived on the action, the flow of money and power through his fingers. Sweetbread needed direct access to pull the strings of a cast of puppets. Corless needed to own the assets of the political theater. Burr only required the touch and feel of the strings. For him power was a stage dance and he needed to be the choreographer.

Burr, the thirteen-term Republican congressman from central Indiana was an inexorable force in Washington. Nearly three decades ago the state legislature gerrymandered a congressional district of the wealthy and privileged, thus granting them a personal representative. The framers of the Constitution would have been pleased at the preservation of the white male landowner as controlling electorate. Nearly eighty percent of registered voters in his district were loyal conservatives. Burr actively reaped the benefits from the seniority system in Congress, which guaranteed the choice chairmanships to anyone who survived enough re-elections.

Interstate Commerce and the Interior committees were his chosen chairmanships. Corless paid heavily to sustain Burr. In return, legislation roadblocks from Burr's committees allowed the uninterrupted roll of waste-filled boxcars into Indiana despite the green protests. The top drawer of power was foreign affairs and appropriations. Only natural longevity stood in his way of attaining all three. Then who knows? The presidency?

"Now come around the cart here, Grant. I know you'll want a picture with me for your office," commandeered the public official, "and Grant, can you switch the bags for me. I need you to drive. My right knee's a little out of sorts."

"It's Graham."

The pathologist hesitated for a moment, considering whether to insist on being addressed as Dr. O'Dell. All knew David Burr by his public persona on television. Graham viewed Burr as an arrogant embarrassment to the state. Once he had called for the use of nuclear bombs to be dropped on the Middle East. Much to the chagrin of his staunch Israeli supporters, he was forced to acknowledge that "the possible collateral damage renders that solution problematic because it might damage Holy Land structures."

Burr referred to welfare mothers as alley cats. In his most red-faced moment of alliteration, he described public schools as "left-wing liberal laboratories of licentiousness." The district teachers and soccer moms winced, but still voted a straight Republican ticket. Indiana, where basketball is the focus of school programs, continues to rank lowest in academic achievement of the midwestern states.

Sweetbread, sensing that Graham was not celebrity struck by Burr, intervened with purpose, "Graham's our ace today. And with your shots too, David," he quickly dabbed in with his brown-nosing brush, "we should be a strong contender. Graham's the best we've got at the hospital. And who among us likes to lose?"

The first straightforward truth had been spoken. Graham O'Dell was a scratch handicap golfer. Sweetbread had demanded O'Dell join and anchor their team today as a ringer, certainly not for socializing. Whispering Pines was a favorite course to the advanced golfer. Old money was highly stacked, and the Indianapolis well-to-do boys had built themselves a golfing monument at Whispering Pines.

Graham gave in to the temptation of the personal splendor experienced from the course. On two previous occasions during his tenure he had prostituted himself to play golf with Sweetbread. Golf with David Burr would greatly eclipse the previous lows of golf with Sweetbread.

The initial six holes were a monologue disparaging the evil liberal bleeding-hearts. Burr complained that the groundkeepers at the course were illegal immigrants who ought to be shipped back to Mexico.

Graham defended them. "The workers do a wonderful job at conditioning the course, a job that Americans are unwilling to perform."

Burr shouted at Graham from within the cart, "The only reason the Mexicans have jobs in the States is that welfare money makes it too easy for able bodied Americans to stay supplied with drugs. Cut off the welfare, that's my back-to-work program."

Later Graham bristled when Burr remarked, "AIDS is a Christian blessing to eliminate pagans in Africa and homosexuals in America."

A young naive college co-ed was driving a drink cart. Burr asked her if she would like to do an internship in Washington. "Really get to know Congress from the inside," he said with a wink.

Burr told her how he flew to Washington early on Monday mornings, therefore he had a standing reservation every Sunday night at the Airport Hyatt Regency. He invited her over to his room that Sunday evening, handing her a card with his hotel room number in pencil on the back.

Graham was aghast and relieved when she said she was babysitting for a niece. This proposition reminded Graham of a scandal Burr had survived. Of course he could survive any scandal; Burr was unbeatable.

Three years ago it was reported that Burr had a child out of wedlock, whom he was supporting with hush money. He denied it vehemently. The local press supported the purity of their great congressman. Graham, however, knew the truth.

His friend, Sergeant Carl Withers of the police department was the uncle to Burr's bastard son, David Withers. The sister of the Sergeant had been a Congressional aid in his office after college and prey to the public servant. For seventeen years money had passed to her for support of their son and bribery for the hush. Graham knew the money came from an un-traceable source and was funneled through Withers.

The second six holes found Graham annoyed with requests for free medical advice. Burr demanded an authoritative and professional explanation for his variable cholesterol level, the value of niacin in reducing heart attacks, and the amount of dietary fiber, zinc, and anti-oxidants which Dr. O'Dell thought advisable.

Burr was proud and shameless about his use of free medical care. He explained how he didn't go to doctors at home because congressmen got free use of the military hospital at Bethesda. The problem was the hour commute each way from his office. Couldn't Graham give him a cortisone shot in his knee?

Graham tried to explain that betamethasone was better and longer lasting than straight cortisone. Lidocaine anesthetic would also be superior to lessen the pain. Burr shook his head. No, he wanted a cortisone shot.

Burr bragged about how much golf he and one senator played at the best clubs on the East Coast: Congressional, Winged Foot, Pine Valley, and Merion. They would cancel committee meetings with minimal notice.

Graham reflected. These men had entire days to plays golf, but not an hour to drive for free medical care. This man, who railed against Medicaid and a National Health Service, was relentless in beseeching a free knee injection from Dr. O'Dell.

**

The Pathology Annual Picnic Fest was the Hoosier subculture variant of Americana. Young girls painted the faces of toddlers to be silly cartoon characters and super-heroes. Retired grandfathers sat in webbed lawn chairs, smoked cigarettes and dripped bake beans down the fronts of their T-shirts and onto their obese midriffs.

Teens hid out of view to smoke cigarettes. Grade school children roamed the park and trees with uncharacteristic freedom from their parents. The children's regulated lives of closely supervised soccer and continuously planned activities yielded little time to experience spontaneous play. They ran with abandon, stopping momentarily to grab a chicken leg or fountain soda. They threw rocks into the woods.

Small children ran and bumped one another seemingly at random. Dr. Green's toddler stumbled about at top speed while his doting father trailed three steps behind. He picked up a dead toad to the horror of his mother.

The adult staff played the annual ritual softball game, which pitted the medical staff and residents against the technical and support personnel. Despite that Dr. Mordecai was the only person on either team to strike out during the slow pitch game, the medical team won. Maddy did not play, but watched and cheered with her guests, Mina and Slurp.

At the conclusion of the opening softball game, the ritual beer keg tapping was accomplished with the losers serving the first beer to the winners. Six years ago, Dr. Sweetbread proclaimed that the softball game must precede beer drinking to minimize losses to the health insurance fund.

Slurp looked almost normal in his golf shirt, but his enthusiastic cheerleading during the softball game vanquished his ruse. The annual awards and stories for the likes of messiest autopsy, greatest blunder, teacher of the year, and least likely to succeed, were bestowed.

Maddy received the "Lost in Space" award for the least likely to be paying attention. A first year resident, Charles Calvert suffered the humiliation of "Most likely to Commit Malpractice Award." The unfortunate resident had dissected a morbidly obese seven hundred and eighty-pound man with boulders of suet everywhere that blobbed over the table like folds of kneaded bread. Poor Charles Calvert in the middle of the prosection was lost in pelvic fat and sliced through the skin. This blind maneuver inadvertently caused the amputation of the corpse's penis. When the body was removed the organ remained on the table, creating an embarrassing legacy of crude humor. Years hence in resident lore he would be immortalized as Charles I, The Penis Pruner.

Charles accepted his award graciously and in good fun. He ducked his head in mock shame, sitting down immediately in the nearest chair next to Slurp, Mina, and Maddy.

Maddy hugged him around the shoulders and offered condolences, "It's all in fun. Believe me, it can be worse." He looked at her in a puzzled expression. "Charles, my second year I got the faculty research award, which is supposed to be for assisting in research. Or in the words of the emcee, researching the faculty. It's common knowledge. You'll hear about my relationship with a chemistry faculty eventually. I just want you to take the ribbing in good fun."

"She was and is doing good research, Charles. And everyone recognized it. Otherwise it would have been a sadistic joke," Mina commented. "She studies blood group antigens on the intimal surfaces of arteries in MI patients."

"How do you do that?" Charles was interested.

"We are using plant lectins, glycoproteins in peanuts, and flowers, and bushes which preferentially bind to cell antigens. Previous research has shown some changes in density of these antigens in damaged intima. We are trying to figure out if the losses of antigen sites come before or after the vessels are damaged," said Maddy.

"Excuse me, doctors, what the hell are you talking about? In working man's terms, please."

"Sorry, Slurp." Maddy looked at Mina who explained.

"Heart attacks occur when blood vessels get clogged. Sometimes the vessels close down with cholesterol clumps called plaques, which is commonly called hardening of the arteries. Other times the arteries just spontaneously clot off. Usually it is a combination of both. Anyway, blood types: O, A, and B are actually complex sugars on the surfaces of red cells. Well, it turns out that artery-lining cells, called the intima, also have these sugars. Maddy is testing whether the density of the sugars on the artery surfaces is related to the clots in heart attacks."

"Oh, sure. I guess that makes sense," said Slurp.

"It's a good project, except when things get too sticky," Maddy punned.

The table laughed. "I need a few more cases of untreated new infarcts before there's enough data to publish. Charles, the department requires us to publish a research project. If you can find a combined clinical pathology and anatomic pathology project, the politics go much easier. It's also less sticky if you don't fool around with your faculty advisor." The table laughed again at Maddy's comfort with her past scandal.

Slurp arose, "I still don't know what in coffee-cake heaven you folks are talking about, but this is a picnic and I need some sweet icing for my long john, and there is one beautiful cheesecake on my radar."

They looked in the direction of a group of men engaged in Frisbee tossing, noticing a bare chested man with muscles attesting familiarity with the gym. Also in view were Doctors Green and Mordecai along with Dr. Green's two-year-old son. Mordecai was videotaping an unsuccessful attempt by Green to induce the moment of first-batted Whiffle Ball.

**

48

By the fourteenth hole, Graham was considering walking off the course. He was infuriated at Burr's cheating. The congressman repeatedly and unashamed nudged his ball unto tufts of grass to improve his lies. Graham felt that golf, while a game of self-administered policing, is a game meant to be fun. He could tolerate rule bending by lesser players to make the game more enjoyable. Burr, however, was a capable player in whom the cheating was unnecessary and disgusting.

Even worse for Graham was the blatant cheating of his presumed friends, Sweetbread and Corless. All had enough money to make the bets irrelevant. Sweetbread and Corless had donated five thousand dollars to the children's charity that day. Burr was a non-donating celebrity. The side game Nassau for twenty bucks was symbolic of their world adventures. Most troubling was that the score of the foursome was cheating the rest of the field at the tournament.

Corless wanted the money to waggle at the bar, while Sweetbread was after the bragging rights. Burr would break any rule to capture his friends' money and feel the trophy pass through his fingertips. Graham knew Burr's character was no more honest in serious matters of state.

On hole fifteen the twosome was searching for a ball Burr hit into an area of long grass and small crowded trees. Graham watched Burr pull a ball out of his pocket, drop it behind a tree out of sight to Sweetbread and Corless, and pronounce it found.

Burr looked squarely at Graham, whose eyes revealed his knowledge of the breach, and winked, "The real world works well for those who know how to play the game.

That's why it's full of poor bastards who work for peanuts and welfare scum who lay around and whine. They don't have a clue how the real world works."

Corless drove over and looked at Burr's newfound perfect lie. "You lucky bastard, David. Speaking of the bastard?"

Graham saw the eyebrows of Corless rise into two little question marks. He sensed they were talking about the child of Wither's sister.

"See this little white ball. Watch me whack it. No problem. That's how to handle it. If it doesn't go in the right direction, just step up and whack it."

"Burr, if you hit that nine iron, it won't clear that greenside sand trap," said Corless.

"Buried in the bunker. That sounds like the perfect solution for dealing with that little bastard. Help me with this one, Richard. Can you put your special agent on it?"

"Splendid, old chap, my pleasure. You need to whack one every now and then or you forget how," responded Corless as he and Sweetbread rode away snickering.

Graham bogied the final two holes. He was lost in thought about the meaning of "whacking the bastard." To Sweetbread's dismay, it dropped the team score to second place. As the rest of the foursome headed to the scorer's table to collect their runner-up awards, Graham made a telephone call. He stopped the Congressman at the bagdrop.

"How's that knee holding out?"

"I'm going to get that cortisone shot from you, aren't I, Doc? You're too nice a guy to let a public servant suffer. I know it'll help the swelling."

Graham continued smiling. "Splendid, old chap, my pleasure. Surely we can make it less painful. But I'll need to check some lab work first. I've got syringes and blood drawing tubes in my car. Come over to my trunk. I'll draw some blood, and when everything checks out, I can come by tomorrow and inject your knee. But let's keep this on low volume. You don't want the word out that a pathologist is treating you. And I don't need that publicity either."

"You do know how the world works, O'Dell. You're one of us," beamed Burr. "Totally Q.T. Tomorrow, you come down to the airport Hyatt after nine, my room is always 313, and it'll be our little secret. Here's my card."

"Nine o'clock, 313," Graham read the back of the congressman's card that was identical to the one given the drink girl.

**

Slurp ran up behind Maddy and gently pinched both shoulder creases. "Precious, your sugar plum is ripening on the tree. See that man over there?" He pointed across the park to a man sitting on a three foot high cut utility pole stump, which was one piece of the parking lot barrier. "He sent you this note."

Maddy stared and nodded, "Bruce Comstock!"

"He is a cute one. But I got my own fish on the line. And I can wait no longer to reel him in. See you Monday. You don't have to come in on Sunday, and if they ain't nothing going on, I will be on muscle beach, multiple times. Thank you for the picnic." Slurp kissed her cheek.

Dear Maddy,

I hoped to see you today. I'm leaving tomorrow to tour the country in my camper. I've always wanted to see the National Parks. Keep up the good work. Your project is well enough along, you'll get it published. I wouldn't risk violating our no contact order, although it wouldn't affect me now, I wouldn't dream of making your life difficult. I'll always care deeply for you. Love and Goodbye, as I'm not returning.
Bruce

Maddy looked up through teary eyes and watched Bruce Comstock climb into a cream colored Winnebago camper. She didn't think twice and furtively walked around the park edge, constantly looking over her shoulder to see who might be watching. She skipped around to the side of the camper and tapped on the door.

Bruce opened the door and pulled her inside. He hugged her tightly and spoke into her hair-covered ear. "You are wonderful, Maddy. Have a great life, a great career."

"You're only forty-nine, Bruce."

"I'm done here. I've done some good work."

"You're still a pretty handsome dude." The words from their first embrace fell out of Maddy's mouth. They kissed with an imploding passion; the wall between Pyramus and Thisbe had been removed.

She grabbed his shirt buttons and created her own déjà vu of their initial office tryst. Within minutes the compact bedroom of the camper was decorated with outer and undergarments.

Maddy sat upright straddled over Comstock with palms on his trampoline belly. She bounded up and down, matching his grunting gasps, and accelerating her springboard pace concentrating on her climatic final flourish.

"God, have I missed this," she groaned, "Are you done?"

The moment failed to come as they say. He grew limp and quiet. Maddy stopped and stared. He was blue-faced with blank stare. She lapsed into one of her momentary trances, but her mind was racing. Only seconds transpired before she poked his neck, searching for a carotid pulse.

Absent.

She pounded his chest, twice, a third time. Her hand hurt, so she groped again for a pulse. She breathed into his mouth forcefully. She pumped his chest for two minutes. There was no pulse. Bruce was dead.

She didn't kill him, did she? He must have had a heart attack. Her most convoluted thought was hearing a tipsy Mina warn a future date to be careful as Maddy had a record of finishing-off old men. "Focus!" she screamed internally.

She dressed herself while lost in an ethical fog. She went over the terms of her agreement with Sweetbread like a defense attorney preparing for trial. She was to have no contact with Bruce Comstock. His wife had threatened legal action against the University. Sweetbread responded to the greater horror of bad publicity. The department function and reputation were at stake, which meant the affair was a threat to Sweetbread's supreme authority. The sacrifice of Dr. Gray's career training and future employability was of no concern to him.

She was desperate for guidance. Soap opera logic would have to suffice. Caring for Bruce and caring for herself meant keeping a secret. She arranged the sheets over his naked body. She folded his clothes by his bed to appear he had gone to bed peacefully. She checked the room twice for any evidence belonging to her. She exited quickly and quietly out the door and down the parking lot, looking up in relief to see no one watching.

She failed to see a man with head down and eyes focused into the video viewfinder. Dr. Mordecai had the telephoto lens at full power to capture the Green toddler blowing bubbles. He noticed the unmistakable image of Maddy Gray exiting the Winnebago mausoleum that now held the remains of Bruce Comstock. In front of Maddy he recorded Slurp standing beside a Ford Explorer with a muscle bound man of twenty-five with shaved head and hairless chest.

**

Ten miles north in the parking lot at Whispering Pines Country Club, Dr. Graham O'Dell inserted a 22-gauge needle attached to a twenty-five c.c. syringe into the arm vein of Congressman David Burr. The man winced, then smirked in self-satisfaction at having the chief medical examiner pampering to him like a common manservant. The professional power of Dr. O'Dell flowed into him via the needle. It gave the Congressman the gooseflesh of triumph.

**

The car drove itself toward Maddy's apartment. Her mind was a prison cell with Winnebago walls. The image of Bruce Comstock blue and lifeless refused to vacate the cell. She pumped his chest over and over. She raided the room frantically for something to aid her. She searched the room afterward for evidence of her presence. Shooting pangs of guilt sent her sorting through her purse, checking for sunglasses, hairbrush, earrings, anything she might have left behind.

Wahoh, wahoh, wahoh yanked her into the present. The police siren and flashing lights closed in near her rear bumper as the cars came to a curbside halt. Maddy had no idea where she had been, how fast she had traveled, or if she had violated any traffic controls.

"My, my, if isn't the good Dr. Gray. You were driving erratically. I'd like you to get out of the car," Officer Maconi instructed in a tone of unveiled contempt.

"I've had a very stressful afternoon. I was daydreaming…"

"Out of the car! How much have you been drinking?" he demanded.

"Maybe a beer or two at a picnic earlier. I'm not drunk," she protested.

"Do you consent to a blood alcohol breath analysis? Failure to consent is grounds for automatic suspension of your driving privileges for not less than 180 days. The full penalties of conviction for driving while intoxicated apply. A nolo-contendere conviction of driving under the influence, a class B misdemeanor in this state, will be rendered, and is not subject to appeal."

"What? I told you. I may have not been paying attention."

"Do you refuse the breath exam, Ma'am?" he gritted his teeth.

She submitted and the registered level of 0.03 percent was well below the legally permissible limit of 0.08. Having anticipated the result, Maconi suffered no disappointment. "Dr. Gray, I'm pleased to see you are a fine citizen obeying your duty to drink responsibly. Might I remind you of your responsibility to punish drunks who run over little old men? Someone's going to jail for the old man. I hope it isn't you. Life will be a lot easier the sooner you get with program. Consider this your final probation."

Maddy noticed how deep blue his eyes looked against the blue of his uniform. But the beauty of such eyes was lost in eddies of anger and pain that swirled in his irises, swirls of a primitive and violent color.

**

JUNE 3, SUNDAY, The Random Ranger

Sergeant Carl Withers hurried through the automatic sliding doors of the emergency department at Charity Hospital. His head leaned forward looking ahead, while his feet dodged the sleepy relatives of the Saturday night casualties. The midnight darkness outside contrasted with the bright fluorescent lighting and whiteness of the patient bay walls and linens. Withers flashed his badge and introduced himself to the ER attending, a bearded young man with a stocky neck appearing thicker under the collar of a dangling stethoscope.

"Officer Withers, Eldred Smith is in bay four. We're sorry to have gotten you out of bed, but he insisted. He has refused to talk with any of our security, counselors, or the police," apologized the doctor.

"How bad is it?"

"He's been beaten up pretty thoroughly, but so far we haven't found anything serious. He's got a three-inch stab wound in the chest that we're most concerned about. We drained some blood and put in a chest tube. Now we wait and see. We've got the chest team ready for surgery," explained the attending while carefully watching Withers's eyes for signs of comprehension. Reading of eyes is a learned medical skill not listed in the medical school curriculum. He misjudged that Withers had understood.

"You think he might not make it to surgery?" Withers leaked some of his concealed apprehension.

"I'm sorry, I misled you. He's fine. Mr. Smith's lung immediately re-inflated and his chest is clear."

"Then you can take him to surgery?" came from Withers' confused face.

"He won't need surgery unless he bleeds more or his lung loses more air. Many times the knife wounds are clean and seal right up. He's really lucky. A few centimeters toward the center and his heart would have been lacerated. I wouldn't tell that to Mr. Smith. Patients can have enough trouble dealing with after effects without piling on the what-ifs. But I'm telling you in case you need a witness for attempted murder," offered the physician.

County Hospital was colloquially known as "the knife and gun club." Staff physicians were inexorably committed to cooperation with the local law enforcement agencies.

"You want to see him now?"

**

Slurp's face was multi-colored with fresh bruises mottling his African complexion. His face was gourd like with right jaw larger than left and the right eyelid swollen shut. Intravenous lines were rooted in each arm. A ten by six-inch thick white gauze bandage was in place over his left chest. From under the bandage a clear plastic catheter drooped over the sheets and ran into a plastic and paper canister partially filled with blood-tinged fluid.

"Carl, my man, whatchu doing up so late? I'd offer you a drink, but I already asked. They low on bourbon tonight," Slurp wheezed out in a dull, drugged, strained whisper followed by a cough and a groan. His uptown sass had reverted to the street slang of his youth.

Withers got close to Slurp's face and compassionately stroked his forehead. "What happened, Slurp? Who?"

"He tried to kill me, Carl. Right here, he cut me," Slurp pointed to his left chest. "Left me out in a soybean field to die, that muffucker. You help me, Carl? When he finds out, he gonna want to finish the job. You help me, Carl?" coughed Slurp followed by an agonizing groan in recoil.

Slowly Carl pieced together the narrative of Slurp leaving the Pap Fest with Shad. His real name was Paul Duval according to the car registration, which Slurp snooped at while Paul was purchasing beer at a Seven-Eleven. Three beers later in a quiet soybean field, the muscle-bound homophobe was getting his jollies by queer-whacking. When Slurp retaliated with a solid kick to the groin, Duval pulled his ten-inch blade and inserted it with vengeance. He poured out the last beer on what he believed to be Slurp's dead face, laughed and drove away.

Slurp used his last reserve of energy to dial 4-1-1 on his cell phone to summon an ambulance.

Slurp was afraid. He had just been shown death's door and it was still open. He was sure Duval would get to him before the police would even open the file for a "queer nigger." He had told no one else and promised Withers to keep it so.

"Don't worry, Slurp. Get some sleep," comforted Withers.

**

Maddy awoke early Sunday. Thoughts of Bruce Comstock as lover and dead man agitated her like machine wash and rinse cycles throughout the night.

The darkness outside didn't match the 8:45 clock face. She listened and heard the faintest of drizzle. The flowers along her apartment foundation would be grateful. Her car certainly would benefit form a little rinse. The thoughts of her car led her to anger focused on Joseph Maconi. Stopping her with a bogus excuse was an abuse of power, but pressuring her to rule the auto accident a homicide was unethical. Her immediate fantasy was to break his kneecaps with a baseball bat, gangland style.

She imagined a full-time career as a Mafia hit-woman. No, she wasn't the type to kill for a living. Could she ever kill anyone? She did not think so.

Perhaps she had missed the point. The woman was legally drunk. Next time she might run over a child. Maddy could prevent that by changing her opinion from accident to homicide. It would get Maconi off her back. Next she thought of Dr. O'Dell. He had led her to the conclusion of innocence. He believed the woman had handled her vehicle normally and that the blood alcohol level was not the issue. Whoever the old man walked into would have run him over.

Then a question flashed before her, the quality of the evidence. Was the breath analysis accurate? Or worse, could the police have falsified the evidence? Certainly Joseph Maconi had the capacity and the willfulness to falsify evidence.

A bolt of lightning crackled and zigzagged overhead, followed with thunder. Maddy's thoughts reverted to Bruce Comstock. Had his first act in Heaven been to induce rain over Maddy? Had his body been discovered yet? She jumped up to the dresser and turned on the local radio channel. She was now an active member of the "The Breakfast Club."

The next ten minutes seemed endless as she waited for the nine o'clock headlines. A rap singer was busted for cocaine possession. The President pretended that a crafted press release defining Alaskan clean oil drilling was spontaneous and sincere. The latest pole on whether a young actress's breasts were real was favoring natural due to the success of a publicity release. Each news item was trivial. She listened for thirty minutes without hearing the name of her ex-lover. She reached for the dial to shut it off when a bulletin was announced.

"In local news, the police have just released a preliminary report that indicates the Random Ranger serial killer has struck again. Police have tested a loose bullet found near the body of a shooting victim. Paul Duval, a 28 year-old city native, was found dead in a farmer's field south of the city around 4 a.m. after an anonymous call. Preliminary ballistics identified the bullet markings as similar to eight unsolved murders over the last seven years. The so-called Random Ranger has thus far eluded all attempts of law enforcement capture, in great part due to the seemingly randomness of his victims, the timing, and the murder scenes. Anyone with information about this or other crimes should contact the police directly."

That was it. No mention of Bruce Comstock came from the radio. Should she notify the police? What if his body was rotting in the camper? She dismissed this sentimentality. As a pathologist, rotting corpses were natural occurrences without the common maudlin sentiment of desecration. The sooner the better for cosmic recycling, she thought. Perhaps his body was in the morgue. The radio news producers had to pick and choose. A university man found dead in his camper wouldn't make the news next to a serial killer. There was only one way to find out.

** **

The old concrete basement hallway of Charity Hospital had been clean, uncluttered and deserted on the two previous days. At ten a.m. Sunday morning it was the tail of a circus parade of reporters, police officers, detectives, laboratory technicians, and F.B.I. leading to the morgue doors. Maddy remembered having to shoulder block the heavy doors open on Friday. Today the doors were wedged open with visitors.

Maddy nudged her way through the crowd. The flowing single file lines of agents entering and exiting the doors resembled sidewalk ants dismantling an apple core. Two technicians were removing fingernails from the hands. Each hand had been covered with clear plastic bags and tied around the wrists like boxing gloves. Photographers with huge cameras flashed images from multiple angles. Two women in scrubs held magnifying lenses over the skin, scanning for trace evidence. They used camel hair paintbrushes to rake all dirt and fibers, seen and possibly seen, into clear plastic vials and bags. Each piece of evidence was labeled as to location. Tattered and blood soaked clothes were cut free and bagged. Maddy thought she could make out a powder burn and gunshot wound from across the room, but wasn't sure.

Richard was dressed in his scrub suit along with another diener. Slurp was nowhere to be seen. She scanned the other two tables that held equipment and leather cases belonging to the technicians. Bruce's body wasn't out. She wondered how to gracefully peek into the body refrigerator drawers in front of twenty people.

Graham spoke to her. "Didn't anyone tell you that Sunday was your day off? Or did you just come down to rubberneck with the rest of the city?" Graham noticed a little embarrassment in her face and rescued her. "You're the most dedicated resident we've had in some time. As long as you're here, we'll put you to work. As soon as they're done with the evidence collection, we'll have our turn."

Maddy changed clothes and re-entered a room that now held only eight people compared with the crowd of twenty, minutes previously. Graham was in charge now and his first act was to clear the morgue of non-essential observers. He introduced the police officers, Sergeant Withers with the city police, and F.B.I. observer, Thane Hatcher. He suggested that Hatcher explain to Maddy the F.B.I.'s involvement with a local homicide.

Thane said, "The local police invited the F.B.I. into the case. Although they are doing an excellent job, it is typical for city police to invite the F.B.I. to safeguard their reputation. The local political hotcake created by a loose serial killer commands it. The F.B.I. is as stumped as anyone in the Random Ranger killings, but the next clue may be the icebreaker."

Thane was clean-shaven with light brown hair. Maddy thought he was average to nice looking for a man in his late twenties. Perhaps he'd be handsomer at age forty. Thane chatted during the autopsy, disclosing that he had graduated from law school at age twenty-five and gone immediately into service with the agency. He was a junior agent working primarily as a homicide detective assistant. He admitted that the F.B.I. held little hope in solving the Random Ranger investigation, which is why they sent him instead of a senior agent.

Thane watched Maddy with long glances. Maddy noticed them as short stares. She was undecided whether his attention was annoying or flattering.

Graham discussed the three bullet wounds. All three were to the chest and visible after Richard cut away the bullet-perforated and blood-soaked sleeveless muscle shirt. Maddy's thoughts returned to the picnic and the human horror of violent death. Corpse indifference was easy for a pathologist unless she had met the person living. She had seen Duval with his shirtless chest yesterday as directed by Slurp's finger.

"Where's Slurp?" she nervously changed the subject.

"Didn't you hear, Dr. Gray? It's awful. He's upstairs in ICU about half-dead and beat up. He figures some guys jumped him and he caught a knife in the side. He can't remember much. Lucky thing, they almost got his heart, the doctor said," said Richard.

"He's doing very well," Graham answered Maddy's unspoken question. "He has a chest stab wound. They clamped the tube this morning and the attending said he should be ready for discharge tomorrow. Now look at *these* chest wounds."

Graham meticulously took Maddy into his tutorial. He first had her count the wounds. There were four. Were there four bullets? Or were three of the holes from entry and one an exit wound? Maddy was confused until Graham handed her a stack of body x-rays.

Two bullets were clearly present in the chest. The third bullet had fallen out of the shirt when the police inspected the body. The police immediately ran ballistic checks on the bullet, confirming that the muzzle-bore scratches were identical with each of the Random Ranger murders. For public relations, the prompt release of evidence confirmation would give the appearance of openness and competence. Delayed information bred suspicion.

Patiently three bullet tracks were uncovered. One lacerated the right ventricle and aorta. The chest was filled with blood, which when suctioned out, revealed an intact bullet and a thin sheet of copper metal. Another bullet had traveled through the left lung and imbedded in the posterior chest with minimal bleeding.

A third entry wound was near the right nipple underlying the bloody shirt stain. The exit wound of outward and jagged skin and fat was in the dead center of the chest.

Graham asked Maddy, "Now tell me the order of firing. Before you say you don't know, because you do know; take some time to think. Then take some more time." Withers and Hatcher were relieved that Graham warned them not to help.

Maddy stood still for what seemed an eon. Then the magic of intuition cast its spell. She identified the third bullet as the one through the lungs because of the minimal bleeding along the tract. The third bullet had been flattened against the thoracic spine. The bone, although splintered, was not particularly hemorrhagic.

As for the fatal lesion, she was sure the bullet that transected the aorta caused exanguination into the chest cavity. That bullet was pristine because it had been slowed down by the heart muscle and aorta and must have missed the bones, tumbling about into the chest. She was stumped to explain the exact path of the other bullet, but correctly surmised it had entered near the right nipple and was first, because of the large shirt bloodstain.

Graham praised her lavishly. He further explained that the nipple area bullet had immediately hit a rib bone and traveled like a hockey puck on ice along the rib surface and exited several inches to the left. The torn surface arteries had a few seconds to profusely bleed before the next bullet lacerated the aorta. Blood pressure rapidly decreased and by the time the third bullet struck little bleeding capacity remained.

The morgue door burst open and a nearly breathless Percival Mordecai entered in running shorts and sweaty T-shirt. "Let me see. Why didn't anyone call me?"

Graham and Maddy looked at each other, exchanging eye rolls. Richard reminded him, he was not on call this Sunday. Percival continued his undisguised personal fascination with the Random Ranger.

"Two, no, three shots, all to the chest? Execution style, I think. Three rapid fire hits, just like half of the previous cases."

Thane's interest perked at Percival's suggestion. "Executed for what, do you think? Drugs? Money, organized crime?"

Percival smiled in delight. "I don't want to intrude on you and Sergeant Withers's territory, but I think this Ranger character is muscular and in clean health. My guess is that he isn't involved in drugs. Money, corporate money is more likely. Quick, close range, one, two, three shots and no other evidence except the bullets."

Thane looked to Graham for an opinion to substantiate or refute Mordecai. Maddy also looked to Graham, to judge how he would respond to his forensic fellow literally running on stage and stealing his show. She imagined slapping him and telling him to mind his own business. She remembered when she was eight, explaining the Girl Scout code to her mother when her brother rudely interrupted with a bragging session of two home runs in Little League.

"Officer Hatcher and Sergeant Withers, I'd pay attention to Dr. Mordecai. He has a remarkable intuition. I can't take any credit away from my astute fellow. He's a hard worker. Any other ideas, Percival?"

Mordecai basked in the moment's glory, hiding a smile. He shook his head with sham humility.

Next Graham pointed to a small metal flake on the bottom of the autopsy table. Stuck with fat to the stainless steel top was a two-millimeter metallic gray sheet that looked like a fingernail clipping. Percival jumped to attention and grabbed a pair of plastic forceps. Richard asked if he wanted some gloves. The dieners and doctors chuckled knowing Percival was too excited to care about contracting disease. Thane and Withers weren't sure what to think. Percival picked up the fragment of steel and twirled it within the forceps before his eyes.

"Always handle metal evidence with plastic. It looks like a jacket shard. If it matches the bullet type, I'd guess the last shot was fired above the body. These size fragments rarely go more than a foot, but they can fall straight down." He held the forceps out to Withers who bagged the evidence.

Maddy admired Graham's smooth acceptance of Percival's intrusion. A lesser man with an insecure ego would have grandstanded the jacket fragment to put Percival in his place. Instead Graham fed him the evidence like mother to infant. Maddy felt her attraction to Dr. O'Dell dangerously increase. She caught herself staring.

The case was announced closed. Maddy waited outside the door as the others exited the morgue room. The intense midday autopsy had distracted her from her initial mission to investigate the whereabouts of Bruce Comstock.

She waited for the morgue to empty, then she reentered to examine the refrigerator contents. She pulled open the middle body drawer of the refrigerator. Her head entered the hole and looked both ways. Just one body was present, the late muscle-bound Paul Duval. The lower row was empty. Comstock was busy rotting under the hot June sun in the Winnebego.

A hand touched her shoulder. She banged her head on the top of the doorway.

"Lose something?" asked the piercing and inquisitive voice of Percival Mordecai. Maddy was instantly aware of two simultaneous feelings. She was embarrassed and rapidly searching for a bogus explanation for her position. She was also uncomfortable with the creepy touch and being alone in the morgue with Percival. Maddy was fairly certain he was physically harmless. His creepiness was the way he looked at her and his impossible attempts at conversation.

"Just checking what's in the hold for tomorrow," she said.

"Have some chewing gum?" asked Percival which seemed odd and out of the blue to Maddy. Her polite refusal was insufficient. He unwrapped a stick of gum partially and with a huge grin delivered it up to her mouth. She let the gum enter her gaped mouth.

"We've got one coming in. I checked with security. A University Hospital professor found dead in a Winnebago at the picnic park we were at yesterday."

Maddy choked out her gum just as Thane entered the room.

"I didn't know him, he was in clinical chemistry," Percival continued as speechless Maddy stood there. Percival grabbed a paper towel and picked up her gum. "Let me get that. It isn't very good is it? You'll get to do him tomorrow, unless there's some reason you cannot." Percival gently placed the towel-wrapped gum into the trash can.

Thane spoke, unknowingly to Maddy's rescue, "Dr. Gray, would you like to get some lunch? On the department, I could use your help with some details for my report."

"Sure," Maddy strode quickly behind Thane. Mordecai watched them leave. After the door was closed, he retrieved the towel-wrapped gum and tucked it into his lab coat pocket.

**

Maddy's Honda Civic strained to follow the pace of Thane's Saab convertible, exceeding the 25-mph speed limit of the inner city through-streets. Six blocks from the hospital the newly-familiar siren and flashing lights of Officer Maconi's overtime-only patrol car filled her back windshield. As Maconi approached her car, Hatcher walked toward Maconi.

"Get back in your car, this is police business that doesn't include you," Maconi scowled and reached for his gun. Thane opened his badge and announced, "F.B.I., she's with me on a homicide investigation."

"Doesn't give her the right to speed in my city," Maconi tapped on her window and Maddy opened it.

"Actually we can, but it wasn't necessary. Officer, she was following me. If you feel the need to write a citation, it should go to me," persisted Thane to the annoyance of Maconi. The policeman narrowed his eyes and poked his head into Maddy's car.

"You're out of time, and I'm out of patience, doctor. Where'd you get the little helper-boy?" Maconi motioned Thane back to his car and headed toward the squad. Thane apologized to Maddy.

"You know I'm not that hungry, but I could use a beer." Thane agreed to follow her to the Internal Medicine Room.

**

Sunday afternoons were slow with blue-collar locals watching baseball and playing illegal scratch-off gambling cards. Thane and Maddy searched unsuccessfully for a clean table, then asked for a damp rag to clean the least disgusting one.

"So what questions did you have?"

"Have you studied any of these Random Ranger victims? The press calls them random, but five are middle level white-collar guys in government, insurance, and industry. I think that's what prompted Dr. Mordecai's comments. The other four are two known black gang-bangers, a computer salesman, and this gym attendant from today."

"Yeah, so?"

"I thought you might have some women's intuition. I don't think the agency cares at all. Who do they have investigating? Me, a junior nobody. But as long as I'm here, I'd like to do a credible job. I'd take any help."

"Mr. Hatcher, I've been on the forensic service for three days. I don't know anything."

"Thane, please. You honed right in on the bullet tracks. What I don't understand is why there's no public sense of desperation."

"The guy strikes once a year, execution style. The cases just don't generate media pizzazz. Richard or Slurp could help you more than I could."

She smiled remembering the fun she had had with Slurp and Mina on Friday in the same bar. She made herself a promise to stop at the hospital and visit Slurp that evening.

"What's so funny," Thane commented to her smile.

"Nothing, I was thinking of Slurp. He's in the hospital. Did you know he got beat up and stabbed last night?"

"Who?"

"Slurp? He's a diener at the morgue."

"What's a diener?"

"A morgue helper. I think the word comes from German to assist. Slurp's a cutie. He talks constantly."

"Cute sounds like competition," Thane floated a trial of his true intentions in code.

"Depends on whether you're chasing girls or boys," she indicated with wrist flap that Slurp was not interested in women.

"Weak competition, I can handle that." Thane succeeded in bringing Maddy to laughter.

"You don't really have any questions, do you? This is a date, isn't it?" teased Maddy.

"As far as the F.B.I. is concerned, this is official business, which means I can use their credit card for meals, shelter, airline tickets, disguises, whatever. You won't turn me in for fraud and abuse, I hope?"

"No, officer, I can tell you about real police abuse. Joseph Maconi, he's the one that stopped us on the way over. He's stalking me." Maddy took the next beer to detail how Maconi was attempting to coerce Maddy to change an accident ruling to a homicide.

"Guys like that make it tough for all law enforcement. I'll check him out for you. Maconi, you said?" Thane jotted his name on his notepad.

"Joseph. Slurp mentioned something about the Michael Johnson case. Ever heard of it?"

"That's like asking about Rodney King, or Diallo, the Haitian man who was sex tortured in New York. Every enforcement academy has to deal with police actions and brutality. Michael Johnson was handcuffed and in the squad car. He was killed by a shot to the head that blew out the back windshield. The police investigation ruled the handcuffed kid got the officer's gun somehow and shot himself."

"So Maconi is famous," Maddy said.

"Five years later, he's still working even though the city paid out millions in civil damages."

"Maconi works desk Monday through Friday. He wasn't allowed back on the beat until recently. Apparently he takes overtime to drive the squad car nights and weekends. I wonder who he hassles besides me?"

"Power Ranger with a gun and a badge."

"Is that what drew you to the F.B.I., Thane?" asked Maddy in a sincere though sarcastic tone.

"I hope not. I always thought law and order and justice were honorable goals."

"If I call your mother, will she tell me you are honorable?"

"She would if she were still alive."

"Oh, I'm sorry."

"Don't be. I axe murdered her when I was seven."

After several seconds of quiet he laughed. "Yes, she would say I am honorable and barely any trouble whatsoever. Would you like her Denver phone number? She and my father are fine. So is my only sister, who also lives in Denver. They are all wonderful people who keep busy breeding cocker-spaniels."

Maddy laughed then arose to signal her intention to exit. Her laugh ended and her face turned serious.

"Thane, I do have a favor to ask. Is there anything you can do to get Maconi off my back, short of me changing the old man's death certificate?"

Thane took her hand and kissed the back of it. "Anything, milady. Of course in return, I will require a real date, as in dinner Tuesday evening. I get to pick this time. I know I'm spoiled, but I do like restaurants where they clean the tables for you."

"Don't waste any time, do you, officer?"

"I'm only here a few weeks, unless something special happens."

"Like what?"

"I catch a serial killer."

"You're so romantic. Tell the F.B.I., thanks for the brew." Maddy departed, satisfied with her enlistment of Thane Hatcher's help with Maconi.

He wasn't her type, too young. She mustn't lead him on. He's much too young unlike Dr. O'Dell. In college she had discovered her general disinterest in men her own age. Frustratingly, the less attention she paid young men, the more desperately they pursued her. At least she would be spared a rejection scene, when a near-future flight would return him to the home office.

**

Sundown was at 8:26 p.m. The warm June afternoon air was cooling. Updraft from the hot asphalt created visible air eddies in the parking lot. Graham was a half-hour early to the Hyatt Hotel. He spent several minutes in his car, studying the surrounding cars. All were empty. Most were white with four doors, late model American compacts and mid-sizes, rental cars for airport travelers. Cycles of thunder and whistling from aircraft landing and taxiing behind him drowned out the usual city noises.

Graham O'Dell waited patiently fifteen more minutes, then entered via the side entrance to the hotel. He thanked the man who had a key-card to open the door. He flipped up the hood on his nylon navy windbreaker and jogging suit. Although overdressed for the June heat, the jogging attire would go unnoticed, disguising O'Dell as an idiotic exerciser, who bundled up to sweat himself into a near coma.

He ascended the two flights of back stairs with head down and out of direct line to the fish-eye surveillance camera. Graham checked the hallway and his watch. At 8:42 a young slender woman quietly exited room 313. Graham estimated her age at most to be twenty-eight. Like Graham she didn't look about and moved in rapid anonymity. He gently knocked at 313.

David Burr, wearing a white bathrobe with hotel logo, motioned him to enter. The bedspread was pulled up in a minimal effort to conceal the twisted sheets, or as Graham punned to himself the trysted sheets.

"Doc, good to see you. My knee's been asking me all day, is it shot time yet?" chuckled Burr. "You know, O'Dell, I appreciate this a ton. I also appreciate the discreet type of person you are. You know, the media hounds get a hold of this news and they'd make me out to be dying. This is strictly Q.T. between you and me. Can I get you a soda? I don't keep any liquor in the room. Wouldn't want to look like a fucking Ted Kennedy, would I?"

"Of course not. Let's take a look at that sore joint. Don't mind these, professional habit," explained O'Dell as he put on pair of latex examining gloves. "This will hurt some until the anesthetic kicks in. Are you sure you don't have any anesthetic or steroid allergies?"

Graham produced two twenty-c.c. syringes. One was empty and one was filled with fluid. Graham scrubbed the knee area. He handed Burr a paper with a simple consent statement permitting him to inject the knee with betamethasone and lidocaine. The second line indicated Burr was unaware of any allergies.

"Just a professional necessity in case there are any complications. No one will ever see it, as long as you don't try to sue me for practicing orthopedics instead of pathology."

"Shucks, Doc, you don't have to worry about that," assured Burr who immediately winced, "Owwww."

"Sign it: and the anesthetic goes in faster." Graham paused after removing about 15 c.c. of cloudy yellow knee fluid. He looked up to see Burr rapidly writing on the paper.

"You docs and the paper work are worse than lawyers. Ooow, that's better."

"Now just lay back, relax, and watch the TV. I don't want you out of bed until morning. I don't want to give that needle tract and joint space any reason to bleed. Do you understand?" sternly cautioned Graham.

"Tomorrow I've got a busy day. I can't be laying about."

"You won't feel a thing tomorrow, guaranteed." Graham gathered both syringes, capping the needles, then wrapping them in his latex gloves. As Graham was leaving, Burr requested a golf rematch in the near future, "On Congress."

"Love to."

Burr thought, "O'Dell is great. He's discrete and not just about medicine. He didn't tell Sweetbread or Corless about moving his ball. He could be trusted."

75

**

"Hello Precious, you are so sweet. I am fit as a fiddle. Lookie here, they took out my chest tube. I can go home first thing tomorrow. Doc Simms is my chest man, and let me tell you, he has got one gorgeous chest. Doc said I could go back to work when I felt like it. Stitches come out in five days. I can do anything in two weeks. Just a flesh wound. Like in the old western movies."

Maddy smiled. They chatted a few minutes until Maddy had to clear the air.

"Have you seen the news today, Slurp? The Random Ranger? Paul Duval?" She stared at Slurp. Her eyes demanded an answer.

"I didn't do it. I was in the hospital with a fucking plastic hose wrapped around my heart all night. I had nothing to do with Mr. Meatmarket's closeout sale. You've got to believe me, Precious. I am not the murdering kind. I got enough bodies already in the morgue. I don't need to whack any extras."

"I believe you. I just thought you might have some idea."

"I didn't say nothing to anyone except that some guy jumped me, I don't know who. No questions asked. I didn't kill Paul Duval. He probably met up with the Random Ranger and was surprised to learn that 9 millimeters is a lot tougher than his road house biceps. Bad luck. I can't deny my pleasure with the outcome. You and Withers I can trust. He tried to kill me. I don't need the police hounding me. I'm sticking to the story that I don't know who stabbed me."

Maddy grinned. "I'm not about to say anything. But I want you to promise me something in return."

Slurp sat up in bed, winced as he grabbed his sore chest stitches, then opened his arms. "If I can do it, it is done."

"Remember the man who gave you the note to give to me?" Slurp nodded and Maddy continued. "He's a little bit dead right now."

"I didn't kill him either."

"I know that."

"He'll still be a little dead later, so what's the problem?" Slurp raised one eyebrow anticipating the worst to come.

"It is complicated. We used to have a special relationship, which caused us both a lot of trouble. The hospital chief, Sweetbread, prohibited me from seeing him. I would appreciate it if you didn't mention him or the note, if anyone should ask. I don't need a lot of questions either," Maddy asked with a nervous smile and forced grin.

"Precious, you poor thing. I hate it when a man makes you so jealous he drives a lover to…"

"No Slurp, I didn't hurt him or anything. I think he had a heart attack or maybe a stroke. The point is that I wasn't allowed to see him. No good could come from anyone knowing that he tried to see me on Saturday. Just like you. No good comes of the police investigating you for revenging a beating, when you didn't do it, right?" Maddy forced her grin again.

"I feel my memory fading. You have gotten yourself into a lot shit in three short days," concluded Slurp who was immediately sorry when beads of water appeared at the corner of Maddy's eyes and rolled over cheeks. She sat down on the bed and tucked her head into Slurp's white gauze bandage and quietly sobbed. He stifled a painful grunt, and stroked her brown hair down to her shoulders.

**

Maddy left Charity Hospital knowing that less than twelve hours later she would face the body of Bruce Comstock. She would have to pretend no deep sorrow as her hand forced the scalpel through the fat and muscle of the belly. She had performed over a hundred autopsies, but never on a person she personally knew, let alone a lover. Bodies from time immemorial have been dressed in finery, perfumed, and ritually grieved. It would be impossible to feign scientific distance from Bruce. Her fear was breaking down and weeping, unable to perform her task.

Maddy could call in sick, that time honored working-caste practice of avoiding unpleasantry. But she was a professional. Could it really be that difficult?

Her daydreaming was abruptly halted by the now familiar *wahoh, wahoh, wahoh* of Officer Maconi's siren. Maddy was instantly irate. Maconi was riding shotgun and a second officer approached Maddy. "I'll need to see your license and insurance registration, ma'am. Do you know you were weaving across the white lines? Have you been drinking, ma'am?"

Maddy was dazed. Was she now enemy number one of the entire city police force? Maconi rapidly surfaced with Breathalyzer in hand. Unseen was the drop of vodka he inserted into the mouthpiece. Maconi's one-sided smile doubled when the reading produced 0.10, a value exceeding the legal limit of 0.08.

They impounded her car and headed for the downtown lockup, despite Maddy's protest that she hadn't had any alcohol for over four hours and that they could call Officer Hatcher of the F.B.I. or Slurp for verification. She repeatedly stated the impossibility of her being intoxicated.

Handcuffing, fingerprinting and brusquely rude police personnel humiliated Maddy, which bred an intense anger. The police officers ignored her requests for a witnessed blood sample for confirmation. She screamed for an attorney. She was told her requests for counsel would be granted when they were done processing her.

The lockup cell had four cots, two wooden benches and an open commode and sink. There were two bizarrely dressed women with ratted hair who were incoherently drug dazed. Another woman was obese and foul smelling and mumbling to herself. Maddy suspected she was schizophrenic. Two Hispanic ladies were arguing in Spanish.

Maddy succumbed to the realization that she could no longer hold her urine. The mumbling and swearing in foreign dialect ceased when Maddy stood. It immediately resumed when she sat on the stool. The absence of toilet paper was some solace to Maddy. It made the event on the open toilet a few seconds shorter.

At four a.m. Maddy opened the door to her apartment. Her bondsman, Mina, attempted to first console Maddy, then persuade her against homicidal threats toward Maconi. Vengeance had replaced the sobbing self-pity comforted by Slurp at the hospital.

"I may have finally found a purpose for my life, putting cops behind bars."

"Get some sleep, Maddy," said Mina.

79

**

JUNE 4, MONDAY, Inside and Personal

It was a hazy heavy morning in need of the late morning burn-off. Maddy felt surprisingly refreshed after two hours of sleep and drove Mina's car to the hospital. Mina didn't have clinic duty until eleven and had the ulterior motive of using her need for a ride to call a male friend whom she dated occasionally. Theoretically, Maconi should be back to desk investigations on Monday morning. He wouldn't know Maddy would be driving Mina's car unless he was sicker than she imagined.

Maddy found herself obsessed with the fantasy of obtaining a gun to protect herself from Maconi. Cops wore Kevlar bullet-retardant vests, so she would have to aim for his head to hit the face or the skull. Alas it was only fantasy. Maddy wasn't inclined to enjoy life in prison. She contented herself to wait for divine justice, like Paul Duval's encounter with the Random Ranger.

Turning the corner one block from Charity she was jolted into hyper-vigilant anxiety by rapid Morse Code like police horns, *reer-reer-eer-up*! She pulled the car to the right wondering what traffic law she could have violated only to have a county sheriff squad car pass her in two seconds of flourish. Paranoia was a new experience and unwelcome.

The sight at Charity was more carnival than hospital. Two ambulances and three television station vans lined the front entrance like travel trucks for a house of horrors. She noticed Thane's Saab in the front row. Multiple police agencies were mulling around as camera crews were moving electrical cables.

Her immediate scenario of terror was Bruce Comstock. Had Maconi been watching her at the picnic and seen her enter the Winnebago? Was he conspiring to frame her as a murderess? Had he invited the entire casts of Police Story and Law and Order for the moment of denouement and arrest?

"Morning, Precious," came a sweet familiar voice.

"Slurp, what are you doing?"

"They just discharged me fifteen minutes ago, but damn if I going to miss the biggest brunch we've ever had."

"What's going on?"

"Honey, you have got to invest in a radio."

Maddy impatiently responded with open palms and outstretched fingers while mouthing the words, "What?"

"Burr's dead. You know that Nazi, homophobic, in your face, right wing asshole Congressman. A maid found him dead at the Hyatt last night at bed turndown. Probably natural, but everyone I know certainly would have killed him. Then we've got to do your Comstock boy, delicately. Plus some young idiot tried to outrun a squad car last night, killing a woman and her baby in a crash. And we have the usual aftershocks of the Random Ranger from yesterday. That's ringing the bell big time."

"Whew, is that all?" commented Maddy in relief that the Burr case did not involve her.

"I'm sure Richard needs us stat. No wallowing in self pity, come on."

The morgue hallway was filled with reporters, policeman and suits. By the time Maddy had changed clothes and entered the morgue it was apparent three active arguments were in progress.

Richard demanded Slurp get home and rest. Slurp insisted Richard not try to diener four cases with only one other assistant. Doctors Green and Mordecai were having a heated discussion over who did which case. Doctor O'Dell and Sergeant Withers were fussing and growling in very low volume voices. Something about Withers should take the day off. Each corner of the room serially increased in volume as voices competed to be heard.

Finally Graham shouted. "Silence, please. We've got a lot of work to do today. Slurp, are you working?"

"He needs to be in bed," immediately commented Richard.

"I asked Slurp, Richard," continued Graham in a firm but soft tone intended to calm the proceedings.

"I'm here, boss."

"Fine, that's your decision. Doctors Green and Mordecai will cover the woman and baby with Richard. Slurp, you and Dr. Gray take the forty-nine-year-old chemist. I'll handle the Congressman."

Graham had not finished speaking. Moans and protests immediately began to crescendo. Mordecai wanted the experience of a federal investigation. Surprisingly his second choice was the Comstock corpse. Dr. Green was feeling second tier. They usually alternated important homicides. Graham had done the Random Ranger post yesterday. The unwritten rule was the next big "H" was for Dr. Green.

Graham reminded him that most likely Burr had died in his sleep, not by homicide. Besides, Sgt Withers and he had begun earlier with blood draws for toxicology studies and evidence collection. Graham would help Maddy, after he finished the Burr case. Dr. O'Dell pronounced, "All grousing is complete. Work begins pronto."

The photographers shot multiple angled views of the congressman. Uncharacteristically they draped a folded towel over his genitals. Normally nude photographs were sufficient, but the possibility of seeing their work on network news or the Internet, caused the photographers to err on the side of dignity to protect themselves from criticism. One photographer commented, "A great towel, covers Burr's ass and ours at the same time."

Hatcher was collecting final data from the autopsy of Paul Duval. He had the dual assignment to relay details of the post mortem on Burr to the Washington office. If any signs of foul play were discovered, the F.B.I. would take over the investigation of the death of the Legislator. Thane greeted Maddy formally followed by a flirtatious smile. The gesture escaped neither Slurp nor Mordecai.

Mordecai nosed about and immediately pointed out the swollen knee and needle puncture wound. Graham stoically thanked him for his excellent observations. Mordecai looked at the arm spot where Graham had drawn his blood specimen on Saturday. He concluded it was several days old, and quietly passed on any further comment.

Meanwhile Dr. Green perfunctorily listed the multiple trauma injuries of the young woman and child. The driver who had attempted to outrun the police was in intensive care but probably would survive to go to trial. To the dismay of Maddy, the local police investigator assigned was Maconi.

He began ranting immediately about the worthless scum who deserved the death penalty, but the soft courts would only give him twenty years, parole after seven. Dr. Green asked about any previous record. The policeman cited three previous arrests as evidence that the boy's recalcitrant character warranted his extermination: marijuana possession, illegal passing, and speeding 75 in a 45-mph zone, along with two curfew violations.

Dr. Green commented on the disproportionate number of minority and young people who were convicted in that north suburban court. Richard supported the assertion that the north suburban court was racist.

"You got that right. I took my cousin to court up there and four out of five guys in the room were brothers. You tell me: how does a county with one percent black folk find all them niggers?"

"Traffic tickets and reefer wouldn't make a white boy a hardened criminal," said Slurp.

Maddy at the adjacent table kept silent no longer. "It's terrible that these two innocent people are dead. However, I can understand how a constant hassling by the police would make him want to run," she interjected with bile rising.

"He's a fucking rotten kid, period," said Maconi.

"Maybe he was a victim of trumped up charges and police who make up traffic violations or plant marijuana in cars?" Maddy's eyes bore through him.

"Good law abiding people, who cooperate with civil servants, don't have any trouble," Maconi grinned in triumph.

Slurp placed a towel over Comstock's head so Maddy wouldn't see him. Slurp volunteered to perform the dissection, which relieved Maddy. The first slow cut of the scalpel opened the skin. She touched the skin and felt in her memory the gray-haired chest skin that had brushed against her breasts.   Lifeless, the remains of Bruce Comstock lay before her, the memories of a gentle but passionate man remained.

She watched in pain as Slurp disassembled the shape of Bruce Comstock. Her stomach cramped. She ached for the autopsy to end. She had no way out of the situation. Paradoxically, the anger and contempt she felt for Maconi and the police was useful in helping her through the examination.   Provoking the police with innuendoes of harassment and racism gave her energy and distraction.

Bruce was a human entity that included body, thoughts, experiences, and a presence in a unique segment of time. She couldn't isolate and analyze a single organ apart from the whole. She was "over him," the times of obsessing and missing his company, but the memories, the history was permanent.

She understood for the first time the concept of an eternal life. Thoughts, actions, and interactions with friends and family were something that could be forgotten, but not destroyed. Her future, although unknown to her now, was a part of the complete entity, the life of Madison Gray.

Mordecai was interested in the body of Bruce Comstock almost ignoring his assistant duties with Dr. Green.   He suggested the possibility of bruising on Comstock's abdomen, but he couldn't be certain, as the bloated body had been in the hot trailer nearly 36 hours. Maddy made no comment. Otherwise, the external skin and features of the body were intact and unremarkable.

Slurp continued opening the chest and belly and removed the sternum. He looked at Maddy in effect requesting permission to proceed.   She knew she must personally examine the heart and lungs for evidence of an acute myocardial infarct. Slurp pinched the main pulmonary arteries. The time had come for Maddy to take over.

"You better check this out."

The head and upper chest vessels were suffused with blood, which is not unusual in sudden death. Maddy was surprised upon opening the pericardium to discover a bulging right ventricle.

She took scissors and entered the pulmonary artery. A large rope-like thrombus of yellow and purple red was coiled in the artery and plugged the pulmonic valve of the heart. There was no question this was a giant and fatal PE, pulmonary thrombo-embolus. Maddy was relieved to have found an easy explanation for his demise. The case would be completed quickly.

"Thank God. No doubt about this PE." Maddy spontaneous leaked her relief. The others responded to her comment with confused looks. Recurring fears of finding no cause of death and having a long drawn out investigation that somehow could expose her contact with him were abating. She was optimistic at this point that Maconi wouldn't find a reason to hassle her, that Sweetbread wouldn't discover her liaison which had violated her terms of continued residency, and that the venom of Mrs. Comstock would not be released.

Thane Hatcher, another F.B.I. agent, and Sgt Withers were discussing something with Dr. Graham and Mordecai. Maddy was unable to make out their words as Slurp started the noisy grinding whir of a Stryker saw over Comstock's skull.

"OK if I harvest the squash?"

To expedite the pace of an autopsy, Slurp routinely began the brain removal while the pathologist finished the examination of the retroperitoneum and pelvis. The morgue crew called brain, "squash," due to its orange hue and greasy pudding-like texture.

"Doctor Green, he's got a mass back here." Maddy consulted Green, who was strolling past examining the police report on his case. He just happened to be the closest pathologist. She wasn't confused or asking for guidance, but delighted to share an exciting finding. She could have shown Slurp who would have nodded his head and kept sawing, but he wouldn't share in the thrill of discovery. Dr. Green looked in and beamed a broad smile.

"The entire aorta is encased with metastatic nodes. He's pretty young. It could be embryonal carcinoma. Examine the testicles," offered the immediately interested Dr. Green.

"Pair of oysters coming right up," said Slurp.

The testicles, nicknamed for their white tunica alba covering, were searched as the potential source of the primary cancer. With her right hand on his scrotum and her left inside his pelvis beneath her pelvic bone, she pushed the testicles one at a time into her left hand. Slurp handed her a scalpel and like gelding a pig, cut free the two-inch oval organs. The covering shell of the testicles glistened like the mother-of-pearl lining of an oyster shell.

The professional excitement of finding, first the pulmonary thrombembolus as cause of death and now the unknown tumor across the aorta, allowed her to forget Bruce Comstock for a moment. The agony returned with the symbolic act of removing his testicles and slicing them in her palm. A defiling pain shot across her chest.

"Normal," commented Dr. Green as she thinly sliced the milky tunica covering down through the stringing brown center of the testicles, "keep drilling, he's got a primary cancer somewhere."

Maddy's eyes watered. Her grief was leaking. The disappointment of the testicles bored Dr. Green, who walked away, resuming his reading. Maddy told Slurp that she needed a break.

"Slurp, would you remove the rest of the organs? Be careful not to damage the inferior vena cava or the iliac vessels. We need to see if we can find the origin of this PE," instructed Maddy confidently. She was in her area of expertise, cardiovascular medical diseases. She began to walk away as Mordecai approached with a plastic bag and scissors.

He leaned over the corpse and rolled the belly skin out of the way to expose the penis. Using the scissors he cut a large swatch of pubic hair from around the shaft of the penis, deposited the hair into the plastic bag, zip-locked the top, and smiled impishly toward Maddy.

"What are you doing?" She asked with the intonation that inserted 'the fuck' between what and are.

"Getting a control sample to go with the Congressman's. Sergeant and the F.B.I. say the surveillance cameras at the Hyatt showed a woman entering and leaving the night he died. If she was a sex partner, there should be traces of nucleated squames and DNA. The lab likes to run a parallel control specimen to judge the cell staining and recovery. Thank you for the advancement of forensic science." Mordecai walked away smugly.

The short night, the trauma of lockup, and the dissection of a loved one had made Maddy shaky, a combination of irritation and nausea. The thought of discovering a woman's cells, her cells, fresh from Bruce was the last gagging stress. She ran to the ladies locker room to vomit. Slurp stood at the table bewildered and holding up the gallbladder.

At the other end of the room, Dr. James Sweetbread entered. He was dressed in a starched and bleached unblemished lab coat with his name embroidered in giant bright red cursive letters over the left chest pocket. He power-strutted into the room and looked about searchingly. He seemed disappointed to have to talk to Graham.

"Graham, damn, this is a shock. I just saw David last Saturday. Hell, you golfed with us, remember? I thought he looked well. Took Corless and I for a pocketful. This is a huge loss for the community. He was powerful. Environment and budget committees. I don't think we can replace him. So what do you think? Was it murder?" The hospital chief cut to the chase.

"Acute MI. Fresh clot in the L.A.D. Nothing else important."

"In the what?" said Sweetbread innocently displaying his administrational lost-touch with clinical medicine.

"L.A.D., left anterior descending coronary artery."

"Of course," Sweetbread said dismissively.

"Dr. Gray is working on Professor Comstock. You are probably interested in that case too," said Graham.

"Not anymore. He retired and doesn't matter," said Sweetbread.

"What about the knee?" Mordecai interjected. "Fresh needle marks, we'll need to wait for toxicology."

"He's been complaining about that knee for two years. He told me that you, Graham, were going to help him," Sweetbread bantered on.

"I did. I injected that knee with some steroids this weekend. In fact I saw him at the hotel about nine last night to check up on him. He seemed fine."

Mordecai retreated like a scolded dog. He was so proud of discovering a needle mark amid the leg hairs. He never dreamed it was the work of his program director.

"I thought it was a girl that the police were interested in talking to?"

"There was a man on the security video also, but we couldn't see his face," the F.B.I. associate of Thane Hatcher offered.

"I'm your needle man. When I left him, he looked good and satisfied. He was in a bathrobe ready for bed. Gossip travels fast doesn't it? Let the girl be. She can't be held accountable for his heart attack. What good does scandalizing do? Ruin the already miserable life a young woman and the Congressman's family? He's dead. Who among us is perfect?"

Withers was listening intently to these comments. Graham shot him a look. Withers pretended disinterest and sat down on an empty bench.

Graham ended his sermon and the autopsy by gently pulling off the green latex gloves and pitching them into the thirty-gallon garbage can lined with bright orange plastic and abundant stickers of "Hazardous Biological Waste." Graham pointed at the labels. "Biological waste, an accurate label for all of us someday."

Maddy returned from the barf closet with hair combed and her washed face still slightly damp. All eyes glanced her way. Sweetbread stared. Graham looked at her deeply then turned to the room.

"Attention! It's been a hell-of-a-day. I'll need an hour to trim the sections, shower, and finish the paperwork. Then drinks are on me at the Internal Medicine Room. Dinner is on Dr. Green."

"I can't. I've got toddler swim at 5:30," protested Green above the cheers of Richard and Slurp.

"I was kidding. I wouldn't allow my staff to eat there anyway. But we do all need a drink." Graham picked up the file folder and tissue trim jar.

Sweetbread continued to stare at Maddy. As she attempted to pass him to return to her autopsy, his broad chest stopped her. He firmly grasped her shoulder. "Dr. Gray, we need to have a conference about your social difficulties. Three p.m. tomorrow, my office. I'll send Dr. O'Dell a notice to make sure you're released for the rest of the afternoon." He turned abruptly and departed with the same power-strut he had used to enter.

"Damn," she said to herself. Somehow he had discovered her meeting with Comstock. She looked forward to a drink. Was this the worst day of her life? No, but up to this point it was the most difficult.

Slurp stood over the neatly exposed great vessels of the abdomen and both kidneys. "Precious," he quietly summoned her attention.

The inferior vena cava was plugged an inch thick with a soft gray mass of cancer thrombus which grew up the renal vein from the right kidney. The organ was three quarters replaced by tumor, the obvious site of the primary cancer. The tumor growing up the vein was the origin of the pulmonary thrombo-embolus. Maddy realized her pushing on his belly during sex had dislodged the thrombus.

It was clear to Maddy now. Bruce had learned of his advanced terminal cancer and had decided to spend the remaining months travelling in his camper. She recalled her trite statement that he was too young to retire at forty-nine. He preferred to secret his cancer rather than accept pity, particularly the ingenuine pity which he might be unable to discern. Both he and his true friends would suffer less not knowing. Maddy smiled gently knowing she had given him a few moments of final pleasure, even it she had slightly shortened his life.

Slurp interrupted her contemplation with the delivery of a 1450-gram brain. "Succotash on the scale."

The normal dura wrapped the brain hemispheres in a sheet of tough protective parchment. Maddy thought of Descartes' belief that he had localized the anatomic site of the soul in the brain's base of the pineal. She hesitated again, unable to desecrate her former lover. Then she rationalized, who better than one who respects and loves him? Still, a small tear trickled out of the corner of her eye as she cut into his brain.

She snipped the small vessels attaching the brain to the dura with scissors. She noticed each little red vessel as it threaded along the meningeal surface, then disappeared into the cortical gray matter of the brain surface. She took a large knife, 18 inches long and 1½ inches deep, and sliced off the front tips of the brain with difficulty. The greasy white matter smeared on the cutting board.

"Do we have another knife, Slurp?" she asked automatically with the drag of the blade. "I'm sorry, you must be tired."

"Precious, we got whatever you need. I guess Richard ain't got around to sharpening the brain blades."

Richard wasn't about to let the gentle jab go unreturned. "Damn straight, we had a *busy* weekend. *Busier* when certain lover boys don't show up for work. Too *busy* getting themselves stabbed and all."

Slurp gave her a new knife, "Thanks for asking. I am quite tired and this bandage is tight as a corset. But I'll make it. And I'm still beautiful, which is the most important thing."

They all laughed. Maddy held a section of brain in prolonged examination.

Slurp continued, "You going to finish cutting that brain or stare it to death? They'll be closing the Medicine Room before you get done with this case. I never miss the opportunity to drink beer on Dr. God."

"Slurp, would you go get Dr. Graham or Dr. Green?"

Slurp returned with Dr. O'Dell who was dressed in golf shirt and beige khaki pants. His work required immediately changing into scrub clothes so he often wore casual clothes like shorts in the summer. Graham kept black slacks, white shirt, and tie in his locker for unscheduled professional meetings and court appearances.

He also kept a sport coat and two suits, one pinstriped and one navy with vest. These outfits were strictly for TV, for the high-profile cases when news teams of reporters and cameramen would accost him outside the courthouse and attempt to gain additional information. He never talked with the press during an active trial, but often the image of him declining an interview would appear on the six o'clock. He didn't wish to look sloppy on TV. Minutes earlier

Sweetbread had announced David Burr's heart attack at a press conference which Graham avoided.

Maddy pointed to multiple brain slices displaying discreet lesions of bubbly deep purple. They were rounded and one to three millimeters in diameter.

"I've never seen metastases look like this. The lesions look more like hemangiomas. What do you think?" Maddy asked in typical consultation, pathologist to pathologist.

Early in training, the pathology resident wonders about all findings, but only has the courage to ask occasional questions. She was advanced after three years and knew this was an unusual pattern, just as she had known Dr. Green would take professional delight in her discovery of Bruce Comstock's fatal cancer.

Dr. Graham concentrated intensely at the ½ inch slices of brain lined up in order from frontal cortex through occiput along the top of the cutting board. The cerebellum was quartered on the lower left of the board. The chain of mid-brain, mesencephalon, pons, and medulla from the lower brain above its connection to the spinal cord sections followed. The slices were arranged like thinly sliced sausage patties on the lower right hand part of the board.

"Kidney's the primary, huh? Any medical history about the family?" asked Graham as he looked over the body and refocused on the brain slices. He took out his reading glasses for a closer look at the bubbly red lesions of the cortical gray matter.

"I'd suggest two things. First, try to get his medical history from his family doctor or wife. Then read about Von-Hippel-Lindau disease. And hurry up. Let's not make a career out of one case. I'm not saving any beer for Slurp."

**

The dictation of autopsy A-0577, Bruce Comstock, was slow for Maddy. She failed in her attempts to stop thinking of him as a person. The description of organs and tumor nodules, parts of a corpse, seemed to belong to someone else.

She took the unfinished tape out of the recorder and left it aside with the case folder. She combed the pathology office searching the bookshelves for textbooks. She chose several tomes, titles from general pathology, neuropathology, vascular, and hereditary disease. Normally she would choose the latest edition by date. This search was for information, and she chose the thickest text in each section.

She opened each book to the index section and fingered down to Von-Hippel-Lindau disease. Each text seemed to have only a paragraph and the same old journal references.

Dr. O'Dell was on the bulls-eye. The disease, which she had only vaguely heard about once in medical school, involved multiple vascular lesions, including blood vessel tumors, called hemangioblastomas in the cerebellum. What was completely unknown to her was the association of kidney cancer with the disease. The kidney cancers often occurred at younger age and were more aggressive than typical kidney carcinoma. If the brain lesions were indeed vascular malformations, Bruce Comstock likely had Von-Hippel-Lindau. If he had any relatives with hemangioblastoma, it was certain.

Ordinarily, any doctor would swell with pride at such a discovery that was professionally interesting. For a pathologist discovering information of use to the living and future family members was as wonderful as it was rare.

Maddy knew the downside. Her ethical responsibility required her to contact Bruce's wife to obtain his family history from her. This was the most complicated day of her life.

**

Maddy drove to the Internal Medicine Room and pulled into the white limestone gravel lot. She parked the car but left it running for air-conditioning and dialed Mina. Mina had promised to retrieve Maddy's car from the police lock-up to save her the agony of dealing with the police. The hectic day had pushed the car-swapping task to low priority.

"Hello, what's the matter? Can't you get your car door open?" Mina answered in one breath.

"Mina, where are you?"

"You're wasting my minutes." Mina hung up and tapped on the glass.

Maddy laughed to see her, then laughed again at Mina's explanation. She had seen Maddy drive Mina's car off campus. She followed her, knowing the only reason she would turn west from campus was a happy hour stop at the Internal Medicine Room.

"So what's the scoop on Congressman Burr?" asked Mina as she gulped at a frosty mug. Beer foam covered her mouth and dripped down her chin. Slurp and Maddy giggled.

Thane Hatcher chivalrously produced a monogrammed handkerchief and offered it for sanitary sacrifice. Mina grabbed the brown paper towel roll on the table instead, but smiled in appreciation.

"Is it public record yet, Dr. O'Dell?" Maddy directed this question for permission to discuss his case.

Graham nodded and raised his glass silently. He chugged the remainder of his beer and put a fifty-dollar bill on the table. "There aren't any secrets when the press is in the hallway. I've got to be running. Everyone, thanks for a hard day. See you tomorrow."

"Dr. O'Dell," Maddy followed him toward the door, "I was reading about Von-Hippel-Lindau. I think you nailed it. Thanks."

"Really? Picking up those vessels in the brain was the key. Few residents have your eye for gross pathology. Ever think about forensics? Unlike surgical work with the microscope, forensics is mostly gross pathology, if you like that. Then there's the evil of mankind, which helps to make it interesting."

Maddy was paying more attention to the graying hairline of his temples and his broad chest. For a moment she fantasized accepting a fellowship solely to work with Dr. O'Dell. She spontaneously reached out and hugged him. He hugged back. Maddy then wondered if she had over-stepped appropriate boundaries.

Maddy detailed to Mina the heart attack findings. Mina asked if the F.B.I. was involved. Thane explained the F.B.I. was just there only as an observer. He refused to gossip about the alleged woman who had visited Burr's room. Thane did acknowledge the press stories and rumors about women chasing. Slurp and Richard joked that perhaps the mysterious woman had screwed him to death. Maddy's stomach contracted as she thought of Comstock.

97

"Speaking of acute MI's, how's your blood group binding site research coming?" Mina sensed Maddy's uneasiness and changed the topic abruptly away from the subject of married man and younger woman.

"I haven't had time. But I need about ten more. I was hoping to get it done this month, but Slurp won't let me autopsy any obvious heart cases."

Maddy jabbed Slurp in the side. He reeled in pain as she had hit dead center his stab wound area. Richard pretended to be afraid of Maddy and used it as excuse to pack up Slurp and leave. The group's noise level was no longer the highest in the room Mina opened her eyes wide and leaned forward to ask Thane how the Random Ranger investigation was going. Her interest was less a curiosity concerning the murders than an opportunity to hear him talk. The beer had awakened her desire for male contact. Her shoulder movements were dramatic and her inspirations and chest expansions full. Thane couldn't help watching her, even as he spoke to Maddy.

"The press calls the murders random. The only link is the same gun according to the reporters. Three were young men, two black and one Hispanic. Three were white collar Caucasians, two from Environ Technologies and one, an accountant. And the other three were low life types: a convicted child molester, an alcoholic construction worker, and the last guy, a thug from a boxing gym. The reporters are bored because there isn't much newsworthy excitement. Who really cares about these victims? My job is to find a pattern within the randomness.

Each of the nine victims has been male. The rate of murder is only one each year. The killer isn't in a hurry. There is no evidence of sexual assault or body mutilation.

Some seem like calculated executions, the others distant gunshots resembling sniper shots."

"And? What's your theory?" Mina seductively smiled waving her hands palm side up.

"It seems very random," deadpanned Thane.

Maddy laughed loudly and burped. She then pushed her beer away and explained to Thane the trumped up D.U.I. charge on which Maconi had arrested her.

Mina added, "That's it. Of course, that's why Sweetbread has called you into his office tomorrow. He has a direct line to the police department. My first year, I was at a party that got busted. I was caught smoking a joint and they arrested me for usage. They had it on videotape. Next morning I get a notice to meet Sweetbread and he knows all about it. He tells me how I won't get my DEA license and that my career is shot."

"You never told me this."

"We didn't start hanging out until my second year."

"What happened?"

"Nothing. He took care of it and I promised not to get into any more trouble."

"Well I've already had my run in with him." Maddy abruptly stopped when she realized this was leading back to Comstock.

Thane tried to disengage from Mina's seductive demeanor and edged closer to Maddy.

"I also asked a contact downtown about Maconi. He's a strange cop. Early in his career he was involved in that Michael Johnson death in his squad car. The kid was handcuffed in the back of the car, but somehow got to Maconi's gun and put the gun in his mouth and committed suicide. The police let him off and put him on desk duty. Only recently has he been allowed to do part-time beat work. He's fired his gun twice in the last year. That's more shots than most cops take in a career. The city paid out huge civil money in settlement to the Johnson family two years ago. Anywhere else he would have been let go. The scuttle-butt is the high brass were pressured to keep Maconi employed."

"Kind of like the O.J. trial, isn't it? Innocent in the criminal investigation, but civil damages were another issue."

"Maddy, while you're at the coroner's office, could you pull the files on the Ranger cases and review them with me?"

"Maconi and Michael Johnson, too, while I'm at it?"

"That sounds vindictive."

"Doesn't the F.B.I. care about justice?" Maddy bargained.

**

After a short discussion to conclude that Maconi wouldn't be in a squad car on a weeknight, the last of the revelers were at their cars. Thane hung on Maddy's door and reminded her of their dinner date the following evening. Maddy drove away. Mina chatted with Thane in the parking lot for several minutes until she talked her way into his car.

**

JUNE 5, TUESDAY, The Throne-Room

<u>Dolochus biflorus</u>, <u>Ulex europus</u>, and <u>Fomes fomentarius</u> vials stood in a row up on the laboratory

counter. Each plant substance, a lectin or sugar-binding chemical, was labeled according to its specific antigen affinity. The affinity allowed it to bind and identify a specific sugar group that dangles from the surfaces of red blood cells. The different dangling sugar chains are identifying markers that are commonly called blood types. Dolochus identifies type A blood; Fomes marks for type B; Ulex binds the sugars of type O blood.

The purpose of Maddy's project, directed by the late Bruce Comstock, Ph.D., was to determine if the density and type of blood group sugars have any relationship to coronary thromboses. Comstock's theory was that mild inflammations in the artery wall would injure the surface and increase the artery's susceptibility to thrombus. The blood vessel linings are bombarded with circulating red blood cells. Does the density of blood cell sugar antigens on the arteries relate to the risk of heart attack? What initially was an excuse to be next to Comstock was now a true research passion.

**

The Breakfast Club had one pop-tart, a seventy-one year old man with Alzheimer's disease who apparently died in his sleep. She signed the death certificate after a thirty-seconds once-over of the body. Maddy was then free to do paper work, research, or take the rest of the day off as along as she could be reached by cell phone. The rest of the morgue team also was free with no autopsies to perform.

Slurp's side was hurting. He went home. Richard took a nap and read a book. Mordecai was in the DNA typing lab.

Tuesday was Graham's day off. Dr. Green was reading journals in his office.

Maddy first reviewed the cancer slides of Bruce Comstock's kidney tumor. She dictated the final report complete with references to Von-Hippel-Lindau disease. Her pride in a thoroughly referenced summary was deflated with the dread of calling Mrs. Comstock. Her home telephone number was on the front of the file. She circled the number and left the file beside the desk phone.

It was nine a.m. and she could devote the rest of the day to her lectin-antigen-binding project. In memory of Bruce Comstock, Ph.D., she felt an urgent duty to complete the project to honor Bruce posthumously by citing him as co-author. The data thus far was producing a negative study in that the blood group density appeared to have no relationship to MI. Journals hate negative studies. The probability of getting it published was low.

Maddy meticulously dropped lectin solutions onto artery sections from clotted coronary arteries. She carefully washed away the excess. Next she applied known red cells which sandwiched to the lectins and identified specific blood groups. Her microscope had a laser assisted color scanner to quantitate the density of the blood group antigens. She compared the staining intensity to vessel walls in the spleen, which she had learned was most similar to normal heart lining cells. The procedure was relatively simple. The most difficult task was searching through the remaining slides to obtain spleen sections. Often pathologists omit spleen sections when the spleen is grossly normal. Cases without spleen sections had to be rejected for Maddy's study.

The records system of the county coroner could be researched by key words. The entry of Michael Johnson revealed eighteen cases. Two were about the right age. One was "gunshot suicide." She ordered the files and x-rays.

Next Maddy typed "coronary thrombus and autopsy." The computer dutifully printed out a list of fully autopsied cases with coronary thromboses, which had microscopic slides. She selected freshness, the ten most recent cases and added the two she knew from her first two days. The old burned woman was of interest to see if blood groups were destroyed by fire. They were not.

David Burr was a minor celebrity. The minor ethical impropriety of keeping and distributing slides of celebrities is well known within the secret inner circles of the pathology profession.

Who among the masses of humanity hasn't a pornographic picture, a shoplifted item, an unregistered gun, or a prevarication? So quickly we forget our own minor ethical improprieties; surely the souvenir collecting of celebrity diseases is harmless.

The pathology equivalent to collecting Elvis scarves is tissue slide collections of celebrities's diseases. Widely circulated tissue slides include President Kennedy's adrenal, which displays evidence of tuberculosis scarring. The President suffered from Addison's disease, which was kept secret from the general public.

On a campaign stop, President Nixon's daughter had an ectopic pregnancy. The circulated slides are labeled, "Tricky Dick's first grandchild." The liver slide of Jeffrey Dahmer has the subtitle, "You are what you eat." Searching the slide boxes of pathologists will unveil the gallbladders, appendices, and vocal cord polyps of the rich and famous. Pathologists do not collect autographs. Maddy was delighted to capture a piece of Congressman Burr. She planned to title the slide, "Heart of the Heartless."

She batch stained all the cases, then went to lunch. She bought a tuna sandwich and Hershey bar at the kiosk off the front lobby. A cold front had passed through during the evening and it was sunny and breezy and only 71 degrees, a perfect day for lunch outside.

Patients were lined up outside the hospital in wheel chairs with attached intravenous poles and pumps. Yellow, white and clear fluids filled their plastic bags. The patients' skins were thin and pale except for bruised spots from venipuncture sites. Maddy thought for a moment about the suffering of the very sick. She wondered how she would respond to her own terminal illness. Would she be stoic, whiny, or depressed? Would remorse bring forth a death-bed confession? She felt mildly guilty that she made a living off of illness and death. The cell phone rang, ending her daydream.

"Mina, what's up, girl?" Maddy answered as she read the caller ID on her cell.

"What are you doing tonight? I'm feeling perky. I was thinking about a movie."

"Thanks, but I've kind of got a date, for dinner."

"What? You dog. Does he have biceps? A job? Probably not both. It is a man, right? I don't suppose he's under fifty."

"Yes, a he, but more job than biceps. And he might even be less than thirty. The F.B.I. guy from the Medicine Room yesterday, Thane Hatcher."

Mina was speechless for five seconds. "So you think he's cute?"

"Sort of. He's the persistent type. Besides an F.B.I. guy is a cop, isn't he? He promises to be gone in a week or so. I was hoping he could help me clean up the crap with Maconi."

"You think he's too young, don't you? Have you ever thought that when you get to be fifty, those fifty-somethings will be pushing eighty?"

"I'll get another fifty-year-old my own age. Then you and my mother will stop lecturing me."

"Sweetbread's in his fifties."

"Just because furniture is old, doesn't make it a valuable antique."

"I'm not joking, Maddy, I'm warning you. Sweetbread's got a reputation for being handsy. Don't let him molest you. I know firsthand."

"Gross."

"When you dump the F.B.I. agent, you tell him I said he's cute and plenty old enough."

**

Twelve stacks of files including the Michael Johnson case were neatly piled next to Maddy's microscope when she returned from lunch. There was a handwritten note, obviously from a woman, written in smooth legible cursive letters. "Dr. Gray, These are the files you requested except for one. Dr. O'Dell has the file on David Burr. He will be back tomorrow. DSW"

Secretaries are wonderful, thought Maddy. She spent the next hour comparing lectin stains in spleen and coronaries in ten cases. One case had no spleen and was rejected. The final case was David Burr. She debated whether to get the slide work done without the file or leave it until the next day. She needed a break and opened the file on Michael Johnson.

The autopsy report was straightforward, too clean, sanitized with no excess words or ambiguous descriptions. Contact gunshot wound inside of mouth had exploded the skull, exiting posteriorly. The bullet reportedly then broke through the back windshield. The police report stated that ballistics concluded one bullet had been fired from the gun of Officer Joseph Maconi. Neither Maconi nor his partner Patrolman Withers could explain how Johnson got control of the gun or managed to fire it.

The conjecture was that the gun was drawn and loose in the squad car. Johnson had kicked off his shoes and maneuvered it with his feet to his lap and then into his mouth. There was nothing new or plausible in the documents. The issue was kinetic energy. Could this caliber of bullet travel through two areas of dense skull bone and then through the rear window? There was no discussion of this crucial question, Michael Johnson's magic bullet.

Maddy reviewed the skull x-rays. The fragments of teeth and bones looked like a constellation map of white dots in a black background.

Her door was open. Percival Mordecai entered and closed the door. What could he want? She quieted her initial thoughts that he might attack her. Still his mere presence was creepy and discomforting.

"Want to see something very interesting?" She nodded okay and Mordecai continued. "See this DNA histogram?"

Mordecai produced a dried gel film with stained bands of DNA lines like little ladders drawn on cellophane. Of course we did these first. He handed her two photomicrographs of cells, hair, and tissue debris.

"Notice the anucleated skin cells and nucleated vaginal squamous cells in both cases!" Mordecai emphasized the word both. "Seems Mr. Burr and Mr. Comstock both had the pleasures of recent heterosexual experience." He stared at Maddy with the voyeuristic pleasure of a sadistic torture.

"This appears to explain the mission of the lady seen by the surveillance cameras, wouldn't you agree?" Mordecai taunted.

"What does it matter? Burr's dead, and he's widely rumored to be a player."

"Yes, yes. But I was referring to the late Mr. Comstock. While videotaping Dr. Green's son attempting to hit a Whiffle Ball, there was a distant image of a mysterious woman, a.k.a. Dr. Gray, quietly sneaking off into a parked trailer."

"You are a despicable snoop with a disgusting imagination. Get out of my office!"

"Certainly, but see these two lines of DNA which match perfectly. One is from the vaginal cells attached to Mr. Comstock. The second came from your chewing gum. There is so little left for me to disgustingly imagine, is there?" Mordecai turned to exit. Maddy sprang forward to close the door and stood with her back blocking it.

"What do you want Mordecai? Why are you doing this to me?" Maddy demanded as Mordecai turned his back and began wandering about the room reading book titles and poking through papers.

He picked up the skull film of Johnson and studied it while responding. "I am merely a fellow trainee, employed by the government to discern the truth. I didn't do anything to you. You are adept enough at self-torture. I don't want anything from you. Not yet anyway. I hear things and I listen. I hear you'd be in a hotbed of trouble if this got out to Sweetbread. Your flirtation with Mr. Comstock was no secret, you know."

"I won't be blackmailed," Maddy hissed.

"I haven't asked for anything. And even if you don't believe me, I'm not your enemy. I was merely sharing professional information. I suggest you be more discreet in the future." Mordecai put the x-ray down and pointed to a triangular piece of metal adjacent a tooth fragment. "I don't know why I find that crown fragment so interesting."

"Are you discreet, Dr. Mordecai?"

"It all depends." He walked away.

She was unsure if Mordecai was dangerous, but convinced he was deranged. She feared and respected his preternatural abilities of observation. Maddy examined the x-ray and turned it upside down. Did Dr. Green know? She needed to find out before her appointment with Sweetbread.

**

"Come in," was the welcoming response of Dr. Green, a man of gentle friendliness without anger, rudeness, or impatience. He was one of the Christian chosen. He was one of God's special cultivars born into a loving, stable, affluent home where strife and violence and sin do not exist. There was only blessed goodness in his home, as it was in the home of each chosen. Maddy wondered what it would have been like to have a parent who lacked impatience and demands of blind obedience.

"Yes, Maddy?"

"I just wanted to let you know I have to see Dr. Sweetbread this afternoon," Maddy stated under the pretext of being informative. She knew Dr. Green didn't expect her to check in and out. "You aren't aware of what he wants to talk to me about, are you?"

Again Maddy was watching for physical signs that Dr. Green knew of her liaison or more importantly that Sweetbread might know. He shook his head, calmly as a Buddhist in meditation. Mordecai hadn't squealed to Green.

Maddy returned to her desk. DSW, Debra Sue Walls, the staff secretary came over the intercom.

"Dr. O'Dell came in and finished the case of David Burr. On his day off, no less. In and out like driving through McDonalds. He doesn't like the high profile ones to go one extra minute. Just get it done and avoid the media he says. I've got the file back if you still need it."

**

She read and studied the file in fine detail, losing track of the time. She noticed her watch: 2:50 p.m. She had ten minutes to cross campus and face the University Chief.

She darted out of her office and ran immediately into the barrel chest of Graham. His arm reached forward to stop her shoulder but slid over her back as her breasts impaled his upper abdomen. The immediate desire to sustain the closeness rendered each speechless for an eon of two seconds. Two simultaneous apologizes were followed by

Maddy's explanation that she was running late to her appointment. She continued walking, rambling incoherently about clustered brain capillaries and the need to discuss the case in more detail. Graham stared speechless in the hallway, contemplating the firmness of a twenty-nine-year-old's breast.

**

A plaque of ebony plastic with wood grain and large polished brass letters hung at eye level right of the doorjamb. It read:

> James Sweetbread, MD
> President and C.E.O.
> University Professional Staff, INC

Ten years previously the state legislature relinquished their employer status of the physician faculty of the University. James Sweetbread organized the medical staff, who were threatening to leave the university system unless given the freedom to control their own billings and greatly increase their incomes. Physicians believed correctly that the University was excessively profiting from their professional work. The new organization increased their pay slightly; it raised Sweetbread's immensely.

David Burr used his control of federal pork programs to pressure the state Republican organization to accept the secession. The new corporation was born with Sweetbread as C.E.O. The name on his stationery was U.P.S. Inc., often written UPSinc, commonly shortened to the last syllable. No one doubted that Sweetbread was the only faucet for

"The Sink." He signed all major contracts. He personally reviewed all salary contracts with physicians. He required all research and grant money designated for professional staff be channeled through the coffers of UPSinc. With 800 doctors, Ph.D.'s and other licensed professionals receiving six figure incomes, the budget for salaries and service contracts was nearly a billion dollars.

James was his first name, as in the King James Bible. James corrected anyone who tried to call him Jim. There is no King Jim in the psyche of James Sweetbread.

His father, a Marine colonel, had lived in the modest luxury afforded the families of military field officers. The best of the perks included house and errand servants of enlisted men and women. Rank was power. When a corporal trembled before his father, James glowed with envy. Someday he would have men tremble beside his desk.

As a boy, Jimmy was athletic enough to make the football and basketball teams through high school. Winning a conference championship his junior year meant nothing compared to becoming team co-captain as a senior. It proved to be a powerful lesson that sharing power and prestige was worse than not having it.

King James's throne-room, as the faculty disparagingly referred to his office suite, was modeled after the royal bedroom suites at Versailles with gilded décor and similar darkly stained woods.

The antechamber housed his two assistants. "Assistant to the President" was the grandiose appellation for the secretary who handled typing, telephone calls, and appointments. Mildred was a flimsy sack of skin encasing her bones like a canvas bag of camping-tent stakes. She was a ninety-pound dowdy matron of sixty years who looked eighty. Her voice was quiet and timid. Her vocalizations were all statement-questions. Maddy had received one earlier, "Dr. Sweetbread is expecting you at three, is that going to be all right?" Her purpose in life was the business of UPS Inc. If she had another life outside the office, no one knew it.

The second woman in the anteroom was Cheryl Sneed. Her fashionable business suit, impeccable nail polish, and barely visible makeup were classy contrasts to Mildred. Her title was Executive Administrator, which was as vague as her formal job description.

She planned and hosted parties to recruit physicians. She served as James's personal travel agent. She met with decorators to redo his office. Cheryl took meeting minutes and schmoozed with board members, the University President, and legislators. She accompanied James on out of town travel. She referred to him as, The Doctor. She held conversation gracefully with disarming smoothness, true to her Georgian debutante background.

"Doctor Sweetbread is expecting you, Dr. Gray. If you wouldn't mind having a chair, I'm sure he'll be off the phone shortly. Could I bring you some cawwfee or Coca Cola?" she offered in an unhurried drawl with genuine-appearing smile. Maddy declined.

She nervously killed the next three minutes, which seemed much longer, observing the signed original artworks and numbered prints behind the secretaries. Maddy was awestruck to see the bold signature of Ronoldo on one painting. He was a living and famous Portuguese impressionist whose work was currently on display at the Chicago Museum of Art. Her immediate thought was the vulnerability to theft of this precious Riviera landscape. She estimated that it cost a hundred thousand dollars.

The Renaissance Royalty of France used the Versailles anteroom for informal visitations, particularly in the afternoon during nap hours. The middle room was for dressing.

In the case of James Sweetbread M.D., President and C.E.O., the middle office chamber was a dressing-down room. The moldings were flowering vines of gilded gold on painted wood. The white wicker chairs were thin with uncomfortable, overly decorated cushions. The chairs surrounded a hard glass top table framed in wicker. The table corners were adorned with gilded flowers matching the wall moldings.

Maddy had been in this room once previously to hear the complaints Mrs. Comstock had lodged in protest to Maddy's "seduction of her faculty husband." The meeting had lasted barely three minutes and concluded with King James's edict dissolving the Comstock-Gray relationship.

Today she was escorted through the center room to the formal office passing a statue of an obese king. Maddy daydreamed about the bed size necessary for King Henry VIII. James directed her to sit on one of two facing oversized and overstuffed couches covered with fine Italian leather.

Unlike the dandy effeminate Rococo and bright wicker of the two outer rooms, the inner chamber was brown and masculine and powerful. The deep coffee bean color of the sofas lay beneath statues of historical leaders. The wall coverings of thick beige woven fabric sprouted guns and medieval armor and paintings of military battles, the décor of a castle war chamber.

"We've got a problem, Dr. Gray, don't we?" He continued, ignoring her open mouth and impending response, "D. U. I. is a serious offense for physicians in training. Do you realize that the licensing board has an automatic supervisory restriction to the license of any physician receiving such a conviction?"

"No, I didn't. What exactly does that entail?"

"You have to go weekly to an alcohol abuse therapy session. The initial assessment and treatment runs between five and eight thousand dollars. That's a lot of money for a resident, isn't it, Dr. Gray? And it is a lot of time away from the University."

Again he ignored her and continued. "But the big problem is I have a University and a state medical school to answer to. Dr. Gray, I can't have any physicians on my staff or in any training program who don't have a clean license. You will be terminated, which in all probability means you'll never get into another program in this country. In short you will have wasted the last seven years of training."

This time he waited a long time until she spoke. "It's a lie, I wasn't drunk. Not even close. I swear it, Dr. Sweetbread. This cop, named Maconi, is hassling me. I know he tampered with the breath test. I'm innocent."

"Maddy, I'd like to call you Maddy, they've got you. You can't beat them. Now, I've got friends at the police station. I am an important man. I can get this thing taken care of, if you'll let me help you." She looked up partly in hope, mostly in puzzlement. He moved over to her couch and sat beside her. "You have a husband or a boyfriend, Maddy?"

"No. I mean, what's that got to do with anything?" she said.

"It makes life a lot easier. You treat me nicely and I can do a lot for you." Sweetbread kissed the back of her neck. She arched her back and jumped up from the couch.

"Whoa! I don't know what you have in mind or think of me."

"I think you are an attractive, bright woman who has the right sense to take care of her career. Look around you. I've got about everything I could want. But I also want you. We'll have a lot a fun. You've proved you don't mind us guys a little older."

"I don't have to take this, and I am leaving."

Sweetbread put his hand in front of the door. "Don't screw up your life, Maddy. Your court date is July 8th. You'll be on the street by 1 p.m. unless..." He paused to become more seductive. "Lighten up. It'll be our little secret. You won't regret it. Friday evening. I'll call you, we'll make each other happy."

He opened his side door which led to a back hallway and then directly outside, circumventing the office secretaries. He had designed this egress specifically for discreet guests. "Think it over. Friday." He closed the door. She spit on it.

Her previous plans were to leave the campus after the appointment and treat herself to a whirlpool. Now, filled with anger, humiliation, and the fear of losing her career, she was ready to fight. The academic competition of college pre-med and the grind of medical school had taught her to take advantage, when bursts of energy presented themselves. She returned to her office with jaw clenched resolve to finish her research project.

Maddy stomped across the parking lot from the White Castle with Nazi-trooper giant-steps. She plowed through the front automatic doors with eyes ahead on the hallway floor. She glazed the shoulder of Graham O'Dell spinning him around as she continued without stopping. She felt no spark this time. Her pond was choking in the scum of men.

"How did the appointment go?" he asked genuinely.

"Sweetbread's an asshole." She kept moving without losing stride.

"Excellent diagnosis, Dr. Gray," Graham responded. Maddy did not turn around, but again felt the warm affection she held for O'Dell.

**

From three forty-five until five Maddy sat at her desk and computer kneading her database. She vigorously and continuously entered red blood cells antigen counts and laser density readings. It was complete. She was satisfied and proud. As she reached for the F-1 key to exit, she remembered the unfinished slides of David Burr. Maddy activated the laser microscopic slide reader and dutifully measured the splenic artery walls. The <u>Dolochus biflorus</u> lectin demonstrated some of the strongest binding in her entire series. Maddy considered how the stressful personality type A, which had absolutely nothing to do with red blood cell type A, was nonetheless appropriate for David Burr.

Her thoughts were interrupted by the static-filled intercom. "Dr. Gray, this is Debra. There's a woman here to see you. Can I send her back?"

"Sure," responded Maddy without hesitation. Must be Mina, she thought.

Leona Comstock had features suggesting descent along a rodent lineage. Despite no discernible tail, she resembled a five foot two mouse. She crept about quietly. She nervously nibbled with her teeth. Her high pitched chirping voice was irritating. She wore a thick gray wool coat with fur trim thick as a squirrel's tail.

The June cold front meant a cool summer temperature that day of seventy-one degrees, but hardly necessitated a coat, let alone the dull ecru headscarf of a Russian peasant. She wore no makeup.

"I'm Leona Comstock, and I know who you are."

Maddy's back arched in readiness for verbal combat. She searched for the words to make this awkward scene more civil. "I'm sorry about Mr. Comstock. I was going to call…"

Leona bypassed Maddy's open mouth and launched into a soliloquy. "I worry a lot. I don't have to worry about Bruce anymore. I hope he's in a better place. You're a pretty girl. I was never pretty. I was born on a farm. We worked for everything. We didn't have anything given to us. Father wasn't pleased when I went to university, but he approved of Bruce. I washed glassware in the chemistry department. I've always worked. I don't know if Bruce ever dated anyone before me. I liked him well enough to marry him. I always worried though. You can't keep a man if you don't have the desire. Well, I've never really had any interest in that area. I worried somebody like you'd come around some day. Men and their hormones. So when I found out about his carrying on with you, the young doctor, I was worried he would be gone. Then what? What would I

117

do about a pension if he runs off with a young woman? Kill myself? I made a lot of trouble for you. I'm sorry for that. I was just worried. I'm not stupid or cruel. I could tell you made him happy, and I couldn't. When I called today for the autopsy results and death certificate, the secretary, Miss Walls, said it was pending, that there was some more research you had to do. I was worried he had something awful, not that he might have given to me. I knew I wouldn't sleep until…"

"Mrs. Comstock, Leona," Maddy loudly cut in, "I am sorry, too, about last year. As for Mr. Comstock, Bruce died of cancer. It's not catching, and you or I didn't cause it. It was kidney cancer. We think it's a hereditary type. Do you know if anyone of his relatives had any blood vessel diseases, tumors of the brain, or kidney cancer?"

A tear welled in corner of her eye, beaded on her lower eyelashes as she stared ahead, then fell onto her folded hands as she lowered her head. "We had a son. I wanted a child. After he was born I moved into the nursery, not so much to be next to the baby as to get a bed of my own. Anyway, I was worried when he started falling down. Calvin was only three. They tried to operate on the back of his brain. He had a hand-basket-tumor or some such name. I was worried before the surgery that he would have an ugly scar. I never worried that he wouldn't survive the operation. Guess maybe I'm not such a good worrier," Leone smiled wanly at her self-effacing joke.

"Hemangioblastoma? Could the 'hand-basket-tumor' have been that, a hemangioblastoma?" Maddy wondered, then asked Leona directly.

"I suppose. It makes more sense that the brain tumor would have a medical name. You probably think I'm ignorant. But at the time, I was a wreck. You can imagine. My son had just died. I was afraid Bruce would leave me after that. We didn't have much in common. What would I do if he left? I couldn't make enough money to live on as a part-time technician. I was so afraid that I'd have to go home and become a burden to my sister. No, I think I'd rather be dead. Bruce liked his work. He was a good man. I tried not to worry, but when he found you, I was desperate. That's why I threatened to blame Dr. Sweetbread's office and make some ugly publicity. I hope you can at least understand if not forgive me."

"No need to worry. We all do the best we can. Leona, your son's tumor and Bruce's kidney cancer are most likely related to a genetic disease called Von-Hippel-Lindau disease. You will need to contact the other members of Bruce's family and have them examined by their doctors. Let me write all these words down."

Leona smiled minimally and shook Maddy's hand at the door, once assured the death certificate would be issued the next day. Leona could file the paper work, and secure her widow's pension. Maddy sighed in relief that all her dreaded thoughts of confronting her lover's wife, including vengeful slurs of paramour, concubine, and harlot had proved groundless.

Leona was only a mouse, relieved that Bruce no longer posed the threat of financial abandonment. She lived the passionless life of her gray wool coat. Maddy felt pity for Bruce. She knew him as a man with passion, torn by the restraints of convention and duty to his wife. She pitied Leona even more. Her energy was spent hiding in the undergrowth of life, a desert rodent shaking behind a cactus canopy, alone.

**

Maddy accessed the university computer on line. As she typed "Calvin Comstock" into the patient inquiry function, the "delayed archiving, please wait" prompt popped up. Twenty seconds later the file card summary from fourteen years ago documented the short life of a three year old boy who had died post operatively from hemangioblastoma. Maddy hand wrote a note for Debra and attached it to the death certificate of Bruce Comstock:

Cause of death: Renal Cell Carcinoma
Secondary to Von Hippel-Lindau Disease
Mechanism: Acute pulmonary embolism
Manner: Natural

Case complete, M. Gray M.D.

Maddy was exhausted. Sweetbread's sexual coercion and the exchange with Leona Comstock had taken its toll. Rising to leave she noticed the last slides of her research project.

Her cell phone rang. Thane Hatcher was calling to discuss final plans for their dinner date.

"I've had a trying day. I don't think I'd be very good company."

"Maddy, that's precisely the reason you need a good relaxing dinner." She was too tired to argue. They agreed to a short evening at a casual Chinese restaurant. Thane would have settled for Taco Bell to see her.

Maddy turned out the light to her office, then turned it back on. She picked up the last slide, the coronary occlusion of David Burr. "Shit," she swore out loud as she realized the <u>Dolochus biflorus</u> stain was completely negative. It would have to be redone. The lights were again turned off, the door locked.

Maddy pushed herself to think of Thane.

She would not become like Leona, but she clearly sympathized with Leona's desperate aversion to being trapped in a farm town.

**

The Wong Wok was testimony that Chinese entrepreneurs do not consult marketing professionals. Instead the restaurant wannabe saves and borrows a few thousands dollars to rent a small rectangular storefront. A name is concocted from any combination of common words like: garden, green, Chinese, dragon, Ming, wok, emperor, red, or a home province. A grill, deep fryer, and refrigerator are purchased. The system of traditional family slavery is invoked. The site is cleaned. The first Board of Health inspection occurs followed by repairs to bring the electrical, washroom, and handicap access up to codes. The issued license is the initial wall decoration, and the door is opened.

The Wong Wok's staff chief was Jian Li, a twenty-eight-year-old matriarch who spoke broken English. Chinese was her overseer dialect to marshal her two brothers, a crippled arthritic grandmother, and a conscripted cousin. The matriarch took all dinner orders and collected all payments between barking commands to the others. One brother was chopper-preparer. The second was grill and fryer man.

121

Grandmother delivered supplies from the shelves and food from the freezers. Jian Li serviced the front counter, packaging carry-outs and waiting the six dining-in tables.

"Washu gitten tudey?"

"Two spring rolls and hot-and-sour soup to start. I'll have the Kung Pao chicken and my good doctor friend will have the Moo shoo pork," Thane ordered slowly with his clearest diction.

"Two soup, one soup?"

"Two soups, two spring rolls for appetizers."

"What mean ap-tizzuh?" she squinted.

Thane shook his head and repeated the order and added a request for hot tea.

"Comwidtea."

It also came with fried rice with small brown things, the exact origin of which Thane and Maddy decided not to speculate. Nor would they ask Jian, fearing they might receive a double order. The food was good. They swapped portions and ranked the dishes for flavor.

The conversation turned to their professional lives. Maddy listened, intending not to discuss her run-in with Sweetbread.

"The Ranger isn't random, he just doesn't have a readily apparent pattern."

Maddy's gender trigger fired, "How do you know it's a he? Don't you think women ever kill people?"

"Except for euthanasia by nurses, 99 percent of serial killers are men. I think it's a hunter-gatherer thing," he tried to keep it light. "Women like to stay close to home, the men enjoy the hunt." She didn't laugh. "Okay, it could be a woman. Here's what I'm seeing. There are three groups of victims: First are the nasty guys: wife beater, gay basher, and child molester. This group would have many enemies and angry family members. These guys were shot at close range without a fight, execution style.

The second batch is the young minorities, guys in the hood. They were gunned down at a distance. The motive could be gang revenge, racism, family feud, who knows.

But they were distance hits, totally unlike the close-up shootings of the three mid-level professionals. That third group of guys wouldn't appear to have any enemies." Thane was thinking out loud.

"Perhaps the woman killer was picking them up Mr. Goodbar style and whacking them for sexual inadequacies."

"Do you have these thoughts often? Is there something I should know in case carnal thoughts should cross my mind?" Thane moved at the opportunity to test her receptiveness to the topic of sex.

"A few have lived." Maddy quipped, then grew silent at the memory of her hands pushing the belly of Bruce Comstock.

"Right, revenge of Mr. Goodbar. The bad ones beat her up. She lures them into a quiet place and blows them away at three inches. But the squirrelly accountants bore her. She meets them at the office after hours. The doors are locked, then she whacks them."

"Do you think the hood boys go to the same bars as Joe 3-piece suit?" Maddy asked, unsure if he was joking.

"That's the beauty of your idea. The hood boys are too young for the bars, so she arranges to meet them on street corners and alleys. When they get within twenty feet of her car, ker-bloom! I think we're ready to turn this case over to the D.A."

"Wouldn't we need a suspect?" Maddy played along.

"Any ideas?"

"Maybe my friend, Mina." Maddy offered flippantly, but Thane's eyes grew wide. "What?" responded Maddy.

"Mina, did she say something to you?"

"About what? Being the Random Ranger? I don't think so. I'm sure I would have remembered that. I was just joking. Mina has to watch herself when she's been drinking. Looking for Mr. Goodbar? Forget it. Beside the D.A. can always come up with a suspect. Just let Maconi frame somebody."

"Has he been around again?" Thane was relieved that Maddy gave no indication she knew of the previous night that he spent acquiescing to Mina's advances.

"No, thank God, but he's done plenty of damage."

"By the way, Maddy, I asked around and there is some talk about dropping your D.U.I."

"Yeah, right. Your buddies, the police, go straight to Sweetbread who says he can get it all straightened out. The only catch is I have to fuck him by Friday. The scum."

"What? Sweetbread offered to trade a get-out-of-jail for a get-into-bed card? That's illegal. That's classic quid-pro-quo sexual harassment. Sue him."

"His word against mine. Like someone would believe the shady-pasted resident of departmental embarrassment and havoc. Indianapolis's finest arrest her as a civic menace to the MADD poster child. Then in desperation of being expelled from her training program, she claims harassment to coerce the professional director to let her sinister and criminal acts continue to be perpetrated upon the innocent public."

"Bad story. Even Gloria Steinem wouldn't believe you."

"Mina tried to warn me, but Sweetbread was all business the last time. I'm screwed."

"Bad pun. I won't let this happen. What did Mina tell you? Did he proposition her?"

"Something about groping hands and her drug license. Apparently he got her off a charge of smoking marijuana."

"We just need a third witness. Two are plausible, but usually with three testimonials a case can be won or at least settled. Do you or Mina know of another woman?"

"That doesn't help me. Even if we got Sweetbread sucked into a suit, my D.U.I. will likely get me kicked out of the residency permanently."

"I've got an idea. Let me talk to some friends at the agency. I'll call you tomorrow."

The two sat quietly finishing dinner. Thane, realizing that his date was a romantic dead end, sympathized, "Sorry it was such a terrible day."

"Actually it wasn't a total loss. I didn't have any autopsies and I almost completed my research project, except for one slide. Wouldn't you know it, the very last slide on David Burr, and the reaction didn't work."

"I don't have a clue what you're talking about."

"None of the red cells in the clotted coronary from the congressman's heart reacted as blood type A. That means the test system failed to work or..." She stopped in mid-sentence and dropped her fortune cookie.

"Or what?" Thane sensed the importance.

"Or that heart section has a totally different blood type. That it wasn't a section from David Burr's heart."

**

JUNE 6, WEDNESDAY, Cause Undetermined

Maddy held the radio set button in the Honda Civic for the requisite three seconds to lock in WXCR. "Excellent Country Radio" devoted the early morning hours to local news and events. Between announcements of "Fiddler on the Roof" performed at 7 pm Friday through Sunday at West Washington Senior High auditorium and Senior Citizens women's quilt show and men's duct-tape sculpture contest, The Breakfast Club morning specials had the greatest chance of air time. Maddy had difficulty imagining who listened to this station or how they got advertisers to keep it afloat.

She detested the fluffy small talk marveling about each baton twirler and basket weaver within twenty miles. Maddy posed the question: When is being nice simply vulgar lying? This was important philosophy, not the drivel of her undergraduate philosophy course. Her optimistic conclusion was that the rest of the population wasn't so stupid. Like herself, they tuned-in for one specific purpose and ignored the mindless banter.

Halfway to County Hospital she listened to the local stories. A 69-year-old woman had been found dead and decaying in her apartment. The influx of roaches into the building had led the exterminators to her deathbed.

The driver of a Ford van with three teenagers had lost control, careened over a downtown underpass and crashed into a concrete pylon. Two passengers were killed and the driver was in critical condition at University Hospital.

The Republican leader of the Senate and the governor announced the selection of Byron Davis to fill the temporary vacancy created at the death of Congressman Burr. It was genuinely newsworthy in that the old name state politicians had been by-passed in the selection of Davis, a financial officer at EnvironTech. While newsworthy, it was no surprise. William Corless was known as the "Golden Goose" of soft money. Byron Davis was his undisguised and fully stringed marionette.

Slurp didn't try to pop-tart fatal motor vehicle accident drivers. Those cases are routinely autopsied for the legal implications of liability. Passengers however can be signed out with any external signs of plausible lethal trauma. After several minutes of cursory inspection, the death certificates are officially completed, "Multiple blunt force injury secondary to motor vehicle accident." The funeral homes are called; the refrigerator drawers are emptied.

The sight of the nubile blonde child of sixteen, lifeless on the morgue gurney, affected Maddy. She had seen dead children at the University. The pale white leukemics and blue cyanotic babies with congenital heart defects looked dead. Those children never seemed normal. Their short lives were sad sagas of suffering by themselves and their families.

Maddy was struck by the aliveness of this dead girl. Her skin was pale yellow like her hair. The front side of her body looked asleep as if a gentle nudge would awaken her to pull the sheet up over her naked body. Maddy could see her flirting with teenage boys and primping her hair.

When her body was turned over the muscles and bones of her back were exposed and raw. The concrete pylon had become a knife-edge slicing her backside away like a cucumber peel. Her spinal cord dangled over the gurney, reminding Maddy of a display at a Jaycee's Halloween Haunted House.

The blonde girl's companion was crushed more typically for a motor vehicle accident. The skull was a bag of jagged broken bones, blood, and shards of scalp loosely attached. Embedded glass fragments glittered. Raggedy Ann limbs were folded and broken. The chest had an MVA signature, a deep groove where the dashboard had crushed it.

It was professionally easier to ignore the pain and disease of eighty-year olds with cancer or strokes. Maddy had a weak spot when the deceased was a young woman. It aroused an inner fear she might squander her own short life. Her heart ached at the tragic sight of these teenage girls in perfect health, annihilated. Although fascinating, forensic pathology was too often too painful an experience.

Dr. Green was vacationing for two days in Florida, indulging his son with Mickey Mouse and the Magic Kingdom. Dr. O'Dell was tied up in a budget committee in the County Hospital executive suite. That left the forensic fellow, Dr. Mordecai, temporarily in charge of the service. He looked over Maddy's shoulder as she signed out the two motor vehicle fatalities. He said nothing, but Maddy could feel his eyes fondling her legs and breasts. Would he try to blackmail her for sex, too?

Maddy readied herself for the stench of the old lady who had laid for ten days in her apartment after dying. She bristled when Mordecai said she could also do the SIDS case afterward. It was only a baby after all, half an hour case at the most, he said. Maddy knew Dr. Green or O'Dell would have only required her to do one of the two cases. Mordecai would stand nearby and watch, lasciviously.

"Nibblings," was how Mordecai described the eroded skin over the arms and legs of 69 year-old Francine Guinn. Mice and rats had chewed a large portion of the exposed extremities and also eaten portholes into the chest hull.

Richard pleaded, "Doctor M, A.S.C.V.D. sign-out and we can save all our noses."

Mordecai insisted, "I have no proof of atherosclerotic or cardiovascular disease. This autopsy is quite necessary to rule out stab wounds." Maddy knew it was a sadistic decision to make her experience the gagging putrid smell.

Slurp, standing behind Mordecai said, "I got your stab wound," while he made a coital gesture running his third finger of his left hand through the circle of the thumb and forefinger of the other.

By weight and odor the decomposing human corpse was equivalent to a hundred rotting rats in a pile. Maddy and Slurp wore double masks, but still required breaks to leave the room to keep from vomiting. Despite the use of huge commercial fans, the stench could be detected throughout the basement of the entire hospital.

Slurp whacked the cockroaches that scurried from the body with his hand. He wore a steel mesh glove for this purpose. "Motherfucking bugs can't be killed no other way. And they move so fast, you only get one shot. Now I like to hit with the palm, then drag the steel mesh a couple of inches, cuz otherwise they take off running soon as you lift up your glove. It's the grinding steel that gets 'em. You got to mill them motherfuckers."

The unwelcome sight of Officer Maconi diffused the unpleasantness of the stench. "Behaving yourself, Doctor?" She pretended not hear. "So what's the verdict. Says in the blotter here that the neighbors haven't seen her in nearly two weeks. They'd know. She was one of those nosy old bags who complained about everything on the block. Blah, blah. One guy puts his garbage out too early, and the dogs tear it up. The teenagers are smoking joints in the alley. The gal downstairs doesn't have to pay rent 'cause she's fucking the landlord. So what's this old bag expect? Like he's interested in poking her. The old bag's husband run off about three years ago. So why are you wasting time on this stink bomb?"

"Officer Maconi, this is new territory. I would have never believed I could ever agree with you about anything. Dr. Mordecai thought it necessary, but we haven't found a thing." Maddy said while winking at Slurp.

"Figures, that squirrelly geek is an idiot." Maconi politely tipped his hat. "Hey, Gray, I heard you're close to a deal on the D.U.I. What happened? Get in touch with your higher power?" Maconi laughed alone as he left with a "pee-yew."

Maddy reflected on the sad state of the woman's life. Her nosiness and grousing had driven away all potential friends and her husband. In New Munich, Indiana she grew up next door to a crotchety old woman whom the children called a witch. Maddy thought that living friendless and alone was equivalent to death. She would call Mina for lunch.

Mordecai, who was observing and exiting every few minutes to escape from the smell, asked for her opinion. "I don't see anything," said Maddy confidently. Mordecai put on a pair of latex gloves and poked into the body and contemplated.

"Undetermined, Natural. Good…," he ran his eyes down the corpse and then down Maddy's body, "Yes, good work."

Cause of death Undetermined was written on the death certificate. The Indianapolis statistics were similar to the national averages. One in five forensic autopsies yielded no cause of death. Disconcerting to the general public, but business as usual for a medical examiners office. Dr. O'Dell had a pet phrase, which was made into a desk plaque,

CAUSE OF DEATH? GOD KNOWS. WE TRY.

Maddy finished the dictation. She categorized the rodent bites, cockroaches, and maggots as evidence of postmortem artifact. The internal organ descriptions were quick and standard. She dictated the cause of death undetermined, pending toxicology. In several days the routine toxicology screen would be negative and the final certificate released. With no evidence of foul play, the opinion was natural death.

She phoned Mina and arranged lunch. Next she gathered all of David Burr's autopsy slides and re-ran the lectin assays for A, B, and H antigens. Group H antigen, abundant in cells of type O blood, is also weakly present in type A and type B tissues. This final case meant her project would be complete within the week.

Maddy's jury was still out on the metaphysical. She favored multiple gods, as only a committee could so thoroughly screw up the universe. If the gods had arranged today's lesson, it was about not living life. The teenage girls frivolously lost their lives en-route to a rock concert.

The old woman had wasted her chance. Her next case of SIDS, sudden infant death syndrome, was a child of five months who never got the chance.

The baby was found dead in her bed when the mother checked on her about nine a.m. It was not unusual for this child to sleep until mid morning.

SIDS has the pretentious quality of a name for something completely unknown. Labeling the unknown allows pediatricians and pathologists and social workers to maintain the charade that they possess some understanding about normal babies who die suddenly.

The grieving process for the families is particularly difficult. Parents feel guilty for failing to protect their child. Did the baby suffocate? Is God punishing the parents? All SIDS cases require autopsy. While intentional suffocation of an infant is nearly impossible to detect, the legal authorities cannot risk not looking. For many parents the diagnosis of SIDS is a relief. For some, however, the guilt is intensified and the grieving prolonged.

Maddy silently shuddered. The baby looked beautiful and healthy. Her rotations at University Hospital had included over forty infant autopsies. These were jaundiced corpses with IV lines, surgical scars, fungating cancers, and deformed congenital monsters. The sight of these medical curiosities, technologically processed through the Children's Hospital intensive care unit, appeared neither human nor alive.

In contrast little Charrise Wilson had pink cherubic skin, stiffened in the cold refrigerator to a doughy solid like mozzarella cheese. The baby girl seemed ready to wake up and smile at any moment. Maddy counted nine shining new teeth, dutifully noting them in on the body diagram.

She had to force her hand to incise the left shoulder for the opening incision. It felt wrong. Surely the child had life remaining. A reflex in Maddy wanted to scream for help. It felt like murder. Maddy looked toward the ceiling and thought. "There may be a God, but fairness isn't one of His traits."

She completed the usual Y-shaped incision with the top V of the Y joining each shoulder with the xyphoid. The Y bottom extended from xyphoid to pubic bone. The exposed organs glistened with delicate surface connective tissue. All were perfectly shaped and positioned. Maddy imaged the desecration a cherubic statue by Rodin.

"Aha!" exclaimed Mordecai before Maddy could speak about the lung section she held up in her hand. "Precisely why we post every one of these babies."

"Do you think it's an abscess? It's only a centimeter," Maddy looked puzzled and needing greater expertise.

"We can do a frozen section to be sure. Get a swab to culture the abscess for bacteria."

"Okay, but does it mean anything?" Maddy was still searching for the significance of the small lung abscess she had uncovered.

"It means this is not a SIDS case. SIDS can only be diagnosed with no abnormalities found. Any infection, no matter how small could give rise to a febrile seizure or a fatal arrhythmia."

Maddy completed the case, while Mordecai continued lecturing. Unfortunately, the diagnosis of broncho-pneumonia with abscess was no less troublesome for the parents. Mrs. Wilson, immediately upon notification, expressed her guilt for not noticing her baby's cough and seeking out her pediatrician. The father's weak excuse on her behalf that his wife was too busy with other duties, conveyed a subtext that he, too, held her accountable. The death might eventually precipitate their divorce. The beautiful little face held fast in Maddy's memory.

**

The lunch bar at the student union building was notorious for tasteless food. The best sandwich was an over-cooked cold hamburger on a stale bun. The iced-tea was adulterated with sugar and imitation raspberry flavoring. French-fries were delicacies iced in cool lard. Mina had free clinic all day and the Union cafeteria was her only chance at lunch. The dermatology department was less than a block away. Maddy and Mina split a musty smelling chicken salad sandwich, potato chips, and bottled water: a light sentence in this Epicurean torture chamber.

"I told you to watch his hands." Mina responded to Maddy's complaint that she should have been more explicit about Sweetbread.

"Yeah, well he's screwing with the wrong nut. Do you know anyone else who has a case against him?"

"What do you mean, anyone else?" Mina's emphasis on the last word clearly implied that she was not to be a part of any run-ins with Sweetbread.

"You will testify that he tried to coerce and fondle you, Mina."

"Nope."

"Mina? Do you intend to let that jerk get away? What about the women who come after us? Maybe the next surgery resident gets mauled or even raped. All because we said nothing."

"Maddy, you don't understand. I've got one year of residency left. Then I can make a real living. I can help thousands of little girls with their pimples. The girls here can take care of themselves."

"You won't testify against Sweetbread? Mina, what kind of friend are you? I need your testimony."

"No. I won't. I'm sorry. And I'd think twice about going after him. He's too powerful." He'll survive and you'll be in Mexico trying to finish a residency. Sorry. I've got to get back to clinic."

Maddy watched her leave. Mina didn't look back. How could Mina be so self-centered to put aside their friendship or the future safety of female residents? The last bite of tasteless chicken salad slid back out of her mouth. She rolled it into a napkin.

Thane had convinced Maddy that three or more accusers could successfully overcome any threat of a backlash by Sweetbread. Mina was no coward and a clear supporter of women. Mina was also bright. Maddy suspected the only reason Mina would refuse to prosecute Sweetbread: Mina had had sex with Sweetbread; and it wasn't all coercion. She liked men, and she enjoyed sex. Maddy could hear Sweetbread starting the same line, "Now Mina, we've got a problem. A conviction on a drug offense and your whole medical career is jeopardized. Perhaps we can help each other out?"

She could imagine Mina seizing the opportunity with a smile, "What did you have in mind?" It had been consensual enough that Mina's testimony would be useless. It would make a fool out of Mina, and ruin Maddy's case against Sweetbread.

Maddy's mind began a contorted game of "what if." She didn't find him physically repulsive. She thought he'd be sexier without the mousse and over-styled razor haircut. He was foolishly primped with over-attention typical of the elite businessman. His pale pink skin of too many showers and not enough sweat repulsed her. She preferred the thick natural look of Bruce Comstock or Graham O'Dell, and perspiration to perfume.

If she had sex with him once, would there be any guarantee he wouldn't try to extort her again? Once, she reasoned, might be a fair swap. The unfairness, she reminded herself, was Maconi's abuse of power and falsifying evidence. Sweetbread's abuse of power was more parasitic; Maconi's more sadistic, but equally evil. Without the D.U.I. charge, Sweetbread wouldn't have the opportunity. Maconi was the one she wanted to skewer, or whip, or better yet, cut his feet off in the desert and let him slowly bake to death.

Maddy continued her daydream as she returned to her County Hospital office. Her navigator was on autopilot. A gentle hand to her shoulder brought her back to the present. Graham O'Dell was dressed in a starched white shirt and blue paisley tie that emphasized a large chest.

"Slurp said you had a nasty one today. Did you have any questions that Dr. Mordecai failed to answer? I apologize for having to be gone. I don't want you to feel abandoned. Once a month the department directors have to listen to Sweetbread justify his existence." It was the first time Maddy had heard Dr. O'Dell not address a colleague as Doctor. Reflexively, Maddy reached out and clutched his arm as if to pull him closer.

She sensed a complex mixture of appreciation, kindness, and fatherly affection that she wished to acknowledge with the gesture. At a more primitive level she felt the presence of strength, the alpha male of our primate ancestors.

"We found nothing in the elderly woman, but the SIDS case turned out to be a death from lung abscess. Do I sign out the final case with you or Dr. Mordecai?" Maddy fought to stay focused on business. She wondered if Graham could detect her school girl crush on him.

"All your cases are my responsibility or Dr. Green's, as are all of Dr. Mordecai's. I can delegate some supervision to Dr. Mordecai, like this morning's prosection, if you'd prefer."

"No, I like you." Maddy's sentenced simply ended.

It should have been, "I'd like to sign them out with you." Her Freudian slip was out. Although she was unashamed of its contents, she feared she had put Graham in an awkward situation. Her sense of decorum rallied to bring up his wife and family to diffuse the awkwardness.

"Does your wife ever visit you at work?" Maddy was drowning. That sounded worse to her than "I like you."

"No, not at all. Well, once she wanted to see a dead body, not an autopsy. We were very young; I was just out of residency. I led her into the morgue not knowing a postmortem was in process. The body and skull were fully open and the diener was about to weigh the brain. My wife screamed, the diener turned toward her, and the brain slid out of his hands and went splat across her brand new Gucci handbag. She hasn't been back."

Maddy laughed and Graham smiled. "She lives in Seattle near our daughter who runs a flower shop in the city market."

"Separated?" Maddy asked in natural continuity of the conversation. At the same time she realized that bringing up his wife to give her some distance had backfired.

"I guess so. Nothing legal, just two thousand miles of comfortable distance," Graham explained in his gentle non-judgmental manner that Maddy found irresistible. She told herself to shut up. Every time she spoke the emotional quicksand rose higher. It was up to chin level now that his wife was not an issue. Maddy fantasized Graham flooded with passion, shutting the door to her office and making love to her atop her desk, taking care not to knock the microscope onto the floor.

If there is a God, one of His angels is named Debra. "Dr. Gray, a Mr. Hatcher from the F.B.I. is on line two. Do you want me to take a message?"

Graham took the cue and waved a hand as he exited, "Bring the slides by tomorrow and we'll sign out those cases."

Flushed and thinking about Graham, Maddy, without hesitation, gave out her home address to Thane and agreed to let him come by later with pizza, wine and a surprise. He had a plan for dealing with Sweetbread.

**

Maddy stood dressed in her long plastic apron next to the lighted cutting board area at the sink. Cold water was running slowly. She opened the block section jars from the two morning autopsies. She poured off the excess formalin preservative and dumped the block sections onto the board. One to two inch rough-cuts of liver, heart, spleen, pancreas, kidney, thyroid, and several additional major organ chunks swam in the formalin jar prepared for trimming.

She selected the specific areas that she wished to examine under the microscope. The excesses of the rough-cuts were trimmed to less than one inch in size. She capped the plastic cassettes in final preparation before the tissue samples were placed into the paraffin processor. The tissue processor would extract the tissue fluids and replace the cellular spaces with paraffin wax to allow thin sectioning for microscopic slides.

The contrasting tissues of Mrs. McGuinn, the roach-eaten busybody, and the baby were more striking after fixation. The decomposing tissues of the former were lifeless and mushy red brown pieces that barely hung together. The baby, whose body was less than four hours dead before refrigeration, was slaughterhouse fresh with bright red spleen and kidneys.

Maddy wondered if crows preferred fresher or older road kills if given a choice. The former would smell better, but the latter would be tenderer. It certainly seemed that the birds in general delighted in the older carcasses. The exception was seagulls, which are very picky. They prefer eyeballs and brains at any age, but will only eat freshly dead fish.

The McGuinn case took twenty-six slides. To reliably state "cause of death, undetermined" all the important organs required sampling, including several slides from the brain and heart conduction system. One representative slice of the great organs of the abdomen, chest, and endocrine systems would otherwise suffice. The baby organs were smaller and the processing cassettes would generally accommodate two. Fifteen slides were prepared.

Maddy sat at her desk. The microscope had survived the fantasy of passion. The histotechnologist delivered four trays of slides she had prepared for staining. Each contained twelve tissue sections from the organs of the late Congressman, David Burr. Lung, kidney, liver, spleen, heart including occluded left main coronary artery, two brain sections, thyroid combined with adrenal, pancreas, stomach, and prostate had been carefully de-paraffinized in organic solvent.

The histotechnologist and Maddy passed the slides through alcohol solutions and back into ionized buffer. The lectin markers for blood type were applied to the entire set of tissues. Next the marker system of dyed antibodies colored the antigen sites. Maddy adjusted her light-sensitive laser reader to quantitate the intensity of staining.

The first tray was the repeat of the type B marker, <u>Fomes fomentarius</u>. All sections were negative. The second tray was a repeat of yesterday's <u>Dolochus biflorus</u> type A marker. Incredulously to Maddy the results were unchanged. All organ samples were positive in normal density except the heart. No staining in the heart muscle, red blood cells, or artery surfaces was detected.

The H substance identified by <u>Ulex europus</u>, the precursor sugar of A and B antigens, is the surface glycoprotein of type O cells. Because it is present as a precursor substance, it is present on all cells in a small amount except type O tissues, which have a high density of staining. All of David Burr's cells showed slight staining, except the heart. The clotted coronary was unequivocal proof of a fatal MI in the left main coronary artery, but it came from a person with type O blood, not the heart of David Burr.

Why? Had someone switched David Burr's heart section with a sample from another person? Who? Mordecai? Was he trying to ruin her research data? Was it the histotechnologist who embedded the sample?

What possible motive? Maddy wondered.

Who else could? Slurp, who delivered the trimmed blocks to the histotechnologist. Many persons could have switched and re-labeled the blocks. She would have to tell Dr. O'Dell of her findings.

The thought of closing his office door and sitting face to face across the duel-headed microscope was erotic. She could flirtatiously say she had something interesting to show him. Maybe their hands would inadvertently touch the coarse adjustment on the microscope. The smoldering embers of passion might burst into flame. She told herself. "You need some serious help with this older man thing."

Her fantasy was doused by a new thought, a horror. Dr. O'Dell could have switched the cassettes. Surely he wouldn't sabotage her research, but what if he was faking an MI. The only plausible purpose was a cover-up, of suicide or murder.

"I'm leaving and locking up, Precious. You need anything?" the sweet voice of Slurp chirped from the doorjamb.

"No, go ahead. Hey Slurp, do you remember who worked with Dr. O'Dell, Monday, when he did the congressman?"

"Sure, me, Sergeant Withers and Dr. God always work together on the front page pastries."

"Why is that, Slurp?"

"We a boat with no leaks." Slurp felt his side. It was still sore, but almost healed. He had told no one, but

Withers. He was proud of his allegiance of silence. The policy kept reporters out of his life.

**

Thane arrived with pizza, Chianti, and a black leather brief case. Embarrassed by the scattered clothes, newspapers, and dirty glasses, Maddy quickly straightened up, stuffing a bra and panties under a sofa cushion. Thane put the pizza on the table and stood quietly awaiting directions. The apartment décor was transitional from college student to urban professional. The bookcase was makeshift concrete blocks and particleboard. The couches were beige leather around a chrome and glass modern coffee table.

"Got a corkscrew?"

"Top drawer, next to the dishwasher. Thane, are you still involved with the Burr case?"

"It's done, I thought. Is there a problem?"

"Yeah. I don't know what it means, but the clotted coronary artery doesn't belong to Burr. It's the only tissue sample from his autopsy that is type O, not type A. Somebody has gone to a lot of trouble to fake his coronary."

"Maybe it was just a simple mix-up. Besides, how could they pull that one over on O'Dell? He examined the heart, didn't he?"

Maddy's mouth was full of pizza. A run of sauce squirted out of her mouth. She giggled, then wiped her mouth. She cleared her throat with a long draw of Chianti.

"It wasn't a mix-up. There's no way. Someone switched a piece of heart at the table, which would have to have been Slurp, Richard, Withers, or O'Dell. They were the only ones near the autopsy. I just can't believe O'Dell would do something like that. Why would he?"

"How about covering up a murder?"

"Killing Burr? What's his motive? O'Dell doesn't care squat about politics."

"Maddy, maybe he cheated him at golf. It's a guy thing." Thane smiled and filled her wine glass."

"I'm keeping track, you know." Maddy pointed to her glass.

"So am I. In fact I'll file a report with the agency tomorrow of the exact amount."

"Seriously, shouldn't we do something?" Maddy persisted.

"Exhume the body?"

"No, look for poison or something."

"I do have the blood sample taken from Burr's autopsy. What would we look for?"

"Special toxicology that wouldn't show up in a general screen. Curare, insulin fragments, botulinum toxin. Can you do that?"

"I could, but I'd need a reason. Maybe you should talk to O'Dell first, before we start a chain of rumors and trouble. You do that first. Ouch!" Thane contorted his mouth and tongue after biting the hard pizza crust. "I've got a tooth that's really been bothering me the last couple of days."

"Let me see." Maddy looked into his mouth. "This one?" she tapped on a molar.

"Oww. Yes."

"You've got a cavity. A pretty good sized one. I'd get it taken care of immediately, before they have to crown it or do a root canal."

"I'm too young to think about root canals. I've only got one filling in my mouth."

"How old are you?"

"Pushing thirty, twenty-nine plus. It'll have to wait. My dentist is back in Washington."

"You can use the walk-in clinic at the dental school."

"Maybe, if it gets worse. I've got a surprise for you in this leather case. Promise me, you know nothing about it."

"What is it?"

"It's a bugging wire and recorder. It's on loan, but no one, I mean no one, can find out. They fire agents for unauthorized bugging. But I thought you could record your Friday meeting with Sweetbread. Once you have him on tape, you can threaten him with a sexual harassment suit and that Mina will testify. Demand that he follow through with getting you off the D.U.I. Am I brilliant or what?"

"You're a cop. You guys are experts in deception. One problem, officer brilliant, Mina won't testify."

"But he doesn't know that."

"You really think we can pull this off? Is this illegal?"

"Coercing employees for sex is illegal. My career is on the line. Hush, hush."

Thane opened the case that held a small cassette recorder and antenna. He pulled out a round disc the size of a half-dollar with a ten-inch wire.

"This goes under your blouse. It has adhesive on the back." He slid his hand under her blouse and pushed the device into place in the middle of her chest between her breasts.

"You go to a lot of work to get your hands into a girl's shirt. Do you use this trick on all your dates?" Maddy tucked her shirt back in. She gave him a cheek kiss in appreciation.

"What? No thank-you sex?"

"Sorry, I'm too wired up."

**

JUNE 7, THURSDAY, The Pancake Man

The alarm was making a strange sound. Her internal clock judged it was too early. Maddy squinted her sleeping eyes to make out 6:18 on the clock. By the fourth ring she realized it was the telephone.

"Maddy, I wanted to catch you before you got to the hospital. Sorry about the early call," Thane apologized.

"Get out of here," Maddy snarled.

"Oops! I'm double sorry."

"I was talking to Tasmin. Get out. I hate cat hair on my pillow."

"I couldn't sleep between thinking about Burr's bogus coronary and this toothache. At least it's after six. I'm having seconds thoughts. I don't think you should confront O'Dell yet. I'll get the special toxicology run on Burr's blood first. Then, only if the tox is negative, can you talk to O'Dell."

"OK."

"Now guess who happened to autopsy all the Random Ranger murders? Every report has pathologist: O'Dell, assistant: Slurp, and officer present: Withers. Does that sound random to you?"

"They like to work together."

"No, I would think statistically they should only be involved in half the cases. And another non-random feature, each autopsy was on a weekend or Monday."

"Maybe the killer has a busy day job. O'Dell staffs Mondays, so he'd normally get those. Still, I can see your point. It's an unlikely probability."

"Do me a favor. Get a computer research of all cases the three of them have done together. One of them may be covering up murders. I think we need some more data before we alert O'Dell."

"Thane, I really can't imagine O'Dell or Slurp. Maybe Withers."

"Maddy, you just don't like cops. But I'll consider your woman's intuition about Withers."

"Call me later. And get that tooth to the dental clinic."

**

The morning radio at WXCR was growing on Maddy. She pictured the DJ and host, Les Bull, as forty pounds overweight, prematurely gray crewcut hair, and bright red cheeks. Surely his real name was Duane or Monty or Buford. He bantered about the corn and soybean crops each morning that brought Maddy images of the rural farmers in her hometown. She should call her mother. He gave personal testimony promoting every advertised product from hemorrhoid cream to his George Foreman grill.

Today he was praising the wonderful decision to name Byron Davis to Congress. A homespun open house was planned for the entire district to meet the new Congressman. His previous boss, William Corless of EnvironTech had invited the entire 600,000 constituents to the corporate headquarters in downtown Indianapolis all day Saturday in several weeks. Lees Bull said he was going for sure and they predicted 30-60,000 people would drop by. Davis will deliver a short address and personally greet everyone who makes it through the line.

How could they predict something like that, Maddy thought? Almost instantly Bull answered that similar events in other states got out five to ten percent of the constituency. Usually less than two percent at a public park, but closer to ten percent when the voters got to gawk a mansion first hand. The enticement factor of EnvironTech corporate headquarters was estimated in between.

When Les got around to the local news, he had the sad tale of a road construction worker who was killed on the outer belt loop the previous night. The worker's job was brooming the new tar sealer in front of the roller-compacter. The man slipped while brooming too close to the roller and his head slid under the giant ten-foot diameter drum. Maddy had been served the morning entrée at The Breakfast Club, a crushed tar broomer.

She entered the morgue. Richard, who usually was all business, was giggling at the sight of "Pancake Man." Maddy gazed at the corpse, which looked like Wimpy with a lollipop face. The roller had crushed his skull instantly. The bones and brains had popped out the back of the skull like a teenager squeezing a pimple. The man's face was completely flat and blackened with tar Al Jolson style. The ambulance crew had laid his flattened glasses over his face, which for some inexplicable aspect of humor, transmogrified the face of a tragic accident victim to a cartoon character with flattened head and balloon body. Maddy laughed and could not stop when Richard lifted up the boneless scalp to reveal the empty cranial cavity. "He doesn't have the brains he was born with."

If Mordecai had a sense of humor, no one had witnessed it today. He stood emotionless as the others enjoyed the macabre joke, then exited without comment. Dr. Green was staffing and looked over the dissection from a distance. "Normal organs, except of course the absent brain. Good thing this isn't Washington, we wouldn't have a diagnosis, would we?" Slurp, Richard, and Maddy lapsed back into their laughing jag.

Maddy felt some guilt about their lack of seriousness, a broach of the ethical responsibility to honor and respect the dead. She tried to imagine the sadness of his family, although when Richard read aloud the report that the deceased lived with his mother, a cook at the Mexican café, Border Burger, the chortle of desecration resumed.

Maconi, the Grim Reaper of jocularity, wandered into the morgue and all flowers of fun wilted instantaneously. "Why do you think the operator ran this guy over? Got anything we could use for evidence?" Maconi fished for blame bait.

"Slurp, did you notice any hand prints on the back?" Maddy deadpanned.

"Didn't see nothing suspicious, Dr. Precious. Just the usual: a knife in the back and a wire around the ankles," said Slurp.

Maconi shook his, sneered at Maddy, then strolled out mumbling something about wasting his time on a fucking accident. Maddy followed him out with her eyes. Blame and retribution drove Maconi. He seemed less personally vindictive to her now. Had he gotten his fill by delivering her to the powers of revenge? Justice was too vague to have any meaning to Maconi. Sacrificing innocents was ritual, not sin.

**

Maddy sat at her desk with Dictaphone in hand. She recorded the weights and shapes of pancake man's inner composite systems of normal organs. Between adrenal and spleen, she paused to gather her thoughts and check the chart notes from the autopsy. "Blunt force trauma to head, secondary to construction vehicle accident, Manner of death: accident."

She closed the file and took it down the hall to Debra for typing. "Dr. Gray, Dr. Sweetbread from the University called while you were in the autopsy suite." Debra handed Maddy a four-inch pink memo slip with a check mark next to the "please return call box." Her fleeting wave of nausea was mixed with relief that the dreaded call had arrived.

"My house is empty tomorrow night except for you, my guest. We're going to have fun, Maddy. Nine o'clock, thirteen, thirteen Sunset and that'll be the end of your troubles with Officer Maconi. Don't be late. I'm not a patient man." James Sweetbread, M.D. commanded.

"I'll be there." Maddy gently hung up the phone and wrote down *1313 Sunset* on the back of the pink memo slip. Mordecai and O'Dell entered from the hallway. Graham tapped on the doorframe and waited for recognition. Mordecai wandered straight in and snooped around.

"Maddy, I've got a short testimony to give at court today at one. You want to see the worst part of the job? I think you'd make a great candidate for our fellowship, but you've got to see court before you ever consider forensic pathology. Believe me, sifting through maggots in the stench of a thirty-day-old field-rot is easier than dealing with lawyers."

"Sure," she said without considering turning Graham down. Maddy imagined that testifying in court would be prestigious, showcasing the pathologist's knowledge. Graham's comment made her reconsider.

Maddy tried to pick up the memo note and put it into her purse inconspicuously, but Mordecai had seen it clearly. 1313 Sunset was an unforgettable address. The incoming residents and fellows were feted at Sweetbread's home every year the first Saturday of July. Mordecai nosily looked at the x-ray view box where Michael Johnson's exploded face and skull still hung. Maddy was unsure if he had seen Sweetbread's address. He tapped his index finger on the triangular sheet of flat metal.

"Come down to my office about 12:45, and we'll leave for the courthouse. We'll have to catch a late lunch after the testimony," said O'Dell. Mordecai, with head swiveling like a radar screen, followed O'Dell out.

Maddy closed the door and telephoned Thane to coordinate plans for the audiotaping. "Remember to get him to speak clearly and closely to your chest. The tape is useless if we can't hear him. The key is to have him offer continued employment on the condition of sex."

They arranged to meet Friday at 8:30 in the parking lot at a nearby Kroger grocery store to test the reception.

**

Criminal Courtroom 4 was at the end of the hall of the fifth floor of the City-County Government Building.

Maddy peaked into Courtroom 3 as she passed. It was in full session. Three fourths of the persons sitting in the pews were black and Hispanic. The police sat at a table in front of the bar. All were white; one was a woman. The defendants were accused of petty theft, driving on suspended driving licenses, moving violations, mostly speeding, and jumping bail. She remembered Richard's cousin and his trip to traffic court.

On the same block outside were mini-skyscrapers filled with suited businessmen and women. Many were falsifying accounting reports, lying about inventories, and marketing false claims of goods and services. Their conscious crimes would never be punished by the likes of Maconi. Partly because they were white, but mostly because they were well dressed.

Graham O'Dell M.D., the first witness, scheduled to appear on the hour, was called to testify at 1:20. "Punctual by lawyer time," whispered O'Dell. The courtroom was sparse with barely ten visitors representing family members of the deceased and the defendant. The state was plaintiff to the domestic murder of a thirty-five year old man.

The slow and simplistic questions began with a litany of Dr. O'Dell's training, residency, board certification, and number of homicides autopsied. Next the prosecutor meticulously went through the autopsy report line by line to trace the bullet path through the brain, skull, scalp and into the wallboard. Graham had tried to speed things along by starting out with the summary that this was unequivocally a homicide secondary to a gunshot to the head.

The defense attorney declined to cross exam. The prosecutor was trying to draw out the gore as long as possible, the defense to stifle it. Graham had remained calm and composed. Maddy watched his style as he faced the jury and made a conscious effort to connect with them. He translated every medical term into simple language. "Glabella, that's a fancy term for the spot, right between the eyes." The questioning dragged along for ninety minutes.

"Did I miss something? You were there for an hour and a half to verify he was shot in the head?" Maddy asked as they left the courthouse.

"The D.A. doesn't have any hard evidence, so she fills up the court time with my testimony to make it appear to the jury that the state has a case. How about that lunch I promised?"

They reached the Oye Stir-Bar at four p.m. The new age martini and seafood bar was noted for shrimp, oysters, and a rainbow assortment of pastel martinis. By mutual agreement the day was over and happy hour had begun. Graham ordered a draft beer; Maddy feigned sophistication by ordering a specialty chartreuse martini made with vodka and a blue-green Curacao.

"What a waste of everybody's time." Maddy said.

"Precisely. It's a stupid game. The D.A. has no rebuttal to the defense's argument that the murder victim had beaten her. The question is whether he was murdered in self-defense. So, she drags out the gory details of the gunshot to try to diffuse the jury's sympathy. The average citizen who is otherwise law abiding, but blows away their spouse, gets about fifteen years, which means parole after five years of hard time. There should have been a plea agreement. This case only went to trial because the D.A. needed something or was feuding with the defense team."

"Like what?" Maddy was getting a discouraging view of the justice system.

"She either needed some publicity or trial time for herself, or she has a bone to pick with the defense attorney, maybe unrelated to this case. The defendant loses big time. Maddy, I don't want you to get cynical. There are mostly honest, good people out there. But everyone, I do believe everyone, gets into a situation at some time where there isn't a clean solution. You're young, but it'll probably happen to you. One of life's scrapes becomes a very dirty wound."

After the second martini, the conversation took a personal turn. Graham had gone to college to be an engineer. The late seventies had seen the close of the rust-belt era of American industry. The job market was bleak for engineers. Graham, who had never considered medicine, took the admission test along with the Graduate Record Examination. His first choice was graduate school in applied physics, a natural application of his engineering training.

Unexpectedly for Graham, he was accepted into medical school. "I was influenced by my fiancé at the time who realized she'd live better with a doctor than an engineer. She was right. She's got a great place on Puget Sound." He laughed and toasted to Maddy. She burped a giggle, then got up to excuse herself to the ladies' room. She slightly tripped and fell onto Graham's shoulder. She smoothly and without hesitation kissed his cheek, "My savior."

Maddy returned with hair combed and clothes freshened. Graham paid the bill and suggested that she not drive after the martini's. "Well, my mother told me not to ride with strangers, but what the hell. Where would you like to go?"

Maddy looked at Graham with come-on eyes. He hadn't
seen that type of look since his twenties, when he was
young and handsome. She was beautiful and he wanted to
make love to her. He knew his body would regret his next
move and hold a grudge against his conscience.

He hailed a taxi and pulled a fifty-dollar bill from his
wallet and handed it to the cabby. "Sir, I need you to take
this beautiful woman home, then pick her up at 7:15
tomorrow morning and deliver her to County Hospital."

"Yes, sir," the cab driver smiled as Graham kissed
Maddy's forehead. She mustered a disappointing, "Thank
you. See you tomorrow."

**

The phone was ringing as Maddy entered her sweltering
apartment. Maddy had gotten up in the middle of the night
and turned off the air-conditioning. Tasmin was meowing
angrily. "Hello, hold on a minute," Maddy answered and
dropped the phone in the same motion. She picked up
Tasmin, comforting her with her right hand as she switched
on the thermostat with her left. She tried the phone with her
left ear, but dropped Tasmin to use her right hand. Tasmin
meowed louder.

"Sorry, I was fiddling with cat."

"Lucky cat," was the response from Thane. Maddy
pushed out of her head the guilt of taking advantage of
Thane Hatcher. She needed him, at least until the
recording. "Have you heard the news?"

"What news?" Maddy's head buzzed from the martinis.
She realized the cab ride had been a good idea. Still, she'd
rather be in bed with Graham right now than talking to

Hatcher on the phone. Had she heard important news on the cab radio? She wasn't sure. She would never drink martinis again. They tasted awful, and got her a kiss on the forehead, hardly better than a handshake.

"Charlene Withers is suing the estate of David Burr for a one-sixth share. She claims her kid is the bastard son of Burr. See?"

"See what?" Maddy was slower and more confused that usual. She reminded herself not to disclose to Thane that she'd been out drinking with Graham O'Dell. No good could come of it. She couldn't risk losing his interest prematurely. She hadn't pursued Thane, but once on the line, it was fair to play him. There was a time for catch and a time for release.

"Don't you get it? Charlene Withers is Sgt. Withers's sister. Withers finds out about Burr fathering his nephew and bam! He kills Burr for money, for his nephew, to avenge him for knocking-up his sister. He's got motive, and the opportunity at the autopsy to fake a coronary."

"Why wouldn't they just sue David Burr? Why do they have to kill him?" Maddy wasn't buying the idea.

"I asked myself the same question. First I thought maybe there's a question about paternity. Then, I said no. Genetics are too good these days. They could compare samples from his other two children. It's the money."

"I don't get it."

"Do the math. Suing for paternity might land child support for a few hundred bucks a week until he's through college. But in the estate settlement, the wife is entitled to half the estate and each kid would get a sixth."

"Doesn't his will dictate where the money goes after death?"

"Exactly why Charlene needs to get her son established as an heir. Apparently she's found out that his will uses the term, 'children,' instead of their specific names."

"Is that enough money to kill over?"

"At least two or three million. Burr's estimated worth is about twenty million, money that's been converted into personal assets from his campaign war chest in Congress, the legal bribes from business and union contributions. I think Withers is the one."

"Sounds far-fetched to me. The cases you asked me to pull-up don't show much. Mordecai and previous fellows did four of the Random Ranger murders, which were only staffed by O'Dell. The rest of the Withers, Slurp, and O'Dell cases seem normally distributed. Sorry to water down your theory, but you can look over the reports. How's your tooth?"

"Much better. I went over to the dental school. They put a filling in it. Said if I hadn't skipped the last two years of regular checkups, it wouldn't have been so deep. It's still tender. They said fillings aren't nearly as bad as crowns or root canals. Another reason to dread getting older. I had to wait two hours, but that gave me a chance to see Charlene Withers on TV."

"What did you say?" Maddy was lost in a new train of thought.

"I said I waited two hours and watched."

"No, the crown and older part. Kids get fillings because they are young, their teeth are stronger, and their cavities are usually smaller. Michael Johnson was only sixteen. Mordecai keeps looking at his teeth. Thane, I want you to get his dental records."

"He's been dead eight years. I can't promise anything. What's in it for me? Do I get tucked in tenderly?" Thane begged shamelessly.

"Not tonight. See you at 8:30 tomorrow." Maddy hung up the phone then spoke out loud, "You should be ashamed of yourself for teasing that little boy."

**

JUNE 8, FRIDAY, Monsters

The doorbell rang twice. In her half-asleep state Maddy wondered if she had heard anything, then relaxed to sleep some more. The doorbell chimed twice again successfully awakening the resident. Her eyes were a blur of mucus requiring three blinks and a thorough rubbing to read the alarm clock. 7:33 on the dial and no alarm light.

She carefully cracked the door with chain guard in place to hear the word, "Taxi."

"Give me fifteen minutes. Sorry, I forgot to set the alarm." Maddy would shower later at the hospital. She sarcastically thought of getting cleaned up for her big date with Sweetbread. She daydreamed about an offensive goat cheese perfume for just such an occasion, as she pulled two handfuls of her thick brown hair back and baled it together with an elastic ribbon. Deciding that no outfit could hide her jump-start, she grabbed a set of surgical scrubs and a white lab coat and successfully camouflaged herself in medical center standard issue.

Tasmin rubbed Maddy's ankles from the bedroom to the kitchen, demanding to be fed. The cat meowed next to the litter box, which reminded Maddy that the filler needed changing. Looking outside she saw the taxi driver glancing at his watch. Maddy opened a can of cat food and put it on the floor not bothering with the feeding dish, then dashed out the door.

The rush out the door reminded her of high school mornings, sleeping to the last minute. Admittedly, pathology training was much more interesting than the drivel of high school English and American history. Maddy remembered the morning ritual of her mother in apron holding an English muffin with strawberry jam on a napkin in the doorway. Maddy would stick out her tongue at the offering as she bounded out the door, dragging book-bag and jacket. She rebuffed the muffin because it was attached to mother. Ten minutes later she would buy a donut and chocolate milk. Twenty minutes later she would arrive at her first class fifteen seconds after the tardy bell.

Maddy was thankful she didn't have children. But if she did, she wouldn't stand at the door with a muffin, even if the latest guru of child psychiatry commanded it. She had no sense of what she would do with a teenage daughter. Like most things in her life, she simply had no plan.

Maddy looked at the row houses in the inner city. Each house was a quaint theater hosting insignificant dramas. Many times she had driven past these houses and never noticed them. The cabby took a slightly different route and ended up at the front patient entrance. He refused an additional five-dollar tip from Maddy, saying he had been overpaid already, and hadn't minded the fifteen-minute wait. Maddy watched as he drove away, inspired with hope for humanity by a man immune from greed.

The canopy extended from the county hospital door to within four feet of the curb. City buses on the six-lane through street kept the air at choking quality with eye-stinging half-burned black diesel fuel. Waiting benches of cleaning women in pink and white uniforms sat patiently with overfilled double-lined grocery sacks on their laps. Maddy nosily maneuvered herself into position to inventory the sack of a black woman who was searching and rearranging the contents.

She had a ten-inch patent-leather black purse on the bottom. A pair of comfortable Keds classic white sneakers for walking after work lay atop the purse. Next was a crochet ring with attached work in progress. Gloves, fold-up umbrella and a word-find puzzle book composed the penultimate layer. The top was hermetically sealed with a sweatshirt bearing the logo of the Indianapolis Colts. A few crevices had fillings of clear plastic bags with crackers and corn snacks.

Travelling by bus, the modern equivalent of Conestoga wagon travel, requires packing only what you can carry. Comfort and survival items are chosen and re-ordered with experience.

Maddy realized she had never actually seen the patient street entrance. Unlike the entrance used by the doctors, where smoking family members and a few patients sat in parked wheel chairs, most of these people were awaiting buses. Hospital workers marched by from the large ground level parking lot across the street. There was a walk signal with a hand-activated button at the curb. Motorists scowled as a single person abruptly halted the traffic, a person whom Maddy immediately recognized.

"Richard, good morning. What are you doing out here? Tell me you're roaming around because we've got a quiet day." Maddy made first contact. Richard recognized the absence of any condescension. He explained he had left the morgue to get some papers out of his car. Maddy felt twinges of class shame at the discovery that Richard and Slurp worked alongside the pathologists, but parked twice as far away.

"Yeah, I wanted to show Slurp these plans I've got for a funeral home. We just need to get the bank to give us the business loan. Trouble be they want fifteen thousand dollars down."

"You want to own a funeral home, Richard?"

"Smith and West's Sons. Get it?"

"Not really." Maddy shrugged her shoulders.

"Slurp Smith and Richard West. We're both sons of Smith and West. Like the guns, Smith and Wesson? We're straight shooters."

"That's clever," Maddy tried to regain her credibility. "You and Slurp think you could work together?" Richard turned his head and rolled his eyes as she continued. "Of course you already work together. I meant as business partners."

"Doctor Precious," a familiar voice interrupted to the rescue of Maddy, "I see you are ready for action. But that white lab coat has got to go by Labor Day. I am thinking dark gray with mauve pinstripes."

"Hi, Slurp. Richard was telling me about your funeral home plans."

"I will run the books and manage operations, because I'm better at that. Slurp is a people person. He can sweet-talk the old widows into buying that special brass-plated casket." Richard said.

"Yes indeed, if there's one thing old Slurp can do right is work these lips." Slurped winked and embarrassed Maddy. "Come on, Doctor Precious, did you listen to the radio?"

"No, I took a cab today."

"We got scrambled eggs and an order of home-style hash. Now look there, Richard. Have you ever seen such beautiful empty eyes in your life? Scrambled eggs is a baby with congenital malformations. Something wrong with the brain development. It died less than two minutes old."

"Baby's are easy, that's less than an hour," Maddy was catching up to Slurp's morning pace.

"That's why Mordecai has volunteered for the quickie. You get the home-style hash: case of a son who beat the hell out his sweet old daddy," Richard explained.

"A Charlie Manson special. The family that slays together stays together. But I didn't tell you the bad part. Your buddy, Maconi, the junkyard dog, is your friendly detective," added Slurp.

**

Wendell Weber and Sons was a notorious family business of junk hauling and piano moving. They also took on tree trimming and firewood distribution, but only as a last resort. They generally delivered the services contracted, but rarely was a customer interested in a re-hire. Their uniforms consisted of dirty blue jeans that reeked of tobacco smoke with a second equally offensive fragrance of unbathed sleeveless T-shirts. Sleeveless shirts allowed full view of the naked women and other vulgar arm tattoos of

161

comic book quality. Mercifully, the fading process of time, combined with the infrequent bathing, obscured the most offensive details.

Wendell, the patriarch of this cash only business, had flawlessly passed on his alcoholic genes to sons, Luther and Martin. The German-Lutheran names were the only known traces of moral or religious affiliation. The three lived together in bachelor squalor on First Street in a small dilapidated bungalow that backed up to the railroad tracks. The accommodations were literally dirt-cheap. The Webers were too drunk most evenings to hear the trains rumble, nor feel the tracks vibrate.

Officer Maconi chronicled the Weber family history in detail. The favorite family pastime was binge drinking followed by family warfare. The Weber's notoriety in the emergency room included multiple fractures, lacerations, and contusions, most often delivered on Friday evenings. The wounds were equally divided between father and sons. On numerous occasions the police had filed battery charges, however, no Weber had ever pressed for prosecution or was willing to testify. The district attorney failed to see that they were a threat to anyone but themselves. The public interest in their case would be best served if they would just kill one another. She got her wish.

"You see, Luther beat the shit out of Wendell a week ago. They finally brought him into the hospital two days ago when he slipped into a coma. One a.m. this morning he's dead. Luther just rang the homicide bell; and I am here to answer." Maconi smiled in contented righteousness.

Maddy, half-listening while reading the hospital chart, commented, "What a family. How can they beat each other up?"

"I imagine they've run out of playmates. But I heard you've got your playbook in order, Doctor." Maconi maintained his smile, now directed toward Maddy specifically.

Was there no honor or privacy to the likes of James Sweetbread? Obviously he had gossiped or bragged to the police department. Maddy was daydreaming if she might also get Sweetbread to confess he had heard from Maconi about the falsified breath test, thus revenging them both.

"Can I open the chest now, Dr. Precious?" Slurp was intent on completing the case and getting Maconi out on the street.

Maddy was shaking her head at the chart lab values.

"I don't have a clue what this low sodium is about. Who's staffing today, Slurp?"

Slurp silently curled his fingers and made an Igor face in the direction of Dr. Mordecai who was drawing notes of the congenital deformities of the baby. "Dr. Mordecai, Dr. Gray has a question. Do you want me to see if Dr. God is available to staff this one?"

"Sure," Mordecai grunted without thinking and without looking up. Slurp winked at Maddy; Maddy threw him a kiss.

**

Graham was at his microscope examining the tissue slides of a gunshot wound in preparation for a court testimony. Maddy knocked on the open door, wondering if he had fully comprehended her come-on and now thought of her as a foolish schoolgirl.

"Come in. You want to see something?" She sat down and noted a section of bloody muscle tissue. "Those black granules are unburned powder. Good confirmation of close range shot. Rarely travel more than a few feet. I'd guess this one to be about a foot away."

"That doesn't seem very far when the bullet is moving 800 feet per second," Maddy encouraged his teaching.

"The blast momentum goes to the bullet. The rest of the powder and solids simply tumble out a few feet after the blast. Big stuff like wadding or jacket fragments fall near the barrel." Graham looked up at her face and allowed himself to enjoy her youthful beauty. "What do you need, Maddy?"

She was unable to respond immediately as his slow rough voice excited her, creating a momentarily lapse into an internal conversation, reminding herself not to act foolishly. She begged herself to be adult and professional. Being twenty-nine with the obsession of a fourteen-year-old was not exciting. It was annoying.

"Maddy? You have something you want me to look at?" Graham raised his voice slightly to enter her daydream. He pointed to the chart and x-rays that she had brought in and put on a chair.

"Yes, I'm about to start this case on a fifty-seven year old guy who died after being beat up by one of his sons."

"That's awful. Freud is right every now and then." Graham couldn't resist the easy joke. Maddy laughed too loudly, violating her internal reminder to be professional.

"I don't know what to make of this low sodium of 107 in the emergency room. I checked his previous admission to the ER. He had a normal, 138, a month ago. The ICU team got it back up, but maybe not soon enough."

Dr. O'Dell's eyebrows perked up. "Anything in the x-rays?"

"Fractured femur and humerus, but they're at least four weeks old according to the radiologist. He does have several large brown belly bruises which are consistent with the recent fight." Maddy continued through the list of charted data. She had seen that hunting dog look in O'Dell's eyes before, when Von-Hippel-Lindau disease was mentioned.

"Is Maconi here for this case?" Graham asked, which seemed out of the blue to the nodding Maddy. "Good. Maybe we can ruin his day."

When she nodded her head Graham rose smoothly and with an arm around Maddy's shoulder gently directed her out of the room in front of him. His touch excited her. She wished he wouldn't. Was he teasing her, pleasing himself, or displaying innocent fondness? The uncertainty, not the physical contact, bothered her.

"Percival, I need to have you and Dr. Gray switch cases this morning. This baby is merely cytogenetic sampling and deformity archiving. You shouldn't be wasting your fellowship on such simplicity. This case is more complicated. You won't mind will you?"

Percival failed to hide his beaming on the compliment. He glared accusingly at Slurp and Richard who simultaneously shook their heads. No, they hadn't put O'Dell up to it. O'Dell handed Percival the case material and left the morgue.

"Here are the diagrams I started." Maddy offered.

"I can do it," snarled Mordecai, unnecessarily. Slurp giggled and choked it off. Percival glared at Slurp. "Something tickle your funny-bone, Mr. Smith?" He added.

"I believe it did, Dr. More-decay," Slurp let out his private dagger, the illicit pronunciation he used maliciously among friends. Percival bit his lip and passed the opportunity to correct to More-deck-eye. Many people inadvertently mispronounced his name, but Slurp's was an undisguised affront, recorded in Percival's inner scorebook.

The monster was a small-for-age infant weighing 2450 grams. Prior to her fourth year of medical school, monster had seemed a slang term of disrespect to Maddy. Her pediatric professors explained the simple veracity and appropriateness of the word.

The face resembled a wrinkled puppet pulled from the bottom of the toy chest. The brows were thick and overhung the small mounded mole-hole eyes. The skull was flat like Pancake Man's for the same reason, no brain inside. Anencephaly, the absence of the cortical brain, comes with distorted facial features. This infant had only a vestigial brainstem and was unable to sustain breathing, hence the death in minutes.

Maddy took soft tissue from the muscle wall of the abdomen as sterilely as possible for cytogenetic studies. The genetic counselors would rule out a parental abnormality and reassure the disappointed parents that the tragic pregnancy was a rare and random event. They could anticipate a future normal pregnancy.

Maddy and Slurp completed the case in thirty-five minutes. Mordecai was still removing the chest organs at the next table.

"Old organized fractures of the left lateral ribcage, T-eight and nine." Percival dictated overhead.

Pathologists differ in their preference for dictation. O'Dell and Gray liked to finish cases and retire to their offices for dictation. Dr.'s Green and Mordecai preferred to dictate tableside as the post mortem proceeded. The advantage of the latter was the inclusiveness of the data as it was discovered. The advantages of dictating afterward included more reflection and editing which yield shorter, more organized final reports.

"Few bruises, but not much else, except for bad alcoholic cirrhosis. You successfully punted this one. I commend your political adroitness, Dr. Gray. Some of us lack the feminine skills of persuasion." Mordecai said openly for all to hear.

Maddy was saved from defensive comment by the loud buzzing of the Stryker bone-saw. Richard exposed the calvarium from ear to ear and was slicing through the half-inch thick bones of the skull table.

"Pop," went the skullcap as Richard pulled on the bone hook. The top of the skull, which looked like a turtle shell, flew over his right shoulder and hit Maconi squarely in the jaw. The sharp edge of the saw-cut bone caused blood to spurt from the cop's chin.

"Motherfucker," was the predicable response from Maconi. Slurp grabbed a gauze strip and applied pressure to the bleeding chin. Richard apologized profusely.

"This guy has chronic liver disease. You need to get needle-stick treatment right away. I'll take you over to employee health when we are done." Maddy's doctoring and maternal instinct came out before she realized what she had committed to do.

"It's just a little cut for christsake."

"She's right, Officer Maconi. You could get AIDS or hepatitis. Who knows? A few shots could save you from some potentially bad diseases." Mordecai, too, had shifted into doctor autopilot.

Maconi hated the dependency of being a patient, but acquiesced, "I'll think about it."

Richard placed the skullcap alongside the head on the autopsy table. He picked up an extra long ten-inch scalpel blade. To remove the brain intact he gently tugged on the tips of the frontal lobes exposing the roofs of the eye sockets. With the tip of the scalpel, he gently severed the cranial nerves in order. First the circuits of smell, the olfactory nerves, were cut from their entrances near the nose plates. Then he severed the optic nerves from back of the eye sockets where the two optic nerves originate. He clipped the remaining nerves down the brainstem like trimming the zest connecting orange and peel. After slicing through the lower medulla, the brain was free of all attachments. Richard plopped it in front of Mordecai onto the trimming board at the foot of the autopsy table.

The delicate transparent blood vessels on the surface made cracked maroon lines over the soft fleshy beige of the cortex. Mordecai rolled the organ in his hands, gently placing it into the white porcelain spring scale hanging from the ceiling over the sink. Mordecai weighed the brain, "Too, small, only 1150 grams." Mordecai pointed out two yellow flat bumps on the underside of the brain. "Mammillary bodies are discolored and atrophied. The liver has a typical shrunken yellow fibrous scarring of cirrhosis. End stage alcoholic toxicity. Piece of cake."

He then cut the brain into quarter inch slices like bread and lined them up sequentially on the table. The brain stem and cerebellum were cut separately and those slices were arranged together on the corner of the table. Mordecai grimaced in confusion. "That looks weird," he said pointing toward the cerebellum and looking up at Maddy.

"Seems somebody's fresh out of icing for that cake," Slurp couldn't resist a cheap stab at Mordecai's pomposity. The prosector reddened with combined anger and embarrassment. He opened his palm to Maddy, soliciting her input, then gave Slurp the squinting eye.

Neuropathology, the arcane subspecialty of the pathology world, is also the weakest academic area for most pathologists. The ability to identify strokes and common tumors is standard course, but the degenerative diseases usually require consultation from an academic neuropathologist.

"The cerebellar white matter doesn't look right," Maddy offered to the agreement and appreciation of Mordecai.

"Isn't that beautiful," the voice of Dr. Green changed the tone from confused to exciting. Green, having entered the morgue unnoticed, was standing behind Maddy.

"I thought you were in Orlando, Doctor G?" Slurp asked.

"My son was frightened by Mickey Mouse and begged to come home. It's a classic," he continued and paused for comment from the blank faces. "See the flat, off color myelin in the cerebellum. It's even more pronounced in the pons." Dr. Green picked a pen out of his shirt pocket and pointed to crumbling brain substance in the pons, the plump bulb at the base of the brain.

"How the fuck would you say that in English?" came the bottom line question from Maconi. Dr. Green looked around patiently allowing Mordecai to speak. He didn't.

Slurp continued his mean streak. "The man's brain is a mess and Dr. More-decay is just dying to tell us all about it." Richard bit his lip hard to suppress his laugh. Mordecai's face became redder. Dr. Green didn't hesitate.

"I guess this is the first one you've had, Percival. End stage alcoholics often become demented from excessive brain cell loss. In their confusion they drink too much water. Diluted blood with very low sodium is toxic and causes breakdown of myelin in the pons. Death is actually hastened when they start eating again. Or, as in this case, the hospital replaces the sodium too quickly. The rapid influx of salt and water kills the nerve sheaths."

"All I need from you is how the beating by his son killed him. I got scum-sucker, sonny-boy in jail for homicide, and I have no desire to send him back out to playschool," Maconi said.

"I can't rule this a homicide. This is death from alcoholism. Natural consequence of addiction, or slow suicide depending how you look at it. Jurisdictions consider alcoholism a disease, therefore this is a natural death," Dr. Green explained.

Maconi was about to blow. Maddy backed up her head and raised her hands signaling not to blame her.

"Motherfucking waste of the morning on this asshole, and now you guys make me turn loose a fucking kid that beats up his old man. This is a sick fucking world," Maconi fumed. "Mordecai, come on, all you have to say is that the beatings made his fucking brain worse and finished him off. We can still get a manslaughter out of this."

"You ever deal in any evidence that isn't manufactured?" Slurp said, again crossing the line into a rude affront. Mordecai, who was waiting for his chance, seized the opportunity to retaliate.

"So sorry to have to end the files on this case, officer. However, I do have something that may help your crusade for justice. Follow me, officer. You may be interested also, Mr. Smith," Mordecai spoke slowly and low-pitched.

Slurp and Maddy walked behind Maconi and Mordecai. They were motioned toward the conference room next to Mordecai's office. Thane Hatcher rounded the corner of the hallway and grabbed Maddy, as she was about to enter the doorway.

"I think I'm ready. We need to test it before you go over there. And I've got the other stuff." Thane whispered to her. Their conversation was interrupted by the appearance of Mordecai.

Mordecai corralled them into the conference room with his left hand, which held a videotape. He mumbled to Thane that the F.B.I. might be interested in the show. He turned on the television, and started the VCR. He paused on a stillframe, which showed Slurp and the latest victim of the Random Ranger leaving the park at the pathology picnic.

"It should please Mr. Smith that you now have some evidence which you haven't had to manufacture." He ejected the tape and tossed it to Maconi. Maddy missed the immediate connection with the Random Ranger. She was focusing on a previous frame of herself entering the camper of Bruce Comstock.

**

"I said I don't know nothing about Paul Duval. I talked to him at the picnic."

"Did you leave with him?" barked the deep voice of Paul Slaughter, F.B.I. interrogator.

Slurp shook his head, "no," hoping to conceal the lie that might be heard in his voice.

"You don't seem to know much of anything."

"No, sir."

"Mr. Smith, on the night of Paul Duval's murder, you were in the hospital."

"I was."

"Did you have any visitors?"

Thane Hatcher's watch read 7:50 p.m. He was to meet Maddy at the Kroger store parking lot in forty minutes. He rose to leave and said he had another appointment to attend. He was stopped cold by the next answer.

Slurp knew the procedures at Charity Hospital. He knew the visitor log at the nurse's station would have Sgt. Carl Withers listed.

"I can't remember. I was hurting and on pain medication, but Sergeant Withers may have come by."

"May have come by?"

Withers's name kept surfacing in suspicious circumstances. Thane stopped his egress to listen. Slurp freely offered, "He's a friendly cop from the morgue. You know the forensic service. Maybe you didn't know that cops could be friendly."

"That's very interesting. Mr. Smith, don't you think it's too coincidental that you happened to get stabbed on the same night and that you are the last person seen with the latest person to be murdered by the Random Ranger? Do you know who might be killing these men? Would you like to personally confess?"

Thane wrote a note to check out Withers on the night of the murder and stuffed it into his pocket. Slurp denied any knowledge and offered no further information claiming, truthfully, he had a lot of morphine on board.

Thane looked at his watch again; he was now late. He walked quickly to his car, jumped in, and pulled away quickly accelerating through the left turn out of the parking lot. The recorder flew hard from the front passenger seat, slamming against the door handle and tumbling onto the floor. The Saab sped toward the grocery mall.

**

Maddy's Civic was parked adjacent to a long line of empty shopping carts in the middle of the lot. She was slowly combing her hair to appear busy. Thane admired her dark brown silky hair. His beautiful Helen of Troy had captured his attention and led him to violate Bureau policy for the first time in his seven years. Unauthorized equipment usage was censurable, but illegal conversation recording was cause for dismissal. This face could launch a thousand vices from him.

"Sorry I'm late. Slaughter thinks the Slurp tape is a break in the Ranger case and is going to keep him and grill him as long as the court will allow. We'll need a beer later. I can fill you in. You got the wire?"

Maddy shook her head in assent. "Let me check." Thane rubbed his hand over her breast to feel the device. She slapped it when he extended the investigation. "You go ahead into Sweetbread's driveway. I'll park around the corner. Give me a test." Thane put the earphones connected to the recorder to his head and motioned to Maddy."

"Testing, this is a test. Operation moldy bread." The signal came through clearly and Thane gave a thumb up.

Next, in one continuous motion, he took off the headset, got out of the car and kissed her on the cheek.

"Break a leg, as they say in the theater, your best performance. I'll be right outside ten seconds away if you need me."

Maddy raised her eyes, "Here's the code: Stop or I'll call the police." Thane smiled, pointed his index finger at her as he got into his car. With headset on he could faintly hear the rhythm of Maddy's heartbeat.

She rehearsed to herself the lines to coyly get Sweetbread to repeat the demand of sex for a work favor. Once clearly recorded, she would reject his offer to complete the evidence. Her goal was out of the house in no more than ten minutes.

The Sweetbread home was modestly nice. The two story five-bedroom brick colonial backed up to a river tributary. The corner lot was sided by an elevated bridge-way over the creek. Passer-byes could view the backyard where Sweetbread and his wife frequently feted the powerful of government and industry. Thane parked just short of the bridge at eye level to the back kitchen windows.

Maddy's car stopped in the circular driveway close to the front door. White Doric columns extended toward the roofline. A flat portico roof opened from the master bedroom suite on to the porch roof above the front door. In the dark behind the portico doors, the large figure of James Sweetbread, sitting in a wicker chair and wearing only a white bathrobe, slowly came to view as Maddy walked toward the front door. The image spoke.

"The door is open, I'll be down."

Maddy entered the foyer. The brown Italian marble floor was purposely dull and simple to not detract from the artwork that crowded the hall. Maddy immediately recognized the Riviera painting by Ronoldo, which she had seen hanging in his office earlier in the week.

Fine art works are the accoutrements of the privileged. They soften the lust for power with a caring façade for the human condition. Lavish business trips, first class air travel, and hundred dollar bottles of wine are the pampering perquisites which the public grants the C.E.O. class. However, John Q. Public is less aware of the process of art collectibles.

As medical power broker and negotiator, Sweetbread had long parted with the little human compassion drizzled upon him during medical school.

The Ronoldo, purchased for ninety-two thousand dollars from the hospital-decorating budget, hung in his office barely long enough to dry. Sweetbread exchanged it for a hundred dollar print from his home.

Not all of James's originals were purchased on the UPSinc. tab. The largest, a Salvatore Dali original on the staircase balcony was a gift from Richard Corless. The C.E.O. expense budget necessarily includes such stylish gifts to fellow C.E.O.s.

"Maddy, to see you is truly the highlight of my day. How about a drink before the highlight of my night?" Sweetbread stroked her hair, not hesitating to initiate physical contact.

"No thank you. I think we should talk."

"Talk would ruin the ambiance. Come here." James pulled the back of her head to position his lips on hers. She struggled free with minimal effort.

"I don't think I can do this. I should never have gotten that D.U.I. Maconi falsified the results. He probably told you it was a falsified breath test. And I shouldn't have to have sex with you keep my job." Maddy realized she had been talking with chin cocked downward toward her chest to amplify the recording.

"Maddy, have that drink. You're just a little nervous. That's understandable. Hey, we're just two nice-looking, fun-loving adults. And if we happen to accomplish some business while we're having fun, it's a bonus, multi-tasking as they say. You look lovely. A gin gimlet, fresh and tart. It'll be perfect." James emphasized the word, tart. He turned his back to her as he moved toward the bar at the side of the family room.

Thane clenched his teeth impatiently as he listened to the banter. Nothing useful as evidence had been said. Maddy's words were not sufficient. Sweetbread had to clearly proposition her with a quid-pro-quo sex-for-work exchange.

"Tell me again, how are you going to help me get rid of this D.U.I.?" Maddy was talking too loudly and James took notice.

"Trust me, I'll take care of it. I'll call some friends at the police department and tell them a friend of mine is a really sweet girl who needs a break. They get a lot of Sweetbread's bread at the Fraternal Order. I'm their friend. They like my friends."

"But what if I refuse to have sex with you, Dr. Sweetbread? Will you refuse to get me off the charge? Will you have me fired?" Maddy impatiently laid out the direct question too clearly.

Thane winced at the bad theater. Next he heard the tone of Sweetbread change to anger. "What are you up to, Gray?"

"Ahhh, ahhhh, you're tearing…" Maddy groaned and then screamed.

"Nice try, bitch."

The wire crackled and stopped. Thane envisioned the scene accurately. Sweetbread smelled a rat. He tore her blouse open and pulled the microphone away from its lead wire. Thane ran out of the car and toward the side of the house. He heard the struggling scream of Maddy.

Thane flung open the unlocked front door running and followed the muted groans. As he entered the family room, Sweetbread's robe was off. He was naked with a leg straddled across Maddy's lower legs. Her blouse was ripped wide open revealing her breasts. Sweetbread had her upper torso pinned with his. One large arm was pressured over her mouth, the other was pulling at her underpants.

Thane was flooded with rage: human, lover, and police officer rage. He reflexively grabbed the nearest weapon. The bright brass fireplace poker had an eagle handle and a colonial style pineapple decoration at the tip. He used his best home-run swing.

Sweetbread's head snapped backwards with a crack the instant the poker struck the center of his forehead. The grunting and struggling ceased seconds after the pineapple tip dented his head. He rolled over motionless.

Maddy gasped and held her hands over her mouth. Instinctively, she moved over to examine him, while wrapping her blouse around her and assembling her skirt. She took his pulse and opened his eyes. She palpated his forehead. "I don't feel any fractures. I think he's just knocked out. His pulse and breathing are fine. Let's get out of here."

Thane carefully picked up the microphone and wire from the bug. Next he wiped off the poker handle with Sweetbread's robe and laid it next to him on the floor. He rolled the sleeping body over on the poker to appear like a fall. He threaded the hands through the armholes of the robe. Finally he instructed Maddy to wash out her gimlet glass and replace it at the bar and not to touch anything else. Thane grabbed several paper napkins at the bar and wiped the door handles as they exited.

Thane disappeared around the side yard. Maddy heard a muffled "shit" as Thane stubbed his foot on a metal downspout opening and tumbled down the back yard until his chin slid into the creek. She started her car and buckled her seat belt. Her headlights came on as she pulled out of the circular driveway. The light revealed a figure arising from a resting position on a curbside fireplug. He stepped into her path. The flashlight beamed into Maddy's face through her open window.

"Have a nice evening, Dr. Gray?" came the unwelcome voice of Officer Maconi. "Or at least good enough to get out of jail free?"

"I hope so." Maddy was unsure where this conversation was going. Had he been there all evening? No, she would have seen his squad car. Had he seen Thane? Again she was unsure.

"Just passing through on my beat. Glad to see you're cooperating with the forces of justice. Have a nice day." Maconi sauntered toward his squad car, twirling his nightstick.

**

Thane sat exhausted on his bed. As he peeled off his T-shirt, a burning pain over his right shoulder announced itself like a late night visitor ringing the doorbell. Several dots of blood soiled the sleeve hem. An inventory of the night's events led him to deduce that the abrasion had occurred when he stumbled over the drain tile and bounced through the edging stones of Sweetbread's creekside landscaping.

Pockets were emptied of wires, quarters, and scraps of paper with written reminders. One read, "track Withers, June 3." Another had Maddy's home and cell phone numbers. It was crinkled and faded from a full week of riding in his pocket.

Thane wondered if Maddy was a Helen of Troy or a cursed Siren calling him toward a whirlpool of trouble. A week ago he had come to Indianapolis as a token investigator on a low profile murder case. He had planned a fortnight of good dinners, novel reading, and doing minimal work. The sight of Maddy had drawn his ship into strange waters. How had he gotten so far off course?

When Sweetbread awoke, would he recognize Thane as his assailant? Would he remain quiet to avoid the accusations of attempted rape? Would there be a trial? An investigation? Would it surface that Thane had performed an unauthorized bugging and utilized agency equipment for personal use: mandatory grounds for dismissal? He could argue that he had probable cause to suspect federal sexual harassment laws were being violated, but where was his court-issued search warrant?

He snickered at himself, "Hatcher needs to hatch a plan." Maddy, he realized, must be suffering a worse trauma. He dialed the first four numbers and then hung up. He would wait and only call with good news. First he would listen to the tape and see if there was enough evidence to coerce Sweetbread into silence and broker Maddy's exoneration.

Thane tiptoed out to the hotel parking lot in his gym shorts. He groaned as his bare foot twisted on a sharp rock. He snatched the recorder from the front seat, then looked around to see an obese elderly woman staring at him, obviously wondering if he were a thief. Thane brandished the car key as proof of ownership, and conspicuously re-locked the door. The woman sneered at his near naked attire. Thane stepped again on the same sharp rock. "Shit," from Thane elicited a raised nose of disgust from the woman.

The casing of the recorder was cracked. Thane remembered a cracking sound when the machine flew off the seat during the car's acceleration out of the parking lot at the police station. By the fourth try to play back the tape, the horror had sunk in. There was no tape recording. Thane concluded the impossibility of trying to convince a jury that Maddy was a victim of attempted rape and that Thane was a knight in shining F.B.I. armor to the rescue.

If he were on the jury, he wouldn't buy it. Sweetbread's attorney would spin the infinitely more plausible scenario that Maddy and Thane had accosted Sweetbread late at night and threatened to harm him unless he dismissed her from the pathology program. An argument ensued and Thane whacked him with the fireplace poker. The only hope was to make Sweetbread believe that he did have an incriminating tape. After all, Sweetbread did know the truth of his guilt.

Thane dialed Maddy's number three times in five minutes and got a busy signal. He then dialed the cell number and got her voice mail. "Maddy, sorry it turned out so badly. Will see you after work. Love you, Thane."

"God, I didn't say that, did I?" Thane was talking to himself. "You aren't talking to your mother. You don't casually use the L word on the voice mail. She's going to think you're a stalker. You idiot. You deserve going straight to bed with no dinner."

**

JUNE 9, SATURDAY, The Cockfighter

Maddy was stuck in a basement with the furnace humming loudly and the air becoming progressively hot and stuffy. The ceiling was collapsing upon her. She could no longer breathe. The humming grew louder. She would die if she couldn't find fresh air. She struggled for one last breath of life. Her chest was crushing under the weight of the ceiling. Her trachea was burning with the pain of suffocation. The ceiling, floor, and her body plunged into a deep ocean.

She awoke gasping for air. Tasmin was purring impatiently and camped on her neck. "Merroww," she whined as Maddy swatted her onto the floor. Tasmin turned with an impertinent glare that said, "Bitch," and then quietly trotted off toward the living room.

Maddy touched the window to feel the temperature of the glass. Maddy's mother, a practical Midwestern housewife, had taught Maddy the temperature forecasting and evaluation technique of feeling window glass.

However, it was June, and the glass was cool from air-conditioning.

She felt silly, but was in need of mothering. She should call her mother. No, she would pay her a visit, if her parents were home for the weekend.

Maddy switched on the radio. Saturday might offer anything for The Breakfast Club. WXCR radio station had a twenty-year-old stand-in DJ for the vacationing Les Bull. She was on a crusade to convert listeners from Merle Haggard to Garth Brooks. Maddy listened impatiently through four songs of cheating lovers, loyal dead dogs, and hard drinking saved by Jesus.

She opened a can of tuna for Tasmin, a special treat for being predictable in a time of chaos. The demands of a resident precluded owning a dog. Cats were low maintenance, even if they were a suffocation hazard. The easiest aspect having a cat was realizing that when Tasmin died, she would hardly miss her.

A forty-seven-year-old man had been fatally stabbed the previous evening, while Maddy and Thane were administering tribal justice to James Sweetbread. The news release indicated that a gambling session had ignited an argument. The assailant escaped and reportedly was unknown to the fellow gamblers. How could the news reporters broadcast such a bogus story? Maddy suspected the police blotter would read differently.

She showered, enjoying the massage of the water spray. As she toweled herself in front of the mirror she noticed several small bruises over her shoulders from the previous evening's assault. She felt good knowing that Sweetbread was nursing the worst headache of his life.

She finished dressing, enjoying a leisurely pace. She absent-mindedly spun her keys around the key ring as she took a final look around the room. Noticing the torn blouse on the floor, she picked it up, stuffed it into a three-quarters full garbage bag, and deposited it into a dumpster at the back of the building. She had parked nearly four feet over the yellow line last night. No ticket must mean her luck was on the upswing.

The morning dew glistened. The air was humid and the temperature rising rapidly. Maddy turned off the air conditioning and opened the windows. She wanted to smell and hear the city. She longed to be free from the medical center. She dreamed of thirteen months hence when she would leave forever. A corner rose bush in full fragrant bloom wafted its sweetness as Maddy stopped at a crossing. She checked the rear view mirror, then remained stopped through the next green light, enjoying the fragrant flowers.

**

Slurp was grinning and prancing about the morgue. "Hello, Doctor Precious, one pop tart and one cherry strudel. Isn't it a glorious morning?" He swung a clipboard toward Maddy and handed her a pen like a symphony conductor summoning the violas. Maddy looked at him and raised one eyebrow.

"I agree. It is a beautiful morning."

Richard walked past them carrying a brain Stryker saw and bone hook. He looked up and commented. "That ain't a speed buzz. He got laid last night." Richard continued setting up the autopsy material alongside a naked Hispanic man on cart number one.

"It was love. Six feet, one hundred eighty pounds of brawn and blue eyes. What a wonderful world. And I just happen to be small, dark and handsome," Slurp twittered.

"Ninety two, dementia, heart failure, end stage renal disease. Need I say more?" Slurp made a pantomime of sawing off his arms. "ARMS OFF!"

"A, R, M, S, O, F, age-related, multi-system, organ failure." Richard offered to move things along. He took the clipboard away from Maddy, checking for the signature, and handed her the police blotter on Felix Hernandez. Richard continued talking.

"Filipino cock-fighter with a long rap sheet of petty scams. Nobody in the community has any information. Police suspect he was doping up his chickens and his gambling cronies got pissed. Probably got stabbed by three or four fellow cock-fighters. Homicide has already taken pictures and gathered routine evidence with Doctor O'Dell. They'll ask around the Filipino community more tomorrow. When nobody talks, they'll let this one go. Withers and the Doc went for coffee. They said, have at it."

Richard took away the police report and showed her his body diagrams of the stab wounds, pointing out each one. Next he handed her a scalpel. "Time to cut."

Maddy performed the autopsy in quiet contemplation. Richard sensed her need for silence and anticipated her needs, handing her instruments without a word. He changed scalpel blades when the cutting edges dragged. He lay large dissecting scissors over the pericardium as she localized the heart. He clamped the rectum and cut string to tie off the bowel ends.

Maddy's thoughts were deep inside. Mr. Hernandez's bronze, dirty skin showed the sun damage from an outdoor work career of fruit picking and grass cutting which preceded his higher paying job as asphalt roofer. His nearly toothless mouth, gray chest hair, and sagging muscles added ten years to his apparent age. The fingernails had been trimmed and bagged for evidence, but black lines of dirt outlined the amputation margins of the nails. Blood-tinged fluid oozed where the scalpel had too closely excised the nails.

There were eleven stab wounds to the chest from at least four different knives. One knife was double edged. It produced a sharp thin cut with tapered tips at both ends of the stab. The other three were single-bladed knife wounds with only one sharp tapered side. Two were five-eighth inches long but differed in width. The third single-edge stab wound was one inch in length and nearly two millimeters wide, a huge knife.

Maddy pictured the hapless man attacked simultaneously by four assailants, while chickens armored with steel spurs hopped and squawked about a smoke-filled basement. Some of the wounds had dried blood; some were clean. All were the judgments of fellow cock-fighters, avenging a breach of chicken-slaughter etiquette.

She wondered how much pain he had felt before losing consciousness. Had his life passed before him? Had he felt guilty, or had he accepted the punishment as his due, like a soldier dying on the battlefield? She thought a more accurate comparison would be a Mafioso member hearing the phrase, "It ain't personal, just bidness."

Mr. Hernandez had black speckled lungs from years of inhaling Marlboro machismo. It saddened Maddy to feel his glistening organs, which had functioned normally until the moment of his death. The fatal stab wound to the left chest had cut the base of the aorta just above the orifices of the coronary arteries. He had lost blood pressure within seconds and exsanguinated internally within the left chest wall. His liver and stomach contents smelled of inexpensive whiskey, the putrid odor of ashtrays and half-empty cocktail glasses the morning following a late party.

Maddy noted that six of the wounds had barely entered the chest and abdomen, the proverbial near miss flesh wounds of cowboy-picture heroes. Would all the assailants be charged with murder if found, or just the one who had hit the aortic bulls-eye?

Her thoughts wandered to the question of justifiable homicide. When examining the victim, it never seems justified. Are there crimes that justify murder, she asked herself? Had Mr. Hernandez tortured chickens, beaten his wife, or gambled away his children's support? Had he cheated other children's fathers out of lunch money? Had Mr. Hernandez ever knifed a cock-fight cheater?

Maddy tossed normal kidneys, adrenals, the spleen, and pancreas into the pan of the weighing scale. Richard dutifully recorded each weight on the worksheet and quietly placed the organs in front of Dr. Gray on her cutting board. She picked up each organ and passed her fingers over the surfaces, feeling the textures. She rinsed excess blood into the sink. She used a knife, twelve inches long and one inch high, similar in size to the fatal weapon. She thinly cut each organ into four millimeter slices like a factory worker, then inspected each widget as it passed her eyes on the assembly line. Young dying children could have lived for years with these normal kidneys, thought Maddy.

She remained quiet until the end of her organ inspection. She looked up toward Slurp and said, "Cherry strudel:

gooey red with lots of slits?" Slurp licked his lips and headed out of the door.

Her report would be the last document in his file, the last sentence in Felix Hernandez's life story. The disinterest of the police was confirmed by their long coffee break. In a usual homicide, officers remained present throughout the examination. They asked questions and took notes to organize the subsequent investigation. Maddy understood that Mr. Hernandez was unimportant not because he was Hispanic, or poor, or a shady character. He simply had no importance to the men who investigated crime. His crimes did not titillate the news media. His daily life was invisible to the mainstream. His assailants were alive and free and would remain so, because their lives were also invisible to the police.

Graham entered the room in blue scrub attire and carrying several papers. He looked over the body cavities. He picked up a metal probe and picked at the lacerated aortic root. Next he inserted the probe into a stab wound in a liver section, which Maddy had reserved for archival fixation in formalin.

"Any surprises?" he asked in earnest. She remained quiet and shook her head.

"Good job. Case is closed then. Maddy, the Sergeant left an envelope for you on my desk."

"I'll be right in. I need to talk to you about something else, too." She turned toward Richard who gestured that he would sew up the corpse and Maddy was free to leave. Richard then rotated his head around the room like a radar antenna obviously searching for Slurp. "Lover boy always seems to disappear when it's time to do the breakfast dishes."

Maddy removed her paper mask, elastic rimmed head cover, and latex gloves in one continuous arm swing from body to garbage can. Next came the surgical apron that she crumbled and dropped into a bright orange bin labeled, "Soiled Laundry, Biohazard." She sighed and breathed deeply, then pulled off her hair band and fluffed down her shoulder-length thick brown hair by pulling her fingers out from the back of her neck. Graham and Richard stared a few seconds. It was an innocent moment when a beautiful woman unwittingly performs an irresistibly sexy movement that a man cannot fail to notice. Richard winked at Graham, who smiled back.

"Holy Mother of God, you won't believe the size of the juicy fruit that just fell off the grapevine!" Slurp sauntered into the suite with hips swinging and lips puckered.

"I hope you can sew while you gossip." Richard handed Slurp the standard autopsy needle, a six-inch long "S"-curved stainless steel implement designed for forceful stabbing. Leather seamstresses use similar needles, as human skin is nearly as tough as cowhide. "And where you been, anyway?"

"I needed a break. I am a stab victim myself, you know."

"You're just disappointed they didn't put it in the right hole." Richard continued his verbal irritation at Slurp.

Graham sensed the need for diplomacy. "What's so newsworthy, Slurp?"

"Burger King just checked into White Castle." All three faces went blank and silent. Slurp raised his arms with wrists bent and palms up. "James Sweetbread just got reeled into University N.I.C.U. Story is they think he had a stroke. They found him down at his house. Fell and hit his head or something. Anyway his nose-in-the-sky golfing buddies were pissed when he didn't show up at the country club. They had his secretary go out to his house, and she found him in his bathrobe out cold on the floor. He was totally naked except for the robe. I think he was jacking his hammer so hard he blew a pipe in the attic." Slurp was in full pantomime masturbating with one hand and exploding the other over his head.

Richard and O'Dell gave short chuckles at Slurp, while Maddy became rigid and pale.

"That's a terrible shame, even if he is a creep." She left to change clothes and venue.

Slurp hollered as she left the room, "Shame, my ass. Ding Dong, let's hope the wicked prick is dead!"

**

Maddy showered and changed to her Saturday clothes of blue jeans and tight-fitting T-shirt. The latter, a gift from Mina on her birthday, advertised in printing over her breasts "Tasmin Slept Here" above a picture of her cat. Like Tasmin, she scurried with short quiet steps rapidly back to her office and closed the door. She found the cell number, dialed, and waited through three rings. The "Hello" was like the gate bell to a racehorse.

"He's in the hospital in a coma for Christ's sake. They're going to figure out it was the poker. When he wakes up, we could be up for assault or attempted murder. Maybe the best defense is a first-strike offense? We could file attempted rape charges on Sweetbread. We've got the tape."

"Maddy, slow down. I don't know what's going to happen. But I can report that the toxicology on the

189

congressman was negative for curare, insulin fragments, the whole list you gave me."

"Thane, what are we going to do?"

"I can't talk right now. I'll call you later." Thane was lying. He had neither an explanation for the empty tape, nor had he hatched a plan. The news that Sweetbread was still unconscious, although serious, was a blessing of delay.

She knocked lightly at Graham's office door. Unlocked, it opened easily with the pressure of her fingers. She accepted the finger curl as an invitation to enter and sit down. With Sweetbread fixed in her mind, she contrasted his office with O'Dell's. There were pictures of international travel to the Swiss Alps, Hawaii, and Alaska. Several small golf trophies sat dust-covered on the top bookshelf. No expensive oil paintings from fashionable artists were present. Sweetbread, Corless, and other C.E.O. club members owned most such works not in the museums. Mildly messy order was the décor, with textbooks, pathology atlases, and a few scattered journal articles on desk and chairs. The remaining books, computer, telephone, and penholder were arranged in useful positions on his desk. A putter and two golf balls idly called for attention in one corner. There was no casting couch for the female residents in need of a favor.

"Here's the envelope from the Sergeant. I'm sure you can do handsomer and younger than old Withers." Graham's joke hit to Maddy's core. As if Graham could read her like an open book, she felt he knew her attraction to older men. She felt embarrassed and excited that he might be responding to her attraction to him. It gave her the focus she needed.

"Dr. O'Dell, I have this terrible dilemma. My research into blood group antigen sites and heart disease has uncovered quite an irregularity." She looked at Graham's silver temples and thick sun-tanned neck. His gentle look and patient listening were captivating. "The case of David Burr doesn't make any sense. The organs are all type A, which was his recorded blood type, but the heart sections with the M.I. were from a type O heart tissue. I was hoping you could clear this up for me." There. She had said it.

"Really? Do you have any ideas?" Graham remained undisturbed, while Maddy searched for any sign of apprehension. She was relieved by his calmness.

"The obvious question is: Why would someone switch the heart tissue? They must have wanted you to think he had an M.I. and stop looking for something else. Or..."

After a few seconds Graham finished her sentence. "Or maybe I needed to have some phony evidence for his heart attack, after I personally poisoned the lout. No, no, I remember now. I went to his motel room the night of his death and injected him with a fatal dose of potassium, or insulin? Something undetectable. Sorry, I'm getting old. I can't remember all these details."

His humorous approach disarmed her. She apologized. "I know you wouldn't kill anybody. I just can't explain it. And I don't know what to do about reporting it."

"Have you told anyone?"

"Thane Hatcher from the F.B.I. That's all, except it may have gotten out in a conversation with Mina. Thatcher suspects Withers might be involved. If we suspected you, I wouldn't be telling you this."

"Before you go to "60 Minutes" with this hoax, you might consider whether someone actually would go through that kind of effort to kill David Burr. Most murderers use handguns because they're quick and easy. On the other hand, the hoax might be that someone in the house wanted to have a little fun with the new resident by switching a heart block to pull your chain."

Maddy turned pale, then reddened. "I feel like such a fool. I've seen too many detective movies lately."

"Real forensic pathology isn't anything like television."

"A joke makes a lot more sense. I am so gullible. You wouldn't do this. Neither would the histo-techs. Slurp and Richard, I'm not so sure about. Not Dr. Green. Mordecai! He's weird enough to think that would be really funny."

"We might never know unless you can get one of them to confess. What's Thatcher's trail on Withers?" Graham moved the conversation.

"The last Random Ranger murder victim, the gym trainer, was last seen on video tape with Slurp at the pathology picnic. Detective Slaughter from homicide thinks if the acquaintance with Slurp isn't coincidental then Slurp is the Random Ranger, and that he killed Duval. Later for an alibi and sympathy, Slurp stabbed himself to get admitted to the hospital. Slaughter thinks he acted way too sick for the shallow wound and fast recovery. Thane Hatcher, on the other hand, knows from the hospital log that Withers came to visit him that night and could have gone out immediately and murdered Duval in revenge. Or who knows, Withers and Slurp may have been acting together. Maybe it has to do with Slurp's amphetamine habit."

"You definitely need to get rid of that television. Slurp wouldn't harm a flea. Duval's time of death was about five in the morning, clearly after Slurp was in the hospital, and after Withers had left for the airport."

"Airport?"

"Withers was on a flight to the Bahamas. Have your friend from the F.B.I. check the airline rosters. He takes vacations to Nassau regularly. Sorry to ruin your wrap-up of the Random Ranger murders. But who knows? Maybe he's written you a full confession." Graham pointed inquisitively at the envelope.

Maddy opened the unsealed flap and took out copies of her three outstanding tickets including the D.U.I. Each was stamped dismissed. There was a notepaper clipped to the top that was printed in masculine handwriting, "In Appreciation, Fraternal Order of Police."

**

Saturday afternoon at the Internal Medicine Room was an eclectic merger of the Indianapolis cultural deserati. The tradesmen were relaxing after having worked the morning from seven until 1 p.m. Six hours of overtime had earned them a belly full of beer and a pork tenderloin sandwich. The journeymen got the breaded oversized cutlets and smothered them with mustard and mayonnaise. The apprentices in their early twenties protected their flat bellies with grilled and bun-less orders sided with coleslaw. The tradesmen tables were well behaved and only loud enough to hear one another.

The boisterous unskilled and under-employed congregated under the television adjacent the pool tables. Long mullet-styled hair often in ponytails required swooshing over the shoulder to allow line of sight while impaling the cue ball. NASCAR racing roared from the television. Cigarettes with long ashes dangled from mouths or actively burned stains on the pool tables. Long-necked beers were ordered from the waitresses, all of whom were called, "Honey." Each billiard ball that rudely failed to drop into the intended pocket brought forth cheers of approval along with profane references to excrement, the Christian messiah, and acts of maternal fornication.

Along the front wall was a brighter section illuminated through a row of glass block windows that began at shoulder height and ran to the ceiling. The tasteless architectural glasswork was long past its late fifties heyday as was the dark wood veneer paneling. The medical center young urban professionals preferred this sunlit and smokeless area. They utilized the facility for its proximity to the hospitals and the price of the beer. White coats were ceremonially removed after ordering and folded over the backs of the tubular steel chairs. Each group paid no attention to the other, except polite tolerance during uncomfortable moments of forced close quartering in the rest rooms.

Mina and Maddy coordinated their simultaneous arrivals via cell phone. Mina had spent the morning at the county free clinic, colloquially referred to as the "scratch and hatch clinic." Inner city children were marched in herds to inspect heads for lice nits. She treated the scratching herdlings for ringworm, scabies, poison ivy or atopic dermatitis until the medicine samples ran out. She wrote prescriptions but realized the unlikelihood of a child getting a medicine that must be purchased. It was simple dermatology practice, but the missionary quality made Mina feel valuable. It was a Saturday rotation that she didn't resent.

"Oh, you're wearing the cat shirt," Mina smiled with appreciation.

"Tasmin hates it. Thinks it makes her look fat, but it was the only thing I had clean," said Maddy. "In truth, this week's nightmare has given me no time for laundry. Mina, have you heard about Sweetbread?"

"Couldn't happen to a nicer guy. There may be a god after all. The bad news is that he's probably going to live. I talked with the chief resident of neurology. Sweetbread's MRI and CAT scans are normal except for a little frontal lobe and brainstem edema. If he's had a stroke it didn't show up on the scans. But you didn't hear that from me, patient confidentiality and all."

"There's no such thing as patient confidentiality, we all know that. Just don't tell Washington. And don't tell anyone what I'm about to tell you."

Maddy became quiet and serious as she explained the events of the prior evening to Mina. She produced the envelope of the dismissed tickets and completed her story, "So when Sweetbread wakes up, I don't know if he'll go after me and Thane or not. I have to have your testimony if we need it."

"You won't need it. You have the tape and the dismissed tickets." Mina objected.

"I can't depend on the tickets. He could easily argue that we had a consensual relationship. Thane bopped him out of jealousy."

"Maddy, I can't confess to using dope in open court. Bam! The licensing Nazis will put me out of business immediately. Having a bogus D.U.I. or a boyfriend that bops somebody won't. I didn't know he was your boyfriend, by the way. Robbing the cradle, are we?"

"He isn't my boyfriend."

"Oh, you're just using his body and his aim with a fireplace poker?"

"Mina, I'm serious. I need your promise. And I'm not sleeping with him."

"Pity, I would."

"Is there anyone you wouldn't sleep with?"

"That is a tough one. Probably just the old geezers you hang out with."

"Bitch," Maddy playfully swatted Mina with her purse and spilled a beer.

Thane Hatcher came through the door swinging a manila envelope. On passing the pool tables the backstroke of a cue stick hit Thane squarely in the Adam's apple. He bent over coughing and gagging and dropped the envelope. It opened releasing papers and x-rays to air-glide under pool tables, bar stools and tables.

The pool player grunted, "Sorry, dude," and slapped him on the back, that insane reflex of purported compassion, which only doubles one's anxiety and discomfort. The pool player's cigarette that hung limp from his lips disposed its nearly two inches of ash upon Thane's lapel pocket. When the ash owner dusted off the pocket, the discovery of Thanes .38 automatic shoulder weapon ignited minor chaos.

"Watch out, he's packing' a fuckin' piece!" the player exclaimed. All conversation ceased. The bartender jumped to re-establish order.

"State law, no firearms allowed in a bar. You check that right here."

Thane reflexively made the mistake of flashing his badge, "F.B.I.," to which one fourth of the patrons, nearly all from the pool tables and several of the tradesmen abandoned their drinks, threw down their gambling scratch-off tickets, and bolted with heads down toward the exits.

"Goddamn, you son-of-a-bitch," cursed the bartender who calculated the afternoon profits had just disappeared. Maddy and Mina scurried about to pick up the x-rays and files. Their opinions of Thane were about to change.

"Stop right there, all of you. Nobody in here is under any investigation. I'm here on a purely social visit with these two ladies. Drinks for the house on me."

The bartender quickly got to work rescuing his clientele from the parking lot. All but two of the patrons returned to their beers, pool, darts, and cigarettes. Maddy felt attracted to Thane's take-command wisdom, a trait that she admired and had typically found in older men. The sight of any young man excited Mina after a cold beer.

"That was quick thinking, cowboy." Mina slapped his thigh and grabbed it as he sat down next to her. He interpreted the thigh contact as a green light signal. The more Mina drank, the greener became the signal. The political problem was how to manage a sure thing with Mina later, while advancing his cause with Maddy. He could use the F.B.I. gun incident to hasten his leave, if need be.

Maddy held the envelope that was re-stuffed with the fallen reports and films. When she held it out to Thane, he pushed it back. "That's for you, the Michael Johnson dental files. Those were easy. His family used the clinic at the dental school, and they keep records forever for research projects."

"Thanks. Thane, I told Mina the whole story."

Mina continued. "A reliable source in neurology says Sweetbread only has some brain swelling. He could wake up any moment. Will the tape keep us out of court? All our jobs are on the line, if this gets public."

Thane hesitated, searching for words.

"What?" said Maddy.

"There is no tape. It is blank. The recorder got banged about in the car and it doesn't work."

"Thane Hatcher, you can't do this to me."

"But Sweetbread doesn't know that. We can bluff him. He's into power. A scandal is worse for him than for us."

"You're just brilliant, officer. I'm out of here. I told my mother I'd visit. Maybe there's one person in this world I can count on. And another thing, Officer Brilliant, your ideas about Withers are dead on arrival. He was on a plane to Nassau the morning of the Random Ranger hit. Do me a favor, go back to wherever you came from, but stay out of my life." Maddy walked away, turning sarcastically so all could hear, "Thanks for the beer, F.B.I. agent."

Mina's hand consolingly squeezed Thane's inner thigh.

**

JUNE 10, SUNDAY, The Old Country

New Munich was indistinguishable from any of a hundred villages in southern Indiana. Boat-loaded German settlers landed at Ellis Island after the Civil War then took trains and ferries down the Ohio River. Land was granted for next to nothing.

The Germans re-established the familiar religious squabbles from the Old Country, segregating into Lutheran-only and Catholic-only villages. Catholic communes were established in the name of Rome; Lutherans perpetuated Martin Luther's tradition of reconfiguring the Church. New Munich was Catholic.

River water and tillable land with ample trees for lumber were necessities. The southern hills of Indiana provided some of the nostalgic landscape of the homeland. Northern Indiana and Illinois were much too flat. Mosquitoes meant the settlers weren't in Germany anymore.

New Munich had never grown past several thousand root-bound transplants. Millers, Schmidts, Machers, and Stadts were partial surnames carrying the trade histories of serf ancestors pre-dating the Reformation.

The Grays were river merchants of English Episcopalian descent. Such families would occasionally lose a son or daughter by marriage into a divergent ethnic community. New Munich's Catholic cultural monolith had captured and converted Maddy's paternal ancestors prior to 1900.

The public school held catechism lessons on Wednesdays. Because the state required taxation to support public schools, the practical and parsimonious German solution was to eliminate the costs of parochial school, and the separation of church and state.

Maddy had no bonding to the Catholic Church. She had no animosity either. She thought the whole process to be a waste of a day off. "Why pray when you can play," she would taunt her friends and parents. The weekend rituals of Mass, confession, and baptism were no more meaningful or useful to Maddy than flipping salt over one's shoulder or avoiding cracks in the sidewalk.

She admired and esteemed her older brother. Eighteen months her elder, he explained to Maddy his two approaches to confession. When forced to attend confession under direct maternal eye, he made up a one line menial transgression, disobeying his father usually sufficed. Full absolution required less than thirty seconds.

The second approach to confession was self-administration. Southern Indiana towns had an elaborate system of canals built at a time when water travel was believed to be the future of trade. Superhighways and railway stops at small towns were yet to be conceived. Her brother would walk along the canal and confess to the water that he was not going to confession. The advantage of this approach was that when his mother would guilt-quiz him on whether he had gone to confession, he could answer an honest, "yes."

Maddy had made her last formal confession at the age of fifteen. Her only trips to Mass since leaving for college had been the weddings of cousins and high school friends. She bided her time in church, pondering the stained glass images of Biblical stories. Maddy imagined small pox, bubonic plague, and cholera, wondering if there were pathologists or death examiners in the ancient world.

Although only one hundred miles from Indianapolis, the cultural divide was oceanic. Several small-manufacturing plants for automobile water pumps and engine mounts employed the majority of the high-school-educated hangers-ons. The pew and barstool counts remained constant. Somehow the rate of deaths, births, marriage recruits, retained homebodies, and escapees like Maddy, balanced out.

Fathers went to work at the factories on weekdays. Evenings were devoted to Catholic League soccer and softball games played on public school athletic fields. Friday nights were bowling leagues. Saturday nights meant euchre games and extra packs of cigarettes. Sunday mornings were spent at Mass. The ritual attendance was followed by an extended family meal of ham and casserole side dishes. Afterwards men watched the sporting matches of the season, women gossiped, and young children played with matches. Older children used matches to light cigarettes.

Maddy slept late while her mother attended early Mass. Her mother kept the rooms of Maddy and her brother like museum exhibits insulated from change, vaults of a previous era. Her junior high posters of blonde-haired pop singers hung undisturbed. A basket of music recordings sat on her desk.

Maddy liked to listen to the old recordings when visiting. She prided herself that she had never wasted money on the vulgar rap CD's her friends felt so smug in owning. Maddy preferred ballads and soft rock. She owned several albums from her parents's generation of Beatles and Bee Gees, nearly all by older male singers. She picked up the top CD, a Phil Collins big seller, *"No Jacket Required,"* and hummed along, "doot, do, do, doot, do, I'm not gonna make it."

Maddy's father declined an invitation to accompany his wife to church. Her father used the complaint of a stiff back this morning. Physical excuses kept him out of church three Sundays out of four. Since Maddy was home, her mother bypassed her usual scowl of disapproval.

On the kitchen table she arranged for Maddy a bowl of frosted cornflakes, orange juice, and a blueberry muffin. Although this was her favorite breakfast in third grade, Maddy's mother had never considered that Maddy might prefer something different. Maddy ate them gratefully and ignored the stale quality of the cereal, which remained in inventory only for her consumption.

After breakfast she visited with her father. He confessed how much better his back felt after being up for several hours. He was busy planning the annual pork chop festival for the fourth of July. Last year they had run out after three hundred pounds of center-cut pork chops. He was unsure whether to order three-fifty this year or stick with the usual. Perhaps last year was a fluke because the weather was exceptionally good. Usually it was hot and humid, but last year a cool spell in the seventies made the New Munich appetites greasier. He would ask the grocer for advice.

Maddy loved the simplicity of her mother. Like a schoolteacher, everything had a time and a place, rightness or wrongness, and a moral imperative. Mother had a comment, criticism, or abhorrence associated with all things: drinking, gambling, rude behavior, stacking glassware, even squeezing out toothpaste. Her maiden name was Einsleiter, loosely translated as one light, but metaphorically, the light bearer of morality.

Maddy went walking before her mother returned from church. She noticed the town did not change, it faded. The paint of the clapboard houses and stores became dull and blistered. Six room bungalows receded into architectural history. Green awnings were rusted or amputated like leper fingers. Air conditioning had made awnings obsolete, but not unseen. Inertia and blind familiarity were the glue that kept them dangling from the window casings.

Maddy remembered her childhood. The Catholic Church, the small town, the soccer games had fully bored her by age twelve. She wanted out. She wanted something different in life, but she had no idea of what. She enjoyed learning and reading. She had only a vague interest in science and medicine, but it gave her an exit from New Munich.

Maddy stopped at the hardware store her father had managed for thirty-two years. It was his only job in New Munich, beginning the year he married her mother. She peered into the tall showcase windows. She saw the same chain saw and snow blower displays that were erected three years ago. The owner, Levi Schmitt, purchased ten units of each during a model-ending sale.

Her father deferred to Levi Schmitt, despite his track record of poor business decisions. He deferred to his wife on all issues of decoration, yard landscaping, and nutrition. He deferred to the editorial column of the newspaper for his political opinion. Most sadly to Maddy, he deferred to the Catholic Church for most of life's decisions.

She had one sibling, her brother. Maddy's mother had used a diaphragm. Maddy discovered the device in high school, and kept the knowledge secret. It was not a topic for family discussion. Maddy was sure her father had no clue that his wife would violate a Catholic directive.

Her father had received a good helping of the southern Indiana gene pool. He was stocky with scant orange hair and freckles. His skin took to the sun poorly. His hairline balded early. Maddy couldn't imagine his mother finding him attractive. She loved him as a soft-spoken daddy.

Her close friends often asked her about her attraction to older men. Maddy was certain it was not because of some Oedipal longing for her father. He was kind and affectionate, but lacked independent thought. She found her father physically unattractive. She didn't idealize him; nor did she pity him or judge his decisions. He was a worker ant, a drone that labored for the queens: his wife and the Church.

Wisdom, dark hair, and graying temples aged to a soft patina were attractive. Adventure and decisiveness were exciting qualities. Her ideal was not a man resembling her father.

Maddy stopped by the drug store to purchase a Sunday newspaper. On the Sabbath New Munich's only open businesses were a gas station and the drug store. Upon returning home she found her mother preparing macaroni and cheese and mashed potatoes, also favorites of Maddy's childhood. Often she resented her mother's failure to accept her adulthood. Today she felt pampered not smothered.

After dinner she relaxed on the porch. It was hot, but the air conditioner in the dining room window had chilled them. The porch was also more suitable for digestion of the starch-based belly stuffing.

Her mother talked of Maddy's old friends who were having babies. The agenda flowed without disguise. This usually annoyed Maddy, but today was a refreshingly predictable source of maternal caring.

"Oh, shit," Maddy gasped as she covered her mouth. Her father picked up the paper as it fell from her lap. In the lower right corner of the front page, the headline read, "Head University Physician Dead, only 56."

**

"I'm sorry I got you into this mess." Maddy began as soon as Thane had said hello. "And I was out of line at the Internal Medicine Room. Thane, I won't…"

"Maddy, shhhhhh! Your cell phone isn't secure. You never know who's listening. Where are you?"

"About 50 minutes south of Indy."

"I'm going to bed. I'll come by your office tomorrow afternoon."

**

JUNE 11, MONDAY, The Telltale Brain

Those working prefer Monday mornings with rain. Golfers favor sunshine. Whispering Pines Country Club, normally closed for course work and maintenance, had a rare corporate outing scheduled. Large outings generated the vulgar necessity of cash flow. Today, Dr. Graham O'Dell was the "A" player recruited to compete in a fund-raising tournament for Children's Memorial Hospital. The news of James Sweetbread's death was the talk of the medical community. Despite O'Dell's general contempt for the man, he appreciated that Sweetbread allowed the physician staff to participate in charity events without having to claim a personal day. Today's event would allow O'Dell to escape the news media, nosy physicians, and other insiders wishing the first hand scoop on Sweetbread's demise. Rain was threatening, but even if the event was cancelled, Graham did not intend to visit County Hospital.

Maddy tuned in the radio for The Breakfast Club menu. The news was treating the Sweetbread death like a simple obituary. Despite being found in his bathrobe, there wasn't enough there to make for interesting copy. The weekend had gone by without a murder or fatal accident.

Maddy anticipated an easy workday. She allowed herself to indulge in the relief that Sweetbread was dead along with her legal problems. Maconi had been at Sweetbread's house to verify that she showed up. Today he was waiting outside the morgue.

"Hey Gray," Maconi came to Maddy and whispered in her ear, "You're a legend down at the station. Fucked old Sweetbread to death, didn't you. Ever consider a younger man who can keep up with you?" He pinched her butt and winked. She swatted his hand and did not comment, but was much relieved that Maconi conveyed no suspicion of manslaughter. She wasn't about to deny sex with Sweetbread. The police might be able to re-instate her D.U.I.

Richard led Maddy to the first refrigerator drawer. There was one sign-out case this morning. Merle Pearl was a seventy-seven year old man with a cardiac pacemaker who had died on the escalator at Lazarus Department store in the downtown mall. He fell on the store escalator and got his hand stuck in the stair assembly stopping the escalator and providing a macabre visual for several hundred shoppers. The children thought the escalator had trapped him. The adults stared in the horrifying realization that they were witnessing an actual death.

Fortunately for Maddy and Richard the widow reported he had complained of chest pains throughout the morning. They both knew he was having another heart attack. He refused to go the hospital. He said he was ready to die. The widow was comfortable with his decision and relieved he was out of pain. There were no issues to resolve.

Dr. Green was staff for the case of James Sweetbread, M.D. Dr. Mordecai would perform the autopsy; and Dr.

Gray would assist. In the dressing room Dr. Green repeated a wisecrack he heard in the hallway from another physician, "This is a reportable case, an exception to the rule that only the good die young." He attempted to treat this autopsy as any routine case. However, Dr. Green spent much of the morning reminding the curious that they were not allowed in the morgue. He closely supervised Drs. Mordecai and Gray knowing that the entire medical center and the Indianapolis News would pay close scrutiny.

Richard was angry that Slurp hadn't come in and hadn't called. "Beefcake brunching," Richard snarled.

Dr. Mordecai was as methodical and observant as ever. He pointed out small scratches on the forearms of the body. Maddy flashed back to the attempted rape and recognized her marks of defense. Her stomach tightened. Mordecai murmured, "Interesting."

There was a large bruise over the forehead with a central diamond-shaped abrasion. Mordecai correlated the mark with the body's final repose on top of the fire poker. He dictated that the impressed abrasion pattern was compatible with the death scene.

To Maddy, Sweetbread's lifeless corpse now looked pathetic, weak, and vulnerable. She felt mixed emotions. He was guilty of assaulting her, but did it warrant his death? Was it really murder, self-defense, or just an accident? She had dragged poor Thane Hatcher into this mess. For a moment she missed the simplicity of New Munich.

The skin of the body was thick and rubbery and difficult to cut, dulling her blade. Two scalpel blades were required to open the chest and abdomen. Even in death he was difficult. As she removed and weighed each organ, she felt progressively more guilty. These were pristine pink organs.

Lungs were soft and air-filled like sponge cake. His heart was a deep red muscle like a rare steak. Tasmin would scratch through a door for such a feast.

Mordecai and Gray had no comments up to this point of the autopsy. They were processing normal tissue with factory-like motions. The expectation that they would find no pathology outside the brain was fulfilled.

Richard incised the scalp from ear to ear. He folded Sweetbread's face forward like slipping off a Halloween mask. Mordecai stopped the dissection to examine the exposed frontal bone area closely. He used the tip of his forceps to point out periosteal bleeding from a hairline fracture. The frontal sinus on the left was filled with bloody fluid, consistent with a small acute fracture. The remaining skull bones were normal.

The turtle shell cut was completed and the skull top was removed. It unveiled the underlying brain, which was slightly swollen and pale. No massive blood collection from a hemorrhagic stroke was present.

Mordecai took over the brain removal as Richard backed away from the autopsy table. He carefully snipped each cranial nerve and then the carotid arteries at the base of the brain. He used scissors to split the thick sheet of dura that covers the hemispheres and folds over the cerebellum. All structures appeared normal and intact.

The brain weighed 1610 grams, slightly heavy from increased fluid as predicted by the admission CAT scans. An area of reddish discoloration was present over the frontal lobe tips, corresponding to the trauma site of the poker injury. Mordecai measured and sketched the injury on the brain diagram. Next he separated the brainstem and cerebellum.

Maddy watched quietly. Richard retrieved Dr. Green from the hallway, where he had escorted out two physician staff onlookers. Richard said, "Excuse me, Doctor Green, Doctor Mordecai is beginning the brain sectioning."

Mordecai stopped to point out the frontal sinus injuries and the frontal lobe discoloration. Both agreed that he had hit the fire poker very hard to fracture bone and contuse the brain. Mordecai bread-loafed the central brain and cortex.

The white and gray matter was boggy, brain edema, the color and texture of peach gelatin. "The brain is swollen, but insufficient to have killed him," Mordecai stated with authority. Dr. Green nodded in agreement.

Next Mordecai sliced the detached cerebellum. Again slight swelling was present. "Not much," he grunted. Mordecai then made several slices through the midbrain, pons, and medulla. He was about to walk away when Dr. Green stepped forward.

"Richard, give me a scalpel." Green then slowly made multiple, delicate one millimeter cuts through the pons. He pointed out round bloody dots only one to two millimeters in diameter. "See, these Maddy, Percival?"

"Dilated blood vessels?" suggested Maddy.

"Actually they are small torn blood vessels. Duret micro-hemorrhages they are called. Duret is the name of the French anatomist who realized their importance."

"Which is?" Maddy inquired innocently.

"The cause of death. We usually see these in a whiplash injury. This is what your car's headrest is designed to prevent. If the brain is rapidly snapped backwards, the small fixed vessels in the brainstem get stretched and then bleed. It doesn't take much bleeding in this area to kill off the cardio-respiratory centers of the brainstem."

Dr. Green seemed like a magical wizard to Maddy. Mordecai's ego was shrinking, but he seized the importance of the finding.

"Dr. Green, do you think there would be enough acceleration upon falling to hyper-extend the neck enough to produce the Duret hemorrhages?"

"Well…"

Mordecai finished his sentence and answered his own question. "Unlikely. When one falls down the brain accelerates slightly forward. It's most likely that someone used the fireplace poker to swat his head like a baseball with a bat, snapping it forcefully backwards. If so, who's the batter? This case reeks of homicide to me."

"I don't know if we can say that yet, Percival. It would take a powerful blow to jerk the head back that quickly."

Richard, Maddy, and Officer Maconi who had been almost asleep on a stool, straightened in unison. Dr. Green offered, "Percival, cut down on the atlas and axis."

Mordecai was alive with excitement. The first cervical vertebra is the atlas, named after the Greek god who held up the world. The orb of the skull sits on the first vertebra. The second vertebra, the axis, is named for an axle-like bony spike that protrudes upward along the spine through the first vertebra. The tooth-like axle is called the odontoid process. Anatomists conjecture it evolved to help distribute the weight of the heavy skull and protect the first vertebra.

This area is not inspected during a routine autopsy. When Mordecai peeled back the coverings of the bone, there was bleeding about the odontoid and the atlas. This evidence of sprain injury supported the hypothesis that Sweetbread's brain injuries were not from a simple fall.

"I should have been more suspicious. A little edema and no blood isn't a lethal fall."

"Don't beat up on yourself, Percival. If you knew everything you wouldn't need a fellowship."

"Homicide?"

Maconi was out the door like a bloodhound on the scent. If this was a felony assault, he had a good idea who might be involved. He didn't hear Dr. Green's response. "Maybe we'll keep it open for now."

**

Homicide detectives combed the estate, which now belonged solely to the widow of James Sweetbread. The family room had been cleaned and vacuumed since Friday. Maconi knew Maddy had been there, so trace fibers or her fingerprints would only prevent her from denying her visit. Besides, she could confess to a consensual visit and passing Maconi on the way out. Would he become a suspect?

"Hey, what's this?" a voice in uniform called as he retrieved a small round metallic device by its dangling wire tail. It lay sheltered from the dew between a rock and the downspout drain tile, exactly where it had ejected from Thane Hatcher's pocket during his tripping over the drain tile. The thumb and forefinger prints would be unmistakable.

**

Maddy sat in her office. She had just finished the final touches to her paper on blood group binding sites. She felt silly about being duped into thinking the heart of David

Burr had been staged for a murder cover-up. She wondered who would have pulled that stunt on her. Only Mordecai or O'Dell himself, she concluded. Mordecai's motivation would be for the shear sadistic pleasure. He was the type to never confess. If O'Dell was the prankster, she was sure he would eventually come forward, probably the last day of her rotation. He would have an honorable reason, like teaching her about her own gullibility, she decided.

She was proud of the work and research of her study. However, the results showed nothing, a negative study suggesting that blood group antigen density in blood vessels had nothing to do with heart disease. Maddy would offer it to several journals. Each would turn it down for publication. Such is the bias with negative studies.

"Doot, do, do, doot, do, I'm not gonna make it," she hummed the Phil Collins song that was stuck in her mind. Thane walked into her office and shut the door.

"Phil Collins from *No Jacket Required.* I was about ten when that came out."

"You ever get a song in your head, and it won't go away? This one's been playing constantly since I heard it in my old room yesterday at my mother's."

"You have a mother? I figured you were a direct spawn from the devil."

"Me?"

"Yes, you. Two weeks ago I was a respectable, innocent, F.B.I. back-lines slug, then I met you."

"I'm sorry. Thane, the autopsy on Sweetbread didn't go well."

"What do they know?"

"Nothing about us. Just that Sweetbread more likely got hit than fell."

"See, there's no end to the cobwebs around this woman." Thane smiled, revealing he was joking. Then he grabbed her neck and pretended to choke her. "No jacket required, straight-jacket required." Thane continued, flapping his hands and darting out his tongue.

"You're in too good a mood for an incipient murder suspect. What's up?"

"Well, have you heard about Slurp?" responded Thane. Maddy gave the negative head oscillation. "Slaughter still considers him the break in the Random Ranger case. He got a court order to search Slurp's apartment. I don't think he expected to find anything. His main purpose was to scare Slurp into revealing whatever he might know. Well, bullseye! They found a spent bullet head that is identical to the Random Ranger's. Slurp said he took it as a souvenir from one of the cases. Slaughter is holding him on suspicion of murder."

"Slurp is the Random Ranger? No."

"Now for my good mood. We're going to the Bahamas."

"What? Are you serious? You do need that straight-jacket, Thane Hatcher."

"Maddy, you want to get Slurp out, don't you? I need your help. I checked out the Bahamas story on Withers. O'Dell was right. Withers left late Saturday night, too early to kill Duval, and came back late Tuesday. But here's the catch: Withers takes a three-day jaunt to Nassau every six months regularly, and an occasional extra sporadic visit. He always pays cash for his ticket. He goes alone. And he's leaving the end of this week, Thursday morning."

"How do you know all this?"

"Airline tickets, immigration records, credit card checks, and cells phone records. This is not moon landing for the F.B.I. We do some things well."

"I missed the 'we' part for the Bahamas."

"Wither's flight gets in at two p.m. We can get there an hour and a half earlier. We rent a car and follow him. I've got two seats reserved, paid for as official business by your benevolent government. You just have to let O'Dell know you need a couple of personal days."

"Do I get to lay out on the beach?"

"Only after we figure out what Withers is up to."

"I still don't get it. Withers seems like a nice cop."

"Intuition. Didn't your mother ever warn you about the nice boys?"

"Like you. Are you going to try to seduce me?"

"Promise."

"I'll have to talk to O'Dell tomorrow. He's off playing golf today."

Thane gave the reservation numbers to Maddy. She promised to call him after talking to her supervisor in the morning. Thane left, pleasantly sauntering in his elevated mood.

**

The Internal Medicine Room was quiet. Monday is a recuperation holiday from weekend excesses. Maddy called and invited Mina to a "plaster party." This was their code word for patching things up. When Mina arrived, there were drinks on the table. The women exchanged the ritual Hershey dark chocolate candy bars and hugged one another.

"I like your style, Maddy. When you have a problem, you kill him."

"Shhh," Maddy giggled. "It probably would be easier to fuck them, like you do."

"Bitch!"

"Slut!" The two hugged again.

"Toast! Friends forever!" The two clanged glasses and sipped the candy red drinks.

"What is this stuff, kool-aid?" Mina shook the glass and peered into the top.

"Bahama Mamas, the official drink of mellow Rastaferians everywhere. I am going to Nassau, Thursday!"

"Get out of here!"

"The F.B.I. has specifically recruited me to join a fact finding expedition in the wilds of the Caribbean."

"Technically, the Bahamas are in the Atlantic Ocean, not the Caribbean. Does the F.B.I. equate with Thane Hatcher?"

"Mina, you're a mind reader."

"I didn't think you liked the young ones."

"It's business. I've told him that."

"Are you going to sleep with him?"

"Of course not."

"Good."

"What do you mean, good? You're the one who's always telling me to find someone my own age."

"Not this one."

"Are you jealous, Mina? Don't tell me."

"I like him. So what?" Mina's tone changed dramatically from playful to angry.

"Why didn't you tell me. Have you been going out?"

"Maybe, yeah."

"Just sleeping in, huh? Is there anybody out there you wouldn't sleep with?"

"Yeah, you." Mina rose up abruptly and flung the Hershey bar back toward Maddy as she fumed out. "Have a nice trip."

**

JUNE 12, TUESDAY, Catch and Release

The snap of a June bug's hard carapace cracking against the window awakened Maddy. She sat up, startled. The brown iridescent scarab lay on its back, panicked and vibrating on the windowsill in a frantic effort to right itself. Maddy turned off the alarm before it could ring. She was ambivalent about the fate of the annoying bug. She questioned, in existential generalities, the merit and criteria to justify capital punishment. Nonetheless, she pulled a tissue out of the box and executed the noisy beetle. Had it not terminated her sleep prematurely, she might have granted it leniency and flipped it outside.

It dawned on her that this was the legal system. One side argued for exoneration, the other for the harshest of punishments and remedies. Unlike the philosophers who drone on to their deathbeds forever locked in quandary, the jurists vote for an outcome, and life is irrevocably changed.

Maddy automatically tuned the radio to the hog report and local news. She did not care whether a case needed autopsy or if she would enjoy a free day. She was ruminating about the best time to call Mina. Morning would be too hectic. Maddy might exacerbate Mina's irritation with her if the dermatology clinic was behind schedule. Maddy decided to wait until after lunch, but she would be unable to enjoy Nassau until she patched the rift.

**

At the city-county police compound, Eldred, a.k.a. Slurp, Smith was being out-processed and awaiting his personal effects before release. The circuit court judge had ordered him released on insufficient evidence. Slurp's story of how he came to possess the Random Ranger spent bullets was believable to the judge who told Slaughter and the district attorney they needed considerably more evidence than last being seen with Duval. The judge did warn Slurp that he was a suspect and not to leave the area without notifying the police.

Meanwhile downstairs on floor four, Withers and Slaughter had a new fish on the line.

**

"You don't know? You don't seem know very much at all, do you, Mr. Thatcher?" Slaughter badgered the F.B.I. agent. "You have no explanation, whatsoever, how your fingerprints got on this espionage device in Doctor Sweetbread's yard."

"No, I do not. Perhaps the police planted it there," Thane flipped.

"You think maybe your fingerprints are just floating around in the air? See this fireplace poker? Do you recognize it?" Slaughter picked up the murder weapon. Hatcher remained calm.

"Don't believe I do."

"One of your floating fingerprints is right here on the neck. Time you answered some questions, you smart-ass little prick. The last thing we do around here is serve up the press with a cop indictment, but you are about one inch from front page news," Slaughter moved his ruddy maroon face into Thane's, spraying him with the wet vapors of his accusations.

"This is bullshit. You guys are trying to frame me. I don't believe a word of it. The bad press is for dirty cops who plant evidence and get caught. Sorry, boys."

"Book him. I've got a whole team of investigators who will vouch for the legitimacy of that wire and those prints." Slaughter walked out of the room and Withers remained.

"Thatcher, I don't know what you were doing at Sweetbread's house, but he ended up dead from that fireplace poker. I don't know if you whacked him, or handed it to whoever did whack him. My point is this: that's water over the dam. You're not a bad guy, but you're not a squeaky clean guy either. Nobody is. Are you hearing me? Before this bad blood gets ugly between the agency and the I.P.D., I'm going to make you an offer. You end your investigations, get out of town, and this little problem of yours won't be a problem anymore. Comprende?"

"But I'm totally innocent," Thane lied without the slightest quiver of his voice.

"So are all your new pals. Welcome to jail. You've got 48 hours until you're meat for the D.A. Take my advice. Walk away, Thane."

Withers motioned to the uniformed cop on the corner chair who produced the mandatory handcuffs. Hatcher was escorted down the hall into the elevator and up to the fifth floor. The book and release desks shared waiting benches. Slurp was waiting for his wallet, keys, and assorted personal effects. The officer signaled Thane to sit down on the bench.

"I didn't do anything," Thane said before Slurp could ask.

"You don't have to tell me, honey. They'd fuckin' lock up Mother Teresa in this Nazi compound."

"Slurp, do me a favor. Tell Maddy I'm here. They won't let me call her, so give her this message. Chase down the Bahamas lead without me. The man wants to deal. He's too anxious to get us out of town. Hound him."

"She's gonna know what that shit means?" Thane nodded and Slurp continued, "You two tight, huh?"

"Not yet."

"All right!"

**

Maddy clutched the steering wheel with one hand and applied a small amount of lipstick and mascara with the other. She combed her hair. The good night sleep had given her the energy to primp today. She rolled up the window to protect her hair and turned on the air conditioning. It was only 72 degrees, but she didn't want to sweat.

The morning news featured the upcoming introductory soiree for Byron Davis, former chief financial officer of EnvironTech, who had been appointed as Representative to fill the vacancy of the late, though still warm in the grave, Congressman Burr. William Corless, C.E.O., wanted "the people of Indianapolis and Indiana to meet their new representative who shared the Hoosier values of family, gun ownership, and the generation of good jobs through partnership with industry."

Corless had paid dearly in campaign contributions, and the Republicans of power acquiesced. They cared little about Davis, only whether he would be electable in sixteen months. Corless's promise to double the soft money influx quashed those doubts.

All registered voters in the congressional district were invited to the office headquarters of EnvironTech Saturday next. Shuttle buses would run continuously from the parking lots at the Keystone corporate center several miles away. Music, food, and drinks were compliments of Mr. Corless. A short address by Mr. Davis would be broadcast to the receiving line crowd.

**

The flashing lights and *wahow, wahow, wahow* of the trailing squad car immediately ruined her tranquil ride. Maddy glanced at her speedometer. She was well within the limit. The "Oh, brother" gut swelling pain returned with the sight of Officer Maconi strutting up to her open window. "Come on, I didn't do anything." Maddy opened.

"You're looking good today, Dr. Gray."

"Does that qualify as probable cause?"

"We serve and protect. It's written on the side of the car. Maddy, you mind if I call you Maddy? We got off on a bad start. I would like to make it up to you. Have any dinner plans this weekend?"

"As a matter of fact I'm going out of town. You know, I really don't care much for cops who have arrested me, particularly on bogus charges. You can take it personally. Is it legal to use the squad car to stop somebody to ask them out?"

"That was a second thought. I wanted you to know something. Your buddy, Thane Hatcher, has been booked for suspicion of murder. They got his prints on a fire-poker and on a wire device they found in Sweetbread's yard. But if he agrees to pull out of town, I think they'll drop it. Professional courtesy. We try to keep the pigs out of the mud. The boys asked if I'd use our close friendship to urge you to convince him to head back to Washington, before he gets a hollow-point tattoo."

Maconi looked closely into her eyes. He saw in her startled face, a mixture of confusion and understanding at his meaning. His mission was accomplished well enough for her to relay the threat to Hatcher.

"Maybe you'll be hungry when you get back into town. Really, no hard feelings." Maconi tipped his hat and walked away.

"It's only Tuesday, what are you doing in a squad car?" Maddy poked her head out the window and asked in earnest.

"I've been such a good boy, they gave me my beat back."

**

Maddy noticed four more June bugs. The brown scarabs had attached themselves to the front door at County Hospital. Their velvety backs glistened in the sun. Maddy speculated that the dull color made them more difficult for birds to see as the beetles feasted on the early summer

221

fruits. In the Mediterranean the June creatures arrive in May and are known as fig eaters.

She flashed back to her earlier moment of beetle execution and experienced a rush of paranoia. Was she a wanted serial killer from the beetle world? She telepathically attempted to assure the four insects that they weren't annoying her; and she had no animosity toward them, nor any intention to harm them. She scratched herself as she passed through the door.

Richard was in an exceptionally good mood. Slurp had called to announce he was free and would be back to work later in the morning. First Slurp needed to stop home and change clothes.

One nursing home Alzheimer's patient was in the morgue. Routinely this death was a direct release to the funeral home after officially notifying the coroner's office. Apparently the family thought the nursing home had neglected the woman or worse, actively participated in euthanasia. Richard shook his head and said he would call the coroner and the nursing home to try to get out of an autopsy.

"The daughter probably hasn't seen her mother in fifteen years, then stuffs her away into a gray-head closet to die. Her unconscious guilt gets projected onto the nursing home. 'They can't do anything right. They're actively killing my mother. They're murderers.' I hate these cases. The old lady got taken care of just fine. Why should we have to bust our butts doing her autopsy to cover the butts of the nursing home staff because of some bitch ass crazy daughter?"

"Who decides if we need to do it?" Maddy hadn't thought through this question before.

"The coroner has the ultimate legal say. If we had a medical examiner's system, Dr. O'Dell could make the call, but Indiana has the good-old-boy coroner system, which means we follow whatever some politician decides. If there's a question, he usually says, "Post 'em." Richard ranted.

"Are there many states with the coroner system?" Maddy inquired.

"Maybe ten, I don't know, all the ones with high rates of intra-family marriage."

"So, does Dr. O'Dell always say no?"

"Doctor O'Dell chooses his battles well. Bottom line, you and Mordecai might as well get started. But I'll try again."

**

Maddy excused herself to telephone the police department. "No calls to prisoners. You can leave Mr. Hatcher a note at the front desk. Have a good day," responded the uniformed agent of service and protection.

Perhaps she should have been nicer to Maconi. It may have facilitated her communication with Hatcher, she wondered, as she returned to the morgue.

"I heard about Slurp and the bullet..." Maddy was cut off. She and Richard turned sharply.

"Possession ain't the same as use. And I'm glad to see you, too," said the breathless Slurp as he entered the morgue.

"I know that you didn't kill anybody."

223

"Well thank you, Precious, I'll take that as a vote of confidence. But I wouldn't presume anything about anybody. I got some bad news. Thane Hatcher…"

"Got booked for suspicion in the Sweetbread case," Maddy completed Slurp's sentence this time.

"He was going in while I was coming out. He gave me a message for you. Something about the man wants to deal so you need to go to the Bahamas without him. All that college education and that boy can't make a coherent sentence. Now don't kill the messenger, but that's exactly what he said."

"I got it Slurp, thanks," said Maddy.

**

She knocked lightly on the door to the office of Graham O'Dell. No one was there. She noticed the golf trophies covered with a thin layer of dust. There was a picture of his daughter with her college sorority sisters next to another picture of his estranged wife who was selling flowers at their daughter's stall in Seattle's city market. Two tiny Vietnamese women were assembling arrangements of cut flowers behind her. Mother and daughter were hugging. Maddy scratched a note asking to meet with him, then returned to the morgue.

Richard had the body diagram completed. The woman had a cholecystectomy scar from her gall bladder removal, which merged with a pink scar over her chest from her second coronary artery bypass operation. The hair was thin and silver gray and bristled straight up like the white, fuzzy top of a dandelion in seed.

"Ever seen an Alzheimer's brain, Dr. Gray?" Percival asked.

"Only in jars and study sets." Maddy confided.

"Good, at least we can use the excuse of education to justify some benefit to this waste of taxpayer money."

That comment provoked a return of today's guilt. While she was mildly annoyed at performing an autopsy with little to no perceived value, she felt profoundly guilty as a co-conspirator with the morgue staff in disrespectfully deriding the life of this human being.

Her guilt receded as Maddy focused on cutting and tearing the adhesions of the pericardium from the chest wall and heart. The two prior heart operations had left a tangle of scar tissue bands encasing the heart. Four of the five grafted vessels from the aorta to the heart had clotted off and closed. Maddy estimated the blood flow to the heart had been barely enough to sustain the woman's bed-ridden state. Doubtless her minimal brain perfusion had worsened her dementia.

Dr. Mordecai had been right that the autopsy would generate little of professional interest. The enlarged fibrotic heart, encased in scar from previous surgeries and heart attacks might have interested the novice medical student, but not a journeyman pathologist. The normal lungs, guts, pancreas and spleen offered nothing. The liver and kidneys showed the withering degenerative effects of atherosclerotic heart disease and would be noted in the final report.

"Well, what do you see?" Mordecai asked in his most Socratic voice as he lifted the brain out of the organ scale. "Eleven-hundred grams, small even for a woman this size."

"Gyri are thin and the sulci a little wide, I guess," Maddy offered cautiously as she ran her fingers over the folds of the brain surfaces.

"Yes, but where? All over? Frontal tips?" Mordecai persisted.

"All over?"

"Not quite, I'd say spotty here in the right frontal cortex, but more so over the temporal and parietal lobes."

Mordecai cut the brain into delicate six to eight millimeter sections and laid them out in sequence. He drew her attention to small cystic fluid collections in the white matter. He pointed with the tip of his scalpel to surface cortical areas of gray scarring "These cystic areas are lacunar infarcts and the cortical lesions also look like ischemic injuries. That makes sense with her history of multiple heart attacks. She was demented all right, but from vascular disease." Mordecai was beaming with pedantic hubris. He stopped and gathered his thoughts.

"But there's no social good that comes from signing this case out as multi-infarct-dementia. You see, the family has been told she has Alzheimer's Disease, technically incorrect. But that diagnosis is well known. It is more prestigious and socially acceptable to go out like Ronald Reagan. If we correct the diagnosis too harshly, the family is confused. They accuse their doctor of being a quack. They convince themselves that their matriarch could have been saved. Then, they may even sue the family doctor."

Maddy, oblivious, asked, "So how do we handle this case?"

"With a delicate balance of professional integrity and political panache. First we wait until we've looked at the brain slides. The sine-qua-non for Alzheimer's is a high density of neuro-fibillary plaques and tangles. Fortunately, all old senile folks have a few. So we can sign out the case as: Clinical Alzheimer's-like dementia with mixed degenerative changes including neuritic plaques. The family and the doctor are happy.

In the body of the report, however, which no one ever reads, is a clear description of multi-infarct-dementia along with the normal concentration of senile plaques. Our pathology conscious is appeased. Who says pathologists don't have a heart?"

Richard was paying close attention and commented to Maddy, "Don't let him fool you. Rumor has it, he is a living heart donor."

Maddy looked at Mordecai, amazed to feel the humanitarian side of his otherwise scary creepiness. True, it was based on professional compassion for the family doctor, but also served the family. She overcame her difficulty believing it, by reminding herself that people are complex and rarely one sided. Maybe Mordecai was more human than she gave him credit.

"Richard is correct. I'm not that nice. The last time I had a similar case, the family kept calling and wanted me testify to the licensing board that their family physician was incompetent. I had the mayor's office on my back and even Sweetbread was threatening me with dismissal from the program. Why? Because half the physicians and nearly all the public doesn't have a clue about dementia. One must learn the danger of being accurate."

**

"I'm going to take a few days off. A quick trip to the Bahamas has come up, all expenses paid. I can't turn it down."

"No problem," Graham smiled and paused watching her. He would not pry, but sensed she needed to say more.

"Actually there's a lot of stuff going on around here. I was going to Nassau with Thane Hatcher to follow Withers. Thane discovered that Withers takes multiple trips to Nassau, the latest on the night of the last Random Ranger killing. You told me that yourself. Well, Thane is convinced that Withers is important. More so now that the cops are holding him in lockup. Withers is pressuring him to give up the investigation and go back to Washington."

"Aren't you a little frightened to go chasing him around the Caribbean?" O'Dell offered.

"It's in the Atlantic, I'm told, which reminds me, I need to call somebody. But Thane may be on to something. Maconi stopped me yesterday and said if we didn't want hollow-point tattoos to get Hatcher off the case. What does that mean? That guy's an idiot."

"He said those words?" Graham's eyes grew wide and serious.

"Hollow-point tattoo? What's that, a dull needle? He's going to hold me down and tattoo across my forehead, 'I will not investigate the cops'?"

"He's talking about a bullet. The cops here use 9 mm hollow-point non-jacketed copper bullets."

"What's the hollow-point?" Maddy was still confused.

"Basic ballistics. The police like ammunition that stops a single suspect. The hollow-point bullets go faster for the same charge of gunpowder because they are lighter. More importantly the hollow point bullets deform easily when they hit. This causes quick damage to the person struck, but the deformed bullets are less likely to travel through the person and injure someone else."

"What about the non-packeted part?" Maddy asked.

"Jacketed. Some bullets have a thin metal sheath around the bullet to alter the flight or velocity characteristics. The police rarely shoot over thirty feet so they don't need fancy flying bullets. The jacket fragments are also a little messier, so the local police have chosen to avoid them."

"Maconi is just trying to scare me, right?"

"He's a loose canon. You and Hatcher better watch yourselves in Nassau."

"He's locked up, remember? I'm on my own."

"I don't think you should risk it." Graham's forcefulness frightened her and surprised him. The two locked their eyes.

"I have to go."

"You can't go alone."

"I will and I am!"

"Then I'll go with you."

Neither asked if the other was serious. They each assumed the other would give up the idea. Maddy spent the next few seconds deciding it would be safer to have a companion, particularly Graham. Graham anticipated a refusal. His bluff was called.

Maddy gave Graham the itinerary and said she'd change Thatcher's reservation to his name. They would leave Thursday morning two hours before Withers. She told Graham to bring sunglasses or other cover-ups to assist their trailing of Withers. Hatcher had reserved two rooms at a hotel, also charged to his F.B.I. account.

**

JUNE 13, WEDNESDAY, The Ides of June

Tasmin was crying a mournful whine at seven a.m. Thunder and lightening abruptly awoke Maddy. Tasmin jumped onto the bed as soon as Maddy's movements conveyed wakefulness. The cat snuggled across her chest for comfort.

"It just a thunderstorm, Tasmin. You're OK." Maddy stroked the cat rhythmically until she began to purr. Maddy did not mind the occasional demand for comfort. Overall, Tasmin was low maintenance, but she was impatient and relentless when she wanted something.

The radio alarm came on. Les Bull gave the price quotes on cattle and hog bellies. Next he read the local news, which to her delight included no murders, accidents or significant tragedies. Maddy felt a surge of energy that seeped into her from the sound of the pelting raindrops outside. She made up her bed, an activity she usually reserved for weekends only. She changed Tasmin's litter box. She watered her two flowerless African violet plants, which were dry and sorely neglected. Maddy wondered if the plants felt tortured, listening to the rain.

After locking her door, she walked out to the street. A water-soaked paper was tucked under the driver-side wiper-blade. Her immediate response was cop hatred for another parking ticket. She noticed her front tires were at the yellow line and her bumper two feet into the restricted zone. She picked up the paper. It was an anonymous note. "Watch out, I've gotten tickets before when I was barely over the yellow line." The note was signed with a simple happy face.

Maddy felt a moment of hope for the world. Then she recognized the handwriting from previous tickets. She looked around for Maconi's squad car. He was watching her every move.

Maddy drove cautiously toward the medical center. She dialed the morgue number on her cell phone and smiled when a familiar voice answered, "Hello, Smith and West's Sons at your service."

"Practicing for the funeral home, Slurp? What's for breakfast?"

"Cold black coffee, Precious. The refrigerator is cold and dark because it ain't been opened all night."

"Good, I'll be in about noon. I've got a few errands to run."

**

Maddy entered the dermatology clinic. She gave a Hershey bar to the office secretary and asked her, "Please give this note and candy to Mina."

The secretary returned several minutes later with a folded note which read, "Come on back, you bitch."

Maddy hugged Mina. Mina introduced Maddy to a young pimply-faced girl of fourteen. Alicia, this is Dr. Gray, a friend of mine. Dr. Gray, this is Alicia. She's been struggling with a little acne problem for the last two years. What do you think?"

"I think you're very lucky to be pretty. Don't worry about the blemishes or anything else from the teenage years. It all gets better with age. I had my share. So did Dr. Mina. Trust me."

"Are you two sisters?" asked Alicia innocently.

"We could pass, couldn't we. Maddy's right, Alicia, your skin will clear up with time. For now, keep up the soap and nightly cream cleansings. We'll see you next month." Alicia smiled.

Maddy returned the smile as the girl left.

"You're a natural. That pretty line was just what she needed to hear."

"She was cute."

"It's not too late to get back into clinical medicine. Why did you go into pathology anyway?" Mina was thinking out loud more than having a definite conversation.

"I like the brutal honesty of organs, tissue, cancers. I couldn't sweet talk patients all day. Dermatology is interesting, but one Alicia is about my limit. Look at how many Hershey bars I go through with you."

"I'm the one who needs to apologize. I have no business being petty jealous over Thane Hatcher. You know how I get after a couple of drinks. Bahamas Mamas no less. Forgive me?"

"You already got the chocolate, slut!"

"Bitch!"

"Thane's being held at the police station, and obviously not going to the Bahamas."

"You said you aren't going to sleep with him, I believe you now."

"I do need a favor. Can you take me to the airport tomorrow and pick me up on Sunday?"

"I'd be glad to, but my car's in the shop for a couple of days."

"I'll pick you up and you can use my car."

"Sure, what time?"

"5:30."

"In the morning? Never."

"Just set the alarm, and try something new."

"Like what?" Mina took the bait.

"Like sleeping alone in your own bed."

"Ooww, good one."

**

The drizzle continued all morning. Maddy arrived at the shopping mall, passing the Kroger and remembering her meeting with Thane on Sweetbread's last evening. She felt guilty that Thane was in lockup for all his trouble, meanwhile she is buying a new swimsuit for Nassau. Plus, his company was paying for her trip. She bargained down her guilt by reminding herself that this was criminal research, not a frivolous junket. Plus, the company's money was tax payments.

She tried on a one-piece with shimmering swirls of lavender, silver, and light blue. The designer had captured the effect of waves breaking. Maddy loved it. It made her feel young and womanly, a feeling easily lost in the years of medical training.

She was beaming with the glow of a successful shopping trip when she entered the morgue. Days without autopsies were ghost town events in the dissection room. The stainless steel tables and scales and counters were antiseptic and dead quiet. The lights were off. Dim sunrays diffused through the translucent glass block windows revealing a faint dust in the air. The humming refrigerators sounded like cicadas, busy lowering the closed morgue temperature to sixty-four degrees.

As Maddy walked through the room, the noise of her hard plastic heels was amplified and resounded by the metal surfaces. This was life: the moments between death and work when the senses are acutely tuned to the timelessness of the present. The moments when plans and agendas fail to intrude.

Slurp peeked into the room. "Well good afternoon, Precious. You are looking good. Mordecai left you the brain slides from yesterday. Said you could finish that case. Nothing else going on. A beautiful rainy day. Doesn't get any better."

"Thanks, Slurp. Was the police station really awful? They've got Thane up there now."

"I figure all cops aren't bad. It's just so hard to find a decent one. Other than Carl, I wouldn't trust any of them. The trouble is they can shoot you, lock you up, fuck-up your life in court, and you can't do anything about it. But a cop can drive anywhere at ninety miles an hours, get drunk, or shake down a donut shop for freebies with never a fear."

"They can't all be that bad, can they?"

"They're all humans. You know anybody who doesn't have a worm hole in his apple or gray stains in their undershorts?"

"Hey, don't make Gray sound like a bad word. My daddy will get you."

"Sorry, Precious."

"Tell me, Slurp. How did you get that Random Ranger bullet?"

"I don't really remember the exact details. But there was a plastic bag in the morgue that I found while cleaning up after one of the drive by shootings. I kept it in my locker for a month. I figured the cops would start asking about it.

After that I just took it home as a souvenir. The cops fuck up just like the rest of us. When Slaughter was interrogating me, I saw his eyes get real wide when I told that story. I knew I was free. He didn't want the press to get a hold of a bungled bullet story."

"Are you sure that Withers is a good guy? Thane thinks otherwise."

"Precious, like I said, when it comes to the shame wardrobe, we all got walk-in closets. Carl takes good care of his sister and nephew, and he's always done right by me. Leave him alone."

"You got any idea why he takes a lot of trips to Nassau?"

"I know he's got business that don't involve me. It sure can't involve you."

"Do you know it's the ides of June today?"

"I thought the ides was in March, the day Julius Caesar was killed. I've been to Shakespeare, you know," Slurp beamed in cultural pride.

"The Romans had beliefs about everything. The ides were near the middle of the month, sometimes the 15th day like the ides of March. Other months, for example June, it's on the thirteenth. Spooky things might happen. The Romans were also spooked by the nones. Those were the ninth days before the ides. Does it seem like a special day to you?"

Slurp looked at her like and pantomimed a screwdriver loosening screws from her head. "I learned that stuff in Latin class. It's raining today. I know you like rain," Maddy pleaded as Slurp left the morgue. He was circling his forefinger around his left ear. It didn't matter. She had a special sensual awareness today.

She stopped at her desk to gather her notes for the trip. She picked up the tray of autopsy slides from the dementia lady. She immediately noticed the small lakes or lacunae of fluid in the white matter of the brain. Her intense clarity made the brain slide neurons appear three-dimensional. She dictated the nature of the old heart disease and the associated chronic congestion of the liver and spleen.

The silver stains showed a few neuro-fibrillary tangles in the temporal lobes. She dictated the density at two or three per high power field, half of what was seen in true Alzheimer's disease. Dr. Mordecai was right, as usual. The dementia was vascular, not the intrinsic degeneration of true Alzheimer's.

The astute pathologist would deduce from the final autopsy report the exact nature of the dementia. Was this deception, diplomacy, or kindness? Only on television were moral issues straightforward. This was real life where nothing passes without the contamination of special interest.

Maddy completed the report and packaged the dictation tape and folder for the secretary. She noticed the x-ray of the head of Michael Johnson. The small sheet of metal adjacent his maxilla loomed out of the picture like Mona Lisa's eyes.

"I'll be on vacation until Tuesday," Maddy informed Debra.

"You too? Dr. O'Dell and Slurp are taking personal days. It's going to be quiet here this weekend. Where are you going, Dr. Gray?"

"Down south to visit a friend."

"A man friend?"

"Yes, a man."

"I want all the juicy details when you get back."

"Would a nice girl kiss and tell?"

"It's twice as romantic, after you share it with another girl."

Maddy smiled. "I'll get back to you on that one."

**

JUNE 14, THURSDAY, New Providence

Maddy's alarm jolted her sleepy brain like an earthquake. After several seconds of bewilderment to determine why it would go off at 4:30, she jumped into the shower. Tasmin was equally annoyed, climbed onto Maddy's bed, and lay on her pillow in protest. Maddy dressed in flamingo pink shorts with matching pink and banana print top. She poured five days of dry cat food into Tasmin's bowl. The cat jumped to the floor sniffed the huge bowl, and then snubbed it with a disgusted hop into the litter box.

Maddy got her largest two bowls from the kitchen and filled them with water. Her packed suitcase was closed upon her dresser. She opened it once more and added a black silk thin strapped nightgown. "Just in case," she whispered out loud.

Mina answered the doorbell on the third ring, dragging a resistant brush through her long brown hair. Maddy had envied its thickness. The people who asked if Mina and Maddy were sisters had over-looked the body and curl of Mina's thick mane compared to Maddy's fine straight-down locks. In comparison, Mina envied Maddy's curves, wondering why someone would want thick hair.

"My apartment key is the gold one next to the car key. Check on Tasmin," said Maddy as she handed her luggage to the curbside attendant. It was 5:55 and the sun was just peaking above the horizon. A few small dark clouds of the previous day's rain lingered low in the eastern sky. The air had the incredibly clarity that lasts less than one day after a rainstorm.

Graham O'Dell sat patiently at the gate reading the morning newspaper and sipping a gourmet coffee from a double walled cup. Maddy noticed him first. He wore long gray slacks and a short-sleeve collarless shirt. She had often seen him in golf shirts, which exacerbated his slight middle aged paunch. This morning he looked soft and quiet. Maddy realized that her planned restraint of foolishness would be difficult. She was determined to enjoy the island and ignore her attraction to O'Dell.

"Graham, I really appreciate your coming along."

"Promise me you'll stay close. We can't be too careful. We don't know what we'll find down there."

"Somehow I can't believe you'd go all the way to Nassau just to be my bodyguard. Why are you really on this plane?"

"Things are getting a little crazy lately. Besides, helping the residents is my job."

**

The captain announced that the final descent into the island of New Providence would take them over several uninhabited coral islands to the northwest and then into airport at the south central part of the island. Maddy awed at the small islands rimmed with the aquamarine shallows extending a half-mile into the water. The western end of New Providence, a collection of wealthy homes and boat docks, slipped under the plane seconds before touchdown.

The glaring noon sun made the humid air more uncomfortable. The two deplaned and leisurely walked the jetway towards customs. The long empty jetway had piped in steel drum music and bright orange carpet. Upon reaching the main terminal and customs clearance, they re-entered air-conditioning. The customs agent stamped their passports after several unenthusiastic questions.

"What is your business in da Bahamas?" the agent asked in slow deep English.

The two glanced at each other. Maddy answered, "Business" at the same time as Graham answered, "Vacation."

"A little fun wid your business, hey mum?" commented the agent who had no genuine interest why they had come to the island. He was offering them a satisfactory and shameless answer. He motioned Maddy and Graham along as the agent handed back their passports. Maddy was in a place where obtaining information would be difficult.

At the baggage claim she experienced the local economy. Men from eighteen to seventy lounged on luggage trolleys inviting each passerby to engage their services of luggage transport. Graham selected the oldest man and clearly instructed him to hold their two suitcases until he returned with his rental car. He made an immediate first installation of ten dollars, which quadrupled the Bahamian's pace.

At the Hertz rental car office they learned the largest car ever available was a sub-compact Toyota Corolla, despite Thane's reservation of a full sized sedan. They waited for the rental car outside the terminal near their bags and the luggage clerk. The Bahamian clerk had little to say except it was hot and the island needed rain. There was a cold front due in a day or two, which the island people hoped would bring rain.

Graham filled the wait by sharing a history of the island. He explained that Europeans colonized the West Indies. The Bahamas are islands to the northeast in the Atlantic Gulfstream. The western and southern islands are true Caribbean. The original Carib Indians were annihilated, as they proved easier to exterminate than to enslave, a genocidal success story.

Slaves were imported into the West Indies from Africa to work the rum and tobacco plantations. Sugar cane fields were suited for growth on the lush volcanic islands. Flat coral islands like New Providence were used for shipping, rum mill production, and as military outposts. New Providence's main colonial power was the British. British style colonial mansions, hotels and gatehouses still line downtown Nassau.

There were two advantages to being a British colony. First, the British, like the Dutch, were early in their abolition of slavery in 1838. Colorful dancers similar to Mardis Gras celebrate the festival of the first freedom called Junkanoo. Historically, slaves, called John Canoes, dressed in African dance costumes danced the cultural and heritage ties to Africa. In the deep-throated English of the African descendants, the dancers became known as Junkanoos. Tourists enjoy the celebrations daily, although officially there are two days for celebrating Junakanoo: Boxing Day and New Years.

Secondly the British favored education and institutional governance to guns. As a result of public education the current Bahamians are more articulate and employable than the slavery descendants of other islands in the West Indies.

Maddy and Graham agreed on their plans of espionage, waiting quietly in the rental car. Withers's plane arrived on schedule at 12:40. At 1:20 he exited the airport door to the street. When they recognized his face, Graham and Maddy hid behind sunglasses and large brimmed hats. She started the Toyota's engine. Withers had only a carry-on bag. He wore business casual gray slacks and a short sleeve sport shirt. Absent the tie, he was dressed for any day of routine investigation. He boarded a cab and headed toward downtown Nassau.

Maddy pulled out sharply into the right lane of traffic. Several honks and raised fists later, she was back into the proper left lane. O'Dell clenched the safety handle over the right doorframe. "Maybe I should drive," he offered, after Maddy stopped abruptly at the first roundabout.

The Bahamian cab behind her skidded to a stop less than one foot behind the Toyota. The horn blared. Maddy stuck her head out the window and smiled. She waved the cabby ahead, almost losing her hat as the taxi sped around her.

"I'm afraid we've lost him."

"No, Maddy, we haven't. There's only one road to town. Speed up a little and we'll catch them. The license plate number was N-37."

After four miles Maddy and Graham crossed the center of the island and emerged along the north shore. Heading east Maddy was on the left side along the ocean. The narrow two-lane road with constant curves was made more dangerous by the distraction of white surf capping

241

aquamarine waves breaking over juts of coral. Sixty-foot tall Causarina pines bordering the highway provided near continuous shade along the oceanfront road.

As they approached town the road widened to a divided four-lane highway. "Dual Carriageway," Maddy read a sign, "Isn't that cute?"

Withers's cab was in the right-hand lane. Graham and Maddy approached close enough to verify the license number, then eased back. The cab looped through the colonial buildings of downtown and dropped Withers at the British Colonial Hotel.

The grand old building, a mixture of Spanish and British architecture proudly displayed tall columns in front with abundant white paint, brass fixtures, and tile floors. Maddy double-parked on the street. She watched Graham enter the ornate front door held open by the white uniformed guesthouse doorman. Graham returned in two minutes.

Withers had checked in, opened his door, left off his bag and returned immediately through the front door. Graham hurried to Maddy's window and instructed her to find a parking space and try to catch up. Withers was nearly two blocks east on Bay Street. Graham broke into a jog. The streets were filled with afternoon shoppers toting bags of perfume and straw goods, which made visual contact with Withers nearly impossible.

Graham slowed to a walk and breathed heavily as Withers turned into the Royal Swiss Commercial Trust. Graham approached the door cautiously to avoid recognition. The street level floor was a typical bank lobby. Along one wall were six tellers in cages with steel bars surrounding small transaction windows. Two large tables with several leather chairs for customers were arranged opposite the tellers. Young bored clerks who appeared desperate for work sat behind the desks. A huge steel vault and safe deposit boxes composed the back wall. Withers was not seen.

Graham entered the front atrium and noticed a stairway to the upper floor. On the wall of the first stair landing was a white rimmed box directory with black felt background and white plastic letters. The second floor listings included several solicitors, two trust agencies, and Galaxy Care Insurance Administrators.

He treaded softly on the marble staircase. The dark wood doors had lettering on the windowed upper half. Withers back could be seen passing through the glass of Galaxy Care. The office consisted of two rooms, two desks, and several large filing cabinets.

A man in a Hawaiian shirt, smoking a cigar, handed Withers a box of bonded copy paper clearly labeled in large print, which Graham could identify through the glass. The man lifted an identical second box, also 18x12x10 inches and labeled "Universal White Bond Paper 500 Sheets." As soon as the two turned toward the door, Graham ducked his head and sprinted to the staircase, descended two steps at a time, and bolted out the front door into the tourist flow.

A young and beautiful female stern sailed past. It instantly yanked his male attention like a junkyard magnet. The flamingo and banana outfit was unmistakable. He raced ahead, gently snuggled her shoulder and pulled her into the doorway at Gucci's. "Maddy, Withers is coming out of the Royal Swiss Trust, four buildings back. Turn slowly and don't stare."

They watched as cab N-37 arrived and pulled over from its orbiting of the block. The two men wriggled into the back with boxes in lap. Maddy and Graham walked briskly in the direction of the cab.

"You get the car, and I'll chase as long as I can."

"Graham, I'll never find you." She ran along side him.

"Traffic is slow downtown; and the city is only a mile wide. Trust me."

"I'm staying with you." She did.

The cab turned one block north to Woodes Rogers Walk along the north shore. The pair ran the short block north just closely enough to see the cab turn right. They stopped and gave up at the corner. The street ran alongside the ocean marking the end of the Nassau city markets.

"There!" Maddy pointed to the cab, which was parked and idling on the ramp to the marina of Prince George's Wharf.

The two men carried their boxes to the near side of the pier where a thirty-foot steel fishing charter was moored. The paper boxes were lowered into the rear fish hold and a padlock secured. Maddy and Graham watched as Withers and the insurance agent returned to the cab. On the far side of the pier passengers from a cruise ship were disembarking. The cab was stuck in a long line of pedestrian tourists.

The fishing charter started its loud dual engines and announced its departure with a growl from its foghorn. Maddy turned about, searching the tourists and shops. The George's Port Tourist Shop was behind her. She ran inside, grabbed a set of binoculars, and returned to the street. The protesting shop owner chased her outside as she read out loud the inscription on the aft of the fishing boat. "Lady Coral, Stuart's Cove, New Providence."

"Thank you, these work fine. I'll take them," Maddy smiled to the shop owner and handed him a credit card.

Maddy and Graham looked at each other and realized they were steamy and covered with sweat. The afternoon June sun had heated the air to 95 degrees. The sidewalk at foot level was 100. "Time for a beer?"

"Not yet. Come on." Graham hurried back up the block and toward the bank and panted as he jogged. "We might have five minutes to get into the Galaxy office. I'll watch from the front landing. See what you can find out."

The cruise ship patrons were oblivious to Withers's taxi. The "no problem, mon" attitude of the cabby was helped by the running meter. Graham and Maddy hurried back to the Galaxy Care office.

The men had left the door unlocked. Maddy noticed there was no telephone. The drawers of the front desk were empty. The second desk had paper, pencils, two decks of playing cards, and paper trimming equipment. The filing cabinets were empty except for the bottom drawer of the largest. Inside the drawer was a fifteen by ten-inch lock box. There were several dozen large envelopes, all of which had one of two addresses: EnvironTech or UPSinc, both of Indianapolis, Indiana. Maddy opened the top two envelopes and each held a stack of hospital bills with patients' names, services, and hospital charges. A cigar box contained fresh stamps of Bahamian issue. A metal wastebasket alongside the desk was empty. Maddy closed the door and whispered to Graham. "Galaxy doesn't do much business except with EnvironTech and UPSinc."

"That could be legitimate. I don't see anything suspicious."

"OK, let's get out of here."

"Good idea."

"Ready for that beer?"

"I know a nice bar next to Stuart's Cove."

"You know everything about this island?"

"I've been to a lot of places. Almost everywhere with golf courses. I'm old, Maddy. Haven't you noticed?"

"They say you're only as old as you feel."

"I can't be that old."

"Are you going to buy me that beer?"

**

They took the same West Bay Street out of town. Graham drove this time, which allowed Maddy to enjoy the ocean view. Maddy watched the afternoon waves spray over the coral rocks. Bahamian natives waded in the surf beside their naked black toddlers who splashed at the junction of foam and sand. Twenty-five minutes from town, Graham turned left into a hillside parking lot.

Across the street from the car park was the Compass Point, a small village of clapboard cottages painted in the Bahamian Junkanoo festival colors of bright pink, blue, yellow, green, and peach. Each separate building had a small wood-railed porch and shuttered windows.

"This is it. Mr. Thatcher obviously knew what he was doing. Out of the way, but first class." Graham escorted her into the restaurant building, which included the hotel front desk.

"A two-bedroom reservation? Is this correct, sir?" inquired the tall thin Bahamian gentleman in a starched white long sleeve shirt. Graham nodded.

They walked past sixteen single-room cottages, each unique with a differing roof color and architectural rearrangements. Two double-bedroom cottages sat behind the gazebo perched above a pier on pilings. The gazebo overlooked the pool to the east and was designed for a westward elevated viewing of the sunset. Maddy and Graham carried in their carry-on bags as the late afternoon service team was attending to their dinner-hour duties in the restaurant. Graham insisted on the upper room, so that Maddy would have easier access to the downstairs bathroom.

"Cocktail hour?"

"Yes, but not here. We've got about an hour of daylight to check out the Lady Coral. Come on, it's only fifteen or twenty minutes away."

"Are you always this much fun?"

"Much worse, if you consult my wife."

Reluctantly Maddy got back in the car for the ten-mile drive to South Ocean. The farther southwest they drove, the more deserted the landscape became. Island brush bushes were interrupted by a few houses and the dirty commercial enterprises of the Bahamian Beer Brewery, the oil burning electricity plant, and Clifton Pier where oil and gas tankers unloaded the petroleum stock for the island's energy consumption. The oceanfront road was littered with American-manufactured and Bahamian-deposited food and beverage wrappings. One isolated hotel, South Ocean, occupied a strip of pristine beach.

The half-hour drive into Nassau along with its isolated location explained South Ocean Hotel's string of revolving-door bankruptcy ownership. Half the time the hotel was operated by the likes of Marriott or Ramada. The other side of the door was receivership by the Bahamian Commonwealth until a new manager was found. Inadequate revenue from low occupancy meant poor maintenance and staff, which in turn attracted fewer future guests. Only the unemployment prevention program of the government kept the operation limping along.

Stuart's Cove was adjacent the South Ocean Hotel. The private marina was one of a chain of dive operations in the Caribbean. The New Providence slip had the fame of having hosted the movie set for *Flipper*. Hollywood studios have worked happily and peacefully several times at this remote island outpost.

Maddy and Graham walked along the planked wharf. Five boats were moored: two dive ships, a wrecked wooden scull leftover from the movie set, and two fishing boats. The Lady Coral was gray-white with blistering paint. The rear fish locker was still padlocked.

"I'm interested in fishing charters. Out there, the Lady Coral, is she available?" asked Graham innocuously.

"Five hundred for a half day, eight-fifty for all day. That's eight to twelve or eight to four. Maximum five riders. Only a hundred a head for the morning if you got five. You want to make a reservation?" rattled-off the white twenty-something man behind the counter.

Clearly he didn't waste time on chitchat. This would make getting information more difficult, thought Graham. He nodded to Maddy to take over the conversation. Maddy stretched her arms out over her head to inspire the attention and loquacious reserve of the young man.

"We were hoping to go out tomorrow." Graham had to bite his lip as she flitted her eyelashes.

"It's chartered tomorrow and Saturday. How about Sunday morning? It's supposed to be nice until a front comes in on Monday." The boy caught himself staring at her chest and looked up abruptly. "The other boat, the MerryTime is just as nice. I can call the captain for the afternoon."

"Such a shame. I really like the Lady Coral. It's my color. Don't I look like coral?" She pulled at her shirt and shorts to demonstrate, but the ultimate purpose was male attention and conversation. "Is it going fishing for two full days?"

"No, it's going to be gone dawn to dusk or later on Friday. That reminds me, I have to fill up both tanks before I leave. A man from the States is taking a day trip to Andros. He comes down two or three times a year and likes the trip, I guess. No fishing gear, just plenty of gas. He's a good, I mean really good, customer. The Lady Coral captain always takes the next day off. Sometimes a full week off afterwards. The MerryTime's just as good as the Lady Coral. I even think it rides better."

"How far is it to Andros? Can that boat go that far?" Maddy smiled conveying a hopeful plea.

"Not too far, inside a hundred miles, about four hours at cruising speed if it's not too choppy."

"We won't be here next week."

Graham stepped forward. "We were really looking forward to an island hop ourselves. How about we hire the MerryTime for the day? Full tanks for cruising, maybe an hour of fishing at the most?"

"All day? You got it."

**

Graham and Maddy walked from Stuart's Cove marina next door to the poolside bar of the South Ocean hotel. While Graham procured two Bahamas Mama rum drinks, Maddy slipped off her shoes and waded in the surf. Calypso steel drum music played in the background. The blue-green cast of the water was growing darker as the sun fell toward the ocean. Graham handed her a drink. Maddy sipped with soft moans of sensuous joy. Turning toward the ocean she hurled the water a seashell.

"Copy paper boxes on a boat? Like Withers is running a floating office printing service for the yacht owners in the Caribbean? What's he smuggling? Cocaine?" Maddy asked bluntly.

"I doubt it. He's not the type."

"Cops have the best dope, right?"

"Not the type."

"What's the type for a drug dealer?"

"High flying. Pun intended. They take risks. They wear flashy clothes. They defy the law, death, and disease. And they don't care who gets killed in the process. That's not Withers. He's a quiet loner. Takes care of his sister and her kid. And…"

"So what! Importing cocaine is great way to make a living." Maddy waited for his reply. Graham was at a loss for words. "And what? You were going to say something."

"Do you think guys who carry around thirty-pound boxes of cocaine would work for cop's pay?"

"Maybe it's a front. Maybe it keeps him clean. Maybe he pays off the vice investigators. Maybe it's a perfect maintenance gig."

"Maybe."

"That's not what you were going say about Withers."

"How do you know that?"

"Female intuition. I am female." The rum had loosened her reserve just enough to be playful. She elbowed him in the mid-section and snuggled up to his arm. Graham summoned his most platonic façade and gave her a hug around the shoulders.

"You are a beautiful young lady, and I don't want anything to happen to you. Withers and the cops like Maconi don't joke about a hollow-point tattoo. We need to stay out of sight of Withers tomorrow. I don't know what we'll run into. I'm serious."

"What's Maconi got to do with Withers?"

"They're both cops. They patrolled together. It's a close society. They are family. The whole squad seemed to know about you and Hatcher and Sweetbread, didn't they?"

"What were you going to tell me about Withers?"

"That he's gay. Why do think he takes care of Slurp? Don't misinterpret. They've never had a love relationship. Withers is usually quiet and gentle. But don't get me wrong. He can be like a wild animal. Don't push him into a corner."

"So is he a nice guy or a crook?"

"There are a lot of crooks who are nice guys, and vice versa."

**

The two pathologists returned to the Compass Point. The front desk had two short lines: one for cottage check-in, one for the restaurant. A red-throated green macaw sat outside its open cage on the desk counter. "Rrrrrk, Hello, Compass Point, hold please. Rrrrrk"

"Two please. Am I OK like this?" Graham asked the maitre d' as he pointed to his casual attire.

"Certainly, sir. You're in the Bahamas. No jacket required." The deep baritone voice of the native reverberated in Maddy's head. The crisp pronunciation of the "t" in jacket evoked images of the Phil Collins album cover of the identical name. The word jacket blew in a cold chill as she imagined a Maconi non-jacketed bullet in the back. Maddy pushed the vision away.

The two sat outside on the painted concrete patio. A border of bricks was painted in blue, green, and yellow to match the shades of the cottages. The hot June air of the day was now a warm refreshing ocean breeze with a hint of mist. The ocean surf was a gentle rhythmic rumble like the nighttime breathing of a lover in deep sleep. They ordered a bottle of Pinot Grigio and a shrimp appetizer. Graham dined on the jerk steak, a rib-eye trimmed with mango chutney and spices. Maddy opted for the tomato sauce dish of Bahamian grouper.

"To Thane Hatcher and the F.B.I.," Maddy toasted as the bottle neared empty.

Graham pointed to his belly as he declined dessert. Maddy had an ice cream roll covered with a thin layer of chocolate icing and finished with fresh sliced peaches. Even the food at the Compass Point was color coordinated with the cottages. Graham excused himself to the restroom. As Maddy ate dessert a large flake of the chocolate icing stuck to her back molar. She loosened it away with her fork. As it hit her tongue she envisioned the x-ray of Michael Johnson's mouth. The flat metal triangle was like the

252

chocolate flake. On her plate was an ice-cream roll like a bullet with a jacket of black icing that separated as the center melted.

The idea arrived like a thunderstorm in the dessert, unexpected and unexplained, but bringing the fluid to germinate new seeds. The cops delivered non-jacketed, hollow-point tattoos. No jacket required on the IPD standard issue 9mm automatic bullets. Michael Johnson had a jacket-like fragment in his mouth. It was thought to be a crown casing. But it might be a bullet jacket related to the nearly identical fragment in the body of Paul Duval.

Maddy passed Graham on the way to the lobby telephone. She dug into her purse for the list of work numbers and her credit card. She thought of her ninth grade English teacher's moral preaching about Lady Macbeth: evil begets evil, lies beget lies, and corruption begets corruption.

"Percival, this is Maddy Gray." She waited for the acknowledging grunts of Dr. Mordecai. "I've got a deal for you. How would you like something really big for your career?"

"I'm listening."

"Hatcher is being held on the basis of your determination of Sweetbread's cause of death. If you ruled the head injuries accidental and consistent with a fall at home, he'd be released."

"I don't think it was an accident."

"But there's enough doubt. But how about a real fish to fry?"

"What have you got?"

"Is it a deal?"

"Depends if the fish is a keeper."

"Fair enough. Remember that metal shadow in Michael Johnson's mouth that you find so interesting…"

Maddy explained the inconsistency of the bullet fragment and police issue of non-jacketed bullets. It was enough evidence to re-open the case and put Mordecai on the front page.

"I'll look over the x-rays and Johnson's dental records to check for the presence of a crowned tooth, before I make a decision."

"Also look over the Random Ranger fragment that came out of Duval. I think they are nearly identical." The words Random Ranger were meat and gravy added to the bone. Maddy knew Mordecai wouldn't wait for the morning to check out x-rays.

She was bargaining to obstruct the legal system. She was creating, not obstructing justice in her mind. The forensic pathology rotation that began June first had taught her much forensics and pathology, but mostly opened her eyes to the operations of the legal system. "Justice system" had become an oxymoron.

She returned to the table energized with her discovery and conspiracy with Mordecai. Maddy insisted on after-dinner drinks, a cognac for Graham and a port wine for herself. Suggesting they finish their drinks on the beach, Maddy signed the check to their cottage and promised to return the glasses in the morning, which was "no problem, mon."

Graham's insides were of whirl of cognac aroma, foolish thoughts of being an old man on a moonlit beach with a youthful beauty of the next generation, the human sensual joys of moist ocean mist, the decrescendo of breaking waves, and sexual longing. He promised himself to love

Maddy as a young woman who needed the mentoring of a professional. He would not allow his lustful interest to become a painful and messy futureless union.

She held his arm the entire length of the beach walk to the end of the pier in front of the gazebo. They stopped at the end of the pier. Maddy looked closely at him. He was unsure if she was about to kiss him. He chastised himself for the fantasy. He turned to face the half moon and sea just in case. "We've got an early day tomorrow, let's turn in."

Back inside the cottage Graham turned out his light and climbed into the loft bed. Maddy was downstairs alone. Graham was proud he successfully avoided an act that might bring him moral remorse. The drone of the surf was loud through the louvered purple window shutters. He closed his eyes and was quickly dreaming.

**

A soft hand rubbed his chest. Maddy clad only in the black spaghetti-strapped negligee, raised the covers and slipped between the sheets. She moved her hand to his chin and turned his face into hers. He pulled back only to gasp for air until he was fully awake and convinced her presence was no longer a fantasy. He returned the kiss, a gentle act with just enough firmness to discover the texture and thickness of her lips, then adjusted the pressure to maximum pleasure.

His arms surrounded her back. His hands dropped along her negligee to discover her bare buttocks. The satin silkiness of the negligee matched the baby-like softness of her skin. With ballerina grace, she sat up, slid off both their nightshirts, and pitched his atop hers bedside on the floor.

255

In continuous movement she resumed her mouth contact with Graham. She opened widely probing with her tongue as she wriggled her breasts into his chest. The delicate creaminess of her breasts bolted energy flashes through his fingertips. The surge spread to his arms and chest, then ignited his groin. He hadn't experienced such urgency in years.

Maddy was swimming in the current of closeness to a man she desired. She grabbed hard the graying hair behind his ears. She bit the muscles in his neck. The wetness of desire was a sea siren beckoning the masculine ship to sail closer. Her thighs opened and she pulled him into her, then moored his legs under hers. They surged with rhythmic thrusts in cadence with the surf. The moist sea air merged with the sweat of their hot naked skin. Maddy was an ocean current that continued undulating until Graham lay quiet and shipwrecked.

Heavy breathing gradually lightened and outside the surf regained its podium. Maddy broke the silence.

"Graham, I've done something I'm not proud of, and it may get you into some hot water."

"Are you kidding. That was the joy of my life. I'm too old to get into trouble. But you're the one we have to protect."

"I'm not talking about sex. I'm a big girl. It's about an autopsy. I've been looking at the old Michael Johnson case. I think the story of him getting the police gun and shooting himself is bogus. The head x-ray has a metal fragment which if it's from a bullet jacket, couldn't have come from a police gun."

"What's the problem? That's quite a laudable achievement, if you can prove it."

"You were the pathologist on the case. It may look like you missed something."

"I'll say it again. I'm too old to worry about trouble. I'm at the age where I have a short time to repair the damage I've done."

"I sold out to Mordecai. I gave him the case in exchange for Thane. If Mordecai agrees to rule Sweetbread an accident, then the cops have to let Hatcher go. I didn't make love to you to tell you this, but Thatcher did play a major role in Sweetbread's demise. He was defending me from Sweetbread's attack, and he clubbed him with the fireplace poker. I am responsible. I have to do something to get him out."

"Maddy, I don't know of anyone who doesn't have some dark secret."

"I suppose you took money out of the collection plate once."

"I did in the Michael Johnson case. Seven years ago, I was up for tenure and promotion. I knew what everyone else knew, that one of the police shot Michael. There was rioting in the streets. The mayor and his political friends were desperate to whitewash the murder. The press was waiting for the pathology and police investigation.

"Sweetbread offered me tenure and department chair to go along with the police story about the suicide. Refusal meant neither. I was having trouble with my wife. I took the easy route and ruled the case was undetermined, but compatible with suicide."

"Was it Withers or Maconi?"

Graham shook his head and shrugged his shoulders. "I don't know. They have maintained a delicate innocence.

We don't want to push either of them too hard. That's why we can't be too careful around Withers tomorrow."

"Maconi is definitely more likely a killer than Withers. I know what an ass he can be. But Thane thinks Withers is the Random Ranger, and he's up to something. You must suspect Withers or you wouldn't be here protecting me."

"Maddy, I think you'd make an excellent forensic pathologist."

"No thanks, I couldn't take the pace. I rather do one than be one." She kissed him and drew back the sheets like a stagehand raising the curtain in preparation for the encore.

**

JUNE 15, FRIDAY, Andros

The lead story of the morning on WXCR was the prosecutor's request to have Michael Johnson's body exhumed, based on new information from the coroner's office. Percival Mordecai M.D. was enjoying a meteoric burst of fame. Out of obscurity the senior forensic pathology fellow had appeared before the Marion County Court to explain the bullet jacket theory and the need to examine directly that little triangle of flat metal. An omnipresent smoldering brushfire of real and perceived racism of the predominantly white police department received a rush of oxygen when the news broke.

The unavoidable hook for the judge was Mordecai's implication that the bullet of Michael Johnson was similar to those of the Random Ranger. Was this coincidence? Was it an act of the Random Ranger? Were the police at the core? Was the suicide story an unnecessary but plausible lie? Were Maconi and Withers perpetrators or puppets? The news sellers had hit the lottery, a juicy plot line with all the social buttons to push. Best for the press, it required no research other than dredging up file stories. Mordecai would be seen wearing neckties from this morning forward.

**

The Coral Lady with Withers and cargo chugged slowly out of the cut coral channel that connected Stuart's Cove marina to the Atlantic Ocean. Immediately, Maddy and Graham boarded the MerryTime and instructed the captain that the day's mission was to follow the Coral Lady to Andros, closely enough to observe, but remain unnoticed.

Captain Charles laughed. "I knows exactly where dey are goin's. I co-piloted da Lady Coral with Mista Withers some days when my bidness is slow, you know, mon. Dey has a favorite divin' hole, midway between da north tip of Andros and da Berry Islands. Dey meet der friends for a lunch, take demselves a dive, and den deys return home. You know, mon, the king mackerels, dey is running. We has a lot more fun if we's go fishin."

"Maybe on the way back, Charles." Graham tapped his wallet to assure the captain that the trip would be most profitable by following Graham's agenda.

Maddy sat at the tip of the bow. The wind brought tears to her eyes. Pelicans and gulls roosted on coral rocks. The clarity of the water mesmerized her. She felt kinship to dreamers who long to sip pina coladas on an island beach, an idea she had previously considered a silly cliché.

Graham sat alongside the captain in the shade of the canopy. The captain opened a waxed surface map of the ocean and islands. A channel of Atlantic Ocean nearly fifty miles wide and three miles deep separated New Providence from Andros. The water changed colors from deep blue to black as they entered the trench. Unlike the clear shallows, the trench waters returned no light. Captain Charles kept the Lady Coral in sight as a speck on the water several miles ahead.

It was nearly noon when the north tip of Andros arose to the left. The MerryTime turned right. "About eight to ten more miles to da north. How close you want to git me to da boat?"

"Close enough to know who they are and what they're doing."

The Lady Coral slowed as the boat reached an area of mangrove islands, sandbars, and coral keys that jutted above the surf. The MerryTime captain turned right and hit full throttle. Maddy bounced off the bow and stumbled to the canopy. The captain explained that he was circling around to the northwest. There was an islet key less than a quarter mile long. The MerryTime could dock on a spot out of view to the Lady Coral and the snorkelers. The captain edged the boat into a pocket in the coral with a rock ledge rising several feet above the gunwale. The center of the key was eight feet high composed entirely of jagged peach streaked gray stone.

Graham handed the binoculars to Maddy as they climbed the wall of coral that rose straight above the gunwale. She slipped and cut her elbow. The algae on the coral burned her wound. Atop the coral isle they could view the Lady Coral. It was anchored alongside a 60-foot yacht of clean

white paint and chrome railing. Three men were
snorkeling. Withers stood on the deck. He was recognizable
through the binoculars by his long slacks and sport shirt.
Maddy could see the transfer of one of the copy paper
boxes from a man to a yacht hand. He was the same Galaxy
Care insurance man seen the previous day. The insurance
man carried aboard the second box. The two men then
disappeared below deck of the yacht.

The Hawaiian-shirted insurance man reappeared within a
minute and climbed back onto The Lady Coral. He stood
alongside Withers.

"My God, you won't believe this."

She handed the binoculars to Graham who confirmed the
presence of a young black man who had climbed out from
the water onto the transfer ship, and removed his snorkeling
gear. It was Slurp.

The gentle surf of the cove nudged the boats in a slow
circle around the anchor. Graham read the name on the aft
panel next to an American flag, "The Cordless Life, Naples,
FL."

"We're all here. We could do autopsies in Nassau,"
Maddy joked.

"Be careful what you ask for."

The Galaxy Care insurance man on the Lady Coral
pointed toward Graham and Maddy. All on both boats
turned their heads toward the coral isle. The man bent down
and raised an automatic rifle. He fired ten, fifteen, twenty
rounds toward Maddy and Graham. The first five arrived
before the audible chamber fire.

The disconnect of the *rattattat* of gunfire from the
explosions of splintering coral confused and immobilized
the defenseless trio. The captain was first to belly crawl

shipward. The two interlopers ran over the crest of the isle. Graham grunted a painful wail and tumbled to the ground. He struggled to continue. Maddy supported him. It was another fifty feet to the boat. The firing ceased as they descended out of sight over the crest of the isle.

"I can't breath," Graham was barely audible.

"Keep going. Help us!" She called to the captain. He leapt out of the boat with speed and terror to assist Graham. The captain propped up Graham against Maddy, then took a position alongside the boat.

"Now push him on top of me. We loads him like a flour bag."

Maddy pushed the gasping Graham headfirst toward the captain. He bent low and sprung upward at the perfect moment to roll Graham into the boat. Maddy recoiled, sliding down and over a jut of coral into the seawater alongside the starboard panel. She splashed through the water to the rear ladder of the boat scraping her shoulder again on the coral shelf. The captain grabbed her arm in a desperate hurry to pull her into the boat. From rail to bench tracks of blood droplets from Graham made a pattern like fox prints in fresh snow.

The crescendo of engine roars from the Cordless Life and the MerryTime frightened pelicans from the marsh trees. The deep black skin of the Bahamian captain hid the terror that his eyes could not.

"We can outrun da Lady Coral, but not dat fancy boat," Captain Charles thought out loud. "How is da doctor?"

"I don't know yet. Do you have a first aid kit?"

"A little one."

Graham was blue and gasping. Maddy tore off his shirt. Two chest holes from the entrance and exit of one bullet drizzled blue blood that turned red as it ran down to his waist. Maddy knew it definitely had lacerated his left lung and maybe his heart. Graham was no longer conversive; he would die within minutes if the heart had been torn. The roar of the speeding engines made talk and hearing difficult.

Maddy lowered her ear to Graham's chest. She heard a hiss from the backside bullet hole with each inspiration attempt.

"Charles, do you have any elastic tape or bandages?" she yelled.

"Jess a Band-Aid."

"Anything else?"

"Duct tape in da tool box."

She accepted. He pointed as he drove. The boat jolted upward as it hit a large wave.

"Sheet, if we don't sinks, I gots an idea. The Lady Coral will be heading back to Nassau. Your friend, he's a need a hospital like dey gots in Grand Bahama. Da Florida boat be going west. It's seventy miles back to Nassau, about a hundred to Freeport. What's you doing wid dat duct tape?"

"He's got a tension pneumothorax."

She immediately felt silly using medical language.

"Air's leaking from his lung. It's his only hope."

She pasted multiple strips of the gray duct tape over his chest alternating vertical and horizontal paths. Within two minutes Graham's color had improved and he regained faint consciousness.

"Freeport's too far. He'll never last that long. Can't you call a rescue helicopter?" she said.

"In da Bahama's?"

"How about the U.S. Coastguard? We're only 150 miles from Miami?"

"I don't know, mum."

"Call!"

Captain Charles went to work on the radio. He contacted the Bahamian navy, which relayed the call to the U.S. Coast Guard. A rescue helicopter was on board a ship in the Straits of Florida ninety miles to the west. The MerryTime was instructed to maintain radio contact. It would take fifty to sixty minutes.

"You can't tell dem da Lady Coral shot your friend, you hear? I gots to live on dis island wid deese people. I don't know whats you people doin' dats so bad, but me and my babies don't need no shootin's."

Maddy cuddled the barely conscious Graham. He started to babble that the island sun was too hot. Maddy realized he was feeling the release of adrenaline from his blood loss. Although cold and shivering, he complained of feeling hot.

"Maddy, I don't mind dying. Better me than you. I've had a good life." He knew he was dying. He coughed up a clot of blood as he tried to smile at her, then slumped over for several seconds. Maddy was unable to determine if Graham was aware of the content of his speech. Graham was determined to speak.

"Burr was a bastard. Had it coming. He was going to kill the boy. He was bad for the country. He cheated his own friends at golf."

"What about Burr, Graham? What boy was he going to kill?"

"A hundred units of insulin, I fixed his knee." Graham slumped over for the last time. The next fifty minutes dragged by in the cold and eerie silence of the unknown fate of Graham. Maddy found a wet suit to cover over the shaking Graham. The seas had risen to three feet and wind was a near gale at 25 to 30 miles per hour.

**

The U.S. Coast Guard helicopter hovered over the MerryTime. Maddy envisioned a halo over the angelic craft. Two crewmen descended with the gurney, each equipped with backpack, rope, and life vest. They rapidly strapped Graham to the cot and hoisted him into the sky. Maddy briefly explained that an unknown person had shot him for unknown reason. When she further stated that he was a doctor on vacation from Indianapolis, the Coast Guard crewman seemed less suspicious. They announced their plans to fly Graham to the Miami University Hospital trauma unit. Maddy was disappointed that she was not allowed to board the helicopter, but relieved that Graham would receive proper medical treatment. She hugged Charles who steered the boat toward Nassau.

**

The MerryTime returned to Stuart's Cove marina shortly after 9 p.m. The Lady Coral was quietly moored with no one around. Maddy thanked the captain and told him to charge Graham's credit card with whatever he thought appropriate. Charles refused and tore up the blank charge slip. "I want no record of dis doin's." She gave him forty dollars cash, all she had.

As she drove back to the Compass Point, her body reminded her that she hadn't eaten except for a morning muffin. At the hotel desk she got cash and ordered a dinner to be delivered to her room. She would not risk being seen in public.

The gale winds, harbingers of the approaching cold front, arrived along the north side of New Providence, creating eight-foot breakers over the coral reefs outside her cottage. The red message light on her phone was the lone light in her room. She turned on the desk lamp and lay on the bed. Who knew she was here? Could it be Withers? The telephone rang. It might be room service, she told herself. She answered cautiously.

"Yes."

A welcome familiar voice came from the receiver. "Maddy, have you heard? Mordecai dropped the Sweetbread homicide call. I'm out, but on administrative leave until the agency investigates. Plus Mordecai wants the Michael Johnson body exhumed. Do you believe that? I know it. Withers is up to something. So, what's he doing in Nassau?"

"I can't talk over the phone. It's bad. I'll tell you tomorrow. I want you to meet me in Naples, Florida."

"What?"

"I'm going to get a flight out of here as soon as I can. You fly into Fort Myers, tomorrow. I'll call you on your cell phone as soon I get back into the States. Naples, tomorrow."

Her hand trembled with the fear of an unfamiliar country and an unknown enemy who had shot and possibly killed Graham. Teardrops trickled down her cheeks. She tried unsuccessfully to call Miami University Hospital. Her tears increased and fell onto the yellow pages as she looked for the local airline entries.

A new sadness arrived, a self-horror that she was cursed to bring sadness, suffering or death to the men she loved and admired.

**

JUNE 16, SATURDAY, Neapolitan Castles

Maddy deplaned the Bahamas Air morning jet at Miami International. She looked back at the yellow and black aircraft in grateful amazement it had made the crossing. The ancient Boeing 707 was close to forty years old. The paint was thin and colorless with worn-through undercoating. Black soot was caked on the wings over the engines. The cockpit glass was scratched to nearly opaque. When the plane touched down, it had bounced heavily and yawed to the left, delivering a thrill to the children and a breathless moment to their parents. She thought of Bruce Comstock's cancer and Graham's bullet to the chest. Death was never more that an instant away, the best reason to value life.

The trip to the medical center was a swim through traffic molasses. Maddy wondered if the trip was even possible on a usual workday. Cuban-American drivers delivered hand signals and accompanying directions in Spanish, ungraciously suggesting Maddy visit the eternal underworld.

Graham was comatose and on life support. He had been taken directly to the trauma room surgical suite where the lung lacerations were oversewn. The duct tape had sealed his chest, allowing sufficient ventilation to keep him alive. He had lost two quarts of blood from the bullet wound causing shock injury to the vital organs of his body.

The battle had begun between the forces of healing and death. His lungs were leaking cells and proteinaceous fluid from injured capillaries into the air spaces. The mechanical ventilator would force oxygen into his lung in hopes of making its way to the bloodstream.

Blood toxins were accumulating. The kidneys were exhausted from the lack of blood flow, analogous to a garbage strike in New York City. His heart and liver were functioning adequately, which gave a distant hope for survival.

Even if Graham's body pulled through, his brain was the big "if." Swollen and injured from the shock and surgery, his brain might not return to normal function even if he survived. Each day that passes without awakening pushes the boat of hope farther out to sea. The hospital transplant nurses were disappointed to learn Maddy was not his daughter. They had already identified Graham as a potential organ donor and a copy of his driver's license with donor permission was taped to the front of his chart. The explanation that he and Maddy were co-workers brought raised eyebrows from one obese nurse. It got worse.

"He has a wife in Seattle and a daughter somewhere, I think," Maddy responded truthfully to the search for nearest relatives.

"You are good friends with the family?" came out of the mouth corner of the nurse as she stuffed a chocolate brownie into her cheek.

"No, he and his wife are unofficially separated."

"I understand." The nurse scanned Maddy's shapely body in sham politeness. She put down her brownie.

The police officer who interviewed Maddy was a jaded veteran of Miami's war on drugs. He accepted her story that they were on a pleasure and fishing trip and got too close to an unknown boat somewhere in the Bahamas, inciting a gunman to open fire. The officer rapidly concluded that whether she was lying or not, he would get no useful information from Maddy. Nor did he care. Graham O'Dell had no criminal record and worked in a police helping profession.

**

At 5 p.m. Maddy's rental car arrived in Naples. The daily late-afternoon thunderstorm was ending. Steamy mist rose from the concrete and asphalt streets. She parked her car in front of an Irish pub in the posh shopping section, Olde Naples on Fifth Avenue.

Thane Hatcher was reading the newspaper at a window-side table. She tapped on the glass and beamed a relieved-to-find-him smile. He waved her in. She sipped a glass of ale while relaying the events of Nassau, the critical condition of Dr. O'Dell, and the reason they had to come to Naples: To search for the Cordless Life.

She omitted the exact sleeping arrangements at the Compass Point, but thanked Thane for the excellent accommodations.

"You look different, good different," Maddy commented spontaneously without thought.

"I think prison changes a man."

"You weren't in prison. You haven't been, and won't be convicted of anything. What did they do to you?"

"They called me agent. Never once did they use my name. Otherwise they treated me fine. But they were viciously and needlessly rude and insulting to the other men. There is no normal toilet privacy. They could have clean pillows and blankets. I doubt a medieval dungeon would have been much worse."

"I'm sorry that I got you into this mess. I seem to have a black widow spider gene when it comes to men."

"I am guilty of lying and accidental homicide, whether justifiable or not." Maddy raised an eyebrow. He quickly added, "Of course it was justified. There just isn't any right and wrong anymore. Take the guys in lockup: most of them have done some pretty bad stuff. But how do you judge? One guy robbed the house of his boss, an asphalt paver who gets jobs by illegal kickbacks to the city contractor. He was pissed off because his boss wanted the crew to work all day Saturday. Tell me, who's the bigger crook?"

"Sometimes people must lie to protect themselves or their jobs. You were actually doing your job. Sweetbread was committing a crime and you used the F.B.I. equipment to fight it. That shouldn't be criminal."

"Apprehending a criminal is different from killing them. I think the term is excessive force."

Her argument was inconsequential. Thane stared out the window. He had changed. The boyish smile and "good deeds make a good boy" attitude were gone. Thane had decided justice was his goal, not compliance with the law. His law enforcement career had lost its innocence.

In contrast Maddy was focused to begin the search. They headed east to the Gordon River. The river mouth flows into the Gulf of Mexico at the south tip of Naples. The river outlet is sided by mansions and boat docks of the country's elite. Upscale marinas pamper the long and sleek multi-million dollar float-toys of the opulent class. Along the northwest bank of the river mouth is Port Royale, the most expensive of housing developments in the city. The largest boats require the expanse of the open river marina slips.

The show pony homes of the ultra-wealthy lay on the gulf side of the Port Royale peninsula. C.E.O.s of multi-national corporations found the building of vacation beach homes an adequate means to divert their interests and disposal of their million-dollar bonuses. They docked boats along the river channel, as the shoreline was too shallow for executive-sized yachts.

The oceanfront "cottages" on south Gordon Drive ranged from twenty to sixty thousand square feet and housed enough art works to fill the museums of several large cities.

Maddy and Thane traversed the entire river boardwalk across from the marina. The Cordless Life was not apparent. They crossed to the marina office that had a spotless waiting office. A blonde woman in her early twenties attended the desk. Her shape and beauty rivaled a Miss America contestant.

The attendant scanned Maddy and Thane like a high-speed computer to determine the wealth and legitimacy of the pair to enter the world of her elite clientele.

"May I help you?" the blonde smiled cooly, firing the first volley in a war of the access control.

"I was looking for a boat. I wanted to show my friend the Cordless Life. I went to a party on it last year. I just wanted him to see it."

"I'm sorry, who are you again?"

"I'm Doctor Gray from Indiana. I don't even remember who the owner was. It was just such a great boat. Of course, how foolish of me. You have to be very careful."

Maddy pulled out her driver's and medical licenses that the woman quickly reviewed.

"I hope I didn't offend you. I'm sorry, but the Corless is out." The woman looked out the window toward the south end of the dock. Only two slips were empty.

"No big deal. It was just something to do today. I love Naples. Thank you," Maddy gushed. Thane recognized and admired Maddy's victory in the information duel, intelligence one-upped the beauty.

**

Maddy called the secretary at the hospital. Debra said the entire department was in social shock over the shooting of Graham. Maddy asked for the details, grateful to learn the department was unaware that she and Graham had been together.

"I had to change plans today, Debra. I don't know exactly when I'll be back. How about Slurp, is he back, yet? I imagine it's pretty busy." Thane marveled again at her talent for pumping information in a seemingly innocent manner.

"He returns Monday. Thank goodness it's been slow."

"Me too. I'm planning on Monday if nothing comes up. See you then, goodbye."

**

Thane called a friend at the agency to request a favor. He wasn't allowed to use the agency resources while on administrative leave. It was a small task to have his friend search the airline files for Eldred Smith's return flight to Indianapolis.

Awaiting the return of The Cordless Life, they drove a mile west to the Gulf to fill the time as tourists. At the Naples fishing pier they walked to the end of the quarter-mile wooden scaffold. Several young boys were casting shrimp bait over the rail with minimal equipment. The older daily fishermen wore hats and sat together in folding chairs. They talked about the local politics not fish. The new mosquito commissioner was cutting back sprays in their neighborhood.

Maddy and Thane lost themselves in the joy of spying a pod of dolphins spraying and leapfrogging above the surface. A brown pelican alit on the rail two feet from Maddy. She instinctively smiled and turned to the bird.

"Well, hello there, Mr. Pelican," she said sweetly. It hissed and raised its feathers to ward her off. Maddy, reflexively, as if swatting Tasmin off her bed, backhanded its belly. The pelican jumped back, tumbled toward the water and barely recovered into flight to avoid striking the surface.

"I think it's illegal to harass the wildlife," Thane teased.

"You've taught me a lot about illegal stuff." She then poked Thane.

The taunt brought thoughts of Mina. She phoned and asked Mina to look in on Tasmin. Mina agreed to stop by on her way to a lawyer party at The Pines. Mina asked to speak to Thane who detailed to her his gratitude of release from jail and contempt with the staff.

The two left the ocean pier and returned by car to the marina boardwalk. One previously empty slip now moored a four-mast sailing yacht, not the Cordless Life. The sun cast long shadows from its descent toward Texas.

More time to kill. They opted to return to the pier area for a beach walk. Eight blocks west of the marina, where the highest-priced real estate met groomed beach, they removed their shoes, and strolled south letting their toes touch the water line. Thane called it, "A gawk-walk tour."

South of the pier mansions arose from the sand like oasis palaces. Teams of Spanish-speaking laborers, wearing long sleeve cotton shirts despite the ninety plus degree heat, were manicuring tropical gardens. With machetes and power tools they trimmed the palm and banana trees, the bushes, the croton plants, and the Bermuda grass.

A Japanese electronic game company C.E.O. owned a sprawling pagoda-style retreat of multiple buildings painted red and deep blue with lacquer gloss finishes like a giant set of Oriental living room furniture. A half-mile farther down the peninsula they reached the construction site of an Italiante villa with arched porches and walkways throughout a sixty thousand square foot main building that would pass for a museum or chic shopping mall in another location. A local beach walker informed them that a nouveau riche telecommunications C.E.O. was the owner.

None of the estates along the executive peninsula had any visible inhabitants, only security guards and the Hispanic leaf-pickers. Occasionally an automobile would be parked near the house. The work trucks and vans were parked on access lanes, auxiliary driveways for the servant class along the edges of the properties.

"Why would someone want a huge showplace that they don't have time to use?" Maddy shook her head. "These lots would be an entire block in New Munich."

"They're pyramids, monuments for the kings to fend off the realization that they are mortal humans no different than the five-dollar-an-hour laborers who generate their wealth.

"Empty temples with guesthouses and secret chambers. You couldn't give me one of these places. I'd feel like a mummy," said Maddy.

"The 'cell phone tower' is its nickname," the beach walker further informed them.

Two doors farther along the beach stood a more modest estate with one eye-catching feature. A white commercial van was conspicuously parked doorside in a location only suitable for a luxury coach. The side of the van had the green earth logo EvTk of the EnvironTech Corporation. A young man with short bleached blonde hair walked out of the side door of the main house and drove off. The Indiana license read EVTK 9.

"That's a familiar Hoosier logo." Maddy said casually as they continued along the beach. She bent down to pick up a spiral orange seashell. "Corless! She said Corless, not Cordless."

"I heard her say that too. Now I get it. Cordless Life is a twist of Corless's name to an ocean lifestyle." Thane confirmed her conclusion. They hurried the twenty minutes back up the beach. The sun touched the horizon. Maddy and Thane jogged eastward toward the marina, glancing over their shoulders to view the spectacular orange disk slip into the Gulf. Thane reached the car and pitched the parking ticket into a trashcan, "Agency perk."

**

As they entered the marina the white van with license plate EVTK 9 drove around them exiting. The Cordless Life was moored in the previously empty slip. Four young men, two blacks and two whites, were disembarking.

"Precious, what are you doing in Naples?"

"Don't fucking precious me. I don't know what you guys are smuggling, but Doctor O'Dell is dead or soon to be."

"What are you talking about?"

"Who do you think was on that reef when your friend opened fire in Andros?"

"Holy shit! Dr. Gray, I swear I don't know nothing."

"What's are you smuggling in those boxes? How did you get this boat?"

"Once or twice a year I get to bring my friends down for some sun and fun." As Slurp continued, Maddy glanced at the other three men. Two had their heads slightly cocked in confusion. They smiled with tilted heads and cocked wrists.

"You call shooting your boss, fun?"

"I didn't shoot anybody. That wasn't our boat. I don't even know who that guy on the Lady Coral was. My job is simple. I just pick up this boat, go snorkeling, and return it."

"Smuggling cocaine is only a minor detail, I suppose," Thane interjected.

"That's paper. Insurance papers they told me. I felt it before. It bends. I told Withers I wasn't doing any drug running, and I ain't. Is Dr. God dead?"

"On life support in Miami. I visited him today, but he isn't responding."

"Who are you working for?" asked Thane.

"Withers. Shit, I don't make no money. How could I afford a trip like this? I don't know what's going on, but

Carl wouldn't lie to me. I go when I get a chance. We were supposed to go two weeks ago, but I got stabbed. That's why I called Carl. He swore there weren't any drugs."

"Let's see the papers."

"They're gone. The van picked up both boxes just a minute ago."

"Who owns this boat?"

"I ain't supposed to know."

"What the fuck does that mean?"

"I was told not to ask, but one time I saw some registration paper in the cabin hold. William Core-lease I think. I swear I don't know nothing."

"Do they always ship papers? Do you ever take them off the boat?"

"Boxes of insurance papers as far as I know, and my job stops at this pier. I don't load or unload anything. It's just a chance to go diving with my friends." A chorus of giggles twittered from the boat.

**

Maddy's Honda Civic was parked at her apartment at 9:22 p.m. Tasmin affectionately deposited the missing fibers from a Persian throw rug onto Mina's ankles. The hairball was a peace offering from an attention-starved cat. The hole in the Persian rug was just retribution for Maddy's desertion. Mina petted the cat and promised to send Maddy home the next day. She opened an offering of canned tuna before leaving.

**

SUNDAY JUNE 17, The Wake

A group of young lawyers from Daniels-Parr law firm had reserved a lavish party room at Whispering Pines Country Club. Peter Emmonds, a handsome thirty-year-old litigation attorney and rising star of the medical malpractice industry, had imbibed heavily enough to mistake Mina as Aphrodite incarnate. His bleary judgment also required that she drive him to his condominium in a wooded and chic section near Geist Reservoir.

While Peter lay naked, snoring and exhausted crosswise in his bed, Mina quietly kissed his forehead. She softly stepped down the front stairs at 3:30 am. She stood in the dark fumbling for the keys to the loaned Civic.

The crickets were chirping, which camouflaged the clicking of the safety release of the Random Ranger's automatic. Two rapid-fire bursts of gunshot preceded the wail and groan of a speeding car. Mina tumbled to the ground. She rolled onto her belly. She made no sound.

**

Mina's body lay dew covered as the mid-June sun peaked over the horizon just south of its solstice apogee. The morning newspaper deliveryman, who drove a rusted Chevy Cavalier, called to the body. He got out of his car and turned back the arm that covered her cheek. One eye was blown out and surrounded by blood and matted hair. The left arm was stiff and snapped the body back to its terminal position. Ants were lining up in four directions for the harvest.

**

Cell phones, radio news, and police investigators brought The Breakfast Club horror to Maddy and Thane. The press was delighted at the possibility of a Random Ranger encore. By the time Thane's car had departed Indianapolis International Airport, Maddy's wailing had moved from grief pangs to sobs of bewilderment.

As Thane entered the city her anger had arrived. She was shouting obscenities at Indianapolis, God, Maconi, Slurp, Withers, the young blonde asshole from EnvironTech whoever he was, and any other mother-fucker who even looked at her cross-eyed. A police investigator who got her cell phone number from the University asked her to come to headquarters to answer questions about Mina.

"I'll be at County Hospital this afternoon. If you catch me there fine, otherwise you can stick your pistol up your ass. I'm going to get the bastard who did this and I'm not going to waste time with the police who couldn't catch a rabbit if it was stuck in the mouth of a retriever." She hung up.

**

Mordecai and Green would jointly perform the autopsy. Maddy refused to talk to any investigator before the autopsy. She demanded to watch every moment of her best friend's last ritual before burial. Dr. Green met with Maddy privately in his office.

"I understand she was a close friend. This isn't professional for you, watching the autopsy. It's personal.

279

You should sit this one out. I can order you out of the morgue."

Maddy regained enough composure from her intermittent weeping to respond with a smile. "Dr. Green, I know myself. The most honoring thing I can do is to hold Mina in my sights. I can handle it. Let me stay."

Dr. Green consented. He had done his due diligence. He had given Maddy permission to excuse herself. He also knew pathologists to be a special breed for whom corpses are a fabric of life to be touched, examined, and held in focus. Dr. Green understood a pathologist's unusual need to process death.

**

The homicide evidence team clipped the nails, brushed the scalp and pubic hair for loose hair and fibers. Each specimen was carefully placed in a clear plastic bag and labeled with its location and the autopsy number A-622. Her naked body was young and looked small on the steel table. Her toenails had peeling purple polish.

The vaginal wash containing semen DNA from Peter Emmonds would provide him with a brief and undeserved tabloid ignominy. The initial insinuations of possible rape and murder would land him raised eyes at the law office, and a newfound difficulty in simple dating.

Mina's organs were normal as the entrails of an Easter lamb. The entire pathological findings were above the jaw-line, and gunshot related.

The first bullet had entered her left temple area and exploded outwardly the contents of the orbit. Orange-tinted brain substance had propelled the eyeball into the street.

The second bullet struck dead center into the parietal bone, sending eggshell fractures throughout the skull bones. Like John Kennedy's brain, what remained was an unorganized pile of gelatin. When Mordecai and Richard removed the flail cranium, it flopped like chicken wire; the brain substance poured out like Jell-O cubes in a broken-glass salad.

Death had been instantaneous. Both bullets were flattened from their pinball paths, ricocheting within the skull. The homicide team used plastic forceps to remove them into plastic bags. The ten o'clock news reported confirmation that the bullets were identical to others from the Random Ranger. A forensic psychologist commented that the serial killer was showing his true colors. He could no longer constrain himself to murder once a year. His pace was accelerating. He was out of control and would strike again soon. The TV and radio replayed the psychologist's statement every hour. The city was alert with fear.

At the conclusion of the autopsy Thane and Maddy stood at Mina's side. The Irish wake is a proven ritual for kick-starting grief. The decedent lying in full view prevents denial. Sustained viewing of the loved one punctures the pockets of pain, draining the abscesses of loss.

She clutched Mina's hand. She kissed her cheek. "She liked you, you know," Maddy said to Thane with tears dropping from her chin.

"I know. I liked her, too."

"Why does shit like this have to happen? Why her? Why not you, or me? Who would randomly fucking kill someone?"

"Maddy, she looked like you. She was driving your car. It wasn't a random shot. You were the target."

"I wish it had been me."

"I wish it weren't anyone."

"We know Withers and Slurp were out of state. I know you suspected Withers."

"Do you wonder if it is a coincidence that Withers is out of town whenever the Ranger strikes?"

"Thane, I fear I may have set up Mordecai with the exhumation."

"If that mouth metal is a jacket fragment, Withers and Maconi and the whole police department are in for a lot of bad publicity. What's another body at this point? We have to tell him."

"Do you think we can trust him?"

**

Mordecai had already left. The bloodhound was combing the street in front of Peter Emmond's condominium. Under his magnifier he spotted two blackened metal shards less than a millimeter that the homicide team had passed over. When he returned to his office, a handwritten note directed him to go to the Internal Medicine Room, "For your own good."

Mordecai listened as Thane theorized that Mina had been mistaken for Maddy. Graham had been shot while he and Maddy were tailing Withers in the Bahamas. They were unsure who was trustworthy, but the safety of Mordecai required a delay in the exhumation until they understood the link between Withers and EnvironTech. Mordecai listened quietly and then softly turned to Maddy.

"I am sorry about the videotape. It was cruel of me to take advantage of you."

Thane looked at Maddy and nodded. Yes, they could trust him.

**

JUNE 18, MONDAY, EnvironTech

Maddy slept until seven. Her body felt new and different this morning. She had not realized her level of accumulated exhaustion. It was sunny. She allowed the pains of grief to surface. A rose bush cane had grown three feet over the last week, covering her bedroom window with cough-drop-red flowers that scratched the glass in the breeze. A bouquet of the gods, she thought, perhaps from Mina.

She made an omelet, forcing herself to eat something. She walked to the corner newsstand to read about Mina. The lead story was a meaningless file replay of the Random Ranger. A more intelligent story came on page six from a junior reporter who emphasized the execution style of the murder. She locked her door. If Mina was an errant target, she could ill afford to turn her back.

The autopsy provided evidence that the firing had come from the street. Witnesses at the party corroborated Peter Emmond's explanation, "She was all over me. She insisted on taking me home herself." One columnist talked about the Ted Bundy types that women find irresistible.

At 7:30 when Maddy determined her mother would be awake, she telephoned. Her mother couldn't talk long. She was hosting a strawberry ice cream social, a great June tradition in New Munich. The rains in May had made the strawberries very juicy this year. Mrs. Gray was oblivious to the Random Ranger, the County Hospital morgue, and pathology in general. Her standard reply to well-meaning questions about her daughter's occupation was, "She is a real doctor; she does medical research." Having made one visit and two calls, Maddy was done with family check-in for the month. She did not tell her mother that she might be in mortal danger.

**

"Today the honorable William Corless, C.E.O. and President, EnvironTech Corporation, cordially invites the voters of central Indiana to a reception in honor of the interim congressional appointee, Byron Davis, CPA. Mr. Davis is an esteemed officer with EnvironTech, the Hoosier company that puts people to work improving the environment."

The invitation took up the entire last page of the first section of the newspaper. Corless had paid double to pre-empt the spot usually held by the weather forecasts.

**

At lunch Maddy met with Mordecai and Thane. Maddy refused food, citing her morning omelet and a general decrease of appetite. She studied the F.B.I. corporate files that Thane brought in a leather satchel, detailed information about EnvironTech. The Indiana based company was an alleged industry leader in toxic waste management and disposal. Indiana law was more lenient regarding the importation of radioactive materials, heavy metals, and polycyclic hydrocarbons. The state legislative committee on environmental legislation prided itself on keeping jobs in Indiana. This meant it was impossible to get any bill out of committee that regulated importation or production of industrial waste.

The flagship factory was situated in south central Indianapolis. Two billion dollars in annual revenue came from processing corporate solid waste. The compaction, treatment, and dissolution into non-toxic by-products earned EVTK, its Wall Street symbol, a corporate green-thumb image for growing profits. EnvironTech bragged in advertisements about its clean run-off after processing. Video shorts featured William Corless holding a tin cup, bending down to the discharge stream into the White River, and drinking the company effluent in testimony of its safety.

Nearly three thousand employees worked at the Indianapolis center. Their health insurance was provided through the University Health Plan and UPSinc. The company's automotive fleet included sixty large trucks and one hundred forty automobiles and delivery vans. The cars were executive lease perks; the vans were the business shuttles. The trucks transported piles of waste material from railroad cars to factory sites.

The main factory had separate areas to treat each type of waste. Metals were salted and dried for export to the desert or recycling to industry. Polycyclic hydrocarbons were held in bacterial pools until degraded to non-toxic common biological compounds, and radioactive materials were concentrated for deposit storage in a Nevada mountain depot. EnvironTech was the highest profit margin company in the toxic waste sector.

Thane's files also listed a satellite operation outside Vincennes in southwestern Indiana. Seven states on the eastern seaboard provided EnvironTech with the bulk of its business, each with shipping stations along railroads.

The glitzy office suites covered the entire top two floors of the administrative building. Of the half million invitees, the twenty-two thousand actually attending were less than the prediction of thirty-five to forty, attributed to the nice weather. Also, Davis, the obvious hand-picked puppet of William Corless, sparked little enthusiasm except to die-hard politicos of the local Republican Party. Byron Davis was smiling and shaking hands at a pace of twelve hundred per hour. Wine, punch, and hors d'oeuvres were served on the executive patio.

Thane and Maddy skipped the interminable reception line in favor of the factory tour. It was clean with the hygienic aroma of a freshly iced urinal. The tour guide was a quality control manager, programmed to tout the purity of the water leaving the plant.

Like medical advertising chants of, "How much they CARE for you," the tour personnel repeatedly stated how devoted EnvironTech was to "PURITY."

The EVTK honey flowed with sickening sweetness from the company drones. The guide couldn't imagine a more perfect company to work for, nor a greater boss than William Corless. Mordecai commented in his curt and caustic monotone, "The man has the soul of Styrofoam."

The back parking lot held parallel rows of huge dump trucks with green doors displaying the EVTK logos. Mordecai said it resembled a Russian military parade on

May Day. Mordecai quickly decoded the arrangement. Cadillac STS's, were lined up one through eight in the first row. Their license plates reading, "EVTK 1" through "8," each with stenciling on the curb to match the tags. Mordecai surmised the executive committee operated these. The second area, for middle executives, had cars numbered 101 and up. The vans were behind the cars with license plates beginning with number 201. The dump trucks were in the back lot.

"Percival, you're like a beagle. You never miss a sniff." Maddy gave him a pat on the back. Thane paid no attention. He also was focused on organization of the fleet.

"Maddy," he motioned her to think, "The Naples van we saw was number nine. Why is it a van instead of a Cadillac? Who's number nine around here?"

"He must be high up, but needs a van for light hauling."

Mordecai took a place in line. Thane and Maddy returned to the administrative wing, pushing through the people lined up to rub palms with Corless and Davis. They began a self-guided tour of the administrative floor.

True to C.E.O. aggrandizement, the wall behind the welcome desk held pictures of the top three executives in stereotypic dark blue suits sitting at their desks. An American flag was over each right shoulder and the EnvironTech banner dangled over the left. Corless was top and center. The C.O.O. below left, and the face of Byron Davis, C.F.O., was lower right. On the far wall was a composite of management and the Board of Trustees. One young face immediately received the index fingers of Maddy and Thane simultaneously, the blonde-haired driver of the van from Naples. "Thank God for corporate arrogance," she whispered to Thane.

At the far end of the hallway, a woman sat behind a reception desk in front of glass doors leading to the executive suites. She had a welcoming smile as Maddy approached. Maddy complimented the secretary on her shoes and matching belt. While the secretary beamed in pride, Maddy pulled her over to the photograph.

"Hello, I'm Dr. Gray, Maddy Gray, from the county coroner's service. This is Thane Hatcher from the F.B.I."

"Connie Snow, assistant to Mr. Corless. Pleased to meet you."

"This one is kind of young and cute. Must be the president's son?"

"No, but he could be. The older men call him the golden boy. Men can be so jealous."

"Tell me about it. So where do the girls hunt this guy down? And don't tell me he's married."

"I don't think he's married. He's Dustin Conrad, the plant C.O.O. in Vincennes. He was here earlier. I think he said something about going to the Statehouse. Good luck. I like the dark haired ones personally."

"This line hasn't shortened all day, you must be exhausted."

"Part of the job. Would you like to meet Mr. Corless and Mr. Davis?"

"Not necessary," Thane declined politely.

"Yes, *I would!*" Maddy raised an eyebrow to Thane.

The secretary waggled her index finger to follow. She opened the top drawer of her desk and took out a set of keys. First she opened a coat closet behind her desk to secure her purse, transporting it from under her desk to the closet. Next she took a large master from the ring and led the three down several back hallways and through a side conference room of the executive office of William Corless. The receiving line filed past the front of his desk. At a momentary break in Mr. Corless's receiving duties, Connie touched his arm from behind.

"Mr. Corless, I'd like to introduce two important guests: Dr. Gray from University Hospitals and Mr. Thatcher from the Federal Bureau of Investigation." Corless beamed with interest. Maddy marveled at Corless's faculty to disarm and enchant those about him.

"Doctor Gray, yes, my good friend, the late Dr. Sweetbread, once mentioned you as a bright and beautiful pathology resident. He certainly wasn't exaggerating. Wouldn't you agree, Mr. Thatcher?"

"I would."

"I understand it's quite busy over there with this Random Ranger character loose and all." Maddy nodded and Corless continued. "Must be fascinating. I'd like to hear about it from a professional like yourself. Please, do come back to my office soon, and fill me in. Will you? I'm dead serious."

"I'd like that, Mr. Corless."

"Anytime. Here's my card. Just check in with my secretary. I promise to clear my calendar."

Corless then turned and introduced Maddy and Thane to Byron Davis. A cold limp handshake loosely coiled Maddy's fingers. The ambiance and ennui of a stuffed antelope head filled his space. He wore an expensive beige Armani business suit. His hair was curly black with gray tips, a backdrop for pale blue eyes without depth.

The secretary escorted the pair back to the front door, retracing their path through the conference room and back corridors. "See, I knew he'd be glad to meet you," she smiled as she reclaimed her purse from the closet and tossed the passkeys back into the top desk drawer.

"He's quite serious about inviting you to visit. He doesn't give out his cards or invitations, unless he is serious. Call me when you're in the neighborhood."

"Perhaps I can take you out to lunch?" Maddy smiled as she received a warm handshake from the secretary. Thane reflected how difficult it would be for the F.B.I. to get into that office, while Maddy had charmed a first-class ticket.

**

Slurp lived in a near northeast section of downtown. New age shops, ethnic restaurants, and four of the six city theaters were located within blocks of Massachusetts Avenue. His apartment was on the second floor over an art studio and gallery. He shared the two-bedroom flat with a revolving door of itinerant hair stylists who worked steady jobs less than a year. A male partnership of two salon owners regularly sent new hires who needed a cheap room to Slurp. He bragged at never having had sex with a paying roommate. He did however feel free reins at seducing any acquaintance the roommate might bring home.

"Give me your gun," Maddy instructed Thane.

"What?"

"You can take the bullets out."

Maddy rushed in as Slurp answered the door and shoved the gun into his face.

"It's spill time, pretty boy, either your brains or the full scoop on Withers and the Random Ranger bullets. My best friend is dead. I may be next. I want some straight answers, Slurp." She clicked off the safety.

"Put that damn thing away. I'm allergic to heavy metal," he said.

She pushed the nose of the gun hard against his forehead.

"I swear I've never seen him with a gun. I had my questions too, but every time the Ranger hit somebody, he was out of town."

Maddy pulled back the gun. "How did you get that bullet?"

"I told you I found it in a plastic bag after we autopsied a case of a drive-by gang-banger. I was going to give it to the police, but when I called, they said I must be mistaken, they had all the bullets. So I kept it. Fuck, the Lone Ranger was always leaving bullets laying around in the movies."

Maddy returned the weapon to Slurp's forehead. "What gang-banger?"

"How would I know?"

"There were only two Random Ranger gang hits. Which one?" Maddy doubled the pressure on his skin. He shook his head no.

"It wasn't either one of those two?" Maddy questioned and Slurp shook his head yes. She withdrew the gun.

"It wasn't a Random Ranger case. That's what I'm saying," he said.

"It was a leftover? Just there in a plastic bag?" Thane said.

"Did someone intend to fake it, to make it look like a Random Ranger killing?" Maddy said.

"I don't know for sure."

"Who was there? Withers, O'Dell, Richard, Maconi?"

"Not Maconi."

"That would explain the different types of victims. The Ranger borrows a few extra bodies from time to time to make it appear random." Thane offered.

"What is Withers smuggling in from the Bahamas? And who shot Graham?" Maddy raised the gun again.

"The insurance guy. I don't know who he is or why he's got to shoot people. All we ever carry is insurance papers, I swear! Cross my heart and hope to go to fairyland. The papers go directly into the van as soon as we hit the Naples marina."

"Why would he have to smuggle insurance papers? Fed Ex would be a lot cheaper than a two hundred mile yacht trip."

"I can't tell you anything that I don't know. I've always been good to you. Stop picking on me."

"Mina is dead, and I am pissed!" Maddy pulled the trigger. Slurp screamed. The firing pin went click.

**

JUNE 22, FRIDAY, Vincennes, IN

All week the air was sticky and the sky overcast like vapors above a stewing pot. People were generally irritable. The work at the morgue dragged. A plethora of motor vehicle accidents kept Maddy mindlessly occupied with inventorying torn aortas, lacerated livers, crushed cranial bones, and limb fractures. Fresh roadkill were easy cases requiring little attention to detail. She needed only to concoct an ample list of lethal injuries and attach it to the report along with the list of additional cuts and contusions as evidence of acute trauma.

Friday morning Maddy worked with Slurp, a born-again sycophant who wouldn't dare cross Maddy. He presented Maddy with detailed drawings for the morning pop-tarts.

"I'm gone the rest of the day," she said.

"Where to, Precious? I mean, Doctor Precious."

"Field trip. With Thane to Vincennes, Indiana."

"Well, don't play with any guns, loaded or unloaded."

**

The small southwestern Indiana city of Vincennes was once a Wabash River trade stop of importance along the Illinois border. The current principal use of the river was a spawning run for catfish. Humans now considered the river a costly nuisance to westbound Illinois traffic, requiring both states to pay dearly to build and maintain bridges.

Several miles northeast of the city the river valley was covered by uninhabited forests and creeks. The EnvironTech, Vincennes Facility was located in the heart of the forest two miles east of the Wabash River. Chain link fencing topped with a helix of razor wire surrounded the large rectangular commercial building. Its cream-colored aluminum siding was painted with the green EvTk logo. The grounds had the appearance of a typical water treatment facility. Along the back perimeter was a chain of collection ponds that included blue algae, visible aeration pumps and grates for regulating discharge along the chain.

Six dump trucks and two cars were visible in the gravel parking area. Two spaces near the front door were occupied. The target vehicle, a cream van with license plates EVTK 9 was parked in a reserved space, closest to the front door. Maddy drove to the plant front gate, and then backed up two hundred yards to pull off road between a cluster of bushes to partially hide her car. The pair walked along the road and through the gate.

Thane stood near the van leased to Dustin Conrad. He pulled out a slim-jim from under his shirt. He slid the flat-hooked metal down along the window, unlocking the driver side door, while Maddy kept watch. No one was in sight.

Thane opened the door just enough to access the rear-hatch release lever. He crawled into the back and sorted through boxes and books. There were directories for the state legislators and the U.S. House of Representative. Thane removed a blanket from behind the driver's seat.

Two boxes, labeled Universal Bond copy paper, were under a blanket. One box was empty. The second had two stacks of computer print paper. He handed one to Maddy. There were reports entitled, EnvironTech Health Insurance Casualties, followed by employee names and a long list of health care conditions, billing codes and prices. The totals at the ends of the reports were each nearly 1.5 million dollars.

"The same type of reports Graham and I saw in Nassau. I still don't get it," said Maddy.

Under the two stacks of reports were four packets of 500-sheet copy paper unopened. As Thane redraped the box in preparation to exit his trespass, he noticed two slight creases dividing the paper packets into thirds. He felt the packets and concluded it was wrapped paper, perhaps drug packages. Running his fingers along the creases it was also apparent that there were three cut stacks. Thane opened a cover seam.

Cut into the copy paper were three rectangular wells. Each well contained 200 pieces of the finest bond paper in circulation. The Uncle Sam issues featured crisp lithographs of Ben Franklin. Thane quickly did the math. Two hundred bills per stack, three wells per package equaled sixty thousand dollars per package. Ten packages were six hundred thousand dollars per box of pertly starched and laundered greenbacks. He closed the open seam as neatly as possible and moved it to the bottom of the box.

"Hurry, get out of there. You won't believe who's here." Maddy pulled Thane out of the van. He banged his head as she shut the van hatch. She led him around the van and through the front door of the plant.

There was no front desk, only an empty hallway with four doors. Maddy turned and pointed through the front glass door at the parking lot where an Indianapolis Police Department squad car was arriving. Joe Maconi got out of the car dressed in street clothes and carrying a velvet cloth bag from a Crown Royal bottle.

Maddy tried a random door; it was locked. The second door selected opened into a small office with two desks and no visible personnel. A man was bent over a wastebasket. He stood up and displayed a blue work shirt. Embroidered on the pocket in cursive writing was the name, "Clay."

"You looking for something?"

"Dustin Conrad. Are we on the right way to his office?"

Clay poked his thumb down the hall and went back to the trash collection. Thane and Maddy nosed their way down the hall. A loud low-pitched grinding sound lightly shook the building for thirty seconds, then stopped.

Conrad's office door was open. They peaked in. "Mr. Conrad?" No response prompted a hurried snoop. The desktop was clear except for a stack of trucking invoices for waste shipments. At the back were two doors, one to a lavatory and one to a small stock room. They were in the stock room when in the hall outside the office boomed the familiar voice of Officer Maconi. They quietly closed the stockroom door. A second voice in a low-class Jersey accent was louder than Maconi's.

"Shit happens."

"Jesus Christ, Maconi, I'm a business man. I don't got time for dumb shit screw-ups like you."

"It was her fuckin' car, I'm telling you. I've seen that green Civic a dozen times. Fuck, I think I've pulled it over more than that. There's one parked down the road just like it. I can finish the job."

"You were supposed to shoot her, not somebody getting into her car. Gimme the gun."

"Her girlfriend looks like her. Shit happens."

"You got the fucking heat? Gimme the fucking heat. I'm gonna fix all this. Now you get the hell out of town for three days and let everybody know you ain't in Indianapolis. I'll show you how to do a fucking hit. Now get the fuck out of here."

A door slammed, followed by silence. Thane drew his automatic from his vest holster and cracked the door. Conrad's office was empty. On the desk was the velvet sack. Maddy touched it and opened the drawstring to reveal an older model .38 caliber handgun.

"Maddy, Conrad was talking about you," said Thane.

"Good? Give me your gun," she said with vicious crazy look.

"We've got to get out of here."

Maddy took the gun from Thane.

"Maddy, that's government property."

"Maconi's gun doesn't look like Government Issue."

She took Thane's gun and exchanged it with the Crown Royal Saturday night special. They exchanged looks about which way to exit. Thane pointed toward a back stairwell. Maddy shrugged her shoulders, and they descended.

**

Joe Maconi slammed on his breaks as he passed the Honda Civic. He got out to bend back the bush branches and view the license plate. He jumped into the squad car and squealed tires toward the plant. Conrad was still at the front door when Maconi burst back into building.

**

"What the fuck now?"

"That's her car, the little bitch's Civic. I checked the plate. She's here."

"You go outside. I'll take the plant."

Maconi drew his gun and searched the front parking lot. Conrad hurried through the first floor to his office to pick up the velvet pouch with Thane's gun. The low-pitched grinding sound again shook the building. He returned rapidly through the front office and stopped Clay.

"Clay, have you seen anyone? A young woman?"

"Yep, I pointed her toward your office. Reckon she got lost?"

"Yeah, we need to find her. Call down to the loading dock."

"Yes, sir."

At the bottom of the stairwell one floor below the offices, Maddy and Thane opened a door into a large concrete-floored room filled with valves, switching machines and laboratory equipment. Two men were sitting at a desk, smoking cigarettes. They stiffened to attention at the sight of the intruders. Simultaneously the telephone rang. One man answered and nodded. He cupped the telephone and yelled, "Hey, you two!"

Thane grabbed Maddy's arm and pulled her toward three large garage doors where trucks entered and dumped their waste into collection vats. Two trucks were unloading waste. The third bay was closed. They bolted toward the garage doors. Maddy spied Maconi at the top of the truck ramp with his back to the door.

Across the loading dock was another door on the far wall. Thane pointed, "Maybe that goes outside." The pair ran across the plant, ducking between the two trucks unloading waste, and passed through the door.

It opened to another stairwell that only descended into the dark. They followed a downward course nearly thirty feet with a full turn under the loading dock. A dim emergency exit sign gave enough light to outline a door at the end of the stairwell. Automatic lights came on as they opened the door. Three large cylindrical machines with thirty-inch intake and ten-inch exit pipes occupied the room. The intakes came from the ceiling tanks to drain the collection vats where the trucks were unloading the waste. The cylinders had floor discharge pipes connected to the outside, which Thane guessed fed into the retention ponds for processing. The writings on the machines included pressure ejection "200 p.s.i." One of the machines activated with a deafening crunching sound and vibrations that shook the floor, causing Thane and Maddy to stumble slightly as they searched for an exit. There was one door, one possible exit.

Thane tried the door behind the grinding ejector and found it locked. Maddy returned to the door they had entered. She met Conrad descending the stairwell with drawn gun.

"Show's over, Missy."

Thane ducked behind the grinder when he heard Conrad's voice. Conrad grabbed Maddy by the neck and put the gun to her head. Thane thought of Maddy, then the fact that Conrad was using his gun. The thought changed to his own murder: Conrad had spotted him.

"I've got just the stage for your curtain call. Drop it! Hands up, boyfriend!" Conrad pushed the gun deeper into Maddy's neck and the velvet bag dropped from its tucked position in Conrad's belt to the floor. Thane surrendered his gun to the floor. Conrad kicked the gun behind the sewage grinder.

Conrad pushed Maddy against the doorframe and opened the lock with a key from his belted spring keychain. He tightened his grip on Maddy's neck and pulled her back. He motioned Thane into the basement chamber and pushed Maddy in after him. She fell onto her knees.

Inside the locked room an automatic light turned on as the door opened. The small rectangular space was empty except for a control panel on one wall. Conrad opened the control panel, revealing electrical switches. At the lower right hand corner of the panel was a keyhole.

Conrad inserted another key from his key ring. The entire back wall rose to expose an elevator entrance. The gun directed Thane and Maddy into the elevator. Conrad pushed the switch. The elevator descended several stories. It opened into a chamber with more plumbing.

Along one wall were pipes at floor level. Thane quickly realized the pipes connected to the grinder machines several floors above. The casing at the base of each grinder purposely hid the pipe penetration of the discharge pipes through the floor and into this secret room.

A ninety-degree elbow-turn downward caused the pipes to disappear into a dark pit. Maddy stood near the edge of the pit. Conrad sat on a pipe.

"You are one major fucking nuisance, doctor. But I appreciate your house call. It saves me a trip to Indianapolis."

"Did Maconi kill Mina?"

"Collateral damage."

"You bastard."

"You would think the police academy could train them better."

"You go to a lot of trouble and traveling to launder money out of the Bahamas. I saw you at Corless's place in Naples," said Maddy.

"You are one nosy bitch. We like to think of it as working capital. It works at the Capitol."

"Why screw with Nassau?"

"It's so clean. Send insurance bills to a made-up company whose income and out-go can't be audited by the IRS. Pay bills, get a huge rebate. All you need is a co-operative C.F.O. to cook the books a little."

"What company can pay excessive health insurance bills?" asked Thane.

"A very profitable one with friends at the University."

"UPSinc!" said Maddy. "As long as you can get the cash back into the country."

"And get rid of nosy bitches. Now, you can either step back into the river pit, or I can shoot you."

"What river?" said Maddy.

"Six hundred and thirty feet below is a nice underground river that feeds the Wabash five miles southwest of here. Do you like Mississippi catfish? They're going to love your cute little ass."

"Excellent run-off for radio-active waste. Very efficient. Grind it up and blow it out under pressure. Nobody knows except the dead shrimp in the Gulf of Mexico. It doesn't cost much to flush it into the river," said Thane.

"We are the most profitable company in the industry. A concentrated six-ton truckload is worth ten grand, when you don't have any processing costs." Conrad pushed Maddy toward the pipe pit. She clasped the center pipe with one foot barely secure on the rim of the pit.

"Bon voyage..." Conrad's sentence was cut off by a shaking roar.

**

The deafening rumble and vibration of the sewage ejectors caused Conrad to slip onto the floor as he pushed Maddy again. Her feet slid over the edge of the pit. As her hips dipped below the surface, terror charged her forearms. She sprung herself up from the pit like a vaulting kangaroo.

Thane seized the flash of opportunity to run at Conrad and grab his right arm. Conrad's empty left fist instinctively coiled around to land squarely in Thane's face. Both handgun and wristwatch came loose and clanged on the concrete. The pair wrestled to the ground. Conrad kneed Thane's groin. The F.B.I. agent collapsed, moaning in pain. His arm and shoulder dropped over the rim of the pit. Thane grabbed Conrad's ankle to stop his descent into the pit.

As Conrad attempted to kick his ankle free from Thane's hand. Maddy grabbed the automatic off the floor. She ran to Conrad's backside and with the gun pounded his head once, twice, and then a third time. He writhed and fell down in a squirming daze.

Thane lost hold of Conrad's ankle. The agent slipped downward into the pit. Maddy screamed. The black widow curse flashed before her eyes as she froze with terror.

Thane clasped the center pipe with sliding hands and legs squeezing for one chance to sustain life. He skidded downward eighteen feet below the floor before stopping, hanging six hundred feet above drowning.

Conrad lurched back to life and tackled Maddy's leg, bringing her to the floor. Her gun fell forward two feet. She stretched along the floor, while kicking her legs and feet in Conrad's face. She regained control of the gun. Conrad twisted her left arm, but she maintained a grasp of the gun in her right. With a backhand acceleration and all the force and remaining energy Maddy could summon, she slammed the gun against his skull three more times. Groans ceased. He was unconscious.

Thane inched upwards along the pipe. "Maddy," he called breathlessly.

"Thane?" Maddy looked into the pit and could see Thane just below the rim. She lay on the edge and extended her hands to help him out of the pit. The ejector again roared. Thane lost his grip. Maddy caught the falling arm of Thane with both of her hands, nearly sliding over the edge.

Thane's free hand grabbed the rim. The ejector became silent. Maddy pulled and Thane was hoisted to safety.

They looked at Conrad. Maddy nodded her head and the pair in silent agreement pushed Conrad over the edge. His head banged on the center discharge pipe as he tumbled into the well. Eight seconds later a faint splash was heard as Conrad's body met the underground river.

"My god. What have we done now?" gasped Maddy.

"Disposing toxic waste. Just like Conrad and Corless did. Look at this sham plant. Those pipes don't go to the collection ponds. No wonder Corless isn't afraid to drink the run-off."

"How are we going to get out of here?"

"Walk."

**

They did. Thane led the way up the stairs, picking up both guns and the velvet Crown Royal bag as they passed through the basement ejector room. He smiled at the two men who were back at the desk, smoking cigarettes. Outside the front door stood Joe Maconi.

"Afternoon, officer. Nice day for a drive down from Indy, don't you agree?" Maddy smiled as she passed him. "Mr. Conrad and I worked things out. He says that he'll be in touch after three days, whatever that means."

"You two talked?"

"Yeah, he's coming to see me in Indy tomorrow."

Maconi smiled in wry satisfaction, stuck a toothpick into the corner of his mouth and drove off in his squad car as the pair hiked down the road toward the Honda.

"You are beyond bad karma. How did you live this long? Or is it just the men near you who get killed?"

"You're still alive."

"Only because we sent Conrad to the Gulf of Mexico in place of me."

"Guys who pollute oceans, who bribe legislators to allow importation of toxic waste, who embezzle, who killed my best friend, they deserve it! Conrad and all the rest of his cronies, too!"

"What are you planning?"

"Let me see that gun."

"Again?" Thane handed her his shoulder automatic.

"Not that one. The one Maconi delivered."

She opened the magazine and examined the .38 caliber lead bullets encased in a thin copper jacket.

"Take off your Kevlar vest."

"Only if you take your shirt off, too."

Maddy aimed the gun at him. Thane delivered his vest. Next she coiled the bulletproof vest several times into a ball over the end of the muzzle and fired. She spit on the bullet and rolled it with her shoe in gravel until it was cool. "See if this bullet doesn't match the Random Ranger. Hey, where are you going?"

Thane was jogging back toward the parking lot. "Conrad left some copy paper for us. He doesn't need it any more. Pull up the car."

"I forgot that cops are experts at stealing evidence."

"I'm on administrative leave."

**

JUNE 25, MONDAY, Beer Talk

A fair weather weekend typically made Monday busy at the morgue. A pile-up on Interstate 465 killed a family of four and a truck driver. The car tried to pass the exact moment the truck was changing lanes. Both the car and the truck glazed the center rail before spinning into a concrete abutment. Maddy and Mordecai each autopsied one driver, while the bodies of the parent and the child were signed out by Dr. Green.

At lunch Maddy rifled through her purse for the business card that William Corless had given her. She dialed and his secretary answered, "Good morning, EnvironTech, how may I help you?"

"Hi, Connie. This is Maddy Gray. Remember me? I would like to take up Mr. Corless on his offer to have me visit. Late in the afternoon would be good. How about Friday?"

"Let me clear this with Mr. Corless, and I'll call you back." The secretary read back the number on the caller I.D., and Maddy confirmed.

"You can tell Mr. Corless that I have an interesting message from Mr. Conrad. It may even be related to the Random Ranger murders that interest him."

**

After work she met Slurp and Thane at the Internal Medicine Room. The news of the day was that Graham O'Dell was being weaned from the ventilator and his lung function was improving. Only now that the endotracheal tube and sedation were removed, would it be possible to assess his brain capacity.

"I hear Doctor God is breathing again. Thank the good lordy, Dr. Precious. I can't take another killing. I have got to get me a new life without homicides."

"You really want out of here? I'll help you, but you've got to come clean," said Maddy.

"Did you and Withers ever kill anybody?" said Thane.

"Never, I swear."

"Did you know that O'Dell whacked Burr, injected him with insulin in his hotel room?"

"Shit. How do you know that?"

"He confessed on his death bed."

"He ain't dead."

"He thought he was on the way out."

"Wait a minute, Maddy. I had Burr's blood checked for insulin fragments and poisons. All were negative. Graham was delirious," said Thane.

"Did he have you switch the heart sections, Slurp?" asked Maddy.

"No, but I saw him cram the heart into the tissue disposal. Then he told me to flip the switch because the drain was running slow. When you discovered the heart tissue didn't match, I suspected he might have."

"Why would he do that, Slurp?"

"Burr had a son with Withers's sister. A few people knew. Burr didn't have anything to do with the child, but he paid her a good deal of money out of his slush fund. The kid was almost eighteen and angry. He wanted his real father, both psychologically and financially, but Burr refused to have any contact with him. Making him a legitimate heir was out of the question. I overheard Doctor God and Carl talking. Doc heard something on the golf course that convinced him that Burr was going to have the kid hit. Withers said he would get Burr first. Doctor God begged Withers to wait."

"Hit by whom?" Thane said.

"One of the Random Ranger hits was an accountant who investigated campaign contributions. Go figure."

"So either the Random Ranger kills the bastard kid on orders from Burr; or Burr's order never got out of his mouth?"

"Where there's a will there's a way."

"What better 'way' than to have your police and pathologists friends investigate a murder that you commit," Maddy said.

Thane poured another beer and asked, "Speaking of cop murders, where's Mordecai with the Johnson exhumation?"

"Withers never killed Johnson."

"According to whom?" said Maddy.

"I believe him," said Slurp.

"But is there any way to prove it?" said Thane.

"Don't you guys read the paper?"

"We've been busy," deadpanned Maddy as Thane's eyes widened in fear that Maddy was about to tell Slurp about Conrad.

"The big dig is set for Wednesday. You ever been to an exhumation?"

"No, what do I wear?" said Maddy.

"Well, the guy they dig up is usually the best dressed person there."

"We wouldn't miss it. Would we, Thane?"

"Wait a minute, you said you'd help me out," reminded Slurp.

"Enough cash to get into the funeral business. You interested?"

"Keep them lips aflappin'."

"Listen up…" Maddy began.

**

JUNE 27, WEDNESDAY, The Exhumation

The exhumation orders set a record by passing process in ten days. The family, state officials, and investigating officers were all notified by overnight certified mail. At the closed judicial hearing the police pleaded against the exhumation, expressing concerns that it would re-ignite the racial fires of the Michael Johnson death. The black community persuaded the family to grant consent, despite concern that the murder would be too painful to re-experience.

Mordecai and the prosecutor's office basked in the constant publicity, but secretly feared that a negative finding would make them look foolish. Mordecai and the DA appeared jointly on television to emphasize the need to put this possibility to rest. They lied when they expressed their hope that the metal fragment would prove unrelated to a bullet jacket.

The Indianapolis News political cartoon featured a large ashtray with a lid labeled INDY. Burning cigarettes with the names of Mordecai, the judge, the police chief, and the mayor lay along the rim of the ashtray. The caption read, "Any more butts to cover?"

The press was not allowed indoors during the exhumation proceeding, however, it was impossible to exclude cameras from the graveside excavation. Telephoto lenses conquered security. The dirt was hand-dug by four court-hired contractors. Four feet below grade was the ceiling of the concrete vault. It was cleared after thirty-five minutes of hand-shoveling. A power casket-lift and winch removed the top to unveil a nearly pristine silver-painted aluminum casket. The gilded brass rails were flaking, otherwise seven years of darkness had produced little noticeable effect since the day Michael's mother had loudly wept in her black dress and veil.

**

The casket was transported by mortuary hearse to County Hospital. A motorcade of police vehicles and television vans interrupted the mid-day traffic. The hearse backed down the steep grade of the loading dock at the rear of the hospital. Police and press vans were not allowed past the sidewalk.

The list of participants included Dr. Green and Dr. Mordecai who were the official examiners. The police association had hired an independent forensic observer, a nationally know expert in forensic pathology from Pittsburgh.

The family was represented by their local minister to insure respectful treatment of Michael's remains. The funeral home owner seized the commercial opportunity to advertise that Hogsdon Mortuary Services provided everything forever, including disinterment. He pledged all the remains would be returned to the plot as undisturbed as possible. Four attorneys from the district attorneys office were rubbernecking the opportunity to gawk and load up on cocktail party gossip.

The usual morgue staff was present along with one official photographer hired by the prosecutor's office. Thane Hatcher represented the F.B.I. as part of the Random Ranger investigation. He had been returned to duty for manpower support in investigating the latest Ranger murder of Mina. His director summarily dismissed the internal investigation in a closed-door session with the police to avoid a public quarrel over possible planted evidence.

In eerie silence, Mr. Hogsdon released the clasps to open the casket lid. Several wriggling insects scurried out from the hinge areas. Yellow satin lined the inside of the casket. The body of Michael Johnson lay undisturbed. The skin was dehydrated and wrinkled like a black raisin.

At first sight the body appeared burned. Closer examination and explanation revealed to Dr. Green that the burn look was post-interment changes. The hair was nearly normal, a shortly cropped Negro coif. The remains of the lips had tightened back and cracked to expose fragmented yellow teeth. The face was distorted due to the gunshot explosion, like a squashed raisin. The photographer snapped pictures from various angles.

The corpse wore a blue suit, which hung baggily now that the body had dehydrated. The feet were covered with black stockings and no shoes. Dr. Mordecai asked the room's observers if there were any questions. There were none. He ordered Richard and Slurp to help lift the body onto an autopsy gurney.

A portable x-ray machine, a six-foot arc of metal casing, was positioned over the head. The young woman who ran the unit was visibly nervous and upset. She worked quickly to produce a film cassette. She shuttled it to the radiology department for developing. The room stood in near silence until she returned. The x-ray verified that the metal fragment in question was still present along the left maxilla.

Mordecai took a scalpel and made a linear incision through the face from the left lip corner to the left ear, incising the upper cheek high above the gum line. Using the Stryker saw, he removed intact, the entire length of the multiply fractured upper jawbone along with the tooth line and roof of the mouth.

Mordecai placed the palm-sized mass of bones and soft tissue on the x-ray unit for confirmation that the fragment was present in the excised bone. While the inspection team awaited the film to develop, Mordecai asked if there were any other issues. He read the court order, which limited the autopsy to search for metallic evidence in the area of the gunshot wound. All agreed that the exhumation had complied with the order; and they had no further questions.

Fredrick Steinmetz, M.D., the expert from Pittsburgh, put on gloves and pompously asked for a probe. He did his best to examine the bullet track. He pulled back the hairs and looked for the exit wound. He tried to appear professorial, but the photographs from the original autopsy were far more valuable than the body was after embalming and burial for seven years. The scalp had a suture line from the mortician's attempt to re-assemble the exploded head. The brain had been removed seven years previously, and the x-ray showed a tissueless air-filled cavity.

The second x-ray confirmed that the metal fragment was in the bone. The four pathologists: Mordecai, Green, Gray, and Steinmetz huddled above the three-inch sheet of bone that lay in front of Dr. Mordecai on the cutting block. Dr. Green inserted a needle into the specimen, marking the area of the fragment.

With dissecting scissors and forceps, Mordecai spread though the rubbery bubble-gum pink embalmed periodontal tissue and found the three millimeter triangular metal fragment. It was green oxidized copper. The photographer switched to a close-up magnifying lens to capture both sides of the metal. Steinmetz used a pocket monocle to compare it with the bullet jacket fragment from Paul Duval.

The specialist concurred with Green and Mordecai that the jacket fragments were similar. They agreed that an elemental assessment of the type of metal and any adherent powder by x-ray dispersion spectroscopy would increase the likelihood that they were from an identical lot of bullets. Their final agreement was an oath of silence prior to Dr. Mordecai's final and official report.

The corpse of Michael Johnson was returned to the casket, the hearse, the cemetery, the plot, and the darkness. Mr. Hogsdon insisted on a re-interment ceremony of five minutes. He correctly estimated it was the precise length to entice a sound bite for the ten-o-clock news.

**

JUNE 29, FRIDAY, EnvironTech Revisited

Tasmin vibrated Maddy's chest as she purred. At 8:45 Maddy called the morgue to confess to Slurp her failure to set the alarm. She'd be a little late to work. She had to shower and fix her hair in preparation for her five p.m. appointment with William Corless.

"One stale muffin left on the stove." Slurp reported that there was an autopsy to perform, a homeless street person found in rigor mortis atop a street grate.

"Good, that won't take too long. After that we'll go over the list one more time. If anything comes up this afternoon, tell Dr. Green I am on a field investigation."

Maddy opened a can of liver-based wet cat food. The whirring sound of the electric opener sent Tasmin into a frenzy, rubbing Maddy's leg and rolling on her back. She stretched and pawed at the kitchen counter and meowed loudly. She jumped onto the table and then across to the counter as the liver fragrance filled the air. In compassion Maddy gave Tasmin the whole can.

**

She deliberately exceeded the speed limit en-route to the hospital. Sure enough, a familiar flashing red light quickly filled her rear-view mirror not ten blocks from her apartment.

"Why, good morning, Officer Maconi. You're probably wondering why I'm late to work and in such a hurry."

"I haven't heard squat from Conrad. Rumor has it, nobody else has either."

"Joe,...Can I call you Joe? We're old buddies by now. Actually, I was going to call you, or drop this off at the police station. Mr. Conrad came by the morgue yesterday. He gave this note to me. He asked me out for Gulf shrimp, but I said to go ahead without me. He must think I'm cuter than you are. Anyway, I told him that I'd track you down.

As promised," Maddy handed the policeman a plain white envelope. He opened it; he read it; and he looked up puzzled.

"You know what this says?"

"Haven't a clue; and I don't care. Can I go now? I've got a date with a homeless lady at the morgue."

"You got any appointments today?"

"As a matter of fact I do. Besides the deceased homeless woman, I'm to see Mr. William Corless in his office at 4:45 p.m. sharp. Not that it's any of your business. Have a good day."

"Slow down! Life's short, you know." Maconi's words were barely audible above the noise of the Civic's engine and squealing tires as she drove off.

**

At 4:30 p.m. Maddy entered the EnvironTech corporate headquarters. She parked in the second parking space in the front executive row, beside the car of William Corless. The C.O.O. had left for the day and his spot was empty. Slot number three was also empty, now that Davis was seated in Washington. She felt smug pride at trespassing on reserved territory of the privileged corporate aristocracy.

It's easy to spend millions on charity, soirees, and political bribes when it's not your money, she thought. Boards of colleges and community art councils lavish praise on the likes of the William Corlesses for their generosity. Dying shrimp in the Gulf of Mexico receive no acknowledgement for their part in making the generosity possible.

Maddy thought her Civic looked quite adequate next to Corless's gold Cadillac STS of the front row. She adjusted her bulky business suit, and checked her hair in the side-view mirror.

**

The secretary, Connie Snow, greeted her with genuine pleasure, "Hello, Dr. Gray."

"Call me Maddy. I feel like we're close friends, Connie."

Maddy delivered a booster shot of flattery, commenting on her silver belt and earrings, and her matching shoes and scarf. Maddy was prepared to continue, but it was unnecessary. The young woman was easy prey to Maddy's puffery.

"Is he in a good mood?" asked Maddy.

"He's been really edgy lately, but he's excited to see you. I know it. Careful, he can be overly friendly at times, if you know what I mean."

"Check. Boys will be boys." said Maddy with a wink.

"Mr. Conrad hasn't been heard from all week. When you said you had a message from him, he got as excited as I've ever seen him."

"Thanks, Connie. Really, we should go out some time, do the town."

"You got any cute doctor friends?"

Maddy winked again and flashed her the OK with her fingers.

"When do you leave, today? Five?"

315

"Actually, I'm out the door as soon as I straighten up the desk. Mr. Corless doesn't allow anything left on my desk when I leave."

"I'll call you." Maddy smiled.

Connie Snow returned the OK sign. Next the secretary excused herself to see if Mr. Corless was available. When Connie was out of sight, Maddy pulled out the top right drawer and took out the keys. She unlocked the coat closet behind the desk and returned the keys.

"You can go back now, Maddy. I'm out of here."

Maddy glanced at her watch.

"Just point me to the ladies room."

**

The Wall Street gurus cited William Corless as a model C.E.O. for "doing the right things right." He had a good product, waste treatment, and made an amazing profit. His office was not filled with pictures of himself shaking hands with presidents or golf professionals. He had no need of celebrity connections, only the power supplied by profits. His office decorations were placards of laminated Wall Street Journal reprints on stained walnut, which touted him as *THE C.E.O.* in heartland America.

**

"So glad you were available this afternoon, Doctor Gray. Please, have a seat. You look lovely, today. And I admire your gloves. So few ladies of your generation avail themselves of the adornment."

316

Maddy smiled in acknowledgement of the compliment. "Thank you. I'm sure that I surprised you. You're probably not used to people actually taking you up on an invitation to visit."

"Quite the contrary. I rarely invite anyone with whom I don't sense a special connection. I understand that my late friend, James Sweetbread, was quite enamored by your talents, and may I say, beauty?"

Maddy smiled again. "Was he a friend of yours?"

"Yes, we played golf, and we were business associates. I believe he was quite fond of you."

"It was more business than pleasure. He wanted me to fuck him in return for his paying off some cop to drop a bogus D.U.I. charge."

"Whoa. I guess I don't need to know anymore about that, do I? You said to Miss Snow that you had a message from Mr. Conrad." Corless looked at his watch and then glanced through the partially closed door to the adjoining conference room.

"I saw him a week ago. He's gone to sea in the Gulf of Mexico. He won't be around for awhile."

"We haven't heard from him since last Friday, either. It is strange that he would go on a cruise without notice."

"Maybe he's in Nassau filing bogus insurance claims. You know the kind: claims with marked-up charges that kickback a few million dollars of excess working capital."

"You little shit."

"Strange that none of the names in these pages or their social security numbers actually work for EnvironTech. They do seem to be copies of bills from other patients treated by the UPSinc H.M.O." Maddy opened her purse, pulled out the insurance list of medical claims, and tossed it onto Corless's desk.

"Where did you get these?" he growled.

"The same place I got the cash. You know the cash, the slush money that you and your chief financial officer embezzle through your Nassau insurance agency. The one that launders bogus health insurance billings from UPSinc into cash, which Withers, the cop that you're blackmailing, smuggles back into the country. About one-point-two million dollars a trip, isn't it, Billy?"

"You cunt!"

The telephone rang and Corless answered with a curt "Yes...what? You've got a wrong number," and hung up.

She reached again into her purse. With her left hand she held up a stack of hundred dollar bills. A tall figure holding a gun appeared in the doorway from the conference room adjoining the C.E.O.'s office.

"What goes around, comes around," said Maconi.

"Whack the nosy little bitch!" Corless demanded.

"I thought you weren't due until 5:15, officer."

"Let's say I called ahead and changed the appointment, which Mr. C never made, and you didn't know about, you lying bitch."

"You're right. I lied. Here Joe, Conrad wanted you to have this, as a Random Ranger bonus." She flung the stack of Ben Franklins toward Maconi's head. It made a three-foot green and black cloud of diversion in his face.

Maddy removed the velvet Crown Royal sack from her purse. She opened it and pointed the gun at Corless's face. "Mina was my friend, you murdering asshole. This is personal, not business."

She fired two shots into the head of William Corless. Hair, scalp and bone fragments exploded over the back of his chair.

She turned toward Maconi whose mouth was wide open. She tossed him her handgun. "Conrad also wanted me to return this. I believe it's yours."

Maddy bolted toward the door. Maconi fired once. It struck in the center of her back, and down she fell, motionless.

Maconi looked at the money pile. He pulled the black plastic trash liner out of a wastebasket beside Corless's desk and stuffed it with the the hundred-dollar bills from the floor. He picked up both guns, returning his automatic to its chest holster and placing the .38 into the velvet pouch. He kicked Maddy who did not respond. He walked slowly out of the office, carrying the garbage sack in one hand, the Crown Royal pouch in the other.

**

At precisely 4:55 p.m. the back seat of the green Honda Civic folded forward. Slurp crawled from the trunk area to the driver's seat. He donned the large straw hat that Maddy had worn when driving into the lot at EnvironTech. Slurp backed out of the parking space and drove to central downtown. He illegally parked along a yellow curb on Monument Circle at the peak of rush hour. Slurp walked into a bank building. He dialed the private line of William Corless.

"Dis de poze offiss?......Sheet."

At 5:05 he withdrew two hundred dollars from the bank ATM. Next he crossed the street and paid $14.45 for

Chinese carryout. He returned to the car and picked up a parking ticket from the windshield. He headed south toward EnvironTech.

At the same moment a cell phone in the hand of Thane Hatcher rang once. The F.B.I. officer was standing outside the entrance to EnvironTech headquarters with Mordecai, police, and two additional F.B.I. agents.

"Didn't go through. I wonder if that was Dr. Gray." Thane pushed buttons and waited four seconds before talking loudly enough to ensure the entire entourage of law enforcement could hear his conversation. "Yes Maddy, we're down at EnvironTech with the arrest warrant. The x-ray dispersion was positive. The metal fragment from Michael Johnson matches the Random Ranger bullet jackets. Maconi's squad's still in the lot. Come on down."

Maconi walked out the front door, carrying the two sacks. Four police officers and three F.B.I. agents held up their badges. One officer approached Maconi. "Joseph Maconi, you're under arrest for the murder of Michael Johnson. You are also under investigation for suspected murder on eight additional counts." The officer continued with his rights, but Maconi would not be silent.

"She did it. That little bitch, Madison Gray. I saw her. With this gun." He opened the velvet bag and pulled out the .38, which instantly got him tackled and handcuffed. His police firearm was also confiscated. The cash bag fell open.

"It's been fired. They both have. Armed robbery to ice the cake, pal," one policeman grunted as he sniffed the guns.

"No! Listen to what I'm trying to tell you. Gray shot Corless up there. Then I shot her as she tried to flee; just doing my professional duty. She got the money from

Corless. I just picked it up. I'm one of you guys, for Christ sake. She's up there dead on the floor. Go see for yourself."

The officers looked at each other. Thane and the other F.B.I. motioned to go ahead and check it out. Inside they found the blood and brains of William Corless strewn over his desk-calendar and dripping from his slumped body. Several hundred-dollar bills were under a side chair.

"Go ahead and get started, I'll call downtown." Thane walked down the hallway. He stood at the secretary's desk pretending to make a call. Slurp came through the front door and stopped next to Thane.

**

As soon as the front hallway became empty, Thane opened the secretary's coat closet. Out stepped Maddy. Slurp handed her ten twenties, a bank receipt, and a parking ticket.

"A parking ticket?"

"Didn't plan that part, did you, Precious?" said Slurp.

"Did you call at five?"

Slurp nodded. She slid him a pair of slightly sooty white gloves. Thane and Maddy exchanged cell phones. The three casually walked through the front door, where numerous police and the press were assembling.

Maddy whispered to Thane, "This Kevlar is killing me. How do you wear this everyday?"

"Dr. Gray, don't leave yet," one of the police officers outside the front door stopped her, "Maconi is jabbering a story that you shot William Corless. And you were listed as a 4:45 appointment."

"I was here earlier for less than five minutes and left for downtown. I returned when Mr. Thatcher called me."

"It only takes five minutes for quick homicide."

"Mr. Corless had asked that I come and see him. He was worried about the disappearance of Dustin Conrad at his Vincennes plant. I saw Conrad a week ago. Mr. Corless wanted to find out about the visit. It seems Mr. Conrad had some scam going about insurance billing or something in the Bahamas. Mr. Corless showed me a list of patient charges which Dr. Sweetbread had billed EnvironTech. It should be on Mr. Corless's desk somewhere.

Well, it turns out that the patients didn't even exist. Mr. Corless wanted to know if I knew anything about Sweetbread, but heck, I'm only a resident. I think Corless was on the trail of a big money embezzlement scheme. Corless wondered if Conrad had disappeared with a lot of money after Sweetbread died."

That statement sent the news reporters to their cell phones.

"Officer Maconi claims to have killed you."

"Do I look dead to you? I saw Maconi go in as I left a few minutes before five. In fact Mr. Corless asked me to leave, because he had another meeting with Officer Maconi. I left in a hurry. I phoned back to Mr. Corless about five, because I thought I had left my sunglasses in his office. I hadn't."

"You were gone at five?"

"Yes, officer. I left and went downtown to pick up some Chinese, which is getting cold in my car. I parked on the circle and first ran into the bank for some cash from an ATM. When I got back, your finest gave me this ticket. Only two minutes later. Don't you guys have some real criminals to chase? Then Agent Hatcher called and informed me that the forensic team and the F.B.I. were about to arrest Officer Maconi."

Thane raised his cell phone. The officer looked at the ATM receipt and the ticket, then waved her away.

"We could check the cell phone calls. I don't think it'll be necessary, unless you've got any white gloves? Maconi says you were wearing white gloves. That's why there won't be any prints on the gun."

"He's been watching too many OJ trials. But, you can search me."

** **

JUNE 30, SATURDAY, New Lives

Jill O'Dell, Graham's wife, had flown to Miami the day after Maddy's visit. She was prepared for his death. She remained at the bedside throughout his hospitalization. When he regained consciousness, she volunteered to return with him to Indianapolis for the duration of his recovery.

Jill opened the door for Thane, Maddy, Slurp, Mordecai, Green, and Richard. The nasal oxygen tubes hung loosely around Graham's neck. He was pale and gaunt, but smiled a broad grin. Maddy placed a bouquet of painted daisies on a coffee table next to his chair.

"I know I'm alive now, this can't be heaven. Oops, I hadn't considered the alternative."

"Doctor God, they can't kill an immortal," said Slurp.

"When will you be back to work, another week?" Richard asked.

"Actually, Richard, I'm not coming back. The shock effects injured my lungs. I might need oxygen for some time. Jill has asked me to move out to Seattle. I think I'll give it a try. I've done enough death for one life."

"Me too, Dr. G, or I should say, we, too. Slurp and I got the financing for the Smith & West's Sons Mortuary Services. Sorry Dr. Green, we're all leaving," smiled Richard. Slurp looked at Thane and Maddy and gave a thumbs-up thank you.

"Why does this feel like a battlefield promotion? Everyone else is gone, and I'm the only one left," said Dr. Green.

"Everyone?" asked Graham.

"Everyone. Maddy has two more months with us. Percival has been making national news. Steinmetz has offered him a partnership in Pittsburgh, starting the first of August."

Graham shook Green's hand. "It's all yours, chief. You'll do fine once you get some decent help. I certainly had it. One question, what's happened to Carl Withers?"

Thane stepped forward, "He's got a plea bargain arrangement for obstruction and he's talking non-stop. He wants to clear his conscience. He swore an affidavit that Corless paid-off a whole slew of people in the Michael Johnson cover-up. Maconi was young and trigger-happy. Michael Johnson was handcuffed in the back seat, screaming obscenities. When Michael called Maconi a 'chicken shit honky pig,' Maconi lost it and fired Johnson's gun into his mouth. The bullet went straight through his head and out the back of his skull, landing free on the back seat. Withers picked up the bullet and took the gun. Maconi fired his gun through the back windshield to stage the suicide."

Dr. Green continued Thane's story. "But Mordecai discovered the jacket fragment, which blew the police cover-up. That was brilliant how you linked the fragments with the Random Ranger, Percival."

"Actually it was Maddy who helped link the bullet jacket fragments. Wither's plea bargain includes his testimony that Corless orchestrated the entire coverup with the police and the coroner's office. Then he blackmailed Maconi into becoming his hit man. He ordered hits on the two EnvironTech execs who threatened to expose the health insurance money laundering. He also had Maconi kill the government accountant who was investigating his buddy, David Burr. All the rest of the Random Ranger cases were planted bullets during body pickups or autopsies. Withers switched bullets to make the killings appear random. He put bullets into cases about once a year to keep the investigators confused. That's his obstruction plea. I was just lucky." Percival sat down.

"What about Duval? Was that faked or ordered?" asked Thane.

"That was faked according to Withers's statement," said Dr. Green.

Percival and Dr. Green rose to leave. At the door they stopped for last remarks.

"We better let Graham get some rest. Besides, somebody has to work today," said Dr. Green.

"This is my last official day. All drinks at the Internal Medicine are on me," said Percival.

**

Slurp said, "Now that we are alone, I'll tell you about Duval. Maconi got his orders through Withers, so Corless didn't have to deal with Maconi directly. Maconi whacked each hit as directed, using Michael Johnson's Random Ranger gun. On his way to the airport, Withers phoned Maconi with the order: 'Mr. C wants Duval taken out.' That's the truth that can't leave this room. Withers is going to get an easy two years for coerced obstruction. The confession and plea bargain don't include ordering the hit on Duval or anybody else," said Slurp.

Graham motioned for Maddy to come close. The others left to allow them privacy. Maddy kneeled down to hear his whispering voice. "No regrets," said Graham.

"Me neither. Have a great life in Seattle." She kissed his forehead.

"I won't ask for anything. Not only about us, I also mean that about the death of Burr. I remember confessing. It was getting crazy. Withers was about to break and shoot him in broad daylight. I figured that Burr was going to die either way. I could get away with it, and save Withers and his nephew. You, Maddy, must do whatever you feel is right. I am not asking for any favors."

"But we tested Burr's blood for insulin fragments?"

"I drew that blood the day before I injected him, specifically to use as an autopsy sample. Withers and I submitted that blood at the time of the post mortem."

"You said we've all got dirty clothes in the closet. You've still got a ways to go to catch up to me."

"One more thing. Get a young one, they'll last longer."

"Graham, Growing up I wanted so badly to get away from New Munich. It was so slow and boring. I've spent half my life daydreaming to escape. Now I know exactly what I am going to do. When I finish next June, I'm going to specialize in dermatopathology."

"A memorial to Mina?"

"Partly. Thanks, Graham." She stroked his cheek.

Jill knocked at the doorway and suggested that Graham should rest.

**

Maddy rode with Thane to Internal Medicine Room to celebrate Percival's last day.

"Maddy, do you think we could ever have a real date? You know, dinner, a movie. Nobody gets killed. Maybe even sex afterwards?"

"Sex? You don't waste any time."

"Rumor has it, men don't last long around you."

"You think you're old enough to handle me?"

"I'll be thirty soon."

"I never believed I'd say this. When I finish my training, I am going to find a dermatopathology job in the quietest town I can find, wherever they ban guns."

"You took the words right out of my mouth. I'm no cop. I don't know right from wrong anymore. Tomorrow I quit."

Thane stopped the car in the middle of a bridge over the White River. He stepped out to the railing and pitched his automatic into the river, one block from the Internal Medicine Room.

**

327

G. H. Ellis

ABOUT THE AUTHOR

G. H. Ellis MD is a practicing pathologist, novelist and playwright in the Indianapolis area. His produced plays are known for dark comedic characters whose dysfunctional exploits often involve dead bodies, mummies, and twisted family relationships. A graduate of Monmouth College and the University of Illinois College of Medicine, he completed pathology training including forensic work at Indiana University. His passions outside medicine and writing include Jungian psychology. Favorite topics include the psychological interpretation of vampirism and other monster motifs. He lives with his attorney/wife, Jan. They have two daughters in college.